COFFINS

COFFINS

♦♦♦

The Vampire Archives

VOLUME 3

EDITED AND WITH AN INTRODUCTION BY
OTTO PENZLER

VINTAGE CRIME BLACK LIZARD
VINTAGE BOOKS
A Division of Random House, Inc.
New York

A VINTAGE CRIME/BLACK LIZARD ORIGINAL, NOVEMBER 2010

Introduction and compilation copyright © 2010 by Otto Penzler

All rights reserved. Published in the United States by Vintage Books, a division of Random House, Inc., New York. Originally published as part of the compilation *The Vampire Archives* in the United States by Vintage Books, a division of Random House, Inc., New York, in 2009. Compilation copyright © 2009 by Otto Penzler. That edition published by arrangement with Quercus Publishing PLC, London.

Vintage is a registered trademark and Vintage Crime/Black Lizard and colophon are trademarks of Random House, Inc.

Owing to limitations on space, permissions to reprint previously published material appear on pages 501–502.

The Library of Congress has cataloged *The Vampire Archives* as follows:
The vampire archives / edited by Otto Penzler.
p. cm.
1. Vampires—Fiction. 2. Horror tales, American. I. Penzler, Otto.
PS648.V35V25 2009
813'.0873808375—dc22
2009008864

ISBN: 978-0-307-74223-0

www.vintagebooks.com

Printed in the United States of America
10 9 8 7 6 5 4 3 2 1

Contents

✦✦✦

OTTO PENZLER	INTRODUCTION	*vii*
ROBERT BLOCH	THE LIVING DEAD	3
PETER TREMAYNE	DRACULA'S CHAIR	13
WILLIAM GILBERT	THE LAST LORDS OF GARDONAL	29
GUY DE MAUPASSANT	THE HORLA	85
ARTHUR CONAN DOYLE	THE ADVENTURE OF THE SUSSEX VAMPIRE	122
BRIAN STABLEFORD	THE MAN WHO LOVED THE VAMPIRE LADY	147
M. R. JAMES	WAILING WELL	181
HARLAN ELLISON	LONELY WOMEN ARE THE VESSELS OF TIME	197
ANNE CRAWFORD	A MYSTERY OF THE CAMPAGNA	204
VASILE ALECSANDRI	THE VAMPIRE	255
ED GORMAN	DUTY	259
STEVE RASNIC TEM	THE MEN & WOMEN OF RIVENDALE	274
BASIL COPPER	DOCTOR PORTHOS	288
ALGERNON BLACKWOOD	THE SINGULAR DEATH OF MORTON	298
EDGAR ALLAN POE	LIGEIA	313
MANLY WADE WELLMAN	WHEN IT WAS MOONLIGHT	337
VICTOR ROMAN	FOUR WOODEN STAKES	359
DION FORTUNE	BLOOD-LUST	376
LUIGI CAPUANA	A CASE OF ALLEGED VAMPIRISM	401
F. PAUL WILSON	MIDNIGHT MASS	421

Introduction

❖❖❖

OTTO PENZLER

In the world of culture and the arts, the vampire began as a literary creation and impressed its image on the Western world as depicted in the books and stories of John Polidori (*The Vampyre*), Sheridan Le Fanu (*Carmilla*), Bram Stoker (*Dracula*), and many others. It is in the more recent invention of film, however, that vampires seized hold of the public imagination, never to let go—never to die.

The first great vampire movie was *Nosferatu* (1922), a silent German expressionist horror film based entirely on Stoker's *Dracula*, but with names changed to avoid paying for the rights. It starred Max Schreck (*schreck* is the German word for fright) as the ugliest vampire ever, a skinny, scuttling ratlike monster named Count Orlok rather than Count Dracula and referred to him as Nosferatu rather than vampire in order to distance itself from potential lawsuits. The filmmaker, F. W. Murnau, was unsuccessful, however, as he was sued for plagiarism and copyright infringement by Stoker's widow and a judge ruled in her favor, ordering all prints of the film to be destroyed; fortunately, a few survived to chill the bones of future generations.

Everything changed in 1931 when Bela Lugosi was signed to star in Universal's classic version of the novel, which had already been a hugely successful stage play. Although producer and director Tod Browning wanted Lon Chaney for the role, the great horror actor died before the film went into production. Lugosi, who had been successful both with audiences and critics on the stage, got the role, metamorphosing Dracula from a repugnant beast to a sexy, well-bred nobleman. His slow, sinister phrasing frightened viewers, even when making such innocuous statements as "I . . . bid you . . . welcome" and "I do not drink . . . wine," which have become so familiar that they have been parodied innumerable times.

Universal, the greatest studio for horror films (it also produced *Frankenstein*, 1931, *The Mummy*, 1932, *The Invisible Man*, 1933, *The Bride of Frankenstein*, 1935, and *The Wolf Man*, 1941), followed its successful *Dracula* by releasing Lugosi's only other vampire movie for the studio, *Mark of the Vampire*, in 1935.

Hammer Films produced seemingly countless vampire films from the late 1950s to the mid-1970s, mostly starring Christopher Lee and Peter Cushing but all cheaply produced in garish color and filled with lots of blood and shapely, half-dressed young women.

More recently, vampires have flourished as handsome, desirable lovers, notably in the motion pictures based on Anne Rice's novel, *Interview with the Vampire* (starring

Tom Cruise, released in 1994) and Stephenie Meyers's phenomenally successful Twilight series (*Twilight, New Moon,* and *Eclipse*).

Bear in mind, however, that not all vampires are desirable sex objects—as this collection will illustrate.

COFFINS

THE LIVING DEAD

$\bullet\bullet\bullet$

ROBERT BLOCH

All day long he rested, while the guns thundered in the village below. Then, in the slanting shadows of the late afternoon, the rumbling echoes faded into the distance and he knew it was over. The American advance had crossed the river. They were gone at last, and it was safe once more.

Above the village, in the crumbling ruins of the great château atop the wooded hillside, Count Barsac emerged from the crypt.

The Count was tall and thin—cadaverously thin, in a manner most hideously appropriate. His face and hands had a waxen pallor; his hair was dark, but not as dark as his eyes and the hollows beneath them. His cloak was black, and the sole touch of color about his person was the vivid redness of his lips when they curled in a smile.

He was smiling now, in the twilight, for it was time to play the game.

The name of the game was Death, and the Count had played it many times.

He had played it in Paris on the stage of the Grand

Guignol; his name had been plain Eric Karon then, but still he'd won a certain renown for his interpretation of bizarre roles. Then the war had come and, with it, his opportunity.

Long before the Germans took Paris, he'd joined their Underground, working long and well. As an actor he'd been invaluable.

And this, of course, was his ultimate reward—to play the supreme role, not on the stage, but in real life. To play without the artifice of spotlights, in true darkness; this was the actor's dream come true. He had even helped to fashion the plot.

"Simplicity itself," he told his German superiors. "Château Barsac has been deserted since the Revolution. None of the peasants from the village dare to venture near it, even in daylight, because of the legend. It is said, you see, that the last Count Barsac was a vampire."

And so it was arranged. The shortwave transmitter had been set up in the large crypt beneath the château, with three skilled operators in attendance, working in shifts. And he, "Count Barsac," in charge of the entire operation, as guardian angel. Rather, as guardian demon.

"There is a graveyard on the hillside below," he informed them. "A humble resting place for poor and ignorant people. It contains a single imposing crypt—the ancestral tomb of the Barsacs. We shall open that crypt, remove the remains of the last Count, and allow the villagers to discover that the coffin is empty. They will never dare come near the spot or the château again, because this will prove that the legend is true—Count Barsac is a vampire, and walks once more."

The question came then. "What if there are sceptics? What if someone does not believe?"

And he had his answer ready. "They will believe. For at night I shall walk—I, Count Barsac."

After they saw him in the makeup, wearing the black cloak, there were no more questions. The role was his.

The role was his, and he'd played it well. The Count nodded to himself as he climbed the stairs and entered the roofless foyer of the château, where only a configuration of cobwebs veiled the radiance of the rising moon.

Now, of course, the curtain must come down. If the American advance had swept past the village below, it was time to make one's bow and exit. And that too had been well arranged.

During the German withdrawal another advantageous use had been made of the tomb in the graveyard. A cache of Air Marshal Goering's art treasures now rested safely and undisturbed within the crypt. A truck had been placed in the château. Even now the three wireless operators would be playing new parts—driving the truck down the hillside to the tomb, placing the *objets d'art* in it.

By the time the Count arrived there, everything would be packed. They would then don the stolen American Army uniforms, carry the forged identifications and permits, drive through the lines across the river, and rejoin the German forces at a predesignated spot.

Nothing had been left to chance. Someday, when he wrote his memoirs . . .

But there was not time to consider that now. The Count glanced up through the gaping aperture in the ruined roof. The moon was high. It was time to leave.

In a way he hated to go. Where others saw only dust and cobwebs he saw a stage—the setting of his finest performance. Playing a vampire's role had not addicted him to the taste of blood—but as an actor he enjoyed the taste of triumph. And he had triumphed here.

"Parting is such sweet sorrow." Shakespeare's line. Shakespeare, who had written of ghosts and witches, of bloody apparitions. Because Shakespeare knew that his audiences, the stupid masses, believed in such things— just as they still believed today. A great actor could always make them believe.

The Count moved into the shadowy darkness outside the entrance of the château. He started down the pathway toward the beckoning trees.

It was here, amid the trees, that he had come upon Raymond, one evening weeks ago. Raymond had been his most appreciative audience—a stern, dignified, white-haired elderly man, mayor of the village of Barsac. But there had been nothing dignified about the old fool when he'd caught sight of the Count looming up before him out of the night. He'd screamed like a woman and run.

Probably Raymond had been prowling around, intent on poaching, but all that had been forgotten after his encounter in the woods. The mayor was the one to thank for spreading the rumors that the Count was again abroad. He and Clodez, the oafish miller, had then led an armed band to the graveyard and entered the Barsac tomb. What a fright they got when they discovered the Count's coffin open and empty!

The coffin had contained only dust that had been scattered to the winds, but they could not know that. Nor could they know about what had happened to Suzanne.

The Count was passing the banks of a small stream now. Here, on another evening, he'd found the girl— Raymond's daughter, as luck would have it—in an embrace with young Antoine LeFevre, her lover. Antoine's shattered leg had invalided him out of the army, but he ran like a deer when he glimpsed the cloaked and grinning Count. Suzanne had been left behind and that was unfortunate, because it was necessary to dispose of her. Her body had been buried in the woods, beneath great stones, and there was no question of discovery; still, it was a regrettable incident.

In the end, however, everything was for the best. Now silly superstitious Raymond was doubly convinced that the vampire walked. He had seen the creature himself, had seen the empty tomb and the open coffin; his own daughter had disappeared. At his command none dared venture near the graveyard, the woods, or the château beyond.

Poor Raymond! He was not even a mayor any more— his village had been destroyed in the bombardment. Just

an ignorant, broken old man, mumbling his idiotic nonsense about the "living dead."

The Count smiled and walked on, his cloak fluttering
in the breeze, casting a batlike shadow on the pathway
before him. He could see the graveyard now, the tilted
tombstones rising from the earth like leprous fingers rotting in the moonlight. His smile faded; he did not like
such thoughts. Perhaps the greatest tribute to his talent as
an actor lay in his actual aversion to death, to darkness
and what lurked in the night. He hated the sight of
blood, had developed within himself an almost claustro-
phobic dread of the confinement of the crypt.

Yes, it had been a great role, but he was thankful it was
ending. It would be good to play the man once more, and
cast off the creature he had created.

As he approached the crypt he saw the truck waiting
in the shadows. The entrance to the tomb was open, but
no sounds issued from it. That meant his colleagues had
completed their task of loading and were ready to go. All
that remained now was to change his clothing, remove
the makeup, and depart.

The Count moved to the darkened truck. And then . . .

Then they were upon him, and he felt the tines of the
pitchfork bite into his back, and as the flash of lanterns
dazzled his eyes he heard the stern command. "Don't
move!"

He didn't move. He could only stare as they surrounded him—Antoine, Clodez, Raymond, and the others, a dozen peasants from the village. A dozen armed

peasants, glaring at him in mingled rage and fear, holding him at bay.

But how could they dare?

The American corporal stepped forward. That was the answer, of course—the American corporal and another man in uniform, armed with a sniper's rifle. They were responsible. He didn't even have to see the riddled corpses of the three shortwave operators piled in the back of the truck to understand what had happened. They'd stumbled on his men while they worked, shot them down, then summoned the villagers.

Now they were jabbering questions at him, in English, of course. He understood English, but he knew better than to reply. "Who are you? Were these men working under your orders? Where were you going with this truck?"

The Count smiled and shook his head. After a while they stopped, as he knew they would.

The corporal turned to his companion. "Okay," he said. "Let's go." The other man nodded and climbed into the cab of the truck as the motor coughed into life. The corporal moved to join him, then turned to Raymond.

"We're taking this across the river," he said. "Hang on to our friend here—they'll be sending a guard detail for him within an hour."

Raymond nodded.

The truck drove off into the darkness.

And it was dark now—the moon had vanished behind a cloud. The Count's smile vanished, too, as he glanced around at his captors. A rabble of stupid clods, surly and ignorant. But armed. No chance of escaping. And they kept staring at him, and mumbling.

"Take him into the tomb."

It was Raymond who spoke, and they obeyed, prodding their captive forward with pitchforks. That was when the Count recognized the first faint ray of hope. For they prodded him most gingerly, no man coming close, and when he glared at them their eyes dropped.

They were putting him in the crypt because they were afraid of him. Now the Americans were gone, they feared him once more—feared his presence and his power. After all, in their eyes he was a vampire—he might turn into a bat and vanish entirely. So they wanted him in the tomb for safekeeping.

The Count shrugged, smiled his most sinister smile, and bared his teeth. They shrank back as he entered the doorway. He turned and, on impulse, furled his cape. It was an instinctive final gesture, in keeping with his role—and it provoked the appropriate response. They moaned and old Raymond crossed himself. It was better, in a way, than any applause.

In the darkness of the crypt the Count permitted himself to relax a trifle. He was offstage now. A pity he'd not been able to make his exit the way he'd planned, but such were the fortunes of war. Soon he'd be taken to the American headquarters and interrogated. Undoubtedly there would be some unpleasant moments, but the worst that could befall him was a few months in a prison camp.

And even the Americans must bow to him in appreciation when they heard the story of his masterful deception.

It was dark in the crypt, and musty. The Count moved about restlessly. His knee grazed the edge of the empty coffin set on a trestle in the tomb. He shuddered involuntarily, loosening his cape at the throat. It would be good to remove it, good to be out of here, good to shed the role of vampire forever. He'd played it well, but now he was anxious to be gone.

There was a mumbling audible from outside, mingled with another and less identifiable noise—a scraping sound. The Count moved to the closed door of the crypt and listened intently; but now there was only silence.

What were the fools doing out there? He wished the Americans would hurry back. It was too hot in here. And why the sudden silence?

Perhaps they'd gone.

Yes. That was it. The Americans had told them to wait and guard him, but they were afraid. They really believed he was a vampire—old Raymond had convinced them of that. So they'd run off. They'd run off, and he was free, he could escape now . . .

So the Count opened the door.

And he saw them then, saw them standing and waiting, old Raymond staring sternly for a moment before he moved forward. He was holding something in his hand, and the Count recognized it, remembering the scraping sound that he'd heard.

It was a long wooden stake with a sharp point.

Then he opened his mouth to scream, telling them it was only a trick, he was no vampire, they were a pack of superstitious fools . . .

But all the while they bore him back into the crypt, lifting him up and thrusting him into the open coffin, holding him there as the grim-faced Raymond raised the pointed stake above his heart.

It was only when the stake came down that he realized there's such a thing as playing a role too well.

DRACULA'S CHAIR

◆◆◆

PETER TREMAYNE

Maybe this is an hallucination. Perhaps I am mad. How else can this be explained?

I sit here alone and helpless! So utterly alone! Alone in an age which is not mine, in a body which is not mine. Oh God! I am slowly being killed—or worse! Yet what is worse than death? That terrifying limbo that is the borderland of Hell, that state that is neither the restful sleep of death nor the perplexities of life but is the nightmare of undeath.

He is draining me of life and yet, *yet is it me who is the victim*? How can I tell him that the person he thinks I am, the person whose body my mind inhabits, is no longer in that body? How can I tell him that *I* am in the body of his victim? *I* . . . a person from another time, another age, another place!

God help me! He is draining me of life and I cannot prevent him!

When did this nightmare begin? An age away. I suppose it began when my wife and I saw the chair.

We were driving back to London one hot July Sunday

afternoon, having been picnicking in Essex. We were returning about mid-afternoon down the A11, through the village of Newport, when my wife suddenly called upon me to pull over and stop.

"I've just seen the most exquisite chair in the window of an antique shop."

I was somewhat annoyed because I wanted to get home early that evening to see a vintage Humphrey Bogart film on the television, one I'd never seen before even though I have been a Bogart fan for years.

"What's the point?" I muttered grumpily, getting out of the car and trailing after her. "The shop's shut anyway."

But the shop wasn't shut. Passing trade on a Sunday from Londoners was apparently very lucrative and most antique shops in the area opened during the afternoons.

The chair stood like a lone sentinel in the window. It was square in shape, a wooden straight-backed chair with sturdy arms. It was of a plain and simple design, dark oak wood yet with none of the ornate woodwork that is commonly associated with such items. The seat was upholstered in a faded tapestry work which was obviously the original. It was a very unattractive upholstery for it was in a faded black with a number of once white exotic dragon's heads. The same upholstery was reflected in a piece which provided a narrow back rest—a strip a foot deep thrust across the middle of the frame. My impression of the chair was hardly "exquisite"—it was a squat, ugly, and aggressive piece. Certainly it did not seem worth the £100 price ticket which was attached by string to one arm.

My wife had contrary ideas. It was, she felt, exactly the right piece to fill a corner in my study and provide a spare chair for extra guests. It could, she assured me, easily be re-upholstered to fit in with our general colour scheme of greens and golds. What was wanted, she said, was a functional chair and this was it. She was adamant and so I resigned myself to a minimum of grumbling, one eye on my watch to ensure I would not miss the Bogart film. The transaction was concluded fairly quickly by comparison with my wife's usual standard of detailed questioning and examination. Perhaps the vendor was rather more loquacious than the average antique dealer.

"It's a very nice chair," said the dealer with summoned enthusiasm. "It's a Victorian piece of eastern European origin. Look, on the back you can actually see a date of manufacture and the place of origin." He pointed to the back of the chair where, carved into the wood with small letters, was the word "Bistritz" and the date "1887." The dealer smiled in the surety of knowledge. "That makes it Romanian in origin. Actually, I purchased the piece from the old Purfleet Art Gallery."

"The Purfleet Art Gallery?" said I, thinking it time to make some contribution to the conversation. "Isn't that the old gallery and museum over which there were some protests a few months ago?"

"Yes, do you know the place? Purfleet in Essex? The gallery was housed in an ancient building, a manor house called Carfax, which was said to date back to medieval times. The old gallery had been there since the late Victorian period but had to close through lack of government subsidies, and the building is being carved up into apartments."

I nodded, feeling I had, perhaps, made too much of a contribution.

The antique dealer went on obliviously.

"When the gallery closed, a lot of its *objets d'art* were auctioned and I bought this chair. According to the auctioneer's catalogue it had been in the old house when the gallery first opened and had belonged to the previous owner. He was said to have been a foreign nobleman . . . probably a Romanian by the workmanship of the chair."

Finally, having had her fears assuaged over matters of woodworm, methods of upholstery, and the like, the purchase was concluded by my wife. The chair was strapped to the roofrack of my car and we headed homewards.

The next day was Monday. My wife, who is in research, had gone to her office while I spent the morning in my study doodling on pieces of paper and vainly waiting for a new plot to mature for the television soap-opera that I was scripting at the time. At mid-day my wife telephoned to remind me to check around for some price quotations for re-upholstering our purchase. I had forgotten all about the chair, still strapped to the roofrack of my car. Feeling a little guilty, I went down to the garage and untied it, carrying it up to my study and placing it in the alloted corner with a critical eye. I confess, I did not like the thing; it was so square and seemed to somehow challenge me. It is hard to define what I mean but you have, I suppose, seen certain types of people with thrust-out jaws, square and aggressive? Well, the chair gave the same impression.

After a while, perhaps in response to its challenge, I decided to sit down in the chair, and as I sat, a sudden coldness spread up my spine and a weird feeling of unease came over me. So strong was it that I immediately jumped up. I stood there looking down at the chair and feeling a trifle self-conscious. I laughed nervously. Ridiculous! What would my friend Philip, who was a psychiatrist, say to such behaviour? I did not like the chair but there was no need to create physical illusions around my distaste.

I sat down again and, as expected, the cold feelings of unease were gone—a mere shadow in my mind. In fact, I was surprised at the comfort of the chair. I sat well back, arms and hands resting on the wooden arm rests, head leaning against the back, legs spread out. It was extremely comfortable.

So comfortable was it that a feeling of deep relaxation came over me, and with the relaxation came the desire to have a cat-nap. I must confess, I tend to enjoy a ten minute nap just after lunch. It relaxes me and stimulates the mind. I sat back, closed my drooping eyelids, and gently let myself drift, drift . . .

It was dark when I awoke.

For an instant I struggled with the remnants of my

dreams. Then my mind cleared and I looked about me.
My first thought was the question—how long had I slept?
I could see the dark hue of early evening through the tall
windows. Then I started *for there were no tall windows in
my study nor anywhere in our house*!

Blinking my eyes rapidly to focus them in the darkened room, I abruptly perceived that I was not in my
study, nor was I in any room that I had ever seen before. I
tried to rise in my surprise and found that I could not
move—some sluggish feeling in my body prevented me
from coordinating my limbs. My mind had clarity and
will but below my neck my whole body seemed numb.
And so I just sat there, staring wildly at the unfamiliar
room in a cold sweat of fear and panic. I tried to blink
away the nightmare, tried to rationalize.

I could move my head around and doing so I found
that I was sitting in the same chair—that accursed chair!
Yet it seemed strangely newer than I remembered it. I
thought, perhaps it was a trick of the light. But I discovered that around my legs was tucked a woolen blanket
while the top half of me was clad in a pajama jacket over
which was a velvet smoking jacket, a garment that I knew
I had never owned. My eyes wandered around the room
from object to unfamiliar object, each unfamiliar item
causing the terror to mount in my veins, now surging
with adrenaline. I was in a lounge filled with some fine
pieces of Victoriana. The chair in which I sat now stood
before an open hearth in which a few coals faintly glim-
mered. In one corner stood a lean, tall grandfather clock,

whose steady tick-tock added to the oppressiveness of the scene. There was, so far as I could see, nothing modern in the room at all.

But for me the greatest horror was the strange paralysis which kept me anchored in that chair. I tried to move until the sweat poured from my face with the effort. I even tried to shout, opening my mouth wide to emit strange choking-like noises. What in God's name had happened to me?

Suddenly a door opened. Into the room came a young girl of about seventeen holding aloft one of those old brass oil lamps, the sort you see converted into electric lamps these days by "trendy" people. Yet this was no converted lamp but a lamp from which a flame spluttered and emitted the odour of burning paraffin. And the girl! She wore a long black dress with a high button collar, with a white linen apron over it. Her fair hair was tucked inside a small white cap set at a jaunty angle on her head. In fact, she looked like a serving maid straight out of those Victorian drama serials we get so often on the television these days. She came forward and placed the lamp on a table near me, and then started, seeing my eyes wide open and upon her. I tried to speak to her, to demand, to exhort some explanation, to ask what the meaning of this trickery was, but only a strangled gasp came from my throat.

The girl was clearly frightened and bobbed what was supposed to be a curtsy in my direction before turning to the door.

"Ma'am! Ma'am!" Her strong Cockney accent made the word sound like "Mum!" "Master's awake, ma'am. What'll I do?"

Another figure moved into the room, tall, graceful, wearing an elegant Victorian dress hung low at the shoulders, and leaving very little of her bust to the imagination. A black ribbon with a cameo was fastened to her pale throat. Her raven black hair was done up in a bun at the back of her head. Her face was small, heart-shaped, and pretty. The lips were naturally red though a trifle sullen for her features. The eyes were deep green and seemed a little sad. She came towards me, bent over me, and gave a wan smile. There was a strange, almost unnatural pallor to her complexion.

"That's all, Fanny," she said. "I'll see to him now."

"Yes, ma'am." The girl bobbed another curtsy and was gone through the door.

"Poor Upton," whispered the woman before me. "Poor Upton. I wish I knew whether you hurt at all? No one seems to know from what strange malady you suffer."

She stood back and sighed sorrowfully and deeply.

"It's time for your medication."

She picked up a bottle and a spoon, pouring a bitter-smelling amber liquid which she forced down my throat. I felt a numbing bitterness searing down my gullet.

"Poor Upton," she sighed again. "It's bitter I know but the doctor says it will take away any pain."

I tried to speak; tried to tell her that I was not Upton, that I did not want her medicine, that I wanted this play-

acting to cease. I succeeded only in gnashing my teeth
and making inarticulate cries like some wild beast at bay.
The woman took a step backwards, her eyes widening in
fright. Then she seemed to regain her composure.

"Come, Upton," she chided. "This won't do at all. Try
to relax."

The girl, Fanny, reappeared.

"Doctor Seward is here, ma'am."

A stocky man in a brown tweed suit, looking like some
character out of a Dickens novel, stepped into the room
and bowed over the woman's proffered hand.

"John," smiled the woman. "I'm so glad you've come."

"How are you, Clara," smiled the man. "You look a trifle weary, a little pale."

"I'm alright, John. But I worry about Upton."

The man turned to me.

"Yes, how is the patient? I swear he looks a little more
alert today."

The woman, Clara, spread her hands and shrugged.

"To me he seems little better, John. Even when he
seems more alert physically he can only growl like a
beast. I try my best but I fear . . . I fear that . . ."

The man called John patted her hand and gestured
her to silence. Then he came and bent over me with a
friendly smile.

"Strange," he murmured. "Indeed, a strange afflic-
tion. And yet . . . yet I do detect a more intelligent gleam
in the eyes today. Hello, old friend, do you know me. It's
John . . . John Seward? Do you recognise me?"

He leaned close to my face, so close I could smell the scent of oranges on his breath.

I struggled to break the paralysis which gripped me and only succeeded in issuing a number of snarls and grunts. The man drew back.

"Upon my word, Clara, has he been violent at all?"

"Not really, John. He does excite himself so with visitors. But perhaps it is his way of trying to communicate with us."

The man grunted and nodded.

"Well, the only remedy for pain is to keep dosing him with the laudanum as I prescribed it. I think he is a little better. However, I shall call again tomorrow to see if there is a significant improvement. If not, I will ask your permission to consult a specialist, perhaps a doctor from Harley Street. There are a number of factors that still puzzle me—the anaemia, the apparent lack of red blood corpuscles or hemoglobin. His paleness and languor. And these strange wounds on his neck do not seem to be healing at all."

The woman bit her lip and lowered her voice.

"You may be frank with me, John. You have known Upton and me for some years now. I am resigned to the fact that there can only be a worsening of his condition. I do fear for his life."

The man glanced at me nervously.

"Should you talk like this in front of him?"

The woman sighed. "He cannot understand, of that I am sure. Poor Upton. Just to think that a few short days ago he was so full of life, so active, and now this strange disease has cut him down . . ."

The man nodded.

"You have been a veritable goddess, Clara, charity herself, nursing him constantly day and night. I shall look in again tomorrow, but if there is no improvement I shall seek permission to call in a specialist."

Clara lowered her head as if in resignation.

The man turned to me and forced a smile.

"So long, old fellow . . ."

I tried to call, desperately tried to plead for help. Then he was gone.

The minutes dragged into hours as the woman, Clara, who was supposed to be my wife, sat gazing into the fire, while I sat pinioned in my accursed chair opposite to her. How long we sat thus I do not truly know. From time to time I felt her gaze, sad and thoughtful, upon me. Then I became aware, somewhere in the house, of a clock commencing to strike. A few seconds later it was followed by the resonant and hollow sounds of the grandfather clock. Without raising my head I counted slowly to twelve. Midnight.

The woman Clara abruptly sprung from her chair and stood upright before the fire.

As I looked up she seemed to change slightly — it is hard to explain. Her face seemed to grow coarser, more bloated. Her tongue, a red glistening object, darted nervously over her lips making them moist and of a deeper red than before, contrasting starkly to the sharp whiteness of her teeth. A strange lustre began to sparkle in her eyes. She raised a languid hand and began to massage her neck slowly, sensually.

Then, abruptly, she laughed—a low voluptuous chuckle that made the hairs on my neck bristle.

She gazed down at me with a wanton expression, a lascivious smile.

"Poor Upton." Her tone was a gloating caress. "He'll be coming soon. You'll like that, won't you? Yet why he takes you first, I cannot understand. Why *you*? Am I not full of the warmth of life—does not warm, rich young blood flow in my veins? Why *you*?"

She made an obscene, seductive gesture with her body.

The way she crooned, the saliva trickling from a corner of those red—oh, so red—lips, made my heart beat faster yet at the same time, the blood seemed to deny its very warmth and pump like some ice-cold liquid in my veins.

What new nightmare was this?

How *he* appeared I do not know.

One minute there was just the woman and myself in the room. Then he was standing there.

A tall man, apparently elderly although his pale face held no aging of the skin; only the long white moustache which drooped over his otherwise clean-shaven face gave the impression of age. His face was strong—extremely strong, aquiline with a high-bridged nose and peculiarly arched nostrils. His forehead was loftily domed and hair grew scantily round the temples but profusely elsewhere. The eyebrows were massive and nearly met across the bridge of the nose.

It was his mouth which captured my attention—a mouth set in the long pale face, fixed and cruel looking, with teeth that protruded over the remarkably ruddy lips whose redness had the effect of highlighting his white skin and giving the impression of an extraordinary pallor. And where the teeth protruded over the lips, they were white and sharp.

His eyes seemed a ghastly red in the glow of the flickering fire.

The woman, Clara, took a step toward him, hands out as if imploring, a glad cry on her red wanton lips, her breasts heaving as if with some wild ecstasy.

"My Lord," she cried, "you have come!"

The tall man ignored her. His red eyes were upon mine, seeming to devour me.

The woman raised a hand to massage her throat.

"Lord, take me first! Take me now!"

The tall man took a stride towards me, drawing back an arm and pushing her roughly aside.

"It is he that I shall take first," he said sibilantly, with a strange accent to his English. "You shall wait your turn which shall be in a little while."

The woman made to protest but he stopped her with an upraised hand.

"Dare you question me?" he said mildly. "Have no fear. You shall be my bountiful wine press in a while. But first I shall slake my thirst with him."

He towered over me as I remained helpless in that chair, that accursed chair. A smile edged his face.

"Is it not just?" whispered the tall man. "Is it not just that having thwarted me, you, Upton Welsford, now become everything that you abhorred and feared?"

And while part of my mind was witnessing this obscene hallucination, another part of it began to experience a strange excitement—almost a sexual excitement as the man lowered his face to mine . . . closer came those awful red eyes to gaze deep into my soul. His mouth was open slightly, I could smell a vile reek of corruption. There was a deliberate voluptuousness about his movements that was both thrilling and appalling—he licked his lips like some animal, the scarlet tongue flickering over the white sharp teeth.

Lower came his head, lower, until it passed from my sight and I could hear the churning sound of his tongue against his teeth and could feel his hot breath on my neck. The skin of my throat began to tingle. Then I felt the soft shivering touch of his cold lips on my throat, the hard indent of two sharp white teeth!

For a while, how long I could not measure, I seemed to fall into a languorous ecstasy.

Then he was standing above me, smiling down sardonically, a trickle of blood on his chin. My blood!

"There is one more night to feast with him," he said

softly. "One night more and then, Upton Welsford, you shall be my brother."

The woman exclaimed in anger.

"But you promised! You promised! When am I to be called?"

The tall man turned and laughed.

"Aye, I promised, my slender vine. You already bear my mark. You belong to me. You shall be one with me, never fear. Immortality will soon be yours and we shall share in the drinking. You will provide me with the wine of life. Have patience, for the greatest wines are long in the savouring. I shall return."

Then to my horror the man was gone. Simply gone, as if he had dissolved into elemental dust.

For some time I sat in horror staring at the woman who seemed to have retreated into a strange trance. Then the grandfather clock began to chime and the woman started, as if waking from a deep sleep. She stared in amazement at the clock and then towards the window where the faint light of early dawn was beginning to show.

"Good Lord, Upton," she exclaimed, "we seemed to have been up all night. I must have fallen asleep, I'm sorry."

She shook herself.

"I've had a strange dream. Ah well, no matter. I'd better get you up to bed. I'll go and wake poor Fanny to help me."

She smiled softly at me as she left the room; there was

no trace of the wanton seductress left on her delicate features.

She left me sitting alone, alone in my prison of a chair.

I sit here alone and helpless. So utterly alone! Alone in an age which is not mine, in a body which is not mine. Oh God! I am slowly being killed—or worse! Yet what is worse than death? That terrifying limbo that is the borderland of Hell, that state that is neither the restful sleep of death nor the perplexities of life but is the nightmare of undeath.

And where is this person . . . the Upton Welsford whose body I now inhabit? Where is he? Has he, by some great effort of will, exchanged his body with mine? Is he even now awakening from that cat-nap sometime in the future? Awakening in my body, in my study, to resume my life? Is he doing even as I have done? What does it all mean?

Maybe this is an hallucination. Perhaps I am mad. How else can all this be explained?

THE LAST LORDS OF GARDONAL

♦♦♦

WILLIAM GILBERT

I

One of the most picturesque objects of the valley of the Engadin is the ruined castle of Gardonal, near the village of Madaline. In the feudal times it was the seat of a family of barons, who possessed as their patrimony the whole of the valley, which with the castle had descended from father to son for many generations. The two last of the race were brothers; handsome, well-made, fine-looking young men, but in nature they more resembled fiends than human beings—so cruel, rapacious, and tyrannical were they. During the earlier part of his life their father had been careful of his patrimony. He had also been unusually just to the serfs on his estates, and in consequence they had attained to such a condition of comfort and prosperity as was rarely met with among those in the power of the feudal lords of the country; most of whom were arbitrary and exacting in the extreme. For several years in the latter part of his life he had been subject to a severe illness, which had confined him to the castle, and the management of his possessions and the government of his serfs had thus fallen into the hands of his sons. Although the old baron had placed so much power in their hands, still he was far from resigning his own authority. He exacted a strict account from them of the manner in which they performed the different duties he had intrusted to them; and having a strong suspicion of their character, and the probability of their endeavouring to conceal their misdoings, he caused agents to watch them secretly, and to report to him as to the correctness of the statements they gave. These agents, possibly knowing that the old man had but a short time to live, invariably gave a most favourable description of the conduct of the two young nobles, which, it must be admitted, was not, during their father's lifetime, particularly reprehensible on the whole. Still, they frequently showed as much of the cloven foot as to prove to the tenants what they had to expect at no distant day.

At the old baron's death, Conrad, the elder, inherited as his portion the castle of Gardonal, and the whole valley of Engadin; while to Hermann, the younger, was assigned some immense estates belonging to his father in the Bresciano district; for even in those early days, there was considerable intercourse between the inhabitants of that northern portion of Italy and those of the valley of the Engadin. The old baron had also willed, that should either of his sons die without children his estates should go to the survivor.

Conrad accordingly now took possession of the castle

and its territory, and Hermann of the estates on the southern side of the Alps; which, although much smaller than those left to his elder brother, were still of great value. Notwithstanding the disparity in the worth of the legacies bequeathed to the two brothers, a perfectly good feeling existed between them, which promised to continue, their tastes being the same, while the mountains which divided them tended to the continuance of peace.

Conrad had hardly been one single week feudal lord of the Engadin before the inhabitants found, to their sorrow, how great was the difference between him and the old baron. Instead of the score of armed retainers his father had kept, Conrad increased the number to three hundred men, none of whom were natives of the valley. They had been chosen with great care from a body of Bohemian, German, and Italian outlaws, who at that time infested the borders of the Grisons, or had found refuge in the fastnesses of the mountains—men capable of any atrocity and to whom pity was unknown. From these miscreants the baron especially chose for his bodyguard those who were ignorant of the language spoken by the peasantry of the Engadin, as they would be less likely to be influenced by any supplications or excuses which might be made to them when in the performance of their duty. Although the keeping of so numerous a body of armed retainers might naturally be considered to have entailed great expense, such a conclusion would be most erroneous, at least as far as regarded the present baron, who was as avaricious as he was despotic. He contrived to support his soldiers by imposing a most onerous tax on his tenants, irrespective of his ordinary feudal imposts; and woe to the unfortunate villagers who from inability, or from a sense of the injustice inflicted on them, did not contribute to the uttermost farthing the amount levied on them. In such a case a party of soldiers was immediately sent off to the defaulting village to collect the tax, with permission to live at free quarters till the money was paid; and they knew their duty too well to return home till they had succeeded in their errand. In doing this they were frequently merciless in the extreme, exacting the money by torture or any other means they pleased; and when they had been successful in obtaining the baron's dues, by way of further punishment they generally robbed the poor peasantry of everything they had which was worth the trouble of carrying away, and not unfrequently, from a spirit of sheer mischief, they spoiled all that remained. Many were the complaints which reached the ears of the baron of the cruel behaviour of his retainers; but in no case did they receive any redress; the baron making it a portion of his policy that no crimes committed by those under his command should be investigated, so long as those crimes took place when employed in collecting taxes which he had imposed, and which had remained unpaid.

But the depredations and cruelties of the Baron Conrad were not confined solely to the valley of the Engadin. Frequently in the summer-time when the snows had melted on the mountains, so as to make the road practicable for his soldiers and their plunder, he would make a raid on the Italian side of the Alps. There they would rob and commit every sort of atrocity with impunity; and when they had collected sufficient booty they returned with it to the castle. Loud indeed were the complaints which reached the authorities of Milan. With routine tardiness, the government never took any energetic steps to punish the offenders until the winter had set in; and to cross the mountains in that season would have been almost an impossibility, at all events for an army. When the spring returned, more prudential reasons prevailed, and the matter, gradually diminishing in interest, was at last allowed to die out without any active measures being taken. Again, the districts in which the atrocities had been committed were hardly looked upon by the Milanese government as being Italian. The people themselves were beginning to be infected by a heresy which approached closely to the Protestantism of the present day; nor was their language that of Italy, but a patois of their own. Thus the government began to consider it unadvisable to attempt to punish the baron, richly as he deserved it, on behalf of those who after all were little worthy of the protection they demanded. The only real step they took to chastise him was to get him excommunicated by the Pope; which, as the baron and his followers professed no religion at all, was treated by them with ridicule.

It happened that in one of his marauding expeditions in the Valteline, the baron, when near Bormio, saw a young girl of extraordinary beauty. He was only attended at the time by two followers, else it is more than probable he would have made her a prisoner and carried her off to Gardonal. As it was he would probably have made the attempt had she not been surrounded by a number of peasants, who were working in some fields belonging to her father. The baron was also aware that the militia of the town, who had been expecting his visit, were under arms, and on an alarm being given could be on the spot in a few minutes. Now as the baron combined with his despotism a considerable amount of cunning, he merely attempted to enter into conversation with the girl. Finding his advances coldly received, he contented himself with inquiring of one of the peasants the girl's name and place of abode. He received for reply that her name was Teresa Biffi, and that she was the daughter of a substantial farmer, who with his wife and four children (of whom Teresa was the eldest) lived in a house at the extremity of the land he occupied.

As soon as the baron had received this information, he left the spot, and proceeded to the farmer's house, which he inspected externally with great care. He found it was of considerable size, strongly built of stone, with iron bars to the lower windows, and a strong well-made oaken door which could be securely fastened from the inside. After having made the round of the house (which he did alone), he returned to his two men, whom, in order to avoid suspicion, he had placed at a short distance from the building, in a spot where they could not easily be seen.

"Ludovico," he said to one of them who was his lieutenant, and invariably accompanied him in all his expeditions, "mark well that house; for some day, or more probably night, you may have to pay it a visit."

Ludovico merely said in reply that he would be always ready and willing to perform any order his master might honour him with; and the baron, with his men, then left the spot.

The hold the beauty of Teresa Biffi had taken upon the imagination of the baron actually looked like enchantment. His love for her, instead of diminishing by time, seemed to increase daily. At last he resolved on making her his wife; and about a month after he had seen her, he commissioned his lieutenant Ludovico to carry to Biffi an offer of marriage with his daughter; not dreaming, at the moment, of the possibility of a refusal. Ludovico immediately started on his mission, and in due time arrived at the farmer's house and delivered the baron's message. To Ludovico's intense surprise, however, he received from Biffi a positive refusal. Not daring to take back so uncourteous a reply to his master, Ludovico went on to describe the great advantage which would accrue to the farmer and his family if the baron's proposal were accepted. Not only, he said, would Teresa be a lady of the highest rank, and in possession of enormous wealth both in gold and jewels, but that the other members of her family would also be ennobled, and each of them, as they grew up, would receive appointments under the baron, besides having large estates allotted to them in the Engadin Valley.

The farmer listened with patience to Ludovico, and when he had concluded, he replied—

"Tell your master I have received his message, and that I am ready to admit that great personal advantages might accrue to me and my family by accepting his offer. Say, that although I am neither noble nor rich, that yet at the same time I am not poor; but were I as poor as the blind mendicant whom you passed on the road in coming hither, I would spurn such an offer from so infamous a wretch as the baron. You say truly that he is well known for his power and his wealth; but the latter has been obtained by robbing both rich and poor, who had not the means to resist him, and his power has been greatly strengthened by engaging in his service a numerous band of robbers and cut-throats, who are ready and willing to murder any one at his bidding. You have my answer, and the sooner you quit this neighbourhood the better, for I can assure you that any one known to be in the service of the Baron Conrad is likely to meet with a most unfavourable reception from those who live around us."

"Then you positively refuse his offer?" said Ludovico.

"Positively, and without the slightest reservation," was the farmer's reply.

"And you wish me to give him the message in the terms you have made use of?"

"Without omitting a word," was the farmer's reply. "At the same time, you may add to it as many of the same description as you please."

"Take care," said Ludovico. "There is yet time for you to reconsider your decision. If you insist on my taking your message to the baron, I must of course do so; but in that case make your peace with heaven as soon as you can, for the baron is not a man to let such an insult pass. Follow my advice, and accept his offer ere it is too late."

"I have no other answer to give you," said Biffi.

"I am sorry for it," said Ludovico, heaving a deep sigh; "I have now no alternative," and mounting his horse he rode away.

Now it must not be imagined that the advice Ludovico gave the farmer, and the urgent requests and arguments he offered, were altogether the genuine effusions of his heart. On the contrary, Ludovico had easily perceived, on hearing the farmer's first refusal, that there was no chance of the proposal being accepted. He had therefore occupied his time during the remaining portion of the interview in carefully examining the premises, and mentally taking note of the manner in which they could be most easily entered, as he judged, rightly enough, that before long he might be sent to the house on a far less peaceable mission.

Nothing could exceed the rage of the baron when he heard the farmer's message.

"You cowardly villain!" he said to Ludovico. "Did you allow the wretch to live who could send such a message to your master?"

"So please you," said Ludovico. "What could I do?"

"You could have struck him to the heart with your dagger, could you not?" said the baron. "I have known you to do such a thing to an old woman for half the provocation. Had it been Biffi's wife instead you might have shown more courage."

"Had I followed my own inclination," said Ludovico, "I would have killed the fellow on the spot; but then I could not have brought away the young lady with me, for there were too many persons about the house and in the fields at the time. So I thought, before acting further, I had better let you hear his answer. One favour I hope your excellency will grant me, that if the fellow is to be punished you will allow me to inflict it as a reward for the skill I showed in keeping my temper when I heard the message."

"Perhaps you have acted wisely, Ludovico," said the baron, after a few moments' silence. "At present my mind is too much ruffled by the villain's impertinence to think calmly on the subject. Tomorrow we will speak of it again."

Next day the baron sent for his lieutenant, and said to him—

"Ludovico, I have now a commission for you to execute which I think will be exactly to your taste. Take with you six men whom you can trust, and start this afternoon for Bormio. Sleep at some village on the road, but let not one word escape you as to your errand. Tomorrow morning leave the village—but separately—so that you may not be seen together, as it is better to avoid suspicion. Meet again near the farmer's house, and arrive there, if possible, before evening has set in, for in all probability you will have to make an attack upon the house, and you may thus become well acquainted with the locality before doing so; but keep yourselves concealed, otherwise you will spoil all. After you have done this, retire some distance, and remain concealed till midnight, as then all the family will be in their first sleep, and you will experience less difficulty than if you began later. I particularly wish you to enter the house without using force, but if you cannot do so, break into it in any way you consider best. Bring out the girl and do her no harm. If any resistance is made by her father, kill him; but not unless you are compelled, as I do not wish to enrage his daughter against me. However, let nothing prevent you from securing her. Burn the house down or anything you please, but bring her here. If you execute your mission promptly and to my satisfaction, I promise you and those with you a most liberal reward. Now go and get ready to depart as speedily as you can."

Ludovico promised to execute the baron's mission to the letter, and shortly afterwards left the castle accompanied by six of the greatest ruffians he could find among the men-at-arms.

Although on the spur of the moment Biffi had sent so defiant a message to the baron, he afterwards felt considerable uneasiness as to the manner in which it would be received. He did not repent having refused the proposal, but he knew that the baron was a man of the most cruel and vindictive disposition, and would in all probability seek some means to be avenged. The only defence he could adopt was to make the fastenings of his house as secure as possible, and to keep at least one of his labourers about him whom he could send as a messenger to Bormio for assistance, and to arouse the inhabitants in the immediate vicinity, in case of his being attacked. Without any hesitation all promised to aid Biffi in every way in their power, for he had acquired great renown among the inhabitants of the place for the courage he had shown in refusing so indignantly the baron's offer of marriage for his daughter.

About midnight, on the day after Ludovico's departure from the castle, Biffi was aroused by some one knocking at the door of his house, and demanding admission. It was Ludovico, for after attempting in vain to enter the house secretly, he had concealed his men, determining to try the effect of treachery before using force. On the inquiry being made as to who the stranger was, he replied that he was a poor traveller who had lost his way, and begged that he might be allowed a night's lodging, as he was so weary he could not go a step further.

"I am sorry for you," said Biffi, "but I cannot allow you to enter this house before daylight. As the night is fine and warm you can easily sleep on the straw under the windows, and in the morning I will let you in and give you a good breakfast."

Again and again did Ludovico plead to be admitted, but in vain; Biffi would not be moved from his resolution. At last, however, the bravo's patience got exhausted, and suddenly changing his manner he roared out in a threatening tone, "If you don't let me in, you villain, I will burn your house over your head. I have here, as you may see, plenty of men to help me to put my threat into execution," he continued, pointing to the men, who had now come up, "so you had better let me in at once."

In a moment Biffi comprehended the character of the person he had to deal with; so, instead of returning any answer, he retired from the window and alarmed the inmates of the house. He also told the labourer whom he had engaged to sleep there to drop from a window at the back and run as fast as he could to arouse the inhabitants in the vicinity, and tell them that his house was attacked by the baron and his men. He was to beg them to arm themselves and come to his aid as quickly as possible, and having done this, he was to go on to Bormio on the same errand. The poor fellow attempted to carry out his master's orders; but in dropping from the window he fell with such force on the ground that he could only move with difficulty, and in trying to crawl away he was observed by some of the baron's men, who immediately set on him and killed him.

Ludovico, finding that he could not enter the house either secretly or by threatenings, attempted to force open the door, but it was so firmly barricaded from within that he did not succeed; while in the meantime Biffi and his family employed themselves in placing wooden faggots and heavy articles of furniture against it, thus making it stronger than ever. Ludovico, finding he could not gain an entrance by the door, told his men to look around in search of a ladder, so that they might get to the windows on the first floor, as those on the ground floor were all small, high up, and well barricaded, as was common in Italian houses of the time; but in spite of all their efforts no ladder could be found. He now deliberated what step he should next take. As it was getting late, he saw that if they did not succeed in effecting an entrance quickly the dawn would break upon them, and the labourers going to their work would raise an alarm. At last one man suggested that as abundance of fuel could be obtained from the stacks at the back of the house they might place a quantity of it against the door and set fire to it; adding that the sight of the flames would soon make the occupants glad to effect their escape by the first-floor windows.

The suggestion was no sooner made than acted upon. A quantity of dry fuel was piled up against the house door to the height of many feet, and a light having been procured by striking a flint stone against the hilt of a

sword over some dried leaves, fire was set to the pile.
From the dry nature of the fuel, the whole mass was in
a blaze in a few moments. But the scheme did not
have the effect Ludovico had anticipated. True, the family rushed towards the windows in the front of the house,
but when they saw the flames rising so fiercely they retreated in the utmost alarm. Meanwhile the screams
from the women and children—who had now lost all
self-control—mingled with the roar of the blazing element, which, besides having set fire to the faggots and
furniture placed within the door, had now reached a
quantity of fodder and Indian corn stored on the ground
floor.

Ludovico soon perceived that the whole house was in
flames, and that the case was becoming desperate. Not
only was there the danger of the fire alarming the inhabitants in the vicinity by the light it shed around, but he
also reflected what would be the rage of his master if the
girl should perish in the flames, and the consequent punishment which would be inflicted on him and those under his command if he returned empty-handed. He now
called out to Biffi and his family to throw themselves out
of the window, and that he and his men would save
them. It was some time before he was understood, but at
last Biffi brought the two younger children to the window, and, lowering them as far as he could, he let them
fall into the arms of Ludovico and his men, and they
reached the ground in safety.

Biffi now returned for the others, and saw Teresa

standing at a short distance behind him. He took her by the hand to bring her forward, and they had nearly reached the window, when she heard a scream from her mother, who being an incurable invalid was confined to her bed. Without a moment's hesitation, the girl turned back to assist her, and the men below, who thought that the prey they wanted was all but in their hands, and cared little about the fate of the rest of the family, were thus disappointed. Ludovico now anxiously awaited the reappearance of Teresa—but he waited in vain. The flames had gained entire mastery, and even the roof had taken fire. The screams of the inmates were now no longer heard, for if not stifled in the smoke they were lost in the roar of the fire; whilst the glare which arose from it illumined the landscape far and near.

It so happened that a peasant, who resided about a quarter of a mile from Biffi's house, had to go a long distance to his work, and having risen at an unusually early hour, he saw the flames, and aroused the inmates of the other cottages in the village, who immediately armed themselves and started off to the scene of the disaster, imagining, but too certainly, that it was the work of an incendiary. The alarm was also communicated to another village, and from thence to Bormio, and in a short time a strong band of armed men had collected, and proceeded together to assist in extinguishing the flames. On their arrival at the house, they found the place one immense heap of ashes—not a soul was to be seen, for Ludovico and his men had already decamped.

The dawn now broke, and the assembled peasantry made some attempt to account for the fire. At first they were induced to attribute it to accident, but on searching around they found the dead body of the murdered peasant, and afterwards the two children who had escaped, and who in their terror had rushed into a thick copse to conceal themselves. With great difficulty they gathered from them sufficient to show that the fire had been caused by a band of robbers who had come for the purpose of plundering the house; and their suspicion fell immediately on Baron Conrad, without any better proof than his infamous reputation.

As soon as Ludovico found that an alarm had been given, he and his men started off to find their horses, which they had hidden among some trees about a mile distant from Biffi's house. The daylight was just breaking, and objects around them began to be visible, but not so clearly as to allow them to see for any distance. Suddenly one of the men pointed to an indistinct figure in white some little way in advance of them. Ludovico halted for a moment to see what it might be, and, with his men, watched it attentively as it appeared to fly from them.

"It is the young girl herself," said one of the men. "She has escaped from the fire; and that was exactly as she appeared in her white dress with her father at the window. I saw her well, and am sure I am not mistaken."

"It is indeed the girl," said another. "I also saw her."

"I hope you are right," said Ludovico, "and if so, it will

be fortunate indeed, for should we return without her we may receive but a rude reception from the baron."

They now quickened their pace, but, fast as they walked, the figure in white walked quite as rapidly. Ludovico, who of course began to suspect that it was Teresa attempting to escape from them, commanded his men to run as fast as they could in order to reach her. Although they tried their utmost, the figure, however, still kept the same distance before them. Another singularity about it was, that as daylight advanced the figure appeared to become less distinct, and ere they had reached their horses it seemed to have melted away.

II

Before mounting their horses, Ludovico held a consultation with his men as to what course they had better adopt; whether they should depart at once or search the neighbourhood for the girl. Both suggestions seemed to be attended with danger. If they delayed their departure, they might be attacked by the peasantry, who by this time were doubtless in hot pursuit of them; and if they returned to the baron without Teresa, they were almost certain to receive a severe punishment for failing in their enterprise. At last the idea struck Ludovico that a good round lie might possibly succeed with the baron and do something to avert his anger, while there was little hope of its in the slightest manner availing with the enraged peasantry. He therefore gave the order for his men to

mount their horses, resolving to tell the baron that Teresa
had escaped from the flames, and had begged their assistance, but a number of armed inhabitants of Bormio
chancing to approach, she had sought their protection. A
great portion of this statement could be substantiated by
his men, as they still fully believed that the figure in white
which they had so indistinctly seen was the girl herself.
Ludovico and his men during their homeward journey
had great difficulty in crossing the mountains, in consequence of a heavy fall of snow (for it was now late in the
autumn). Next day they arrived at the castle of Gardonal.

It would be difficult to describe the rage of the baron
when he heard that his retainers had been unsuccessful
in their mission. He ordered Ludovico to be thrown into
a dungeon, where he remained for more than a month,
and was only then liberated in consequence of the baron
needing his services for some expedition requiring special skill and courage. The other men were also punished, though less severely than their leader, on whom,
of course, they laid all the blame.

For some time after Ludovico's return, the baron occupied himself in concocting schemes, not only to secure the girl Teresa (for he fully believed the account
Ludovico had given of her escape), but to revenge himself on the inhabitants of Bormio for the part they had
taken in the affair; and it was to carry out these schemes
that he liberated Ludovico from prison.

. . .

The winter had passed, and the spring sun was rapidly melting the snows on the mountains, when one morning three travel-stained men, having the appearance of respectable burghers, arrived at the Hospice, and requested to be allowed an interview with the Innominato. A messenger was despatched to the castle, who shortly afterwards returned, saying that his master desired the visitors should immediately be admitted into his presence. When they arrived at the castle they found him fully prepared to receive them, a handsome repast being spread out for their refreshment. At first the travellers seemed under some restraint; but this was soon dispelled by the friendly courtesy of the astrologer. After partaking of the viands which had been set before them, the Innominato inquired the object of their visit. One of them, who had been evidently chosen as spokesman, then rose from his chair, and addressed their host as follows:

"We have been sent to your excellency by the inhabitants of Bormio, as a deputation, to ask your advice and assistance in a strait we are in at present. Late in the autumn of last year, the Baron Conrad, feudal lord of the Engadin, was on some not very honest expedition in our neighbourhood, when by chance he saw a very beautiful girl, of the name of Teresa Biffi, whose father occupied a large farm about half a league from the town. The baron, it appears, became so deeply enamoured of the girl that he afterwards sent a messenger to her father with an offer of marriage for his daughter. Biffi, knowing full well the infamous reputation of the baron, unhesitatingly declined his proposal, and in such indignant terms as to arouse the tyrant's anger to the highest pitch. Determining not only to possess himself of the girl, but to avenge the insult he had received, he sent a body of armed retainers, who in the night attacked the farmer's house, and endeavoured to effect an entrance by breaking open the door. Finding they could not succeed, and after murdering one of the servants who had been sent to a neighbouring village to give the alarm, they set fire to the house, and with the exception of two children who contrived to escape, the whole family, including the young girl herself, perished in the flames. It appears, however, that the baron (doubtless through his agents) received a false report that the young girl had escaped, and was taken under the protection of some of the inhabitants of Bormio. In consequence, he sent another body of armed men, who arrived in the night at the house of the podesta, and contrived to make his only son, a boy of about fifteen years old, a prisoner, bearing him off to the baron's castle. They left word, that unless Teresa Biffi was placed in their power before the first day of May, not only would the youth be put to death, but the baron would also wreak vengeance on the whole town. On the perpetration of this last atrocity, we again applied to the government of Milan for protection; but although our reception was most courteous, and we were promised assistance, we have too good reason to doubt our receiving it. Certainly up to the present time no steps have been taken in the matter, nor has a single soldier been sent, although the time named for the death of the child has nearly expired. The townsmen therefore, having heard of your great wisdom and power, your willingness to help those who are in distress, as well as to protect the weak and oppressed, have sent us to ask you to take them under your protection; as the baron is not a man to scruple at putting such a threat into execution."

The Innominato, who had listened to the delegate with great patience and attention, told him that he had no soldiers or retainers at his orders; while the baron, whose wicked life was known to him, had many.

"But your excellency has great wisdom, and from all we have heard, we feel certain that you could protect us."

"Your case," said the Innominato, "is a very sad one, I admit, and you certainly ought to be protected from the baron's machinations. I will not disguise from you that I have the power to help you. Tell the unhappy podesta that he need be under no alarm as to his son's safety, and that I will oblige the baron to release him. My art tells me that the boy is still alive, though confined in prison. As for your friends who sent you to me, tell them that the baron shall do them no harm. All you have to do is, to contrive some means by which the baron may hear that the girl Teresa Biffi has been placed by me where he will never find her without my permission."

"But Teresa Biffi," said the delegate, "perished with her father; and the baron will wreak his vengeance both on you and us, when he finds you cannot place the girl in his power."

"Fear nothing, but obey my orders," said the Innominato. "Do what I have told you, and I promise you shall have nothing to dread from him. The sooner you carry out my directions the better."

The deputation now returned to Bormio, and related all that had taken place at their interview with the Innominato. Although the result of their mission was scarcely considered satisfactory, they determined, after much consideration, to act on the astrologer's advice. But how to carry it out was a very difficult matter. This was, however, overcome by one of the chief inhabitants of the town—a man of most determined courage—offering himself as a delegate to the baron, to convey to him the Innominato's message. Without hesitation the offer was gratefully accepted, and the next day he started on his journey. No sooner had he arrived at the castle of Gardonal, and explained the object of his mission, than he was ushered into the presence of the baron, whom he found in the great hall, surrounded by a numerous body of armed men.

"Well," said the baron, as soon as the delegate had entered, "have your townspeople come to their senses at last, and sent me the girl Teresa?"

"No, they have not, baron," was the reply, "for she is not in their custody. All they can do is to inform you where you may possibly receive some information about her."

"And where may that be?"

"The only person who knows where she may be found

is the celebrated astrologer who lives in a castle near Lecco."

"Ah now, you are trifling with me," said the baron sternly. "You must be a great fool or a very bold man to try such an experiment as that."

"I am neither the one nor the other, your excellency; nor am I trifling with you. What I have told you is the simple truth."

"And how did you learn it?"

"From the Innominato's own lips."

"Then you applied to him for assistance against me," said the baron, furiously.

"That is hardly correct, your excellency," said the delegate. "It is true we applied to him for advice as to the manner in which we should act in case you should attack us, and put your threat into execution respecting the son of the podesta."

"And what answer did he give you?"

"Just what I have told you—that he alone knows where Teresa Biffi is to be found, and that you could not remove her from the protection she is under without his permission."

"Did he send that message to me in defiance?" said the baron.

"I have no reason to believe so, your excellency."

The baron was silent for some time; he then inquired of the delegate how many armed retainers the Innominato kept.

"None, I believe," was the reply. "At any rate, there were none to be seen when the deputation from the town visited him."

The baron was again silent for some moments, and seemed deeply absorbed in thought. He would rather have met with any other opponent than the Innominato, whose reputation was well known to him, and whose learning he dreaded more than the power of any noble-man—no matter how many armed retainers he could bring against him.

"I very much suspect," he said at last, "that some deception is being practised on me. But should my suspicion be correct I shall exact terrible vengeance. I shall detain you," he continued, turning abruptly and fiercely on the delegate; "as a hostage while I visit the Innominato; and if I do not succeed with him, you shall die on the same scaffold as the son of your podesta."

It was in vain that the delegate protested against being detained as a prisoner, saying that it was against all rules of knightly usage; but the baron would not listen to reason, and the unfortunate man was immediately hurried out of the hall and imprisoned.

Although the baron by no means liked the idea of an interview with the Innominato, he immediately made preparations to visit him, and the day after the delegate's arrival he set out on his journey, attended by only four of his retainers. It should here be mentioned, that it is more than probable the baron would have avoided meeting the Innominato on any other occasion whatever, so great was the dislike he had to him. He seemed to be acting under some fatality; some power seemed to impel him in his endeavours to obtain Teresa which it was impossible to account for.

The road chosen by the baron to reach the castle of the Innominato was rather a circuitous one. In the first place, he did not consider it prudent to pass through the Valteline; and in the second, he thought that by visiting his brother on his way he might be able to obtain some particulars as to the character of the mysterious individual whom he was about to see, as his reputation would probably be better known among the inhabitants of the Bergamo district than by those in the valley of the Engadin.

The baron arrived safely at his brother's castle, where the reports which had hitherto indistinctly reached him of the wonderful power and skill of the astrologer were fully confirmed. After remaining a day with his brother, the baron started for Lecco. Under an assumed name he stayed here for two days, in order that he might receive the report of one of his men, whom he had sent forward to ascertain whether the Innominato had any armed men in his castle; for, being capable of any act of treachery himself, he naturally suspected treason in others. The man in due time returned, and reported that, although he had taken great pains to find out the truth, he was fully convinced that not only were there no soldiers in the castle, but that it did not, to the best of his belief, contain an arm of any kind—the Innominato relying solely on his occult power for his defence.

Perfectly assured that he had no danger to apprehend, the baron left Lecco, attended by his retainers, and in a few hours afterwards he arrived at the Hospice, where his wish for an interview was conveyed to the astrologer. After some delay a reply was sent that the Innominato was willing to receive the baron on condition that he came alone, as his retainers would not be allowed to enter the castle. The baron hesitated for some moments, not liking to place himself in the power of a man who, after all, might prove a very dangerous adversary, and who might even use treacherous means. His love for Teresa Biffi, however, urged him to accept the invitation, and he accompanied the messenger to the castle.

The Innominato received his guest with stern courtesy; and, without even asking him to be seated, requested to know the object of his visit.

"Perhaps I am not altogether unknown to you," said the baron. "I am lord of the Engadin."

"Frankly," said the Innominato, "your name and reputation are both well known to me. It would give me great satisfaction were they less so."

"I regret to hear you speak in that tone," said the baron, evidently making great efforts to repress his rising passion. "A person in my position is not likely to be without enemies, but it rather surprises me to find a man of your reputation so prejudiced against me without having investigated the accusations laid to my charge."

"You judge wrongly if you imagine that I am so," said the Innominato. "But once more, will you tell me the object of your visit?"

"I understood," said the baron, "by a message sent to me by the insolent inhabitants of Bormio, that you know the person with whom a young girl, named Teresa Biffi, is at present residing. Might I ask if that statement is correct?"

"I hardly sent it in those words," said the Innominato. "But admitting it to be so, I must first ask your reason for inquiring."

"I have not the slightest objection to inform you," said the baron. "I have nothing to conceal. I wish to make her my wife."

"On those terms I am willing to assist you," said the astrologer. "But only on the condition that you immediately release the messenger you have most unjustly confined in one of your dungeons, as well as the young son of the podesta, and that you grant them a safe escort back to Bormio, and further, that you promise to cease annoying the people of that district. Do all this, and I am willing to promise you that Teresa Biffi shall not only become your wife, but shall bring with her a dowry and wedding outfit sufficiently magnificent even for the exalted position to which you propose to raise her."

"I solemnly promise you," said the baron, "that the moment the wedding is over, the delegate from Bormio and the son of the podesta shall both leave my castle perfectly free and unhampered with any conditions; and moreover that I will send a strong escort with them to protect them on their road."

"I see you are already meditating treachery," said the Innominato. "But I will not, in any manner, alter my offer. The day week after their safe return to Bormio Teresa Biffi shall arrive at the castle of Gardonal for the wedding ceremony. Now you distinctly know my conditions, and I demand from you an unequivocal acceptance or refusal."

"What security shall I have that the bargain will be kept on your side?" said the baron.

"My word, and no other."

The baron remained silent for a moment, and then said—

"I accept your offer. But clearly understand me in my turn, sir astrologer. Fail to keep your promise, and had you ten times the power you have I will take my revenge on you; and I am not a man to threaten such a thing without doing it."

"All that I am ready to allow," said the Innominato, with great coolness, "that is to say, in case you have the power to carry out your threat, which in the present instance you have not. Do not imagine that because I am not surrounded by a band of armed cut-throats and miscreants I am not the stronger of the two. You little dream how powerless you are in my hands. You see this bird," he continued, taking down a common sparrow in a wooden cage from a nail in the wall on which it hung. "It is not more helpless in my hands than you are; nay more, I will now give the bird far greater power over you than I possess over it."

As he spoke he unfastened the door of the cage, and the sparrow darted from it through the window into the air, and in a moment afterwards was lost to sight.

"That bird," the astrologer went on to say, "will follow you till I deprive it of the power. I bear you no malice for doubting my veracity. Falsehood is too much a portion of your nature for you to disbelieve its existence in others. I will not seek to punish you for the treachery which I am perfectly sure you will soon be imagining against me without giving you fair warning; for, a traitor yourself, you naturally suspect treason in others. As soon as you entertain a thought of evading your promise to release your prisoners, or conceive any treason or ill feeling against me, that sparrow will appear to you. If you instantly abandon the thought no harm will follow; but if you do not a terrible punishment will soon fall upon you. In whatever position you may find yourself at the moment, the bird will be near you, and no skill of yours will be able to harm it."

The baron now left the Innominato, and returned with his men to Lecco, where he employed himself for the remainder of the day in making preparations for his homeward journey. To return by the circuitous route he had taken in going to Lecco would have occupied too much time, as he was anxious to arrive at his castle, that he might without delay release the prisoners and make preparations for his wedding with Teresa Biffi. To pass the Valteline openly with his retainers—which was by far the shortest road—would have exposed him to too much danger; he therefore resolved to divide his party and send three men back by his brother's castle, so that they could return the horses they had borrowed. Then he would disguise himself and the fourth man (a German who could not speak a word of Italian, and from whom he had nothing therefore to fear on the score of treachery) as two Tyrolese merchants returning to their own country. He also purchased two mules and some provisions for the journey, so that they need not be obliged to rest in any of the villages they passed through, where possibly they might be detected, and probably maltreated.

Next morning the baron and his servant, together with the two mules, went on board a large bark which was manned by six men, and which he had hired for the occasion, and in it they started for Colico. At the commencement of their voyage they kept along the eastern side of the lake, but after advancing a few miles the wind, which had hitherto been moderate, now became so strong as to cause much fatigue to the rowers, and the captain of the bark determined on crossing the lake, so as to be under the lee of the mountains on the other side. When half way across they came in view of the turrets of the castle of the Innominato. The sight of the castle brought to the baron's mind his interview with its owner, and the defiant manner in which he had been treated by him. The longer he gazed the stronger became his anger against the Innominato, and at last it rose to such a point that he exclaimed aloud, to the great surprise of the men in the boat, "Some day I will meet thee again, thou insolent villain, and I will then take signal vengeance on thee for the insult offered me yesterday."

The words had hardly been uttered when a sparrow, apparently driven from the shore by the wind, settled on the bark for a moment, and then flew away. The baron instantly remembered what the Innominato had said to him, and also the warning the bird was to give. With a sensation closely resembling fear, he tried to change the current of his thoughts, and was on the point of turning his head from the castle, when the rowers in the boat simultaneously set up a loud shout of warning, and the baron then perceived that a heavily-laden vessel, four times the size of his own, and with a huge sail set, was running before the wind with great velocity, threatening the next moment to strike his boat on the beam; in which case both he and the men would undoubtedly be drowned. Fortunately, the captain of the strange bark had heard the cry of the rowers, and by rapidly putting down his helm, saved their lives; though the baron's boat was struck with so much violence on the quarter that she nearly sank.

The Baron Conrad had now received an earnest that the threat of the Innominato was not a vain one, and feeling that he was entirely in his power, resolved if possible not to offend him again. The boat continued on her voyage, and late in the evening arrived safely at Colico, where the baron, with his servant and the mules, disembarked, and without delay proceeded on their journey. They continued on their road till nightfall, when they began to consider how they should pass the night. They looked around them, but they could perceive no habitation or shelter of any kind, and it was now raining heavily. They continued their journey onwards, and had almost come to the conclusion that they should be obliged to pass the night in the open air, when a short distance before them they saw a low cottage, the door of which was open, showing the dim light of a fire burning within. The baron now determined to ask the owner of the cottage for permission to remain there for the night; but to be certain that no danger could arise, he sent forward his man to discover whether it was a house standing by itself, or one of a village; as in the latter case he would have to use great caution to avoid being detected. His servant accordingly left him to obey orders, and shortly afterwards returned with the news that the house was a solitary one, and that he could not distinguish a trace of any other in the neighbourhood. Satisfied with this information, the baron proceeded to the cottage door, and begged the inmates to afford him shelter for the night, assuring them that the next morning he would remunerate them handsomely. The peasant and his wife—a sickly-looking, emaciated old couple—gladly offered them all the accommodation the wretched cabin could afford. After fastening up the mules at the back of the house, and bringing in the baggage and some dry fodder to form a bed for the baron and his servant, they prepared some of the food their guests had brought with them for supper, and shortly afterwards the baron and his servant were fast asleep.

Next morning they rose early and continued on their journey. After they had been some hours on the road, the baron, who had before been conversing with his retainer, suddenly became silent and absorbed in thought. He rode on a few paces in advance of the man, thinking over the conditions made by the Innominato, when the idea struck him whether it would not be possible in some way to evade them. He had hardly entertained the thought, when the sparrow flew rapidly before his mule's head, and then instantly afterwards his servant, who had ridden up to him, touched him on the shoulder and pointed to a body of eight or ten armed men about a quarter of a mile distant, who were advancing towards them. The baron, fearing lest they might be some of the armed inhabitants of the neighbourhood who were banded together against him, and seeing that no time was to be lost, immediately plunged, with his servant, into a thick copse where, without being seen, he could command a view of the advancing soldiers as they passed. He perceived that when they came near the place where he was concealed they halted, and evidently set about examining the traces of the footsteps of the mules. They communed together for some time as if in doubt what course they should adopt, and finally, the leader giving the order, they continued their march onwards, and the baron shortly afterwards left his place of concealment.

Nothing further worthy of notice occurred that day; and late at night they passed through Bormio, fortunately without being observed. They afterwards arrived safely at the foot of the mountain pass, and at dawn began the ascent. The day was fine and calm, and the sun shone magnificently. The baron, who now calculated that the dangers of his journey were over, was in high spirits, and familiarly conversed with his retainer. When they had reached a considerable elevation, the path narrowed, so that the two could not ride abreast, and the baron went in advance. He now became very silent and thoughtful, all his thoughts being fixed on the approaching wedding, and in speculations as to how short a time it would take for the delegate and the youth to reach Bormio. Suddenly the thought occurred to him, whether the men whom he should send to escort the hostages back, could not, when they had completed their business, remain concealed in the immediate neighbourhood till after the celebration of the wedding, and then bring back with them some other hostage, and thus enable him to make further demands for compensation for the insult he considered had been offered him. Although the idea had only been vaguely formed, and possibly with but little intention of carrying it out, he had an immediate proof that the power of the astrologer was following him. A sparrow settled on the ground before him, and did not move until his mule was close to it, when it rose in the air right before his face. He continued to follow its course with his eyes, and as it rose higher he thought he perceived a tremulous movement in an immense mass of snow, which had accumulated at the base of one of the mountain peaks. All thought of treachery immediately vanished. He gave a cry of alarm to his servant, and they both hurried onwards, thus barely escaping being buried in an avalanche, which the moment afterwards overwhelmed the path they had crossed.

The baron was now more convinced than ever of the tremendous power of the Innominato, and so great was his fear of him, that he resolved for the future not to contemplate any treachery against him, or entertain any thoughts of revenge.

The day after the baron's arrival at the castle of Gardonal, he ordered the delegate and the podesta's son to be brought into his presence. Assuming a tone of much mildness and courtesy, he told them he much regretted the inconvenience they had been put to, but that the behaviour of the inhabitants of Bormio had left him no alternative. He was ready to admit that the delegate had told him the truth, although from the interview he had with the Innominato, he was by no means certain that the inhabitants of their town had acted in a friendly manner towards him, or were without blame in the matter. Still he did not wish to be harsh, and was willing for the future to be on friendly terms with them if they promised to cease insulting him—what possible affront they could have offered him it would be difficult to say. "At the same time, in justice to myself," he continued (his natural cupidity gaining the ascendant at the moment),

"I hardly think I ought to allow you to return without the payment of some fair ransom."

He had scarcely uttered these words when a sparrow flew in at the window, and darting wildly two or three times across the hall, left by the same window through which it had entered. Those present who noticed the bird looked at it with an eye of indifference—but not so the baron. He knew perfectly well that it was a warning from the astrologer, and he looked around him to see what accident might have befallen him had he continued the train of thought. Nothing of an extraordinary nature followed the disappearance of the bird. The baron now changed the conversation, and told his prisoners that they were at liberty to depart as soon as they pleased; and that to prevent any misfortune befalling them on the road, he would send four of his retainers to protect them. In this he kept his promise to the letter, and a few days afterwards the men returned, reporting that the delegate and the son of the podesta had both arrived safely at their destination.

III

Immediately after the departure of his prisoners, the baron began to make preparations for his wedding, for although he detested the Innominato in his heart, he had still the fullest reliance on his fulfilling the promise he had made. His assurance was further confirmed by a messenger from the astrologer to inform him that on the next Wednesday the affianced bride would arrive with her suite, and that he (the Innominato) had given this notice, that all things might be in readiness for the ceremony.

Neither expense nor exertion was spared by the baron to make his nuptials imposing and magnificent. The chapel belonging to the castle, which had been allowed to fall into a most neglected condition, was put into order, the altar redecorated, and the walls hung with tapestry. Preparations were made in the inner hall for a banquet on the grandest scale, which was to be given after the ceremony; and on a dais in the main hall into which the bride was to be conducted on her arrival were placed two chairs of state, where the baron and his bride were to be seated.

When the day arrived for the wedding, everything was prepared for the reception of the bride. As no hour had been named for her arrival, all persons who were to be engaged in the ceremony were ready in the castle by break of day; and the baron, in a state of great excitement, mounted to the top of the watch-tower, that he might be able to give orders to the rest the moment her cavalcade appeared in sight. Hour after hour passed, but still Teresa did not make her appearance, and at last the baron began to feel considerable anxiety on the subject.

At last a mist, which had been over a part of the valley, cleared up, and all the anxiety of the baron was dispelled; for in the distance he perceived a group of travellers approaching the castle, some mounted on horseback and some on foot. In front rode the bride on a superb white palfrey, her face covered with a thick veil. On each side of her rode an esquire magnificently dressed. Behind her were a waiting woman on horseback and two menservants; and in the rear were several led mules laden with packages. The baron now quitted his position in the tower and descended to the castle gates to receive his bride. When he arrived there, he found one of the esquires, who had ridden forward at the desire of his mistress, waiting to speak to him.

"I have been ordered," he said to the baron, "by the Lady Teresa, to request that you will be good enough to allow her to change her dress before she meets you."

The baron of course willingly assented, and then retired into the hall destined for the reception ceremony. Shortly afterwards Teresa arrived at the castle, and being helped from her palfrey, she proceeded with her lady in waiting and a female attendant (who had been engaged by the baron) into her private apartment, while two of the muleteers brought up a large trunk containing her wedding dress.

In less than an hour Teresa left her room to be introduced to the baron, and was conducted into his presence by one of the esquires. As soon as she entered the hall, a cry of admiration arose from all present—so extraordinary was her beauty. The baron, in a state of breathless emotion, advanced to meet her, but before he had reached her she bent on her knee, and remained in that position till he had raised her up. "Kneel not to me, thou lovely one," he said. "It is for all present to kneel to thee in adoration of thy wonderful beauty, rather than for thee to bend to any one." So saying, and holding her hand, he led her to one of the seats on the dais, and then, seating himself by her side, gave orders for the ceremony of introduction to begin. One by one the different persons to be presented were led up to her, all of whom she received with a grace and amiability which raised her very high in their estimation.

When the ceremony of introduction was over the baron ordered that the procession should be formed, and then, taking Teresa by the hand, he led her into the chapel, followed by the others. When all were arranged in their proper places the marriage ceremony was performed by the priest, and the newly-married couple, with the retainers and guests, entered into the banqueting hall. Splendid as was the repast which had been prepared for the company, their attention seemed for some time more drawn to the baron and his bride than to the duties of the feast. A handsomer couple it would have been impossible to find. The baron himself, as has been stated already, had no lack of manly beauty either in face or form; while the loveliness of his bride appeared almost more than mortal. Even their splendid attire seemed to attract little notice when compared with their personal beauty.

After the surprise and admiration had somewhat abated, the feast progressed most satisfactorily. All were in high spirits, and good humour and conviviality reigned throughout the hall. Even on the baron it seemed to produce a kindly effect, so that few who could have seen him at that moment would have imagined him to be the stern, cold-blooded tyrant he really was. His countenance was lighted up with good humour and friendliness. Much as his attention was occupied with his bride, he had still a little to bestow on his guests, and he rose many times from his seat to request the attention of the servants to their wants. At last he cast his eye over the tables as if searching for some person whom he could not see, and he then beckoned to the major domo, who, staff of office in hand, advanced to receive his orders.

"I do not see the esquires of the Lady Teresa in the room," said the baron.

"Your excellency," said the man, "they are not here."

"How is that?" said the baron, with some impatience. "You ought to have found room for them in the hall. Where are they?"

"Your excellency," said the major domo, who from the expression of the baron's countenance evidently expected a storm, "they are not here. The whole of the suite left the castle immediately after the mules were unladen and her ladyship had left her room. I was inspecting the places which I had prepared for them, when a servant came forward and told me that the esquires and attendants had left the castle. I at once hurried after them and begged they would return, as I was sure your excellency would feel hurt if they did not stay to the banquet. But they told me they had received express orders to leave the castle directly after they had seen the Lady Teresa lodged

safely in it. I again entreated them to stay, but it was useless. They hurried on their way, and I returned by myself."

"The ill-bred hounds!" said the baron, in anger. "A
sound scourging would have taught them better manners."

"Do not be angry with them," said Teresa, laying her
hand gently on that of her husband's. "They did but obey
their master's orders."

"Some day, I swear," said the baron, "I will be re-
venged on their master for this insult, miserable churl
that he is!"

He had no sooner uttered these words than he looked
round him for the sparrow, but the bird did not make its
appearance. Possibly its absence alarmed him even more
than its presence would have done, for he began to dread
lest the vengeance of the astrologer was about to fall on
him, without giving him the usual notice. Teresa, perceiving the expression of his countenance, did all in her
power to calm him, but for some time she but partially
succeeded. He continued to glance anxiously about him,
to ascertain, if possible, from which side the blow might
come. He was just on the point of raising a goblet to his
lips, when the idea seized him that the wine might be
poisoned. He declined to touch food for the same reason.
The idea of being struck with death when at the height of
his happiness seemed to overwhelm him. Thanks, however, to the kind soothing of Teresa, as well as the ab-

sence of any visible effects of the Innominato's anger, he at last became completely reassured, and the feast proceeded.

Long before the banquet had concluded the baron and his wife quitted the hall and retired through their private apartments to the terrace of the castle. The evening, which was now rapidly advancing, was warm and genial, and not a cloud was to be seen in the atmosphere. For some time they walked together up and down on the terrace; and afterwards they seated themselves on a bench. There, with his arm round her waist and her head leaning on his shoulder, they watched the sun in all his magnificence sinking behind the mountains. The sun had almost disappeared, when the baron took his wife's hand in his.

"How cold thou art, my dear!" he said to her. "Let us go in."

Teresa made no answer, but rising from her seat was conducted by her husband into the room which opened on to the terrace, and which was lighted by a large brass lamp which hung by a chain from the ceiling. When they were nearly under the lamp, whose light increased as the daylight declined, Conrad again cast his arm round his wife, and fondly pressed her head to his breast. They remained thus for some moments, entranced in their happiness.

"Dost thou really love me, Teresa?" asked the baron.

"Love you?" said Teresa, now burying her face in his

bosom. "Love you? Yes, dearer than all the world. My very existence hangs on your life. When that ceases my existence ends."

When she had uttered these words, Conrad, in a state of intense happiness, said to her—

"Kiss me, my beloved."

Teresa still kept her face pressed on his bosom; and Conrad, to overcome her coyness, placed his hand on her head and gently pressed it backwards, so that he might kiss her.

He stood motionless, aghast with horror, for the light of the lamp above their heads showed him no longer the angelic features of Teresa, but the hideous face of a corpse that had remained some time in the tomb, and whose only sign of vitality was a horrible phosphoric light which shone in its eyes. Conrad now tried to rush from the room, and to scream for assistance—but in vain. With one arm she clasped him tightly round the waist, and raising the other, she placed her clammy hand upon his mouth, and threw him with great force upon the floor. Then seizing the side of his neck with her lips, she deliberately and slowly sucked from him his life's blood; while he, utterly incapable either of moving or crying, was yet perfectly conscious of the awful fate that was awaiting him.

In this manner Conrad remained for some hours in the arms of his vampire wife. At last faintness came over him, and he grew insensible. The sun had risen some hours before consciousness returned. He rose from the ground horror-stricken and pallid, and glanced fearfully around him to see if Teresa were still there; but he found himself alone in the room. For some minutes he remained undecided what step to take. At last he rose from his chair to leave the apartment, but he was so weak he could scarcely drag himself along. When he left the room he bent his steps towards the courtyard. Each person he met saluted him with the most profound respect, while on the countenance of each was visible an expression of intense surprise, so altered was he from the athletic young man they had seen him the day before. Presently he heard the merry laughter of a number of children, and immediately hastened to the spot from whence the noise came. To his surprise he found his wife Teresa, in full possession of her beauty, playing with several children, whose mothers had brought them to see her, and who stood delighted with the condescending kindness of the baroness towards their little ones.

Conrad remained motionless for some moments, gazing with intense surprise at his wife, and the idea occurred to him that the events of the last night must have been a terrible dream and nothing more. But he was at a loss how to account for his bodily weakness. Teresa, in the midst of her gambols with the children, accidentally raised her head and perceived her husband. She uttered a slight cry of pleasure when she saw him, and snatching up in her arms a beautiful child she had been playing with, she rushed towards him, exclaiming—

"Look, dear Conrad, what a little beauty this is! Is he not a little cherub?"

The baron gazed wildly at his wife for a few moments, but said nothing.

"My dearest husband, what ails you?" said Teresa. "Are you not well?"

Conrad made no answer, but turning suddenly round staggered hurriedly away, while Teresa, with an expression of alarm and anxiety on her face, followed him with her eyes as he went. He still hurried on till he reached the small sitting-room from which he was accustomed each morning to issue his orders to his dependants, and seated himself in a chair to recover if possible from the bewilderment he was in. Presently Ludovico, whose duty it was to attend on his master every morning for instructions, entered the room, and bowing respectfully to the baron, stood silently aside, waiting till he should be spoken to, but during the time marking the baron's altered appearance with the most intense curiosity. After some moments the baron asked him what he saw to make him stare in that manner.

"Pardon my boldness, your excellency," said Ludovico, "but I was afraid you might be ill. I trust I am in error."

"What should make you think I am unwell?" inquired the baron.

"Your highness's countenance is far paler than usual, and there is a small wound on the side of your throat. I hope you have not injured yourself."

The last remark of Ludovico decided the action that

the events of the evening had been no hallucination. What stronger proof could be required than the marks of his vampire wife's teeth still upon him? He perceived that some course of action must be at once decided upon, and the urgency of his position aided him to concentrate his thoughts. He determined on visiting a celebrated anchorite who lived in the mountains about four leagues distant, and who was famous not only for the piety of his life, but for his power in exorcising evil spirits. Having come to this resolution, he desired Ludovico immediately to saddle for him a sure-footed mule, as the path to the anchorite's dwelling was not only difficult but dangerous.

Ludovico bowed, and after having been informed that there were no other orders, he left the room, wondering in his mind what could be the reason for his master's wishing a mule saddled, when he generally rode only the highest-spirited horses. The conclusion he came to was, that the baron must have been attacked with some serious illness, and was about to proceed to some skilful leech.

As soon as Ludovico had left the room, the baron called to one of the servants whom he saw passing, and ordered breakfast to be brought to him immediately, hoping that by a hearty meal he should recover sufficient strength for the journey he was about to undertake. To a certain extent he succeeded, though possibly it was from the quantity of wine he drank, rather than from any other cause, for he had no appetite and had eaten but little.

He now descended into the courtyard of the castle, cautiously avoiding his wife. Finding the mule in readiness, he mounted it and started on his journey. For some time he went along quietly and slowly, for he still felt weak and languid, but as he attained a higher elevation of the mountains, the cold breeze seemed to invigorate him. He now began to consider how he could rid himself of the horrible vampire he had married, and of whose real nature he had no longer any doubt. Speculations on this subject occupied him till he had entered on a path on the slope of an exceedingly high mountain. It was difficult to keep footing, and it required all his caution to prevent himself from falling. Of fear, however, the baron had none; and his thoughts continued to run on the possibility of separating himself from Teresa, and on what vengeance he would take on the Innominato for the treachery he had practised on him, as soon as he should be fairly freed. The more he dwelt on his revenge, the more excited he became, till at last he exclaimed aloud, "Infamous wretch! Let me be but once fairly released from the execrable fiend you have imposed upon me, and I swear I will burn thee alive in thy castle, as a fitting punishment for the sorcery thou hast practised."

Conrad had hardly uttered these words, when the pathway upon which he was riding gave way beneath him, and glided down the incline into a tremendous precipice below. He succeeded in throwing himself from his mule, which, with the *débris* of the rocks, was hurried over the precipice, while he clutched with the energy of despair at each object he saw likely to give him a moment's support. But everything he touched gave way, and he gradually sank and sank towards the verge of the precipice, his efforts to save himself becoming more violent the nearer he approached to what appeared certain death. Down he sank, till his legs actually hung over the precipice, when he succeeded in grasping a stone somewhat firmer than the others, thus retarding his fall for a moment. In horror he now glanced at the terrible chasm beneath him, when suddenly different objects came before his mind with fearful reality. There was an unhappy peasant, who had without permission killed a head of game, hanging from the branch of a tree, still struggling in the agonies of death, while his wife and children were in vain imploring the baron's clemency.

This vanished and he saw a boy with a knife in his hand, stabbing at his own mother for some slight offence she had given him.

This passed, and he found himself in a small village, the inhabitants of which were all dead within their houses; for at the approach of winter he had, in a fit of ill-temper, ordered his retainers to take from them all their provisions; and a snowstorm coming on immediately afterwards, they were blocked up in their dwellings, and all perished.

Again his thoughts reverted to the position he was in, and his eye glanced over the terrible precipice that yawned beneath him, when he saw, as if in a dream, the house of Biffi the farmer, with his wife and children around him, apparently contented and happy.

As soon as he had realized the idea, the stone which he had clutched began to give way, and all seemed lost to him, when a sparrow suddenly flew on the earth a short distance from him, and immediately afterwards darted away. "Save but my life," screamed the baron, "and I swear I will keep all secret!"

The words had hardly been uttered, when a goatherd with a long staff in his hand appeared on the incline above him. The man perceiving the imminent peril of the baron, with great caution, and yet with great activity, descended to assist him. He succeeded in reaching a ledge of rock a few feet above, and rather to the side of the baron, to whom he stretched forth the long mountain staff in his hand. The baron clutched it with such energy as would certainly have drawn the goatherd over with him, had it not been that the latter was a remarkably powerful man. With some difficulty the baron reached the ledge of the rock, and the goatherd then ascended to a higher position, and in like manner drew the baron on, till at last he had contrived to get him to a place of safety. As soon as Conrad found himself out of danger, he gazed wildly around him for a moment, then dizziness came over him, and he sank fainting on the ground.

When the baron had recovered his senses, he found himself so weak that it would have been impossible for him to have reached the castle that evening. He therefore willingly accompanied the goatherd to his hut in the mountains, where he proposed to pass the night. The man made what provision he could for his illustrious guest, and prepared him a supper of the best his hut afforded; but had the latter been composed of the most exquisite delicacies, it would have been equally tasteless; for Conrad had not the slightest appetite. Evening was now rapidly approaching, and the goatherd prepared a bed of leaves, over which he threw a cloak, and the baron, utterly exhausted, reposed on it for the night, without anything occurring to disturb his rest.

Next morning he found himself somewhat refreshed by his night's rest, and he prepared to return to the castle, assisted by the goatherd, to whom he had promised a handsome reward. He had now given up all idea of visiting the anchorite, dreading that by so doing he might excite the animosity of the Innominato, of whose tremendous power he had lately received more than ample proof. In due time he reached home in safety, and the goatherd was dismissed after having received the promised reward. On entering the castle-yard the baron found his wife in a state of great alarm and sorrow, and surrounded by the retainers. No sooner did she perceive her husband, then, uttering a cry of delight and surprise, she rushed forward to clasp him in her arms; but the baron pushed her rudely away, and hurrying forwards, directed his steps to the room in which he was accustomed to issue his orders. Ludovico, having heard of the arrival of his master, immediately waited on him.

"Ludovico," said the baron, as soon as he saw him, "I want you to execute an order for me with great promptitude and secrecy. Go below, and prepare two good horses for a journey; one for you, the other for myself. See that we take with us provisions and equipments for two or three days. As soon as they are in readiness, leave the castle with them without speaking to any one, and wait for me about a league up the mountain, where in less than two hours I will join you. Now see that you faithfully carry out my orders, and if you do so, I assure you you will lose nothing by your obedience."

Ludovico left the baron's presence to execute his order, when immediately afterwards a servant came into the room, and inquired if the Lady Teresa might enter.

"Tell your mistress," said the baron, in a tone of great courtesy and kindness, "that I hope she will excuse me for the moment, as I am deeply engaged in affairs of importance; but I shall await her visit with great impatience in the afternoon."

The baron, now left to himself, began to draw out more fully the plan for his future operations. He resolved to visit his brother Hermann, and consult him as to what steps he ought to take in this horrible emergency; and in case no better means presented themselves, he determined on offering to give up to Hermann the castle of Gardonal and the whole valley of the Engadin, on condition of receiving from him an annuity sufficient to support him in the position he had always been accustomed to maintain. He then intended to retire to some distant country, where there would be no probability of his being followed by the horrible monster whom he had accepted as his wife. Of course he had no intention of receiving Teresa in the afternoon, and he had merely put off her visit for the purpose of allowing himself to escape with greater convenience from the castle.

About an hour after Ludovico had left him, the baron quitted the castle by a postern, with as much haste as his enfeebled strength would allow, and hurried after his retainer, whom he found awaiting him with the horses. The baron immediately mounted one, and followed by Ludovico, took the road to his brother's, where in three days he arrived in safety. Hermann received his brother with great pleasure, though much surprised at the alteration in his appearance.

"My dear Conrad," he said to him, "what can possibly have occurred to you? You look very pale, weak, and haggard. Have you been ill?"

"Worse, a thousand times worse," said Conrad. "Let us go where we may be by ourselves, and I will tell you all."

Hermann led his brother into a private room, where Conrad explained to him the terrible misfortune which had befallen him. Hermann listened attentively, and for some time could not help doubting whether his brother's mind was not affected; but Conrad explained everything in so circumstantial and lucid a manner as to dispel that idea. To the proposition which Conrad made, to make over the territory of the Engadin Valley for an annuity,

Hermann promised to give full consideration. At the same time, before any further steps were taken in the matter, he advised Conrad to visit a villa he had, on the sea-shore, about ten miles distant from Genoa; where, in quiet and seclusion, he would be able to recover his energies.

Conrad thanked his brother for his advice, and willingly accepted the offer. Two days afterwards he started on the journey, and by the end of the week arrived safely, and without difficulty, at the villa.

On the evening of his arrival, Conrad, who had employed himself during the afternoon in visiting the different apartments as well as the grounds surrounding the villa, was seated at a window overlooking the sea. The evening was deliciously calm, and he felt such ease and security as he had not enjoyed for some time past. The sun was sinking in the ocean, and the moon began to appear, and the stars one by one to shine in the cloudless heavens. The thought crossed Conrad's mind that the sight of the sun sinking in the waters strongly resembled his own position when he fell over the precipice. The thought had hardly been conceived when some one touched him on the shoulder. He turned round, and saw standing before him, in the full majesty of her beauty—his wife Teresa!

"My dearest Conrad," she said, with much affection in her tone, "why have you treated me in this cruel manner? It was most unkind of you to leave me suddenly without giving the slightest hint of your intentions."

"Execrable fiend," said Conrad, springing from his chair, "leave me! Why do you haunt me in this manner?"

"Do not speak so harshly to me, my dear husband," said Teresa. "To oblige you I was taken from my grave, and on you now my very existence depends."

"Rather my death," said Conrad. "One night more such as we passed, and I should be a corpse."

"Nay, dear Conrad," said Teresa. "I have the power of indefinitely prolonging your life. Drink but of this," she continued, taking from the table behind her a silver goblet, "and tomorrow all ill effects will have passed away."

Conrad mechanically took the goblet from her hand, and was on the point of raising it to his lips when he suddenly stopped, and with a shudder replaced it again on the table.

"It is blood," he said.

"True, my dear husband," said Teresa. "What else could it be? My life is dependent on your life's blood, and when that ceases so does my life. Drink then, I implore you," she continued, again offering him the goblet. "Look, the sun has already sunk beneath the wave; a minute more and daylight will have gone. Drink, Conrad, I implore you, or this night will be your last."

Conrad again took the goblet from her hand to raise it to his lips; but it was impossible, and he placed it on the table. A ray of pure moonlight now penetrated the room, as if to prove that the light of day had fled. Teresa, again transformed into a horrible vampire, flew at her husband, and throwing him on the floor, fastened her teeth on the half-healed wound in his throat. The next morning, when the servants entered the room, they found the baron a corpse on the floor; but Teresa was nowhere to be seen, nor was she ever heard of afterwards.

Little more remains to be told. Hermann took possession of the castle of Gardonal and the valley of the Engadin, and treated his vassals with even more despotism than his brother had done before him. At last, driven to desperation, they rose against him and slew him; and the valley afterwards became absorbed into the Canton of the Grisons.

THE HORLA

✦✦✦

GUY DE MAUPASSANT

May 8. What a lovely day. I have spent all the morning
lying in the grass in front of my house, under the enormous plane tree that shades the whole of it. I like this part
of the country and I like to live here because I am attached to it by old associations, by those deep and delicate roots which attach man to the soil on which his
ancestors were born and died, which attach him to the
ideas and usages of the place as well as to the food, to local expressions, to the peculiar twang of the peasants, to
the smell of the soil, of the villages, and of the atmosphere itself.

I love my house in which I grew up. From my windows I can see the Seine which flows alongside my garden, on the other side of the high road, almost through
my grounds, the great and wide Seine, which goes to
Rouen and Havre, and is covered with boats passing to
and fro.

On the left, down yonder, lies Rouen, that large town,
with its blue roofs, under its pointed Gothic towers.
These are innumerable, slender or broad, dominated by

the spire of the cathedral, and full of bells which sound through the blue air on fine mornings, sending their sweet and distant iron clang even as far as my home; that song of the metal, which the breeze wafts in my direction, now stronger and now weaker, according as the wind is stronger or lighter.

What a delicious morning it was!

About eleven o'clock, a long line of boats drawn by a steam tug as big as a fly, and which scarcely puffed while emitting its thick smoke, passed my gate.

After two English schooners, whose red flag fluttered in space, there came a magnificent Brazilian three-master; it was perfectly white, and wonderfully clean and shining. I saluted it, I hardly knew why, except that the sight of the vessel gave me great pleasure.

May 12. I have had a slight feverish attack for the last few days, and I feel ill, or rather I feel low-spirited.

Whence come those mysterious influences which change our happiness into discouragement, and our self-confidence into diffidence? One might almost say that the air, the invisible air, is full of unknowable Powers whose mysterious presence we have to endure. I wake up in the best spirits, with an inclination to sing. Why? I go down to the edge of the water, and suddenly, after walking a short distance, I return home wretched, as if some misfortune were awaiting me there. Why? Is it a cold shiver which, passing over my skin, has upset my nerves and given me low spirits? Is it the form of the clouds, the color of the sky, or the color of the surrounding objects

which is so changeable, that has troubled my thoughts as
they passed before my eyes? Who can tell? Everything
that we touch, without knowing it, everything that we
handle, without feeling it, all that we meet, without
clearly distinguishing it, has a rapid, surprising, and inexplicable effect upon us and upon our senses, and,
through them, on our ideas and on our heart itself.

How profound that mystery of the Invisible is! We
cannot fathom it with our miserable senses, with our eyes
which are unable to perceive what is either too small or
too great, too near to us, or too far from us—neither the
inhabitants of a star nor of a drop of water; nor with our
ears that deceive us, for they transmit to us the vibrations
of the air in sonorous notes. They are fairies who work
the miracle of changing these vibrations into sounds, and
by that metamorphosis give birth to music, which makes
the silent motion of nature musical . . . with our sense of
smell which is less keen than that of a dog . . . with our
sense of taste which can scarcely distinguish the age of
wine!

Oh! If we only had other organs which would work
other miracles in our favor, what a number of fresh things
we might discover around us!

May 16. I am ill, decidedly! I was so well last month! I
am feverish, horribly feverish, or rather I am in a state of
feverish enervation, which makes my mind suffer as
much as my body. I have, continually, that horrible sensation of some impending danger, that apprehension of
some coming misfortune, or of approaching death; that

presentiment which is, no doubt, an attack of some illness which is still unknown, which germinates in the flesh and in the blood.

May 17. I have just come from consulting my physician, for I could no longer get any sleep. He said my pulse was rapid, my eyes dilated, my nerves highly strung, but there were no alarming symptoms. I must take a course of shower baths and of bromide of potassium.

May 25. No change! My condition is really very peculiar. As the evening comes on, an incomprehensible feeling of disquietude seizes me, just as if night concealed some threatening disaster. I dine hurriedly, and then try to read, but I do not understand the words, and can scarcely distinguish the letters. Then I walk up and down my drawing-room, oppressed by a feeling of confused and irresistible fear, the fear of sleep and fear of my bed.

About ten o'clock I go up to my room. As soon as I enter it I double-lock and bolt the door; I am afraid . . . of what? Up to the present time I have been afraid of nothing . . . I open my cupboards, and look under my bed; I listen . . . to what? How strange it is that a simple feeling of discomfort, impeded or heightened circulation, perhaps the irritation of a nerve filament, a slight congestion, a small disturbance in the imperfect delicate functioning of our living machinery, may turn the most light-hearted of men into a melancholy one, and make a coward of the bravest? Then, I go to bed, and wait for sleep as a man might wait for the executioner. I wait for its coming with dread, and my heart beats and my legs tremble, while my whole body shivers beneath the warmth of the bed-clothes, until all at once I fall asleep, as though one should plunge into a pool of stagnant water in order to drown. I do not feel it coming on as I did formerly, this perfidious sleep which is close to me and watching me, which is going to seize me by the head, to close my eyes and annihilate me.

I sleep—a long time—two or three hours perhaps— then a dream—no—a nightmare lays hold on me. I feel that I am in bed and asleep . . . I feel it and I know it . . . and I feel also that somebody is coming close to me, is looking at me, touching me, is getting on to my bed, is kneeling on my chest, is taking my neck between his hands and squeezing it . . . squeezing it with all his might in order to strangle me.

I struggle, bound by that terrible sense of powerlessness which paralyzes us in our dreams; I try to cry out— but I cannot; I want to move—I cannot do so; I try, with the most violent efforts and breathing hard, to turn over and throw off this being who is crushing and suffocating me—I cannot!

And then, suddenly, I wake up, trembling and bathed in perspiration. I light a candle and find that I am alone, and after that crisis, which occurs every night, I at length fall asleep and slumber tranquilly till morning.

June 2. My condition has grown worse. What is the

matter with me? The bromide does me no good, and the shower baths have no effect. Sometimes, in order to tire myself thoroughly, though I am fatigued enough already, I go for a walk in the forest of Roumare. I used to think at first that the fresh light and soft air, impregnated with the odor of herbs and leaves, would instill new blood into my veins and impart fresh energy to my heart. I turned into a broad hunting road, and then turned toward La Bouille, through a narrow path, between two rows of exceedingly tall trees, which placed a thick green, almost black, roof between the sky and me.

A sudden shiver ran through me, not a cold shiver, but a strange shiver of agony, and I hastened my steps, uneasy at being alone in the forest, afraid, stupidly and without reason, of the profound solitude. Suddenly it seemed to me as if I were being followed, that somebody was walking at my heels, close, quite close to me, near enough to touch me.

I turned round suddenly, but I was alone. I saw nothing behind me except the straight, broad path, empty and bordered by high trees, horribly empty; before me it also extended until it was lost in the distance, and looked just the same, terrible.

I closed my eyes. Why? And then I began to turn round on one heel very quickly, just like a top. I nearly fell down, and opened my eyes; the trees were dancing round me and the earth heaved; I was obliged to sit down. Then ah! I no longer remembered how I had come! What a strange idea! What a strange, strange idea! I did not in the least know. I started off to the right, and got back into the avenue which had led me into the middle of the forest.

June 3. I have had a terrible night. I shall go away for a few weeks, for no doubt a journey will set me up again.

July 2. I have come back, quite cured, and have had a most delightful trip into the bargain. I have been to Mont Saint-Michel, which I had not seen before.

What a sight, when one arrives, as I did, at Avranches, toward the end of the day! The town stands on a hill, and I was taken into the public garden at the extremity of the town. I uttered a cry of astonishment. An extraordinarily large bay lay extended before me, as far as my eyes could reach, between two hills which were lost to sight in the mist; and in the middle of this immense yellow bay, under a clear, golden sky, a peculiar hill rose up, sombre and pointed in the midst of the sand. The sun had just disappeared, and under the still flaming sky appeared the outline of that fantastic rock which bears on its summit a fantastic monument.

At daybreak I went out to it. The tide was low, as it had been the night before, and I saw that wonderful abbey rise up before me as I approached it. After several hours' walking, I reached the enormous mass of rocks which supports the little town, dominated by the great church. Having climbed the steep and narrow street, I entered the most wonderful Gothic building that has ever been built to God on earth, as large as a town, full of low rooms which seem buried beneath vaulted roofs, and lofty galleries supported by delicate columns.

I entered this gigantic granite gem, which is as light as a bit of lace, covered with towers, with slender belfries with spiral staircases, which raise their strange heads that bristle with chimeras, with devils, with fantastic animals, with monstrous flowers, to the blue sky by day, and to the black sky by night, and are connected by finely carved arches.

When I had reached the summit I said to the monk who accompanied me: "Father, how happy you must be here!" And he replied: "It is very windy here, monsieur"; and so we began to talk while watching the rising tide, which ran over the sand and covered it as with a steel cuirass.

And then the monk told me stories, all the old stories belonging to the place, legends, nothing but legends.

One of them struck me forcibly. The country people, those belonging to the Mount, declare that at night one can hear voices talking on the sands, and then that one hears two goats bleating, one with a strong, the other with a weak voice. Incredulous people declare that it is nothing but the cry of the sea birds, which occasionally resembles bleatings, and occasionally, human lamentations; but belated fishermen swear that they have met an old shepherd wandering between tides on the sands around the little town. His head is completely concealed by his cloak and he is followed by a billy goat with a man's face, and a nanny goat with a woman's face, both having long, white hair and talking incessantly and quarreling in an unknown tongue. Then suddenly they cease and begin to bleat with all their might.

"Do you believe it?" I asked the monk. "I scarcely know," he replied, and I continued: "If there are other beings besides ourselves on this earth, how comes it that we have not known it long since, or why have *you* not seen them? How is that *I* have not seen them?" He replied: "Do we see the hundred-thousandth part of what exists? Look here; there is the wind, which is the strongest force in nature, which knocks down men, and blows down buildings, destroys cliffs and casts great ships on the rocks; the wind which kills, which whistles, which sighs, which roars—have you ever seen it, and can you see it? It exists for all that, however."

I was silent before this simple reasoning. That man was a philosopher, or perhaps a fool; I could not say which exactly, so I held my tongue. What he had said had often been in my own thoughts.

July 3. I have slept badly; certainly there is some feverish influence here, for my coachman is suffering in the same way as I am. When I went back home yesterday, I noticed his singular paleness, and I asked him: "What is the matter with you, Jean?" "The matter is that I never get any rest, and my nights devour my days. Since your departure, monsieur, there has been a spell over me."

However, the other servants are all well, but I am very much afraid of having another attack myself.

July 4. I am decidedly ill again; for my old nightmares have returned. Last night I felt somebody leaning on me and sucking my life from between my lips. Yes, he was sucking it out of my throat, like a leech. Then he got up, satiated, and I woke up, so exhausted, crushed, and weak that I could not move. If this continues for a few days, I shall certainly go away again.

July 5. Have I lost my reason? What happened last night is so strange that my head wanders when I think of it!

I had locked my door, as I do now every evening, and then, being thirsty, I drank half a glass of water, and accidentally noticed that the water bottle was full up to the cut-glass stopper.

Then I went to bed and fell into one of my terrible sleeps, from which I was aroused in about two hours by a still more frightful shock.

Picture to yourself a sleeping man who is being murdered and who wakes up with a knife in his lung, and whose breath rattles, who is covered with blood, and who can no longer breathe and is about to die, and does not understand—there you have it.

Having recovered my senses, I was thirsty again, so I lit a candle and went to the table on which stood my water bottle. I lifted it up and tilted it over my glass, but nothing came out. It was empty! It was completely empty! At first I could not understand it at all, and then suddenly I was seized by such a terrible feeling that I had to sit down, or rather I fell into a chair! Then I sprang up sud-

denly to look about me; then I sat down again, overcome
by astonishment and fear, in front of the transparent glass
bottle! I looked at it with fixed eyes, trying to conjecture,
and my hands trembled! Somebody had drunk the water,
but who? I? I without any doubt. It could surely only be I.
In that case I was a somnambulist; I lived, without knowing it, that mysterious double life which makes us doubt
whether there are not two beings in us, or whether a
strange, unknowable, and invisible being does not at
such moments, when our soul is in a state of torpor, ani-
mate our captive body, which obeys this other being, as it
obeys us, and more than it obeys ourselves.

Oh! Who will understand my horrible agony? Who
will understand the emotion of a man who is sound in
mind, wide awake, full of common sense, who looks in
horror through the glass of a water bottle for a little water
that disappeared while he was asleep? I remained thus
until it was daylight, without venturing to go to bed
again.

July 6. I am going mad. Again all the contents of my
water bottle have been drunk during the night—or
rather, I have drunk it!

But is it I? Is it I? Who could it be? Who? Oh! God!
Am I going mad? Who will save me?

July 10. I have just been through some surprising or-
deals. Decidedly I am mad! And yet! . . .

On July 6, before going to bed, I put some wine, milk,
water, bread, and strawberries on my table. Somebody
drank—I drank—all the water and a little of the milk, but

neither the wine, bread, nor the strawberries were touched.

On the seventh of July I renewed the same experiment, with the same results, and on July 8, I left out the water and the milk, and nothing was touched.

Lastly, on July 9, I put only water and milk on my table, taking care to wrap up the bottles in white muslin and to tie down the stoppers. Then I rubbed my lips, my beard and my hands with pencil lead, and went to bed.

Irresistible sleep seized me, which was soon followed by a terrible awakening. I had not moved, and there was no mark of lead on the sheets. I rushed to the table. The muslin round the bottles remained intact; I undid the string, trembling with fear. All the water had been drunk, and so had the milk! Ah! Great God! . . .

I must start for Paris immediately.

July 12. Paris. I must have lost my head during the last few days! I must be the plaything of my enervated imagination, unless I am really a somnambulist, or that I have been under the power of one of those hitherto unexplained influences which are called suggestions. In any case, my mental state bordered on madness, and twenty-four hours of Paris sufficed to restore my equilibrium.

Yesterday, after doing some business and paying some visits which instilled fresh and invigorating air into my soul, I wound up the evening at the Théâtre-Français. A play by Alexandre Dumas the younger was being acted, and his active and powerful imagination completed my cure. Certainly solitude is dangerous for active minds.

We require around us men who can think and talk. When we are alone for a long time, we people space with phantoms.

I returned along the boulevards to my hotel in excellent spirits. Amid the jostling of the crowd I thought, not without irony, of my terrors and surmises of the previous week, because I had believed—yes, I had believed—that an invisible being lived beneath my roof. How weak our brains are, and how quickly they are terrified and led into error by a small incomprehensible fact.

Instead of saying simply: "I do not understand because I do not know the cause," we immediately imagine terrible mysteries and supernatural powers.

July 14. Fête of the Republic. I walked through the streets, amused as a child at the firecrackers and flags. Still it is very foolish to be merry on a fixed date, by Government decree. The populace is an imbecile flock of sheep, now stupidly patient, and now in ferocious revolt. Say to it: "Amuse yourself," and it amuses itself. Say to it: "Vote for the Emperor," and it votes for the Emperor, and then say to it: "Vote for the Republic," and it votes for the Republic.

Those who direct it are also stupid; only, instead of obeying men, they obey principles which can only be stupid, sterile, and false, for the very reason that they are principles, that is to say, ideas which are considered as certain and unchangeable, in this world where one is certain of nothing, since light is an illusion and noise is an illusion.

July 16. I saw some things yesterday that troubled me very much.

I was dining at the house of my cousin, Madame Sable, whose husband is colonel of the 76th Chasseurs at Limoges. There were two young women there, one of whom had married a medical man, Dr. Parent, who devotes much attention to nervous diseases and to the remarkable manifestations taking place at this moment under the influence of hypnotism and suggestion.

He related to us at some length the wonderful results obtained by English scientists and by the doctors of the Nancy school; and the facts which he adduced appeared to me so strange that I declared that I was altogether incredulous.

"We are," he declared, "on the point of discovering one of the most important secrets of nature; I mean to say, one of its most important secrets on this earth, for there are certainly others of a different kind of importance up in the stars, yonder. Ever since man has thought, ever since he has been able to express and write down his thoughts, he has felt himself close to a mystery which is impenetrable to his gross and imperfect senses, and he endeavors to supplement through his intellect the inefficiency of his senses. As long as that intellect remained in its elementary stage, these apparitions of invisible spirits assumed forms that were commonplace, though terrifying. Thence sprang the popular belief in the supernatural, the legends of wandering spirits, of fairies, of gnomes, ghosts, I might even say the legend of

God; for our conceptions of the workman-creator, from whatever religion they may have come down to us, are certainly the most mediocre, the most stupid, and the most incredible inventions that ever sprang from the terrified brain of any human beings. Nothing is truer than what Voltaire says: 'God made man in His own image, but man has certainly paid Him back in his own coin.'

"However, for rather more than a century men seem to have had a presentiment of something new. Mesmer and some others have put us on an unexpected track, and, especially within the last two or three years, we have arrived at really surprising results."

My cousin, who is also very incredulous, smiled, and Dr. Parent said to her: "Would you like me to try and send you to sleep, madame?" "Yes, certainly."

She sat down in an easy chair, and he began to look at her fixedly, so as to fascinate her. I suddenly felt myself growing uncomfortable, my heart beating rapidly and a choking sensation in my throat. I saw Madame Sable's eyes becoming heavy, her mouth twitching and her bosom heaving, and at the end of ten minutes she was asleep.

"Go behind her," the doctor said to me, and I took a seat behind her. He put a visiting card into her hands, and said to her: "This is a looking-glass; what do you see in it?" And she replied: "I see my cousin." "What is he doing?" "He is twisting his mustache." "And now?" "He is taking a photograph out of his pocket." "Whose photograph is it?" "His own."

That was true, and the photograph had been given me that same evening at the hotel.

"What is his attitude in this portrait?" "He is standing up with his hat in his hand."

She saw, therefore, on that card, on that piece of white pasteboard, as if she had seen it in a mirror.

The young women were frightened, and exclaimed: "That is enough! Quite, quite enough!"

But the doctor said to Madame Sable authoritatively: "You will rise at eight o'clock tomorrow morning; then you will go and call on your cousin at his hotel and ask him to lend you five thousand francs which your husband demands of you, and which he will ask for when he sets out on his coming journey."

Then he woke her up.

On returning to my hotel, I thought over this curious séance, and I was assailed by doubts, not as to my cousin's absolute and undoubted good faith, for I had known her as well as if she were my own sister ever since she was a child, but as to a possible trick on the doctor's part. Had he not, perhaps, kept a glass hidden in his hand, which he showed to the young woman in her sleep, at the same time as he did the card? Professional conjurors do things that are just as singular.

So I went home and to bed, and this morning, at about half-past eight, I was awakened by my valet, who said to me: "Madame Sable has asked to see you immediately, monsieur." I dressed hastily and went to her.

She sat down in some agitation, with her eyes on the

floor, and without raising her veil she said to me: "My
dear cousin, I am going to ask a great favor of you."
"What is it, cousin?" "I do not like to tell you, and yet I
must. I am in absolute need of five thousand francs."
"What, you?" "Yes, I, or rather my husband, who has
asked me to procure them for him."

I was so thunderstruck that I stammered out my answers. I asked myself whether she had not really been
making fun of me with Dr. Parent, if it was not merely a
very well-acted farce which had been rehearsed before-
hand. On looking at her attentively, however, all my
doubts disappeared. She was trembling with grief, so
painful was this step to her, and I was convinced that her
throat was full of sobs.

I knew that she was very rich and I continued: "What!
Has not your husband five thousand francs at his disposal? Come, think. Are you sure that he commissioned
you to ask me for them?"

She hesitated for a few seconds, as if she were making
a great effort to search her memory, and then she replied:
"Yes . . . yes, I am quite sure of it." "He has written to
you?"

She hesitated again and reflected, and I guessed the
torture of her thoughts. She did not know. She only knew
that she was to borrow five thousand francs of me for her
husband. So she told a lie. "Yes, he has written to me."
"When, pray? You did not mention it to me yesterday." "I
received his letter this morning." "Can you show it me?"
"No; no . . . no . . . it contained private matters . . . things

too personal to ourselves. . . . I burned it." "So your husband runs into debt?"

She hesitated again, and then murmured: "I do not know." Thereupon I said bluntly: "I have not five thousand francs at my disposal at this moment, my dear cousin."

She uttered a kind of cry as if she were in pain and said: "Oh! Oh! I beseech you, I beseech you to get them for me. . . ."

She got excited and clasped her hands as if she were praying to me! I heard her voice change its tone; she wept and stammered, harassed and dominated by the irresistible order that she had received.

"Oh! Oh! I beg you to . . . if you knew what I am suffering . . . I want them today."

I had pity on her: "You shall have them by and by, I swear to you." "Oh! Thank you! Thank you! How kind you are."

I continued: "Do you remember what took place at your house last night?" "Yes." "Do you remember that Dr. Parent sent you to sleep?" "Yes." "Oh! Very well, then; he ordered you to come to me this morning to borrow five thousand francs, and at this moment you are obeying that suggestion."

She considered for a few moments, and then replied: "But as it is my husband who wants them—"

For a whole hour I tried to convince her, but could not succeed, and when she had gone I went to the doctor. He was just going out, and he listened to me with a smile, and said: "Do you believe now?" "Yes, I cannot help it." "Let us go to your cousin's."

She was already half asleep on a reclining chair, overcome with fatigue. The doctor felt her pulse, looked at her for some time with one hand raised toward her eyes, which she closed by degrees under the irresistible power of this magnetic influence, and when she was asleep, he said:

"Your husband does not require the five thousand francs any longer! You must, therefore, forget that you asked your cousin to lend them to you, and, if he speaks to you about it, you will not understand him."

Then he woke her up, and I took out a pocket book and said: "Here is what you asked me for this morning, my dear cousin." But she was so surprised that I did not venture to persist; nevertheless, I tried to recall the circumstance to her, but she denied it vigorously, thought I was making fun of her, and, in the end, very nearly lost her temper.

There! I have just come back, and I have not been able to eat any lunch, for this experiment has altogether upset me.

July 19. Many people to whom I told the adventure laughed at me. I no longer know what to think. The wise man says: "It may be!"

July 21. I dined at Bougival, and then I spent the evening at a boatmen's ball. Decidedly everything depends on place and surroundings. It would be the height of folly to believe in the supernatural on the Ile de la Grenouillière . . . but on top of Mont Saint-Michel? . . . And in India? We are terribly influenced by our surroundings. I shall return home next week.

July 30. I came back to my own house yesterday. Everything is going on well.

August 2. Nothing new; it is splendid weather, and I spend my days in watching the Seine flowing past.

August 4. Quarrels among my servants. They declare that the glasses are broken in the cupboards at night. The footman accuses the cook, who accuses the seamstress, who accuses the other two. Who is the culprit? It is a clever person who can tell.

August 6. This time I am not mad. I have seen . . . I have seen . . . I have seen! . . . I can doubt no longer . . . I have seen it! . . .

I was walking at two o'clock among my rose trees, in the full sunlight . . . in the walk bordered by autumn roses which are beginning to fall. As I stopped to look at a Géant de Bataille, which had three splendid blossoms, I distinctly saw the stalk of one of the roses near me bend, as if an invisible hand had bent it, and then break, as if that hand had picked it! Then the flower raised itself, following the curve which a hand would have described in carrying it toward a mouth, and it remained suspended in the transparent air, all alone and motionless, a terrible red spot, three yards from my eyes. In desperation I rushed at it to take it! I found nothing; it had disap-

peared. Then I was seized with furious rage against myself, for a reasonable and serious man should not have
such hallucinations.

But was it an hallucination? I turned round to look for
the stalk, and I found it at once, on the bush, freshly broken, between two other roses which remained on the
branch. I returned home then, my mind greatly disturbed; for I am certain now, as certain as I am of the al-
ternation of day and night, that there exists close to me an
invisible being that lives on milk and water, that can
touch objects, take them and change their places; that is,
consequently, endowed with a material nature, although
it is imperceptible to our senses, and that lives as I do, under my roof—

August 7. I slept tranquilly. He drank the water out of
my decanter, but did not disturb my sleep.

I wonder if I am mad. As I was walking just now in the
sun by the river side, doubts as to my sanity arose in me;
not vague doubts such as I have had hitherto, but definite, absolute doubts. I have seen mad people, and I have
known some who have been quite intelligent, lucid, even
clear-sighted in every concern of life, except on one
point. They spoke readily, clearly, profoundly on everything, when suddenly their mind struck upon the shoals
of their madness and broke to pieces there, and scattered
and floundered in that furious and terrible sea, full of
rolling waves, fogs, and squalls, which is called *madness.*

I certainly should think that I was mad, absolutely
mad, if I were not conscious, did not perfectly know my

condition, did not fathom it by analyzing it with the most complete lucidity. I should, in fact, be only a rational man who was laboring under an hallucination. Some unknown disturbance must have arisen in my brain, one of those disturbances which physiologists of the present day try to note and to verify; and that disturbance must have caused a deep gap in my mind and in the sequence and logic of my ideas. Similar phenomena occur in dreams which lead us among the most unlikely phantasmagoria, without causing us any surprise, because our verifying apparatus and our organ of control are asleep, while our imaginative faculty is awake and active. Is it not possible that one of the imperceptible notes of the cerebral keyboard had been paralyzed in me? Some men lose the recollection of proper names, of verbs, or of numbers, or merely of dates, in consequence of an accident. The localization of all the variations of thought has been established nowadays; why, then, should it be surprising if my faculty of controlling the unreality of certain hallucinations were dormant in me for the time being?

I thought of all this as I walked by the side of the water. The sun shone brightly on the river and made earth delightful, while it filled me with a love for life, for the swallows, whose agility always delights my eye, for the plants by the river side, the rustle of whose leaves is a pleasure to my ears.

By degrees, however, an inexplicable feeling of discomfort seized me. It seemed as if some unknown force were numbing and stopping me, were preventing me from going further, and were calling me back. I felt that painful wish to return which oppresses you when you have left a beloved invalid at home, and when you are seized with a presentiment that he is worse.

I, therefore, returned in spite of myself, feeling certain that I should find some bad news awaiting me, a letter or a telegram. There was nothing, however, and I was more surprised and uneasy than if I had had another fantastic vision.

August 8. I spent a terrible evening yesterday. He does not show himself any more, but I feel that he is near me, watching me, looking at me, penetrating me, dominating me, and more redoubtable when he hides himself thus than if he were to manifest his constant and invisible presence by supernatural phenomena. However, I slept.

August 9. Nothing, but I am afraid.

August 10. Nothing; what will happen tomorrow?

August 11. Still nothing; I cannot stop at home with this fear hanging over me and these thoughts in my mind; I shall go away.

August 12. Ten o'clock at night. All day long I have been trying to get away, and have not been able. I wish to accomplish this simple and easy act of freedom—to go out—to get into my carriage in order to go to Rouen—and I have not been able to do it. What is the reason?

August 13. When one is attacked by certain maladies, all the springs of our physical being appear to be broken, all our energies destroyed, all our muscles relaxed; our bones, too, have become as soft as flesh, and our blood as liquid as water. I am experiencing these sensations in my moral being in a strange and distressing manner. I have no longer any strength, any courage, any self-control, not even any power to set my own will in motion. I have no power left to will anything; but someone does it for me and I obey.

August 14. I am lost. Somebody possesses my soul and dominates it. Somebody orders all my acts, all my movements, all my thoughts. I am no longer anything in myself, nothing except an enslaved and terrified spectator of all the things I do. I wish to go out; I cannot. He does not wish to, and so I remain, trembling and distracted, in the armchair in which he keeps me sitting. I merely wish to get up and to rouse myself so as to think that I am master of myself: I cannot! I am riveted to my chair, and my chair adheres to the ground in such a manner that no power could move us.

Then, suddenly, I must, I must go to the bottom of my garden to pick some strawberries and eat them, and I go there. I pick the strawberries and eat them! Oh, my God! My God! Is there a God? If there be one, deliver me! Save me! Succor me! Pardon! Pity! Mercy! Save me! Oh, what sufferings! What torture! What horror!

August 15. This is certainly the way in which my poor cousin was possessed and controlled when she came to borrow five thousand francs of me. She was under the power of a strange will which had entered into her, like another soul, like another parasitic and dominating soul. Is the world coming to an end?

But who is he, this invisible being that rules me? This unknowable being, this rover of a supernatural race?

Invisible beings exist, then! How is it, then, that since the beginning of the world they have never manifested themselves precisely as they do to me? I have never read of anything that resembles what goes on in my house. Oh, if I could only leave it, if I could only go away, escape, and never return! I should be saved, but I cannot.

August 16. I managed to escape today for two hours, like a prisoner who finds the door of his dungeon accidentally open. I suddenly felt that I was free and that he was far away, and so I gave orders to harness the horses as quickly as possible, and I drove to Rouen. Oh, how delightful to be able to say to a man who obeys you: "Go to Rouen!"

I made him pull up before the library, and I begged them to lend me Dr. Herrmann Herestauss' treatise on the unknown inhabitants of the ancient and modern world.

Then, as I was getting into my carriage, I intended to say: "To the railway station!" but instead of this I shouted—I did not say, I shouted—in such a loud voice that all the passersby turned round: "Home!" and I fell back on the cushion of my carriage, overcome by mental agony. He had found me again and regained possession of me.

August 17. Oh, what a night! What a night! And yet it seems to me that I ought to rejoice. I read until one o'clock in the morning! Herestauss, doctor of philosophy and theogony, wrote the history of the manifestation of all those invisible beings which hover round man, or of whom he dreams. He describes their origin, their domain, their power; but none of them resembles the one which haunts me. One might say that man, ever since he began to think, has had a foreboding fear of a new being, stronger than himself, his successor in this new world, and that, feeling his presence, and not being able to foresee the nature of that master, he has, in his terror, created the whole race of occult beings, of vague phantoms born of fear.

Having, therefore, read until one o'clock in the morning, I went and sat down at the open window, in order to cool my forehead and my thoughts, in the calm night air. It was very pleasant and warm! How I should have enjoyed such a night formerly!

There was no moon, but the stars darted out their rays in the dark heavens. Who inhabits those worlds? What forms, what living beings, what animals are there yonder? What can they do more than we can? What do they see which we do not know? Will not one of them, some day or other, traversing space, appear on our earth to conquer it, just as the Norsemen formerly crossed the sea in order to subjugate nations more feeble than themselves?

We are so weak, so defenseless, so ignorant, so small,

we who live on this particle of mud which revolves in a drop of water.

I fell asleep, dreaming thus in the cool night air, and when I had slept for about three-quarters of an hour, I opened my eyes without moving, awakened by I know not what confused and strange sensation. At first I saw nothing, and then suddenly it appeared to me as if a page of a book which had remained open on my table turned over of its own accord. Not a breath of air had come in at my window, and I was surprised, and waited. In about four minutes, I saw, I saw, yes, I saw with my own eyes, another page lift itself up and fall down on the others, as if a finger had turned it over. My armchair was empty, appeared empty, but I knew that he was there, he, and sitting in my place, and that he was reading. With a furious bound, the bound of an enraged wild beast that springs at its tamer, I crossed my room to seize him, to strangle him, to kill him! But before I could reach it, the chair fell over as if somebody had run away from me—my table rocked, my lamp fell and went out, and my window closed as if some thief had been surprised and had fled out into the night, shutting it behind him.

So he had run away; he had been afraid; he, afraid of me!

But—but—tomorrow—or later—some day or other—I should be able to hold him in my clutches and crush him against the ground! Do not dogs occasionally bite and strangle their masters?

August 18. I have been thinking the whole day long. Oh, yes, I will obey him, follow his impulses, fulfill all his wishes, show myself humble, submissive, a coward. He is the stronger; but the hour will come—

August 19. I know—I know—I know all! I have just read the following in the *Revue du Monde Scientifique*: "A curious piece of news comes to us from Rio de Janeiro. Madness, an epidemic of madness, which may be compared to that contagious madness which attacked the people of Europe in the Middle Ages, is at this moment raging in the Province of San-Paolo. The terrified inhabitants are leaving their houses, saying that they are pursued, possessed, dominated like human cattle by invisible, though tangible beings, a species of vampire, which feed on their life while they are asleep, and who, besides, drink water and milk without appearing to touch any other nourishment.

"Professor Don Pedro Henriquez, accompanied by several medical savants, has gone to the Province of San-Paolo, in order to study the origin and the manifestations of this surprising madness on the spot, and to propose such measures to the Emperor as may appear to him to be most fitted to restore the mad population to reason."

Ah! Ah! I remember now that fine Brazilian three-master which passed in front of my windows as it was going up the Seine, on the 8th day of last May! I thought it looked so pretty, so white and bright! That Being was on board of her, coming from there, where its race originated. And it saw me! It saw my house which was also white, and it sprang from the ship onto the land. Oh, merciful heaven!

Now I know, I can divine. The reign of man is over, and he has come. He who was feared by primitive man; whom disquieted priests exorcised; whom sorcerers evoked on dark nights, without having seen him appear, to whom the imagination of the transient masters of the world lent all the monstrous or graceful forms of gnomes, spirits, genii, fairies, and familiar spirits. After the coarse conceptions of primitive fear, more clear-sighted men foresaw it more clearly. Mesmer divined him, and ten years ago physicians accurately discovered the nature of his power, even before he exercised it himself. They played with this new weapon of the Lord, the sway of a mysterious will over the human soul, which had become a slave. They called it magnetism, hypnotism, suggestion—what do I know? I have seen them amusing themselves like rash children with this horrible power! Woe to us! Woe to man! He has come, the—the—what does he call himself—the—I fancy that he is shouting out his name to me and I do not hear him—the—yes—he is shouting it out—I am listening—I cannot—he repeats it—the—Horla—I hear—the Horla—it is he—the Horla—he has come!

Ah! The vulture has eaten the pigeon; the wolf has eaten the lamb; the lion has devoured the sharp-horned buffalo; man has killed the lion with an arrow, with sword, with gunpowder; but the Horla will make of man what we have made of the horse and of the ox; his chattel, his slave, and his food, by the mere power of his will. Woe to us!

But, nevertheless, the animal sometimes revolts and kills the man who has subjugated it. I should also like— I shall be able to—but I must know him, touch him, see him! Scientists say that animals' eyes, being different from ours, do not distinguish objects as ours do. And my eye cannot distinguish this newcomer who is oppressing me.

Why? Oh, now I remember the words of the monk at Mont Saint-Michel: "Can we see the hundred-thousandth part of what exists? See here; there is the wind, which is the strongest force in nature, which knocks men, and blows down buildings, uproots trees, raises the sea into mountains of water, destroys cliffs and casts great ships on the breakers; the wind which kills, which whistles, which sighs, which roars—have you ever seen it, and can you see it? It exists for all that, however!"

And I went on thinking: my eyes are so weak, so imperfect, that they do not even distinguish hard bodies, if they are as transparent as glass! If a glass without tinfoil behind it were to bar my way, I should run into it, just as a bird which has flown into a room breaks its head against the window-panes. A thousand things, moreover, deceive man and lead him astray. Why should it then be surprising that he cannot perceive an unknown body through which the light passes?

A new being! Why not? It was assuredly bound to come! Why should we be the last? We do not distinguish it any more than all the others created before us! The reason is, that its nature is more perfect, its body finer and more finished than ours, that ours is so weak, so awkwardly constructed, encumbered with organs that are always tired, always on the strain like machinery that is too complicated, which lives like a plant and like a beast, nourishing itself on air, herbs, and flesh, an animal machine which is a prey to maladies, to malformations, to decay; broken-winded, badly regulated, simple and eccentric, ingeniously badly made, at once a coarse and a delicate piece of workmanship, the rough sketch of a being that might become intelligent and grand.

We are only a few, so few in this world, from the oyster up to man. Why should there not be one more, once that period is passed which separates the successive apparitions from all the different species?

Why not one more? Why not, also, other trees with immense, splendid flowers, perfuming whole regions? Why not other elements besides fire, air, earth, and water? There are four, only four, those nursing fathers of various beings! What a pity! Why are there not forty, four hundred, four thousand? How poor everything is, how mean and wretched! Grudgingly produced, roughly constructed, clumsily made! Ah, the elephant and the hippopotamus, what grace! And the camel, what elegance!

But the butterfly, you will say, a flying flower? I dream of one that should be as large as a hundred worlds, with wings whose shape, beauty, colors and motion I cannot even express. But I see it—it flutters from star to star, refreshing them and perfuming them with the light and harmonious breath of its flight! And the people up there look at it as it passes in an ecstasy of delight!

What is the matter with me? It is he, the Horla, who haunts me, and who makes me think of these foolish things! He is within me, he is becoming my soul; I shall kill him!

August 19. I shall kill him. I have seen him! Yesterday I sat down at my table and pretended to write very assiduously. I knew quite well that he would come prowling round me, quite close to me, so close that I might perhaps be able to touch him, to seize him. And then—then I should have the strength of desperation; I should have my hands, my knees, my chest, my forehead, my teeth to strangle him, to crush him, to bite him, to tear him to pieces. And I watched for him with all my over-excited senses.

I had lighted my two lamps and the eight wax candles on my mantelpiece, as if with this light I could discover him.

My bedstead, my old oak post bedstead, stood opposite to me; on my right was the fireplace; on my left, the door which was carefully closed, after I had left it open for some time in order to attract him; behind me was a very high wardrobe with a looking-glass in it, before which I stood to shave and dress every day, and in which

I was in the habit of glancing at myself from head to foot every time I passed it.

I pretended to be writing in order to deceive him, for he also was watching me, and suddenly I felt—I was certain that he was reading over my shoulder, that he was there, touching my ear.

I got up, my hands extended, and turned round so quickly that I almost fell. Eh! Well? It was as bright as at midday, but I did not see my reflection in the mirror! It was empty, clear, profound, full of light! But my figure was not reflected in it—and I, I was opposite to it! I saw the large, clear glass from top to bottom, and I looked at it with unsteady eyes; and I did not dare to advance; I did not venture to make a movement, feeling that he was there, but that he would escape me again, he whose imperceptible body had absorbed my reflection.

How frightened I was! And then, suddenly, I began to see myself in a mist in the depths of the looking-glass, in a mist as it were a sheet of water; and it seemed to me as if this water were flowing clearer every moment. It was like the end of an eclipse. Whatever it was that hid me did not appear to possess any clearly defined outlines, but a sort of opaque transparency which gradually grew clearer.

At last I was able to distinguish myself completely, as I do every day when I look at myself.

I had seen it! And the horror of it remained with me, and makes me shudder even now.

August 20. How could I kill it, as I could not get hold
of it? Poison? But it would see me mix it with the water;
and then, would our poisons have any effect on its impal-
pable body? No—no—no doubt about the matter—
Then—then?—

August 21. I sent for a blacksmith from Rouen, and ordered iron shutters for my room, such as some private hotels in Paris have on the ground floor, for fear of burglars,
and he is going to make me an iron door as well. I have
made myself out a coward, but I do not care about that!

September 10. Rouen, Hôtel Continental. It is done—
it is done—but is he dead? My mind is thoroughly upset
by what I have seen.

Well then, yesterday, the locksmith having put on the
iron shutters and door, I left everything until midnight,
although it was getting cold.

Suddenly I felt that he was there, and joy, mad joy,
took possession of me. I got up softly, and walked up and
down for some time, so that he might not suspect anything; then I took off my boots and put on my slippers
carelessly; then I fastened the iron shutters, and, going
back to the door, quickly double-locked it with a pad-
lock, putting the key into my pocket.

Suddenly I noticed that he was moving restlessly
round me, that in his turn he was frightened and was ordering me to let him out. I nearly yielded; I did not, however, but putting my back to the door, I half opened it,
just enough to allow me to go out backward, and as I am

very tall my head touched the casing. I was sure that he had not been able to escape, and I shut him up alone, quite alone. What happiness! I had him fast. Then I ran downstairs; in the drawing-room, which was under my bedroom, I took the two lamps and I poured all the oil on the carpet, the furniture, everywhere; then I set fire to it and made my escape, after having carefully double-locked the door.

I went and hid myself at the bottom of the garden, in a clump of laurel bushes. How long it seemed! How long it seemed! Everything was dark, silent, motionless, not a breath of air and not a star, but heavy banks of clouds which one could not see, but which weighed, oh, so heavily on my soul.

I looked at my house and waited. How long it was! I already began to think that the fire had gone out of its own accord, or that he had extinguished it, when one of the lower windows gave way under the violence of the flames, and a long, soft, caressing sheet of red flame mounted up the white wall, and enveloped it as far as the roof. The light fell on the trees, the branches, and the leaves, and a shiver of fear pervaded them also! The birds awoke, a dog began to howl, and it seemed to me as if the day were breaking! Almost immediately two other windows flew into fragments, and I saw that the whole of the lower part of my house was nothing but a terrible furnace. But a cry, a horrible, shrill, heartrending cry, a woman's cry, sounded through the night, and two garret windows were opened! I had forgotten the servants! I saw their terror-stricken faces, and their arms waving frantically.

Then overwhelmed with horror, I set off to run to the village, shouting: "Help! Help! Fire! Fire!" I met some people who were already coming to the scene, and I returned with them.

By this time the house was nothing but a horrible and magnificent funeral pile, a monstrous funeral pile which lit up the whole country, a funeral pile where men were burning, and where he was burning also, He, He, my prisoner, that new Being, the new master, the Horla!

Suddenly the whole roof fell in between the walls, and a volcano of flames darted up to the sky. Through all the windows which opened on that furnace, I saw the flames darting, and I thought that he was there, in that kiln, dead.

Dead? Perhaps? — His body? Was not his body, which was transparent, indestructible by such means as would kill ours?

If he were not dead? — Perhaps time alone has power over that Invisible and Redoubtable Being. Why this transparent, unrecognizable body, this body belonging to a spirit, if it also has to fear ills, infirmities, and premature destruction?

Premature destruction? All human terror springs from that! After man, the Horla. After him who can die every day, at any hour, at any moment, by any accident, came the one who would die only at his own proper hour, day, and minute, because he had touched the limits of his existence!

No—no—without any doubt—he is not dead—Then—then—I suppose I must kill myself! . . .

THE ADVENTURE OF THE
SUSSEX VAMPIRE

✦✦✦

ARTHUR CONAN DOYLE

Holmes had read carefully a note which the last post had brought him. Then, with the dry chuckle which was his nearest approach to a laugh, he tossed it over to me.

"For a mixture of the modern and the mediæval, of the practical and of the wildly fanciful, I think this is surely the limit," said he. "What do you make of it, Watson?"

I read as follows:

46, Old Jewry
Nov. 19th
Re Vampires
Sir:

Our client, Mr. Robert Ferguson, of Ferguson and Muirhead, tea brokers, of Mincing Lane, has made some inquiry from us in a communication of even date concerning vampires. As our firm specializes entirely upon the assessment of machinery the matter hardly comes within our purview, and we have therefore recommended Mr. Ferguson to call upon you and lay the

matter before you. We have not forgotten your success-
ful action in the case of Matilda Briggs.

  We are, sir,

  Faithfully yours,
  Morrison, Morrison, and Dodd
  per E. J. C.

"Matilda Briggs was not the name of a young woman, Watson," said Holmes in a reminiscent voice. "It was a ship which is associated with the giant rat of Sumatra, a story for which the world is not yet prepared. But what do we know about vampires? Does it come within our purview either? Anything is better than stagnation, but really we seem to have been switched on to a Grimms' fairy tale. Make a long arm, Watson, and see what V has to say."

I leaned back and took down the great index volume to which he referred. Holmes balanced it on his knee, and his eyes moved slowly and lovingly over the record of old cases, mixed with the accumulated information of a lifetime.

"Voyage of the *Gloria Scott*," he read. "That was a bad business. I have some recollection that you made a record of it, Watson, though I was unable to congratulate you upon the result. Victor Lynch, the forger. Venomous lizard or gila. Remarkable case, that! Vittoria, the circus belle. Vanderbilt and the Yeggman. Vipers. Vigor, the Hammersmith wonder. Hullo! Hullo! Good old index. You can't beat it. Listen to this, Watson. Vampirism in Hungary. And again, Vampires in Transylvania." He turned over the pages with eagerness, but after a short intent perusal he threw down the great book with a snarl of disappointment.

"Rubbish, Watson, rubbish! What have we to do with walking corpses who can only be held in their grave by stakes driven through their hearts? It's pure lunacy."

"But surely," said I, "the vampire was not necessarily a dead man? A living person might have the habit. I have read, for example, of the old sucking the blood of the young in order to retain their youth."

"You are right, Watson. It mentions the legend in one of these references. But are we to give serious attention to such things? This Agency stands flat-footed upon the ground, and there it must remain. The world is big enough for us. No ghosts need apply. I fear that we cannot take Mr. Robert Ferguson very seriously. Possibly this note may be from him, and may throw some light upon what is worrying him."

He took up a second letter which had lain unnoticed upon the table while he had been absorbed with the first. This he began to read with a smile of amusement upon his face which gradually faded away into an expression of intense interest and concentration. When he had finished, he sat for some little time lost in thought, with the letter dangling from his fingers. Finally, with a start, he aroused himself from his reverie.

"Cheeseman's, Lamberley. Where is Lamberley, Watson?"

"It is in Sussex, south of Horsham."

"Not very far, eh? And Cheeseman's?"

"I know that country, Holmes. It is full of old houses which are named after the men who built them centuries ago. You get Odley's and Harvey's and Carriton's— the folk are forgotten but their names live in their houses."

"Precisely," said Holmes coldly. It was one of the peculiarities of his proud, self-contained nature that though he docketed any fresh information very quietly and accurately in his brain, he seldom made any acknowledgment to the giver. "I rather fancy we shall know a good deal more about Cheeseman's, Lamberley, before we are through. The letter is, as I had hoped, from Robert Ferguson. By the way, he claims acquaintance with you."

"With me!"

"You had better read it."

He handed the letter across. It was headed with the address quoted.

Dear Mr. Holmes [it said]:

I have been recommended to you by my lawyers, but indeed the matter is so extraordinarily delicate that it is most difficult to discuss. It concerns a friend for whom I am acting. This gentleman married some five years ago a Peruvian lady, the daughter of a Peruvian merchant, whom he had met in connection with the importation of nitrates. The lady was very beautiful, but the fact of her foreign birth and of her alien religion always caused a separation of interests and of feelings between husband and wife, so that after a time his love may have cooled towards her and he may have come to regard their union as a mistake. He felt there were sides of her character which he could never explore or understand. This was the more painful as she was as loving a wife as a man could have—to all appearance absolutely devoted.

Now for the point which I will make more plain when we meet. Indeed, this note is merely to give you a general idea of the situation and to ascertain whether you would care to interest yourself in the matter. The lady began to show some curious traits quite alien to her ordinarily sweet and gentle disposition. The gentleman had been married twice and he had one son by the first wife. This boy was now fifteen, a very charming and affectionate youth, though unhappily injured through an accident in childhood. Twice the wife was caught in the act of assaulting this poor lad in the most unprovoked way. Once she struck him with a stick and left a great weal on his arm.

This was a small matter, however, compared with her conduct to her own child, a dear boy just under one year of age. On one occasion about a month ago this child had been left by its nurse for a few minutes. A loud cry from the baby, as of pain, called the nurse back. As she ran into the room she saw her employer, the lady, leaning over the baby and apparently biting his neck. There was a small wound in the neck from which a stream of blood had escaped. The nurse was so horrified that she wished to call the husband, but the lady implored her not to do so and actually gave her five pounds as a price for her silence. No explanation was ever given, and for the moment the matter was passed over.

It left, however, a terrible impression upon the nurse's mind, and from that time she began to watch her mistress closely and to keep a closer guard upon the baby, whom she tenderly loved. It seemed to her that even as she watched the mother, so the mother watched her, and that every time she was compelled to leave the baby alone the mother was waiting to get at it. Day and night the nurse covered the child, and day and night the silent, watchful mother seemed to be lying in wait as a wolf waits for a lamb. It must read most incredible to you, and yet I beg you to take it seriously, for a child's life and a man's sanity may depend upon it.

At last there came one dreadful day when the facts could no longer be concealed from the husband. The nurse's nerve had given way; she could stand the strain no longer, and she made a clean breast of it all to the man. To him it seemed as wild a tale as it may now seem to you. He knew his wife to be a loving wife, and, save for the assaults upon her stepson, a loving mother. Why, then, should she wound her own dear little baby? He told the nurse that she was dreaming, that her suspicions were those of a lunatic, and that such libels upon her mistress were not to be tolerated. While they were talking a sudden cry of pain was heard. Nurse and master rushed together to the nursery. Imagine his feelings, Mr. Holmes, as he saw his wife rise from a kneeling position beside the cot and saw blood upon the child's exposed neck and upon the sheet. With a cry of horror, he turned his wife's face to the light and saw blood all round her lips. It was she—she beyond all question—who had drunk the poor baby's blood.

So the matter stands. She is now confined to her room. There has been no explanation. The husband is half demented. He knows, and I know, little of vampirism beyond the name. We had thought it was some wild tale of foreign parts. And yet here in the very heart of the English Sussex—well, all this can be discussed with you in the morning. Will you see me? Will you use your great powers in aiding a distracted man? If so, kindly wire to Ferguson, Cheeseman's, Lamberley, and I will be at your rooms by ten o'clock.

Yours faithfully,
Robert Ferguson

P. S. I believe your friend Watson played Rugby for Blackheath when I was three-quarter for Richmond. It is the only personal introduction which I can give.

"Of course I remembered him," said I as I laid down the letter. "Big Bob Ferguson, the finest three-quarter Richmond ever had. He was always a good-natured chap. It's like him to be so concerned over a friend's case."

Holmes looked at me thoughtfully and shook his head.

"I never get your limits, Watson," said he. "There are unexplored possibilities about you. Take a wire down, like a good fellow. 'Will examine your case with pleasure.'"

"*Your* case!"

"We must not let him think that this Agency is weak-minded. Of course it is his case. Send him that wire and let the matter rest till morning."

Promptly at ten o'clock next morning Ferguson strode into our room. I had remembered him as a long, slab-sided man with loose limbs and a fine turn of speed which had carried him round many an opposing back. There is surely nothing in life more painful than to meet the wreck of a fine athlete whom one has known in his prime. His great frame had fallen in, his flaxen hair was scanty, and his shoulders were bowed. I fear that I roused corresponding emotions in him.

"Hullo, Watson," said he, and his voice was still deep and hearty. "You don't look quite the man you did when I threw you over the ropes into the crowd at the Old Deer Park. I expect I have changed a bit also. But it's this last day or two that has aged me. I see by your telegram, Mr. Holmes, that it is no use my pretending to be anyone's deputy."

"It is simpler to deal direct," said Holmes.

"Of course it is. But you can imagine how difficult it is when you are speaking of the one woman whom you are bound to protect and help. What can I do? How am I to go to the police with such a story? And yet the kiddies have got to be protected. Is it madness, Mr. Holmes? Is it something in the blood? Have you any similar case in your experience? For God's sake, give me some advice, for I am at my wit's end."

"Very naturally, Mr. Ferguson. Now sit here and pull yourself together and give me a few clear answers. I can assure you that I am very far from being at my wit's end, and that I am confident we shall find some solution. First of all, tell me what steps you have taken. Is your wife still near the children?"

"We had a dreadful scene. She is a most loving woman, Mr. Holmes. If ever a woman loved a man with all her heart and soul, she loves me. She was cut to the heart that I should have discovered this horrible, this incredible, secret. She would not even speak. She gave no answer to my reproaches, save to gaze at me with a sort of wild, despairing look in her eyes. Then she rushed to her room and locked herself in. Since then she has refused to see me. She has a maid who was with her before her marriage, Dolores by name—a friend rather than a servant. She takes her food to her."

"Then the child is in no immediate danger?"

"Mrs. Mason, the nurse, has sworn that she will not leave it night or day. I can absolutely trust her. I am more uneasy about poor little Jack, for, as I told you in my note, he has twice been assaulted by her."

"But never wounded?"

"No, she struck him savagely. It is the more terrible as he is a poor little inoffensive cripple." Ferguson's gaunt features softened as he spoke of his boy. "You would think that the dear lad's condition would soften anyone's heart. A fall in childhood and a twisted spine, Mr. Holmes. But the dearest, most loving heart within."

Holmes had picked up the letter of yesterday and was reading it over. "What other inmates are there in your house, Mr. Ferguson?"

"Two servants who have not been long with us. One stable-hand, Michael, who sleeps in the house. My wife, myself, my boy Jack, baby, Dolores, and Mrs. Mason. That is all."

"I gather that you did not know your wife well at the time of your marriage?"

"I had only known her a few weeks."

"How long had this maid Dolores been with her?"

"Some years."

"Then your wife's character would really be better known by Dolores than by you?"

"Yes, you may say so."

Holmes made a note.

"I fancy," said he, "that I may be of more use at Lamberley than here. It is eminently a case for personal investigation. If the lady remains in her room, our presence could not annoy or inconvenience her. Of course, we would stay at the inn."

Ferguson gave a gesture of relief.

"It is what I hoped, Mr. Holmes. There is an excellent train at two from Victoria if you could come."

"Of course we could come. There is a lull at present. I can give you my undivided energies. Watson, of course, comes with us. But there are one or two points upon which I wish to be very sure before I start. This unhappy lady, as I understand it, has appeared to assault both the children, her own baby and your little son?"

"That is so."

"But the assaults take different forms, do they not? She has beaten your son."

"Once with a stick and once very savagely with her hands."

"Did she give no explanation why she struck him?"

"None save that she hated him. Again and again she said so."

"Well, that is not unknown among stepmothers. A posthumous jealousy, we will say. Is the lady jealous by nature?"

"Yes, she is very jealous—jealous with all the strength of her fiery tropical love."

"But the boy—he is fifteen, I understand, and probably very developed in mind, since his body has been circumscribed in action. Did he give you no explanation of these assaults?"

"No, he declared there was no reason."

"Were they good friends at other times?"

"No, there was never any love between them."

"Yet you say he is affectionate?"

"Never in the world could there be so devoted a son. My life is his life. He is absorbed in what I say or do."

Once again Holmes made a note. For some time he sat lost in thought.

"No doubt you and the boy were great comrades before this second marriage. You were thrown very close together, were you not?"

"Very much so."

"And the boy, having so affectionate a nature, was devoted, no doubt, to the memory of his mother?"

"Most devoted."

"He would certainly seem to be a most interesting lad. There is one other point about these assaults. Were the strange attacks upon the baby and the assaults upon your son at the same period?"

"In the first case it was so. It was as if some frenzy had seized her, and she had vented her rage upon both. In the second case it was only Jack who suffered. Mrs. Mason had no complaint to make about the baby."

"That certainly complicates matters."

"I don't quite follow you, Mr. Holmes."

"Possibly not. One forms provisional theories and waits for time or fuller knowledge to explode them. A bad habit, Mr. Ferguson, but human nature is weak. I fear that your old friend here has given an exaggerated view of my scientific methods. However, I will only say at the present stage that your problem does not appear to me to be insoluble, and that you may expect to find us at Victoria at two o'clock."

It was evening of a dull, foggy November day when, having left our bags at the Chequers, Lamberley, we drove through the Sussex clay of a long winding lane and finally reached the isolated and ancient farmhouse in which Ferguson dwelt. It was a large, straggling building, very old in the centre, very new at the wings with towering Tudor chimneys and a lichen-spotted, high-pitched roof of Horsham slabs. The doorsteps were worn into curves, and the ancient tiles which lined the porch were marked with the rebus of a cheese and a man after the original builder. Within, the ceilings were corrugated with heavy oaken beams, and the uneven floors sagged into sharp curves. An odour of age and decay pervaded the whole crumbling building.

There was one very large central room into which Ferguson led us. Here, in a huge old-fashioned fireplace with an iron screen behind it dated 1670, there blazed and spluttered a splendid log fire.

The room, as I gazed round, was a most singular mixture of dates and of places. The half-panelled walls may well have belonged to the original yeoman farmer of the seventeenth century. They were ornamented, however, on the lower part by a line of well-chosen modern water-colours; while above, where yellow plaster took the place of oak, there was hung a fine collection of South American utensils and weapons, which had been brought, no doubt, by the Peruvian lady upstairs. Holmes rose, with that quick curiosity which sprang from his eager mind, and examined them with some care. He returned with his eyes full of thought.

"Hullo!" he cried. "Hullo!"

A spaniel had lain in a basket in the corner. It came slowly forward towards its master, walking with difficulty. Its hind legs moved irregularly and its tail was on the ground. It licked Ferguson's hand.

"What is it, Mr. Holmes?"

"The dog. What's the matter with it?"

"That's what puzzled the vet. A sort of paralysis. Spinal meningitis, he thought. But it is passing. He'll be all right soon—won't you, Carlo?"

A shiver of assent passed through the drooping tail. The dog's mournful eyes passed from one of us to the other. He knew that we were discussing his case.

"Did it come on suddenly?"

"In a single night."

"How long ago?"

"It may have been four months ago."

"Very remarkable. Very suggestive."

"What do you see in it, Mr. Holmes?"

"A confirmation of what I had already thought."

"For God's sake, what *do* you think, Mr. Holmes? It may be a mere intellectual puzzle to you, but it is life and death to me! My wife a would-be murderer—my child in constant danger! Don't play with me, Mr. Holmes. It is too terribly serious."

The big Rugby three-quarter was trembling all over. Holmes put his hand soothingly upon his arm.

"I fear that there is pain for you, Mr. Ferguson, whatever the solution may be," said he. "I would spare you all I can. I cannot say more for the instant, but before I leave this house I hope I may have something definite."

"Please God you may! If you will excuse me, gentlemen, I will go up to my wife's room and see if there has been any change."

He was away some minutes, during which Holmes resumed his examination of the curiosities upon the wall. When our host returned it was clear from his downcast face that he had made no progress. He brought with him a tall, slim, brown-faced girl.

"The tea is ready, Dolores," said Ferguson. "See that your mistress has everything she can wish."

"She verra ill," cried the girl, looking with indignant eyes at her master. "She no ask for food. She verra ill. She need doctor. I frightened stay alone with her without doctor."

Ferguson looked at me with a question in his eyes.

"I should be so glad if I could be of use."

"Would your mistress see Dr. Watson?"

"I take him. I no ask leave. She needs doctor."

"Then I'll come with you at once."

I followed the girl, who was quivering with strong emotion, up the staircase and down an ancient corridor. At the end was an iron-clamped and massive door. It struck me as I looked at it that if Ferguson tried to force his way to his wife he would find it no easy matter. The girl drew a key from her pocket, and the heavy oaken planks creaked upon their old hinges. I passed in and she swiftly followed, fastening the door behind her.

On the bed a woman was lying who was clearly in a high fever. She was only half conscious, but as I entered she raised a pair of frightened but beautiful eyes and glared at me in apprehension. Seeing a stranger, she appeared to be relieved and sank back with a sigh upon the pillow. I stepped up to her with a few reassuring words, and she lay still while I took her pulse and temperature. Both were high, and yet my impression was that the condition was rather that of mental and nervous excitement than of any actual seizure.

"She lie like that one day, two day. I 'fraid she die," said the girl.

The woman turned her flushed and handsome face towards me.

"Where is my husband?"

"He is below and would wish to see you."

"I will not see him. I will not see him." Then she seemed to wander off into delirium. "A fiend! A fiend! Oh, what shall I do with this devil?"

"Can I help you in any way?"

"No. No one can help. It is finished. All is destroyed. Do what I will, all is destroyed."

The woman must have some strange delusion. I could not see honest Bob Ferguson in the character of fiend or devil.

"Madame," I said, "your husband loves you dearly. He is deeply grieved at this happening."

Again she turned on me those glorious eyes.

"He loves me. Yes. But do I not love him? Do I not love him even to sacrifice myself rather than break his dear heart? That is how I love him. And yet he could think of me—he could speak to me so."

"He is full of grief, but he cannot understand."

"No, he cannot understand. But he should trust."

"Will you not see him?" I suggested.

"No, no, I cannot forget those terrible words nor the look upon his face. I will not see him. Go now. You can do nothing for me. Tell him only one thing. I want my child. I have a right to my child. That is the only message I can send him." She turned her face to the wall and would say no more.

I returned to the room downstairs, where Ferguson and Holmes still sat by the fire. Ferguson listened moodily to my account of the interview.

"How can I send her the child?" he said. "How do I know what strange impulse might come upon her? How can I ever forget how she rose from beside it with its blood upon her lips?" He shuddered at the recollection. "The child is safe with Mrs. Mason, and there he must remain."

A smart maid, the only modern thing which we had seen in the house, had brought in some tea. As she was serving it the door opened and a youth entered the room. He was a remarkable lad, pale-faced and fair-haired, with excitable light blue eyes which blazed into a sudden flame of emotion and joy as they rested upon his father. He rushed forward and threw his arms round his neck with the abandon of a loving girl.

"Oh, daddy," he cried, "I did not know that you were due yet. I should have been here to meet you. Oh, I am so glad to see you!"

Ferguson gently disengaged himself from the embrace with some little show of embarrassment.

"Dear old chap," said he, patting the flaxen head with a very tender hand. "I came early because my friends, Mr. Holmes and Dr. Watson, have been persuaded to come down and spend an evening with us."

"Is that Mr. Holmes, the detective?"

"Yes."

The youth looked at us with a very penetrating and, as it seemed to me, unfriendly gaze.

"What about your other child, Mr. Ferguson?" asked Holmes. "Might we make the acquaintance of the baby?"

"Ask Mrs. Mason to bring baby down," said Ferguson. The boy went off with a curious, shambling gait which told my surgical eyes that he was suffering from a weak spine. Presently he returned, and behind him came a tall, gaunt woman bearing in her arms a very beautiful child, dark-eyed, golden-haired, a wonderful mixture of the Saxon and the Latin. Ferguson was evidently devoted to it, for he took it into his arms and fondled it most tenderly.

"Fancy anyone having the heart to hurt him," he muttered as he glanced down at the small, angry red pucker upon the cherub throat.

It was at this moment that I chanced to glance at Holmes and saw a most singular intentness in his expression. His face was as set as if it had been carved out of old ivory, and his eyes, which had glanced for a moment at father and child, were now fixed with eager curiosity upon something at the other side of the room. Following his gaze I could only guess that he was looking out through the window at the melancholy, dripping garden. It is true that a shutter had half closed outside and obstructed the view, but none the less it was certainly at the window that Holmes was fixing his concentrated attention. Then he smiled, and his eyes came back to the baby. On its chubby neck there was this small puckered mark. Without speaking, Holmes examined it with care. Finally he shook one of the dimpled fists which waved in front of him.

"Good-bye, little man. You have made a strange start in life. Nurse, I should wish to have a word with you in private."

He took her aside and spoke earnestly for a few minutes. I only heard the last words, which were: "Your anxiety will soon, I hope, be set at rest." The woman, who seemed to be a sour, silent kind of creature, withdrew with the child.

"What is Mrs. Mason like?" asked Holmes.

"Not very prepossessing externally, as you can see, but a heart of gold, and devoted to the child."

"Do you like her, Jack?" Holmes turned suddenly upon the boy. His expressive mobile face shadowed over, and he shook his head.

"Jacky has very strong likes and dislikes," said Ferguson, putting his arm round the boy. "Luckily I am one of his likes."

The boy cooed and nestled his head upon his father's breast. Ferguson gently disengaged him.

"Run away, little Jacky," said he, and he watched his son with loving eyes until he disappeared. "Now, Mr. Holmes," he continued when the boy was gone, "I really feel that I have brought you on a fool's errand, for what can you possibly do save give me your sympathy? It must be an exceedingly delicate and complex affair from your point of view."

"It is certainly delicate," said my friend with an amused smile, "but I have not been struck up to now with its complexity. It has been a case for intellectual deduction, but when this original intellectual deduction is confirmed point by point by quite a number of independent incidents, then the subjective becomes objective and we can say confidently that we have reached our goal. I had, in fact, reached it before we left Baker Street, and the rest has merely been observation and confirmation."

Ferguson put his big hand to his furrowed forehead.

"For heaven's sake, Holmes," he said hoarsely, "if you

can see the truth in this matter, do not keep me in suspense. How do I stand? What shall I do? I care nothing as to how you have found your facts so long as you have really got them."

"Certainly I owe you an explanation, and you shall have it. But you will permit me to handle the matter in my own way? Is the lady capable of seeing us, Watson?"

"She is ill, but she is quite rational."

"Very good. It is only in her presence that we can clear the matter up. Let us go up to her."

"She will not see me," cried Ferguson.

"Oh, yes, she will," said Holmes. He scribbled a few lines upon a sheet of paper. "You at least have the entrée, Watson. Will you have the goodness to give the lady this note?"

I ascended again and handed the note to Dolores, who cautiously opened the door. A minute later I heard a cry from within, a cry in which joy and surprise seemed to be blended. Dolores looked out.

"She will see them. She will leesten," said she.

At my summons, Ferguson and Holmes came up. As we entered the room Ferguson took a step or two towards his wife, who had raised herself in the bed, but she held out her hand to repulse him. He sank into an armchair, while Holmes seated himself beside him, after bowing to the lady, who looked at him with wide-eyed amazement.

"I think we can dispense with Dolores," said Holmes. "Oh, very well, madame, if you would rather she stayed I can see no objection. Now, Mr. Ferguson, I am a busy man with many calls, and my methods have to be short and direct. The swiftest surgery is the least painful. Let me first say what will ease your mind. Your wife is a very good, a very loving, and a very ill-used woman."

Ferguson sat up with a cry of joy.

"Prove that, Mr. Holmes, and I am your debtor forever."

"I will do so, but in doing so I must wound you deeply in another direction."

"I care nothing so long as you clear my wife. Everything on earth is insignificant compared to that."

"Let me tell you, then, the train of reasoning which passed through my mind in Baker Street. The idea of a vampire was to me absurd. Such things do not happen in criminal practice in England. And yet your observation was precise. You had seen the lady rise from beside the child's cot with the blood upon her lips."

"I did."

"Did it not occur to you that a bleeding wound may be sucked for some other purpose than to draw the blood from it? Was there not a queen in English history who sucked such a wound to draw poison from it?"

"Poison!"

"A South American household. My instinct felt the presence of those weapons upon the wall before my eyes ever saw them. It might have been other poison, but that was what occurred to me. When I saw that little empty quiver beside the small bird-bow, it was just what I expected to see. If the child were pricked with one of those arrows dipped in curare or some other devilish drug, it would mean death if the venom were not sucked out.

"And the dog! If one were to use such a poison, would one not try it first in order to see that it had not lost its power? I did not foresee the dog, but at least I understand him and he fitted into my reconstruction.

"Now do you understand? Your wife feared such an attack. She saw it made and saved the child's life, and yet she shrank from telling you all the truth, for she knew how you loved the boy and feared lest it break your heart."

"Jacky!"

"I watched him as you fondled the child just now. His face was clearly reflected in the glass of the window where the shutter formed a background. I saw such jealousy, such cruel hatred, as I have seldom seen in a human face."

"My Jacky!"

"You have to face it, Mr. Ferguson. It is the more painful because it is a distorted love, a maniacal exaggerated love for you, and possibly for his dead mother, which has prompted his action. His very soul is consumed with hatred for this splendid child, whose health and beauty are a contrast to his own weakness."

"Good God! It is incredible!"

"Have I spoken the truth, madame?"

The lady was sobbing, with her face buried in the pillows. Now she turned to her husband.

"How could I tell you, Bob? I felt the blow it would be

to you. It was better that I should wait and that it should come from some other lips than mine. When this gentleman, who seems to have powers of magic, wrote that he knew all, I was glad."

"I think a year at sea would be my prescription for Master Jacky," said Holmes, rising from his chair. "Only one thing is still clouded, madame. We can quite understand your attacks upon Master Jacky. There is a limit to a mother's patience. But how did you dare to leave the child these last two days?"

"I had told Mrs. Mason. She knew."

"Exactly. So I imagined."

Ferguson was standing by the bed, choking, his hands outstretched and quivering.

"This, I fancy, is the time for our exit, Watson," said Holmes in a whisper. "If you will take one elbow of the too faithful Dolores, I will take the other. There, now," he added as he closed the door behind him, "I think we may leave them to settle the rest among themselves."

I have only one further note of this case. It is the letter which Holmes wrote in final answer to that with which the narrative begins. It ran thus:

Baker Street
Nov. 21st
Re Vampires
Sir:
   Referring to your letter of the 19th, I beg to state that I have looked into the inquiry of your client, Mr.

Robert Ferguson, of Ferguson and Muirhead, tea bro-
kers, of Mincing Lane, and that the matter has been
brought to a satisfactory conclusion. With thanks for
your recommendation, I am, sir,

Faithfully yours,
Sherlock Holmes

THE MAN WHO LOVED THE VAMPIRE LADY

◆◆◆

BRIAN STABLEFORD

A man who loves a vampire lady may not die young, but cannot live forever.

—WALACHIAN PROVERB

It was the thirteenth of June in the Year of Our Lord 1623. Grand Normandy was in the grip of an early spell of warm weather, and the streets of London bathed in sunlight. There were crowds everywhere, and the port was busy with ships, three having docked that very day. One of the ships, the *Freemartin*, was from the Moorish enclave and had produce from the heart of Africa, including ivory and the skins of exotic animals. There were rumors, too, of secret and more precious goods: jewels and magical charms; but such rumors always attended the docking of any vessel from remote parts of the world. Beggars and street urchins had flocked to the dockland, responsive as ever to such whisperings, and were plaguing every sailor in the streets, as anxious for gossip as for copper coins. It seemed that the only faces not animated by excitement were those worn by the severed heads that dressed the spikes atop the Southwark Gate. The Tower of London, though, stood quite aloof from the hubbub, its tall and forbidding turrets so remote from the streets that they belonged to a different world.

Edmund Cordery, mechanician to the court of the Archduke Girard, tilted the small concave mirror on the brass device that rested on his workbench, catching the rays of the afternoon sun and deflecting the light through the system of lenses.

He turned away and directed his son, Noell, to take his place. "Tell me if all is well," he said tiredly. "I can hardly focus my eyes, let alone the instrument."

Noell closed his left eye and put his other to the microscope. He turned the wheel that adjusted the height of the stage. "It's perfect," he said. "What is it?"

"The wing of a moth." Edmund scanned the polished tabletop, checking that the other slides were in readiness for the demonstration. The prospect of Lady Carmilla's visit filled him with a complex anxiety that he resented in himself. Even in the old days, she had not come to his laboratory often, but to see her here—on his own territory, as it were—would be bound to awaken memories that were untouched by the glimpses that he caught of her in the public parts of the Tower and on ceremonial occasions.

"The water slide isn't ready," Noell pointed out.

Edmund shook his head. "I'll make a fresh one when the time comes," he said. "Living things are fragile, and the world that is in a water drop is all too easily destroyed."

He looked farther along the bench-top, and moved a crucible, placing it out of sight behind a row of jars. It was impossible—and unnecessary—to make the place tidy, but he felt it important to conserve some sense of order and control. To discourage himself from fidgeting, he went to the window and looked out at the sparkling Thames and the strange gray sheen on the slate roofs of the houses beyond. From this high vantage point, the people were tiny; he was higher even than the cross on the steeple of the church beside the Leathermarket. Edmund was not a devout man, but such was the agitation within him, yearning for expression in action, that the sight of the cross on the church made him cross himself, murmuring the ritual devotion. As soon as he had done it, he cursed himself for childishness.

I am forty-four years old, he thought, *and a mechanician. I am no longer the boy who was favored with the love of the lady, and there is no need for this stupid trepidation.*

He was being deliberately unfair to himself in this private scolding. It was not simply the fact that he had once been Carmilla's lover that made him anxious. There was the microscope, and the ship from the Moorish country. He hoped that he would be able to judge by the lady's reaction how much cause there really was for fear.

The door opened then, and the lady entered. She half turned to indicate by a flutter of her hand that her attendant need not come in with her, and he withdrew, closing the door behind him. She was alone, with no friend or favorite in tow. She came across the room carefully, lifting the hem of her skirt a little, though the floor was not dusty. Her gaze flicked from side to side, to take note of the shelves, the beakers, the furnace, and the numerous tools of the mechanician's craft. To a commoner, it would have seemed a threatening environment, redolent with unholiness, but her attitude was cool and controlled. She arrived to stand before the brass instrument that Edmund had recently completed, but did not look long at it before raising her eyes to look fully into Edmund's face.

"You look well, Master Cordery," she said calmly. "But you are pale. You should not shut yourself in your rooms now that summer is come to Normandy."

Edmund bowed slightly, but met her gaze. She had not changed in the slightest degree, of course, since the days when he had been intimate with her. She was six hundred years old—hardly younger than the archduke— and the years were impotent as far as her appearance was concerned. Her complexion was much darker than his, her eyes a deep liquid brown, and her hair jet black. He had not stood so close to her for several years, and he could not help the tide of memories rising in his mind. For her, it would be different: his hair was gray now, his skin creased; he must seem an altogether different person. As he met her gaze, though, it seemed to him that she, too, was remembering, and not without fondness.

"My lady," he said, his voice quite steady, "may I present my son and apprentice, Noell."

Noell bowed more deeply than his father, blushing with embarrassment.

The Lady Carmilla favored the youth with a smile. "He has the look of you, Master Cordery," she said—a casual compliment. She returned her attention then to the instrument.

"The designer was correct?" she asked.

"Yes, indeed," he replied. "The device is most ingenious. I would dearly like to meet the man who thought of it. A fine discovery—though it taxed the talents of my lens grinder severely. I think we might make a better one, with much care and skill; this is but a poor example, as one must expect from a first attempt."

The Lady Carmilla seated herself at the bench, and Edmund showed her how to apply her eye to the instrument, and how to adjust the focusing wheel and the mirror. She expressed surprise at the appearance of the magnified moth's wing, and Edmund took her through the series of prepared slides, which included other parts of insects' bodies, and sections through the stems and seeds of plants.

"I need a sharper knife and a steadier hand, my lady," he told her. "The device exposes the clumsiness of my cutting."

"Oh no, Master Cordery," she assured him politely. "These are quite pretty enough. But we were told that more interesting things might be seen. Living things too small for ordinary sight."

Edmund bowed in apology and explained about the preparation of water slides. He made a new one, using a pipette to take a drop from a jar full of dirty river water. Patiently, he helped the lady search the slide for the tiny creatures that human eyes were not equipped to perceive. He showed her one that flowed as if it were semiliquid itself, and tinier ones that moved by means of cilia. She was quite captivated, and watched for some time, moving the slide very gently with her painted fingernails.

Eventually she asked: "Have you looked at other fluids?"

"What kind of fluids?" he asked, though the question was quite clear to him and disturbed him.

She was not prepared to mince words with him. "Blood, Master Cordery," she said very softly. Her past acquaintance with him had taught her respect for his intelligence, and he half regretted it.

"Blood clots very quickly," he told her. "I could not produce a satisfactory slide. It would take unusual skill."

"I'm sure that it would," she replied.

"Noell has made drawings of many of the things we *have* looked at," said Edmund. "Would you like to see them?"

She accepted the change of subject, and indicated that she would. She moved to Noell's station and began sorting through the drawings, occasionally looking up at the boy to compliment him on his work. Edmund stood by, remembering how sensitive he once had been to her moods and desires, trying hard to work out now exactly what she was thinking. Something in one of her contemplative glances at Noell sent an icy pang of dread into Edmund's gut, and he found his more important fears momentarily displaced by what might have been anxiety for his son, or simply jealousy. He cursed himself again for his weakness.

"May I take these to show the archduke?" asked the Lady Carmilla, addressing the question to Noell rather than to his father. The boy nodded, still too embarrassed to construct a proper reply. She took a selection of the drawings and rolled them into a scroll. She stood and faced Edmund again.

"We are most interested in this apparatus," she informed him. "We must consider carefully whether to provide you with new assistants, to encourage development of the appropriate skills. In the meantime, you may return to your ordinary work. I will send someone for the instrument, so that the archduke can inspect it at his leisure. Your son draws very well, and must be encouraged. You and he may visit me in my chambers on Monday next; we will dine at seven o'clock, and you may tell me about all your recent work."

Edmund bowed to signal his acquiescence—it was, of course, a command rather than an invitation. He moved before her to the door in order to hold it open for her. The two exchanged another brief glance as she went past him.

When she had gone, it was as though something taut unwound inside him, leaving him relaxed and emptied.

He felt strangely cool and distant as he considered the possibility—stronger now—that his life was in peril.

When the twilight had faded, Edmund lit a single candle on the bench and sat staring into the flame while he drank dark wine from a flask. He did not look up when Noell came into the room, but when the boy brought another stool close to his and sat down upon it, he offered the flask. Noell took it, but sipped rather gingerly.

"I'm old enough to drink now?" he commented dryly.

"You're old enough," Edmund assured him. "But beware of excess, and never drink alone. Conventional fatherly advice, I believe."

Noell reached across the bench so that he could stroke the barrel of the microscope with slender fingers.

"What are you afraid of?" he asked.

Edmund sighed. "You're old enough for that, too, I suppose?"

"I think you ought to tell me."

Edmund looked at the brass instrument and said, "It were better to keep things like this dark secret. Some human mechanician, I daresay, eager to please the vampire lords and ladies, showed off his cleverness as proud as a peacock. Thoughtless. Inevitable, though, now that all this play with lenses has become fashionable."

"You'll be glad of eyeglasses when your sight begins to fail," Noell told him. "In any case, I can't see the danger in this new toy."

Edmund smiled. "New toys," he mused. "Clocks to tell the time, mills to grind the corn, lenses to aid human sight. Produced by human craftsmen for the delight of their masters. I think we've finally succeeded in proving to the vampires just how very clever we are—and how much more there is to know than we know already."

"You think the vampires are beginning to fear us?"

Edmund gulped wine from the flask and passed it again to his son. "Their rule is founded in fear and superstition," he said quietly. "They're long-lived, suffer only mild attacks of diseases that are fatal to us, and have marvelous powers of regeneration. But they're not immortal, and they're vastly outnumbered by humans. Terror keeps them safe, but terror is based in ignorance, and behind their haughtiness and arrogance, there's a gnawing fear of what might happen if humans ever lost their supernatural reverence for vampirekind. It's very difficult for them to die, but they don't fear death any the less for that."

"There've been rebellions against vampire rule. They've always failed."

Edmund nodded to concede the point. "There are three million people in Grand Normandy," he said, "and less than five thousand vampires. There are only forty thousand vampires in the entire imperium of Gaul, and about the same number in the imperium of Byzantium—no telling how many there may be in the khanate of Walachia and Cathay, but not so very many more. In Africa the vampires must be outnumbered three or four thousand to one. If people no longer saw them as demons and demi-gods, as unconquerable forces of evil, their empire would be fragile. The centuries through which they live give them wisdom, but longevity seems to be inimical to creative thought—they learn, but they don't *invent*. Humans remain the true masters of art and science, which are forces of change. They've tried to control that—to turn it to their advantage—but it remains a thorn in their side."

"But they do have power," insisted Noell. "They *are* vampires."

Edmund shrugged. "Their longevity is real—their powers of regeneration, too. But is it really their magic that makes them so? I don't know for sure what merit there is in their incantations and rituals, and I don't think even *they* know—they cling to their rites because they dare not abandon them, but where the power that makes humans into vampires really comes from, no one knows. From the devil? I think not. I don't believe in the devil— I think it's something in the blood. I think vampirism may be a kind of disease—but a disease that makes men stronger instead of weaker, insulates them against death instead of killing them. If that is the case—do you see now why the Lady Carmilla asked whether I had looked at blood beneath the microscope?"

Noell stared at the instrument for twenty seconds or so, mulling over the idea. Then he laughed.

"If we could *all* become vampires," he said lightly, "we'd have to suck one another's blood."

Edmund couldn't bring himself to look for such ironies. For him, the possibilities inherent in discovering the secrets of vampire nature were much more immediate, and utterly bleak.

"It's not true that they *need* to suck the blood of humans," he told the boy. "It's not nourishment. It gives them . . . a kind of pleasure that we can't understand. And it's part of the mystique that makes them so terrible . . . and hence so powerful." He stopped, feeling embarrassed. He did not know how much Noell knew about his sources of information. He and his wife never talked about the days of his affair with the Lady Carmilla, but there was no way to keep gossip and rumor from reaching the boy's ears.

Noell took the flask again, and this time took a deeper draft from it. "I've heard," he said distantly, "that humans find pleasure, too . . . in their blood being drunk."

"No," replied Edmund calmly. "That's untrue. Unless one counts the small pleasure of sacrifice. The pleasure that a human man takes from a vampire lady is the same pleasure that he takes from a human lover. It might be different for the girls who entertain vampire men, but I suspect it's just the excitement of hoping that they may become vampires themselves."

Noell hesitated, and would probably have dropped the subject, but Edmund realized suddenly that he did not want the subject dropped. The boy had a right to know, and perhaps might one day *need* to know.

"That's not entirely true," Edmund corrected himself.

"When the Lady Carmilla used to taste my blood, it did give me pleasure, in a way. It pleased me because it pleased *her*. There *is* an excitement in loving a vampire lady, which makes it different from loving an ordinary woman . . . even though the chance that a vampire lady's lover may himself become a vampire is so remote as to be inconsiderable."

Noell blushed, not knowing how to react to this acceptance into his father's confidence. Finally he decided that it was best to pretend a purely academic interest.

"Why are there so many more vampire women than men?" he asked.

"No one knows for sure," Edmund said. "No humans, at any rate. I can tell you what I believe, from hearsay and from reasoning, but you must understand that it is a dangerous thing to think about, let alone to speak about."

Noell nodded.

"The vampires keep their history secret," said Edmund, "and they try to control the writing of human history, but the following facts are probably true. Vampirism came to western Europe in the fifth century, with the vampire-led horde of Attila. Attila must have known well enough how to make more vampires—he converted both Aëtius, who became ruler of the imperium of Gaul, and Theodosius II, the emperor of the east who was later murdered. Of all the vampires that now exist, the vast majority must be converts. I have heard reports of vampire children born to vampire ladies, but it must be an extremely rare occurrence. Vampire men seem to be much less virile than human men—it is said that they couple very rarely. Nevertheless, they frequently take human consorts, and these consorts often become vampires. Vampires usually claim that this is a gift, bestowed deliberately by magic, but I am not so sure they can control the process. I think the semen of vampire men carries some kind of seed that communicates vampirism much as the semen of humans makes women pregnant—and just as haphazardly. That's why the male lovers of vampire ladies don't become vampires."

Noell considered this, and then asked: "Then where do vampire lords come from?"

"They're converted by other male vampires," Edmund said. "Just as Attila converted Aëtius and Theodosius." He did not elaborate, but waited to see whether Noell understood the implication. An expression of disgust crossed the boy's face and Edmund did not know whether to be glad or sorry that his son could follow the argument through.

"Because it doesn't always happen," Edmund went on, "it's easy for the vampires to pretend that they have some special magic. But some women never become pregnant, though they lie with their husbands for years. It is said, though, that a human may also become a vampire by drinking vampire's blood—if he knows the appropriate magic spell. That's a rumor the vampires don't like, and they exact terrible penalties if anyone is caught trying the experiment. The ladies of our own court, of course, are for the most part onetime lovers of the archduke or his cousins. It would be indelicate to speculate about the conversion of the archduke, though he is certainly acquainted with Aëtius."

Noell reached out a hand, palm downward, and made a few passes above the candle flame, making it flicker from side to side. He stared at the microscope.

"*Have* you looked at blood?" he asked.

"I have," replied Edmund. "And semen. Human blood, of course—and human semen."

"And?"

Edmund shook his head. "They're certainly not homogeneous fluids," he said, "but the instrument isn't good enough for really detailed inspection. There are small corpuscles—the ones in semen have long, writhing tails—but there's more . . . much more . . . to be seen, if I had the chance. By tomorrow this instrument will be gone—I don't think I'll be given the chance to build another."

"You're surely not in danger! You're an important man—and your loyalty has never been in question. People think of you as being almost a vampire yourself. A black magician. The kitchen girls are afraid of me because I'm your son—they cross themselves when they see me."

Edmund laughed, a little bitterly. "I've no doubt they suspect me of intercourse with demons, and avoid my gaze for fear of the spell of the evil eye. But none of that matters to the vampires. To them, I'm only a human, and for all that they value my skills, they'd kill me without a thought if they suspected that I might have dangerous knowledge."

Noell was clearly alarmed by this. "Wouldn't . . ." He stopped, but saw Edmund waiting for him to ask, and carried on after only a brief pause. "The Lady Carmilla . . . wouldn't she . . . ?"

"Protect me?" Edmund shook his head. "Not even if I were her favorite still. Vampire loyalty is to vampires."

"She was human once."

"It counts for nothing. She's been a vampire for nearly six hundred years, but it wouldn't be any different if she were no older than I."

"But . . . she did love you?"

"In her way," said Edmund sadly. "In her way." He stood up then, no longer feeling the urgent desire to help his son to understand. There were things the boy could find out only for himself and might never have to. He took up the candle tray and shielded the flame with his hand as he walked to the door. Noell followed him, leaving the empty flask behind.

Edmund left the citadel by the so-called Traitor's Gate, and crossed the Thames by the Tower Bridge. The houses on the bridge were in darkness now, but there was still a trickle of traffic; even at two in the morning, the business of the great city did not come to a standstill. The night had clouded over, and a light drizzle had begun to fall. Some of the oil lamps that were supposed to keep the thoroughfare lit at all times had gone out, and there was not a lamplight in sight. Edmund did not mind the shadows, though.

He was aware before he reached the south bank that two men were dogging his footsteps, and he dawdled in order to give them the impression that he would be easy to track. Once he entered the network of streets surrounding the Leathermarket, though, he gave them the slip. He knew the maze of filthy streets well enough—he had lived here as a child. It was while he was apprenticed to a local clockmaker that he had learned the cleverness with tools that had eventually brought him to the notice of his predecessor, and had sent him on the road to fortune and celebrity. He had a brother and a sister still living and working in the district, though he saw them very rarely. Neither one of them was proud to have a reputed magician for a brother, and they had not forgiven him his association with the Lady Carmilla.

He picked his way carefully through the garbage in the dark alleys, unperturbed by the sound of scavenging rats. He kept his hands on the pommel of the dagger that was clasped to his belt, but he had no need to draw it. Because the stars were hidden, the night was pitch-dark, and few of the windows were lit from within by candlelight, but he was able to keep track of his progress by reaching out to touch familiar walls every now and again.

He came eventually to a tiny door set three steps down from a side street, and rapped upon it quickly, three times and then twice. There was a long pause before he felt the door yield beneath his fingers, and he stepped inside hurriedly. Until he relaxed when the door clicked shut again, he did not realize how tense he had been.

He waited for a candle to be lit.

The light, when it came, illuminated a thin face, crabbed and wrinkled, the eyes very pale and the wispy white hair gathered imperfectly behind a linen bonnet.

"The Lord be with you," he whispered.

"And with you, Edmund Cordery," she croaked.

He frowned at the use of his name—it was a deliberate breach of etiquette, a feeble and meaningless gesture of independence. She did not like him, though he had never been less than kind to her. She did not fear him as so many others did, but she considered him tainted.

They had been bound together in the business of the Fraternity for nearly twenty years, but she would never completely trust him.

She led him into an inner room, and left him there to take care of his business.

A stranger stepped from the shadows. He was short, stout, and bald, perhaps sixty years old. He made the special sign of the cross, and Edmund responded.

"I'm Cordery," he said.

"Were you followed?" The older man's tone was deferential and fearful.

"Not here. They followed me from the Tower, but it was easy to shake them loose."

"That's bad."

"Perhaps—but it has to do with another matter, not

with our business. There's no danger to you. Do you have what I asked for?"

The stout man nodded uncertainly. "My masters are unhappy," he said. "I have been asked to tell you that they do not want you to take risks. You are too valuable to place yourself in peril."

"I am in peril already. Events are overtaking us. In any case, it is neither your concern nor that of your . . . masters. It is for me to decide."

The stout man shook his head, but it was a gesture of resignation rather than a denial. He pulled something from beneath the chair where he had waited in the shadows. It was a large box, clad in leather. A row of small holes was set in the longer side, and there was a sound of scratching from within that testified to the presence of living creatures.

"You did exactly as I instructed?" asked Edmund.

The small man nodded, then put his hand on the mechanician's arm, fearfully. "Don't open it, sir, I beg you. Not here."

"There's nothing to fear," Edmund assured him.

"You haven't been in Africa, sir, as I have. Believe me, *everyone* is afraid—and not merely humans. They say that vampires are dying, too."

"Yes, I know," said Edmund distractedly. He shook off the older man's restraining hand and undid the straps that sealed the box. He lifted the lid, but not far—just enough to let the light in, and to let him see what was inside.

The box contained two big gray rats. They cowered from the light.

Edmund shut the lid again and fastened the straps.

"It's not my place, sir," said the little man hesitantly, "but I'm not sure that you really understand what you have there. I've seen the cities of West Africa—I've been in Corunna, too, and Marseilles. They remember other plagues in those cities, and all the horror stories are emerging again to haunt them. Sir, if any such thing ever came to London . . ."

Edmund tested the weight of the box to see whether he could carry it comfortably. "It's not your concern," he said. "Forget everything that has happened. I will communicate with your masters. It is in my hands now."

"Forgive me," said the other, "but I must say this: there is naught to be gained from destroying vampires, if we destroy ourselves, too. It would be a pity to wipe out half of Europe in the cause of attacking our oppressors."

Edmund stared at the stout man coldly. "You talk too much," he said. "Indeed, you talk a *deal* too much."

"I beg your pardon, sire."

Edmund hesitated for a moment, wondering whether to reassure the messenger that his anxiety was understandable, but he had learned long ago that where the business of the Fraternity was concerned, it was best to say as little as possible. There was no way of knowing when this man would speak again of this affair, or to whom, or with what consequence.

The mechanician took up the box, making sure that

he could carry it comfortably. The rats stirred inside, scrabbling with their small clawed feet. With his free hand, Edmund made the sign of the cross again.

"God go with you," said the messenger, with urgent sincerity.

"And with thy spirit," replied Edmund colorlessly.

Then he left, without pausing to exchange a ritual farewell with the crone. He had no difficulty in smuggling his burden back into the Tower, by means of a gate where the guard was long practiced in the art of turning a blind eye.

When Monday came, Edmund and Noell made their way to the Lady Carmilla's chambers. Noell had never been in such an apartment before, and it was a source of wonder to him. Edmund watched the boy's reactions to the carpets, the wall hangings, the mirrors and ornaments, and could not help but recall the first time *he* had entered these chambers. Nothing had changed here, and the rooms were full of provocations to stir and sharpen his faded memories.

Younger vampires tended to change their surroundings often, addicted to novelty, as if they feared the prospect of being changeless themselves. The Lady Carmilla had long since passed beyond this phase of her career. She had grown used to changelessness, had transcended the kind of attitude to the world that permitted boredom and ennui. She had adapted herself to a new aesthetic of existence, whereby her personal space became an extension of her own eternal sameness, and innovation was confined to tightly controlled areas of her life—including the irregular shifting of her erotic affections from one lover to another.

The sumptuousness of the lady's table was a further source of astonishment to Noell. Silver plates and forks he had imagined, and crystal goblets, and carved decanters of wine. But the lavishness of provision for just three diners—the casual waste—was something that obviously set him aback. He had always known that he was himself a member of a privileged elite, and that by the standards of the greater world, Master Cordery and his family ate well; the revelation that there was a further order of magnitude to distinguish the private world of the real aristocracy clearly made its impact upon him.

Edmund had been very careful in preparing his dress, fetching from his closet finery that he had not put on for many years. On official occasions he was always concerned to play the part of mechanician, and dressed in order to sustain that appearance. He never appeared as a courtier, always as a functionary. Now, though, he was reverting to a kind of performance that Noell had never seen him play, and though the boy had no idea of the subtleties of his father's performance, he clearly understood something of what was going on; he had complained acidly about the dull and plain way in which his father had made *him* dress.

Edmund ate and drank sparingly, and was pleased to

note that Noell did likewise, obeying his father's instructions despite the obvious temptations of the lavish provision. For a while the lady was content to exchange routine courtesies, but she came quickly enough—by her standards—to the real business of the evening.

"My cousin Girard," she told Edmund, "is quite enraptured by your clever device. He finds it most interesting."

"Then I am pleased to make him a gift of it," Edmund replied. "And I would be pleased to make another, as a gift for Your Ladyship."

"That is not our desire," she said coolly. "In fact, we have other matters in mind. The archduke and his seneschal have discussed certain tasks that you might profitably carry out. Instructions will be communicated to you in due time, I have no doubt."

"Thank you, my lady," said Edmund.

"The ladies of the court were pleased with the drawings that I showed to them," said the Lady Carmilla, turning to look at Noell. "They marveled at the thought that a cupful of Thames water might contain thousands of tiny living creatures. Do you think that our bodies, too, might be the habitation of countless invisible insects?"

Noell opened his mouth to reply, because the question was addressed to him, but Edmund interrupted smoothly.

"There are creatures that may live upon our bodies," he said, "and worms that may live within. We are told that the macrocosm reproduces in essence the microcosm of human beings; perhaps there is a small microcosm within us, where our natures are reproduced again, incalculably small. I have read . . ."

"I have read, Master Cordery," she cut in, "that the illnesses that afflict humankind might be carried from person to person by means of these tiny creatures."

"The idea that diseases were communicated from one person to another by tiny seeds was produced in antiquity," Edmund replied, "but I do not know how such seeds might be recognized, and I think it very unlikely that the creatures we have seen in river water could possibly be of that character."

"It is a disquieting thought," she insisted, "that our bodies might be inhabited by creatures of which we can know nothing, and that every breath we take might be carrying into us seeds of all kinds of change, too small to be seen or tasted. It makes me feel uneasy."

"But there is no need," Edmund protested. "Seeds of corruptibility take root in human flesh, but yours is inviolate."

"You know that is not so, Master Cordery," she said levelly. "You have seen me ill yourself."

"That was a pox that killed many humans, my lady — yet it gave to you no more than a mild fever."

"We have reports from the imperium of Byzantium, and from the Moorish enclave, too, that there is plague in Africa, and that it has now reached the southern regions of the imperium of Gaul. It is said that this plague makes little distinction between human and vampire."

"Rumors, my lady," said Edmund soothingly. "You know how news becomes blacker as it travels."

The Lady Carmilla turned again to Noell, and this time addressed him by name so that there could be no opportunity for Edmund to usurp the privilege of answering her. "Are you afraid of me, Noell?" she asked.

The boy was startled, and stumbled slightly over his reply, which was in the negative.

"You must not lie to me," she told him. "You *are* afraid of me, because I am a vampire. Master Cordery is a skeptic, and must have told you that vampires have less magic than is commonly credited to us, but he must also have told you that I can do you harm if I will. Would you like to be a vampire yourself, Noell?"

Noell was still confused by the correction, and hesitated over his reply, but he eventually said: "Yes, I would."

"Of course you would," she purred. "All humans would be vampires if they could, no matter how they might pretend when they bend the knee in church. And men *can* become vampires; immortality is within our gift. Because of this, we have always enjoyed the loyalty and devotion of the greater number of our human subjects. We have always rewarded that devotion in some measure. Few have joined our ranks, but the many have enjoyed centuries of order and stability. The vampires rescued Europe from a Dark Age, and as long as vampires rule, barbarism will always be held in check. Our

rule has not always been kind, because we cannot toler-
ate defiance, but the alternative would have been far
worse. Even so, there are men who would destroy us—
did you know that?"

Noell did not know how to reply to this, so he simply
stared, waiting for her to continue. She seemed a little
impatient with his gracelessness, and Edmund deliberately let the awkward pause go on. He saw a certain advantage in allowing Noell to make a poor impression.

"There is an organization of rebels," the Lady Carmilla went on. "A secret society, ambitious to discover
the secret way by which vampires are made. They put
about the idea that they would make all men immortal,
but this is a lie, and foolish. The members of this brotherhood seek power for themselves."

The vampire lady paused to direct the clearing of one
set of dishes and the bringing of another. She asked for a
new wine, too. Her gaze wandered back and forth between the gauche youth and his self-assured father.

"The loyalty of your family is, of course, beyond question," she eventually continued. "No one understands
the workings of society like a mechanician, who knows
well enough how forces must be balanced and how the
different parts of a machine must interlock and support
one another. Master Cordery knows well how the cleverness of rulers resembles the cleverness of clockmakers,
do you not?"

"Indeed, I do, my lady," replied Edmund.

"There might be a way," she said, in a strangely distant tone, "that a good mechanician might earn a conversion to vampirism."

Edmund was wise enough not to interpret this as an offer or a promise. He accepted a measure of the new wine and said: "My lady, there are matters that it would be as well for us to discuss in private. May I send my son to his room?"

The Lady Carmilla's eyes narrowed just a little, but there was hardly any expression in her finely etched features. Edmund held his breath, knowing that he had forced a decision upon her that she had not intended to make so soon.

"The poor boy has not quite finished his meal," she said.

"I think he has had enough, my lady," Edmund countered. Noell did not disagree, and, after a brief hesitation, the lady bowed to signal her permission. Edmund asked Noell to leave, and when he was gone, the Lady Carmilla rose from her seat and went from the dining room into an inner chamber. Edmund followed her.

"You were presumptuous, Master Cordery," she told him.

"I was carried away, my lady. There are too many memories here."

"The boy is mine," she said, "if I so choose. You do know that, do you not?"

Edmund bowed.

"I did not ask you here tonight to make you witness

the seduction of your son. Nor do you think that I did. This matter that you would discuss with me—does it concern science or treason?"

"Science, my lady. As you have said yourself, my loyalty is not in question."

Carmilla laid herself upon a sofa and indicated that Edmund should take a chair nearby. This was the antechamber to her bedroom, and the air was sweet with the odor of cosmetics.

"Speak," she bade him.

"I believe that the archduke is afraid of what my little device might reveal," he said. "He fears that it will expose to the eye such seeds as carry vampirism from one person to another, just as it might expose the seeds that carry disease. I think that the man who devised the instrument may have been put to death already, but I think you know well enough that a discovery once made is likely to be made again and again. You are uncertain as to what course of action would best serve your ends, because you cannot tell whence the greater threat to your rule might come. There is the Fraternity, which is dedicated to your destruction; there is plague in Africa, from which even vampires may die; and there is the new sight, which renders visible what previously lurked unseen. Do you want my advice, Lady Carmilla?"

"Do you *have* any advice, Edmund?"

"Yes. Do not try to control by terror and persecution the things that are happening. Let your rule be unkind *now*, as it has been before, and it will open the way to destruction. Should you concede power gently, you might live for centuries yet, but if you strike out . . . your enemies will strike back."

The vampire lady leaned back her head, looking at the ceiling. She contrived a small laugh.

"I cannot take advice such as that to the archduke," she told him flatly.

"I thought not, my lady," Edmund replied very calmly.

"You humans have your own immortality," she complained. "Your faith promises it, and you all affirm it. Your faith tells you that you must not covet the immortality that is ours, and we do no more than agree with you when we guard it so jealously. You should look to your Christ for fortune, not to us. I think you know well enough that we could not convert the world if we wanted to. Our magic is such that it can be used only sparingly. Are you distressed because it has never been offered to you? Are you bitter? Are you becoming our enemy because you cannot become our kin?"

"You have nothing to fear from me, my lady," he lied. Then he added, not quite sure whether it was a lie or not: "I loved you faithfully. I still do."

She sat up straight then, and reached out a hand as though to stroke his cheek, though he was too far away for her to reach.

"That is what I told the archduke," she said, "when he suggested to me that you might be a traitor. I promised him that I could test your loyalty more keenly in my chambers than his officers in theirs. I do not think you could delude me, Edmund. Do you?"

"No, my lady," he replied.

"By morning," she told him gently, "I will know whether or not you are a traitor."

"That you will," he assured her. "That you will, my lady."

He woke before her, his mouth dry and his forehead burning. He was not sweating—indeed, he was possessed by a feeling of desiccation, as though the moisture were being squeezed out of his organs. His head was aching, and the light of the morning sun that streamed through the unshuttered window hurt his eyes.

He pulled himself up to a half-sitting position, pushing the coverlet back from his bare chest.

So soon! he thought. He had not expected to be consumed so quickly, but he was surprised to find that his reaction was one of relief rather than fear or regret. He had difficulty collecting his thoughts, and was perversely glad to accept that he did not need to.

He looked down at the cuts that she had made on his breast with her little silver knife; they were raw and red, and made a strange contrast with the faded scars whose crisscross pattern still engraved the story of unforgotten passions. He touched the new wounds gently with his fingers, and winced at the fiery pain.

She woke up then, and saw him inspecting the marks.

"Have you missed the knife?" she asked sleepily. "Were you hungry for its touch?"

There was no need to lie now, and there was a delicious sense of freedom in that knowledge. There was a joy in being able to face her, at last, quite naked in his thoughts as well as his flesh.

"Yes, my lady," he said with a slight croak in his voice. "I had missed the knife. Its touch . . . rekindled flames in my soul."

She had closed her eyes again, to allow herself to wake slowly. She laughed. "It is pleasant, sometimes, to return to forsaken pastures. You can have no notion how a particular *taste* may stir memories. I am glad to have seen you again, in this way. I had grown quite used to you as the gray mechanician. But now . . ."

He laughed, as lightly as she, but the laugh turned to a cough, and something in the sound alerted her to the fact that all was not as it should be. She opened her eyes and raised her head, turning toward him.

"Why, Edmund," she said, "you're as pale as death!"

She reached out to touch his cheek, and snatched her hand away again as she found it unexpectedly hot and dry. A blush of confusion spread across her own features. He took her hand and held it, looking steadily into her eyes.

"Edmund," she said softly. "What have you done?"

"I can't be sure," he said, "and I will not live to find out, but I have tried to kill you, my lady."

He was pleased by the way her mouth gaped in astonishment. He watched disbelief and anxiety mingle in her expression, as though fighting for control. She did not call out for help.

"This is nonsense," she whispered.

"Perhaps," he admitted. "Perhaps it was also nonsense that we talked last evening. Nonsense about treason. Why did you ask me to make the microscope, my lady, when you knew that making me a party to such a secret was as good as signing my death warrant?"

"Oh Edmund," she said with a sigh. "You could not think that it was my own idea? I tried to protect you, Edmund, from Girard's fears and suspicions. It was because I was your protector that I was made to bear the message. What have you done, Edmund?"

He began to reply, but the words turned into a fit of coughing.

She sat upright, wrenching her hand away from his enfeebled grip, and looked down at him as he sank back upon the pillow.

"For the love of God!" she exclaimed, as fearfully as any true believer. "It is the plague—the plague out of Africa!"

He tried to confirm her suspicion, but could do so only with a nod of his head as he fought for breath.

"But they held the *Freemartin* by the Essex coast for a full fortnight's quarantine," she protested. "There was no trace of plague aboard."

"The disease kills men," said Edmund in a shallow whisper. "But animals can carry it, in their blood, without dying."

"You cannot know this!"

Edmund managed a small laugh. "My lady," he said, "I am a member of that Fraternity that interests itself in everything that might kill a vampire. The information came to me in good time for me to arrange delivery of the rats—though when I asked for them, I had not in mind the means of using them that I eventually employed. More recent events . . ." Again he was forced to stop, unable to draw sufficient breath even to sustain the thin whisper.

The Lady Carmilla put her hand to her throat, swallowing as if she expected to feel evidence already of her infection.

"You would destroy me, Edmund?" she asked, as though she genuinely found it difficult to believe.

"I would destroy you all," he told her. "I would bring disaster, turn the world upside down, to end your rule. . . . We cannot allow you to stamp out learning itself to preserve your empire forever. Order must be fought with chaos, and chaos is come, my lady."

When she tried to rise from the bed, he reached out to restrain her, and though there was no power left in him, she allowed herself to be checked. The coverlet fell away from her, to expose her breasts as she sat upright.

"The boy will die for this, Master Cordery," she said. "His mother, too."

"They're gone," he told her. "Noell went from your table to the custody of the society that I serve. By now they're beyond your reach. The archduke will never catch them."

She stared at him, and now he could see the beginnings of hate and fear in her stare.

"You came here last night to bring me poisoned blood," she said. "In the hope that this new disease might kill even. me, you condemned yourself to death. What did you do, Edmund?"

He reached out again to touch her arm, and was pleased to see her flinch and draw away: that he had become dreadful.

"Only vampires live forever," he told her hoarsely. "But anyone may drink blood, if they have the stomach for it. I took full measure from my two sick rats . . . and I pray to God that the seed of this fever is raging in my blood . . . and in my semen, too. You, too, have received full measure, my lady . . . and you are in God's hands now like any common mortal. I cannot know for sure whether you will catch the plague, or whether it will kill you, but I—an unbeliever—am not ashamed to pray. Perhaps you could pray, too, my lady, so that we may know how the Lord favors one unbeliever over another."

She looked down at him, her face gradually losing the expressions that had tugged at her features, becoming masklike in its steadiness.

"You could have taken our side, Edmund. I trusted you, and I could have made the archduke trust you, too.

You could have become a vampire. We could have shared the centuries, you and I."

This was dissimulation, and they both knew it. He had been her lover, and had ceased to be, and had grown older for so many years that now she remembered him as much in his son as in himself. The promises were all too obviously hollow now, and she realized that she could not even taunt him with them.

From beside the bed she took up the small silver knife that she had used to let his blood. She held it now as if it were a dagger, not a delicate instrument to be used with care and love.

"I thought you still loved me," she told him. "I really did."

That, at least, he thought, might be true.

He actually put his head farther back, to expose his throat to the expected thrust. He wanted her to strike him—angrily, brutally, passionately. He had nothing more to say, and would not confirm or deny that he did still love her.

He admitted to himself now that his motives had been mixed, and that he really did not know whether it was loyalty to the Fraternity that had made him submit to this extraordinary experiment. It did not matter.

She cut his throat, and he watched her for a few long seconds while she stared at the blood gouting from the wound. When he saw her put stained fingers to her lips, knowing what she knew, he realized that after her own fashion, she still loved him.

WAILING WELL

+++

M. R. JAMES

In the year 19— there were two members of the Troop of Scouts attached to a famous school, named respectively Arthur Wilcox and Stanley Judkins. They were the same age, boarded in the same house, were in the same division, and naturally were members of the same patrol. They were so much alike in appearance as to cause anxiety and trouble, and even irritation, to the masters who came in contact with them. But oh how different were they in their inward man, or boy!

It was to Arthur Wilcox that the Head Master said, looking up with a smile as the boy entered chambers, "Why, Wilcox, there will be a deficit in the prize fund if you stay here much longer! Here, take this handsomely bound copy of the *Life and Works of Bishop Ken*, and with it my hearty congratulations to yourself and your excellent parents." It was Wilcox again, whom the Provost noticed as he passed through the playing fields, and, pausing for a moment, observed to the Vice-Provost, "That lad has a remarkable brow!" "Indeed, yes," said the Vice-Provost. "It denotes either genius or water on the brain."

As a Scout, Wilcox secured every badge and distinction for which he competed. The Cookery Badge, the Map-making Badge, the Life-saving Badge, the Badge for picking up bits of newspaper, the Badge for not slamming the door when leaving the pupil-room, and many others. Of the Life-saving Badge I may have a word to say when we come to treat of Stanley Judkins.

You cannot be surprised to hear that Mr. Hope Jones added a special verse to each of his songs, in commendation of Arthur Wilcox, or that the Lower Master burst into tears when handing him the Good Conduct Medal in its handsome claret-coloured case: the medal which had been unanimously voted to him by the whole of Third Form. Unanimously, did I say? I am wrong. There was one dissentient, Judkins *mi.*, who said that he had excellent reasons for acting as he did. He shared, it seems, a room with his major. You cannot, again, wonder that in after years Arthur Wilcox was the first, and so far the only boy, to become Captain of both the School and of the Oppidans, or that the strain of carrying out the duties of both positions, coupled with the ordinary work of the school, was so severe that a complete rest for six months, followed by a voyage round the world, was pronounced an absolute necessity by the family doctor.

It would be a pleasant task to trace the steps by which he attained the giddy eminence he now occupies; but for the moment enough of Arthur Wilcox. Time presses, and we must turn to a very different matter; the career of Stanley Judkins—Judkins *ma.*

Stanley Judkins, like Arthur Wilcox, attracted the attention of the authorities; but in quite another fashion. It was to him that the Lower Master said, with no cheerful smile, "What, again, Judkins? A very little persistence in this course of conduct, my boy, and you will have cause to regret that you ever entered this academy. There, take that, and that, and think yourself very lucky you don't get that and that!" It was Judkins, again, whom the Provost had cause to notice as he passed through the playing fields, when a cricket ball struck him with considerable force on the ankle, and a voice from a short way off cried, "Thank you, cut-over!" "I think," said the Provost, pausing for a moment to rub his ankle, "that that boy had better fetch his cricket ball for himself!" "Indeed, yes," said the Vice-Provost, "and if he comes within reach, I will do my best to fetch him something else."

As a Scout, Stanley Judkins secured no badge save those which he was able to abstract from members of other patrols. In the cookery competition he was detected trying to introduce squibs into the Dutch oven of the next-door competitors. In the tailoring competition he succeeded in sewing two boys together very firmly, with disastrous effect when they tried to get up. For the Tidiness Badge he was disqualified, because, in the Midsummer schooltime, which chanced to be hot, he could not be dissuaded from sitting with his fingers in the ink: as he said, for coolness' sake. For one piece of paper which he picked up, he must have dropped at least six banana skins or orange peels. Aged women seeing him approaching would beg him with tears in their eyes not to carry their pails of water across the road. They knew too well what the result would inevitably be. But it was in the life-saving competition that Stanley Judkins's conduct was most blameable and had the most far-reaching effects. The practice, as you know, was to throw a selected lower boy, of suitable dimensions, fully dressed, with his hands and feet tied together, into the deepest part of Cuckoo Weir, and to time the Scout whose turn it was to rescue him. On every occasion when he was entered for this competition Stanley Judkins was seized, at the critical moment, with a severe fit of cramp, which caused him to roll on the ground and utter alarming cries. This naturally distracted the attention of those present from the boy in the water, and had it not been for the presence of Arthur Wilcox the death-roll would have been a heavy one. As it was, the Lower Master found it necessary to take a firm line and say that the competition must be discontinued. It was in vain that Mr. Beasley Robinson represented to him that in five competitions only four lower boys had actually succumbed. The Lower Master said that he would be the last to interfere in any way with the work of the Scouts; but that three of these boys had been valued members of his choir, and both he and Dr. Ley felt that the inconvenience caused by the losses outweighed the advantages of the competitions. Besides, the correspondence with the parents of these boys had become annoying, and even distressing: they were no longer satisfied with the printed form which he was in the habit of sending out, and more than one of them had actually visited Eton and taken up much of his valuable time with complaints. So the life-saving competition is now a thing of the past.

In short, Stanley Judkins was no credit to the Scouts, and there was talk on more than one occasion of informing him that his services were no longer required. This course was strongly advocated by Mr. Lambart: but in the end milder counsels prevailed, and it was decided to give him another chance.

So it is that we find him at the beginning of the Midsummer Holidays of 19— at the Scouts' camp in the beautiful district of W (or X) in the country of D (or Y).

It was a lovely morning, and Stanley Judkins and one or two of his friends—for he still had friends—lay basking on the top of the down. Stanley was lying on his stomach with his chin propped on his hands, staring into the distance.

"I wonder what that place is," he said.

"Which place?" said one of the others.

"That sort of clump in the middle of the field down there."

"Oh, ah! How should I know what it is?"

"What do you want to know for?" said another.

"I don't know: I like the look of it. What's it called? Nobody got a map?" said Stanley. "Call yourselves Scouts!"

"Here's a map all right," said Wilfred Pipsqueak, ever resourceful, "and there's the place marked on it. But it's inside the red ring. We can't go there."

"Who cares about a red ring?" said Stanley. "But it's got no name on your silly map."

"Well, you can ask this old chap what it's called if you're so keen to find out." "This old chap" was an old shepherd who had come up and was standing behind them.

"Good morning, young gents," he said, "you've got a fine day for your doin's, ain't you?"

"Yes, thank you," said Algernon de Montmorency, with native politeness. "Can you tell us what that clump over there's called? And what's that thing inside it?"

"Course I can tell you," said the shepherd. "That's Wailin' Well, that is. But you ain't got no call to worry about that."

"Is it a well in there?" said Algernon. "Who uses it?"

The shepherd laughed. "Bless you," he said, "there ain't from a man to a sheep in these parts uses Wailin' Well, nor haven't done all the years I've lived here."

"Well, there'll be a record broken today, then," said Stanley Judkins, "because I shall go and get some water out of it for tea!"

"Sakes alive, young gentleman!" said the shepherd in a startled voice. "Don't you get to talkin' that way! Why, ain't your masters give you notice not to go by there? They'd ought to have done."

"Yes, they have," said Wilfred Pipsqueak.

"Shut up, you ass!" said Stanley Judkins. "What's the matter with it? Isn't the water good? Anyhow, if it was boiled, it would be all right."

"I don't know as there's anything much wrong with the water," said the shepherd. "All I know is, my old dog wouldn't go through that field, let alone me or anyone else that's got a morsel of brains in their heads."

"More fool them," said Stanley Judkins, at once rudely and ungrammatically. "Who ever took any harm going there?" he added.

"Three women and a man," said the shepherd gravely. "Now just you listen to me. I know these 'ere parts and you don't, and I can tell you this much: for these ten years last past there ain't been a sheep fed in that field, nor a crop raised off of it—and it's good land, too. You can pretty well see from here what a state it's got into with brambles and suckers and trash of all kinds. You've got a glass, young gentleman," he said to Wilfred Pipsqueak, "you can tell with that anyway."

"Yes," said Wilfred, "but I see there's tracks in it. Someone must go through it sometimes."

"Tracks!" said the shepherd. "I believe you! Four tracks: three women and a man."

"What d'you mean, three women and a man?" said Stanley, turning over for the first time and looking at the shepherd (he had been talking with his back to him till this moment: he was an ill-mannered boy).

"Mean? Why, what I says: three women and a man."

"Who are they?" asked Algernon. "Why do they go there?"

"There's some p'r'aps could tell you who they *was*," said the shepherd, "but it was afore my time they come by their end. And why they goes there still is more than the children of men can tell; except I've heard they was all bad 'uns when they was alive."

"By George, what a rum thing!" Algernon and Wilfred muttered: but Stanley was scornful and bitter.

"Why, you don't mean they're deaders? What rot! You must be a lot of fools to believe that. Who's ever seen them, I'd like to know?"

"*I've* seen 'em, young gentleman!" said the shepherd, "seen 'em from nearby on that bit of down: and my old dog, if he could speak, he'd tell you he've seen 'em, same time. About four o'clock of the day it was, much such a day as this. I see 'em, each one of 'em, come peerin' out of the bushes and stand up, and work their way slow by them tracks towards the trees in the middle where the well is."

"And what were they like? Do tell us!" said Algernon and Wilfred eagerly.

"Rags and bones, young gentlemen: all four of 'em: flutterin' rags and whitey bones. It seemed to me as if I could hear 'em clackin' as they got along. Very slow they went, and lookin' from side to side."

"What were their faces like? Could you see?"

"They hadn't much to call faces," said the shepherd, "but I could seem to see as they had teeth."

"Lor'!" said Wilfred. "And what did they do when they got to the trees?"

"I can't tell you that, sir," said the shepherd. "I wasn't for stayin' in that place, and if I had been, I was bound to look to my old dog: he'd gone! Such a thing he never done before as leave me; but gone he had, and when I came up with him in the end, he was in that state he didn't know me, and was fit to fly at my throat. But I kep' talkin' to him, and after a bit he remembered my voice and came creepin' up like a child askin' pardon. I never want to see him like that again, nor yet no other dog."

The dog, who had come up and was making friends all round, looked up at his master, and expressed agreement with what he was saying very fully.

The boys pondered for some moments on what they had heard: after which Wilfred said: "And why's it called Wailing Well?"

"If you was round here at dusk of a winter's evening, you wouldn't want to ask why," was all the shepherd said.

"Well, I don't believe a word of it," said Stanley Judkins, "and I'll go there next chance I get: blowed if I don't!"

"Then you won't be ruled by me?" said the shepherd. "Nor yet by your masters as warned you off? Come now, young gentleman, you don't want for sense, I should say. What should I want tellin' you a pack of lies? It ain't sixpence to me anyone goin' in that field: but I wouldn't like to see a young chap snuffed out like in his prime."

"I expect it's a lot more than sixpence to you," said Stanley. "I expect you've got a whisky still or something in there, and want to keep other people away. Rot I call it. Come on back, you boys."

So they turned away. The two others said, "Good evening" and "Thank you" to the shepherd, but Stanley said nothing. The shepherd shrugged his shoulders and stood where he was, looking after them rather sadly.

On the way back to the camp there was great argument about it all, and Stanley was told as plainly as he could be told all the sorts of fools he would be if he went to the Wailing Well.

That evening, among other notices, Mr. Beasley Robinson asked if all maps had got the red ring marked on them. "Be particular," he said, "not to trespass inside it."

Several voices—among them the sulky one of Stanley Judkins—said, "Why not, sir?"

"Because not," said Mr. Beasley Robinson, "and if that isn't enough for you, I can't help it." He turned and spoke to Mr. Lambart in a low voice, and then said, "I'll tell you this much: we've been asked to warn Scouts off that field. It's very good of the people to let us camp here at all, and the least we can do is to oblige them—I'm sure you'll agree to that."

Everybody said, "Yes, sir!" except Stanley Judkins, who was heard to mutter, "Oblige them be blowed!"

Early in the afternoon of the next day, the following dia-
logue was heard. "Wilcox, is all your tent there?"

"No, sir, Judkins isn't!"

"That boy is *the* most infernal nuisance ever invented!
Where do you suppose he is?"

"I haven't an idea, sir."

"Does anybody else know?"

"Sir, I shouldn't wonder if he'd gone to the Wailing
Well."

"Who's that? Pipsqueak? What's the Wailing Well?"

"Sir, it's that place in the field by—well, sir, it's in a
clump of trees in a rough field."

"D'you mean inside the red ring? Good heavens!
What makes you think he's gone there?"

"Why, he was terribly keen to know about it yesterday,
and we were talking to a shepherd man, and he told us a
lot about it and advised us not to go there: but Judkins
didn't believe him, and said he meant to go."

"Young ass!" said Mr. Hope Jones. "Did he take anything with him?"

"Yes, I think he took some rope and a can. We did tell
him he'd be a fool to go."

"Little brute! What the deuce does he mean by pinch-
ing stores like that! Well, come along, you three, we must
see after him. Why can't people keep the simplest orders? What was it the man told you? No, don't wait, let's
have it as we go along."

And off they started—Algernon and Wilfred talking rapidly and the other two listening with growing concern. At last they reached that spur of down overlooking the field of which the shepherd had spoken the day before. It commanded the place completely; the well inside the clump of bent and gnarled Scotch firs was plainly visible, and so were the four tracks winding about among the thorns and rough growth.

It was a wonderful day of shimmering heat. The sea looked like a floor of metal. There was no breath of wind. They were all exhausted when they got to the top, and flung themselves down on the hot grass.

"Nothing to be seen of him yet," said Mr. Hope Jones, "but we must stop here a bit. You're done up—not to speak of me. Keep a sharp look-out," he went on after a moment, "I thought I saw the bushes stir."

"Yes," said Wilcox, "so did I. Look . . . no, that can't be him. It's somebody though, putting their head up, isn't it?"

"I thought it was, but I'm not sure."

Silence for a moment. Then:

"That's him, sure enough," said Wilcox, "getting over the hedge on the far side. Don't you see? With a shiny thing. That's the can you said he had."

"Yes, it's him, and he's making straight for the trees," said Wilfred.

At this moment Algernon, who had been staring with all his might, broke into a scream.

"What's that on the track? On all fours—O, it's the

woman. O, don't let me look at her! Don't let it happen!"
And he rolled over, clutching at the grass and trying to
bury his head in it.

"Stop that!" said Mr. Hope Jones loudly—but it was
no use. "Look here," he said, "I must go down there. You
stop here, Wilfred, and look after that boy. Wilcox, you
run as hard as you can to the camp and get some help."

They ran off, both of them. Wilfred was left alone
with Algernon, and did his best to calm him, but indeed
he was not much happier himself. From time to time
he glanced down the hill and into the field. He saw
Mr. Hope Jones drawing nearer at a swift pace, and
then, to his great surprise, he saw him stop, look up and
round about him, and turn quickly off at an angle! What
could be the reason? He looked at the field, and there he
saw a terrible figure—something in ragged black—with
whitish patches breaking out of it: the head, perched on a
long thin neck, half hidden by a shapeless sort of blackened sun-bonnet. The creature was waving thin arms in
the direction of the rescuer who was approaching, as if to
ward him off: and between the two figures the air seemed
to shake and shimmer as he had never seen it: and as he
looked, he began himself to feel something of a waviness
and confusion in his brain, which made him guess what
might be the effect on someone within closer range of
the influence. He looked away hastily, to see Stanley
Judkins making his way pretty quickly towards the
clump, and in proper Scout fashion; evidently picking
his steps with care to avoid treading on snapping sticks or

being caught by arms of brambles. Evidently, though he saw nothing, he suspected some sort of ambush, and was trying to go noiselessly. Wilfred saw all that, and he saw more, too. With a sudden and dreadful sinking at the heart, he caught sight of someone among the trees, waiting: and again of someone—another of the hideous black figures—working slowly along the track from another side of the field, looking from side to side, as the shepherd had described it. Worst of all, he saw a fourth—unmistakably a man this time—rising out of the bushes a few yards behind the wretched Stanley, and painfully, as it seemed, crawling into the track. On all sides the miserable victim was cut off.

Wilfred was at his wits' end. He rushed at Algernon and shook him. "Get up," he said. "Yell! Yell as loud as you can. Oh, if we'd got a whistle!"

Algernon pulled himself together. "There's one," he said, "Wilcox's: he must have dropped it."

So one whistled, the other screamed. In the still air the sound carried. Stanley heard: he stopped: he turned round: and then indeed a cry was heard more piercing and dreadful than any that the boys on the hill could raise. It was too late. The crouched figure behind Stanley sprang at him and caught him about the waist. The dreadful one that was standing waving her arms waved them again but in exultation. The one that was lurking among the trees shuffled forward, and she too stretched out her arms as if to clutch at something coming her way; and the other, farthest off, quickened her pace and came on, nodding gleefully. The boys took it all in in an instant of terrible silence, and hardly could they breathe as they watched the horrid struggle between the man and his victim. Stanley struck with his can, the only weapon he had. The rim of a broken black hat fell off the creature's head and showed a white skull with stains that might be wisps of hair. By this time one of the women had reached the pair, and was pulling at the rope that was coiled about Stanley's neck. Between them they overpowered him in a moment: the awful screaming ceased, and then the three passed within the circle of the clump of firs.

Yet for a moment it seemed as if rescue might come. Mr. Hope Jones, striding quickly along, suddenly stopped, turned, seemed to rub his eyes, and then started running *towards* the field. More: the boys glanced behind them, and saw not only a troop of figures from the camp coming over the top of the next down, but the shepherd running up the slope of their own hill. They beckoned, they shouted, they ran a few yards towards him and then back again. He mended his pace.

Once more the boys looked towards the field. There was nothing. Or, was there something among the trees? Why was there a mist about the trees? Mr. Hope Jones had scrambled over the hedge, and was plunging through the bushes.

The shepherd stood beside them, panting. They ran to him and clung to his arms. "They've got him! In the trees!" was as much as they could say, over and over again.

"What? Do you tell me he've gone in there after all I said to him yesterday? Poor young thing! Poor young thing!" He would have said more, but other voices broke in. The rescuers from the camp had arrived. A few hasty words, and all were dashing down the hill.

They had just entered the field when they met Mr. Hope Jones. Over his shoulder hung the corpse of Stanley Judkins. He had cut it from the branch to which he found it hanging, waving to and fro. There was not a drop of blood in the body.

On the following day Mr. Hope Jones sallied forth with an axe and with the expressed intention of cutting down every tree in the clump, and of burning every bush in the field. He returned with a nasty cut in his leg and a broken axe-helve. Not a spark of fire could he light, and on no single tree could he make the least impression.

I have heard that the present population of the Wailing Well field consists of three women, a man, and a boy.

The shock experienced by Algernon de Montmorency and Wilfred Pipsqueak was severe. Both of them left the camp at once; and the occurrence undoubtedly cast a gloom—if but a passing one—on those who remained. One of the first to recover his spirits was Judkins *mi.*

Such, gentlemen, is the story of the career of Stanley Judkins, and of a portion of the career of Arthur Wilcox. It has, I believe, never been told before. If it has a moral, that moral is, I trust, obvious: if it has none, I do not well know how to help it.

LONELY WOMEN ARE THE
VESSELS OF TIME

♦♦♦

HARLAN ELLISON

After the funeral, Mitch went to Dynamite's. It was a singles' bar. Vernon, the day-shift bartender, had Mitch's
stool reserved, waiting for him. "I figured you'd be in," he
said, mixing up a Tia Maria Cooler and passing it across
the bar. "Sorry about Anne." Mitch nodded and sipped
off the top of the drink. He looked around Dynamite's; it
was too early in the day, even for a Friday; there wasn't
much action. A few dudes getting the best corners at the
inlaid-tile and stained-glass bar, couples in the plush
back booths stealing a few minutes before going home to
their wives and husbands. It was only three o'clock and
the secretaries didn't start coming in till five thirty. Later,
Dynamite's would be pulsing with the chatter and occasional shriek of laughter, the chatting-up and the smell of
hot bodies circling each other for the kill. The traditional
mating ritual of the singles' bar scene.

He saw one girl at a tiny deuce, way at the rear, beside
the glass-fronted booth where the DJ played his disco
rock all night, every night. But she was swathed in
shadow, and he wasn't up to hustling anybody at the

moment, anyhow. But he marked her in his mind for later.

He sipped at the Cooler, just thinking about Anne, until a space salesman from the *Enquirer*, whom he knew by first name but not by last, plopped himself onto the next stool and started laying a commiseration trip on him about Anne. He wanted to turn to the guy and simply say, "Look, fuck off, will you; she was just a Friday night pickup who hung on a little longer than most of them; so stop busting my chops and get lost." But he didn't. He listened to the bullshit as long as he could, then he excused himself and took what was left of the Cooler, and a double Cutty-&-water, and trudged back to a booth. He sat there in the semidarkness trying to figure out why Anne had killed herself, and couldn't get a handle on the question.

He tried to remember *exactly* what she had looked like, but all he could bring into focus was the honey-colored hair and her height. The special smile was gone. The tilt of the head and the hand movement when she was annoyed . . . gone. The exact timbre of her voice . . . gone. All of it was gone, and he knew he should be upset about it, but he wasn't.

He hadn't loved her; had, in fact, been ready to dump her for that BOAC hostess. But she had left a note pledging her undying love, and he knew he ought to feel some deep responsibility for her death.

But he didn't.

What it was all about, dammit, was not being lonely. It was all about getting as much as one could, as best as one could, from as many different places as one could, without having to be alone, without having to be unhappy, without having them sink their fangs in too deeply.

That, dammit, was what it was all about.

He thought about the crap a libber had laid on him in this very bar only a week ago. He had been chatting up a girl who worked for a surety underwriters firm, letting her bore him with a lot of crap about contract bonds, probate, temporary restraining orders and suchlike nonsense, but never dropping his gaze from those incredible green eyes, when Anne had gotten pissed-off and come over to suggest they leave.

He had been abrupt with her. Rude, if he wanted to be honest with himself, and had told her to go back and sit down till he was ready. The libber on the next stool had laid into him, whipping endless jingoism on him, telling him what a shithead he was.

"Lady, if you don't like the way the system works, why not go find a good clinic where they'll graft a dork on you, and then you won't have to bother people who're minding their own business."

The bar had given him a standing ovation.

The Cutty tasted like sawdust. The air in the bar smelled like mildew. His body didn't fit. He turned this way and that, trying to find a comfortable position. Why the hell did he feel lousy? Anne, that was why. But he wasn't responsible. She'd known it was frolic, nothing more than frolic. She'd known that from the moment they'd met. She hadn't been fresh to these bars, she was a swinger, what was all the *sturm und drang* about! But he felt like shit, and that was the bottom line.

"Can I buy you a drink?" the girl said.

Mitch looked up. It seemed to be the girl from the deuce in the rear.

She was incredible. Cheekbones like cut crystal; a full lower lip. Honey hair . . . again. Tall, willowy, with a good chest and fine legs. "Sure. Sit down."

She sat and pushed a double Cutty-&-water at him. "The bartender told me what you were drinking."

Four hours later—and he still hadn't learned her name—she got around to suggesting they go back to her place. He followed her out of the bar, and she hailed a cab. In the back seat he looked at her, lights flickering on and off in her blue eyes as the street lamps whizzed past, and he said, "It's nice to meet a girl who doesn't waste time."

"I gather you've been picked up before," she replied. "But then, you're a very nice-looking man."

"Why, thank you."

At her apartment in the East Fifties, they had a few more drinks; the usual preparatory ritual. Mitch was starting to feel it, getting a little wobbly. He refused a re-fill. He wanted to be able to perform. He knew the rules. Get it up or get the hell out.

So they went into the bedroom.

He stopped and stared at the set-up. She had it hung with white, sheer hangings, tulle perhaps, some kind of very fine netting. White walls, white ceiling, white carpet so thick and deep he lost his ankles in it. And an enormous circular bed covered with white fur.

"Polar bear," he said, laughing a little drunkenly.

"The color of loneliness," she said.

"What?"

"Nothing, forget it," she said, and began to undress him.

She helped him lie down, and he stared at her as she took off her clothes. Her body was pale and filled with light; she was an ice maiden from a far magical land. He felt himself getting hard.

Then she came to him.

When he awoke, she was standing at the other side of the room, watching him. Her eyes were no longer a lovely blue. They were dark and filled with smoke. He felt . . .

He felt . . . awful. Uncomfortable, filled with vague terrors and a limitless desperation. He felt . . . lonely.

"You don't hold nearly as much as I thought," she said.

He sat up, tried to get out of the bed, the sea of white, and could not. He lay back and watched her.

Finally, after a time of silence, she said, "Get up and get dressed and get out of here."

He did it, with difficulty, and as he dressed, sluggishly and with the loneliness in him growing, choking his mind and physically causing him to tremble, she told him things he did not want to know.

About the loneliness of people that makes them do things they hate the next day. About the sickness to which people are heir, the sickness of being without anyone who truly cares. About the predators who smell out such victims and use them and, when they go, leave them emptier than when they first picked up the scent. And about herself, the vessel that contained the loneliness like smoke, waiting only for other containers such as Mitch to decant a little of the poison, waiting only to return some of the pain for pain given.

What she was, where she came from, what dark land had given her birth, he did not know and would not ask. But when he stumbled to the door, and she opened it for him, the smile on her lips frightened him more than anything in his life.

"Don't feel neglected, baby," she said. "There are others like you. You'll run into them. Maybe you can start a club."

He didn't know what to say; he wanted to run, but he knew she had spread fog across his soul and he knew if he walked out the door he was never going to reclaim his feeling of self-satisfaction. He had to make one last attempt . . .

"Help me . . . please, I feel so—so—"

"I know how you feel, baby," she said, moving him through the door. "Now you know how they feel."

And she closed the door behind him. Very softly.

Very firmly.

A MYSTERY OF THE CAMPAGNA

✦✦✦

ANNE CRAWFORD

I

MARTIN DETAILLE'S ACCOUNT OF WHAT
HAPPENED AT THE VIGNA MARZIALI

Marcello's voice is pleading with me now, perhaps because after years of separation I have met an old acquaintance who had a part in his strange story. I have a longing
to tell it, and have asked Monsieur Sutton to help me.
He noted down the circumstances at the time, and he is
willing to join his share to mine, that Marcello may be
remembered.

One day, it was in spring, he appeared in my little studio amongst the laurels and green alleys of the Villa
Medici. "Come, *mon enfant,*" he said, "put up your paints,"
and he unceremoniously took my palette out of my hand.
"I have a cab waiting outside, and we are going in search
of a hermitage." He was already washing my brushes as
he spoke, and this softened my heart, for I hate to do it
myself. Then he pulled off my velvet jacket and took

down my respectable coat from a nail on the wall. I let him dress me like a child. We always did his will, and he knew it, and in a moment we were sitting in the cab, driving through the Via Sistina on our way to the Porta San Giovanni, whither he had directed the coachman to go.

I must tell my story as I can, for though I have been told by my comrades, who cannot know very well, that I can speak good English, writing it is another thing. Monsieur Sutton has asked me to use his tongue, because he has so far forgotten mine that he will not trust himself in it, though he has promised to correct my mistakes, that what I have to tell you may not seem ridiculous, and make people laugh when they read of Marcello. I tell him I wish to write this for my countrymen, not his; but he reminds me that Marcello had many English friends who still live, and that the English do not forget as we do. It is of no use to reason with him, for neither do they yield as we do, and so I have consented to his wish. I think he has a reason which he does not tell me, but let it go. I will translate it all into my own language for my own people. Your English phrases seem to me to be always walking sideways, or trying to look around the corner or stand upon their heads, and they have as many little tails as a kite. I will try not to have recourse to my own language, but he must pardon me if I forget myself. He may be sure I do not do it to offend him. Now that I have explained so much, let me go on.

When we had passed out of the Porta San Giovanni, the coachman drove as slowly as possible; but Marcello was never practical. How could he be, I ask you, with an opera in his head? So we crawled along, and he gazed dreamily before him. At last, when we had reached the part where the little villas and vineyards begin, he began to look about him.

You all know how it is out there; iron gates with rusty names or initials over them, and beyond them straight walks bordered with roses and lavender leading up to a forlorn little casino, with trees and a wilderness behind it sloping down to the Campagna, lonely enough to be murdered in and no one to hear you cry. We stopped at several of these gates and Marcello stood looking in, but none of the places were to his taste. He seemed not to doubt that he might have whatever pleased him, but nothing did so. He would jump out and run to the gate, and return saying, "The shape of those windows would disturb my inspiration," or, "That yellow paint would make me fail my duet in the second act"; and once he liked the air of the house well enough, but there were marigolds growing in the walk, and he hated them. So we drove on and on, until I thought we should find nothing more to reject. At last we came to one which suited him, though it was terribly lonely, and I should have fancied it very *agaçant* to live so far away from the world with nothing but those melancholy olives and green oaks—ilexes, you call them—for company.

"I shall live here and become famous!" he said, decidedly, as he pulled the iron rod which rang a great bell inside. We waited, and then he rang again very impatiently and stamped his foot.

"No one lives here, *mon vieux*! Come, it is getting late, and it is so damp out here, and you know that the damp for a tenor voice—" He stamped his foot again and interrupted me angrily.

"Why, then, have you got a tenor? You are stupid! A bass would be more sensible; nothing hurts it. But you have not got one, and you call yourself my friend! Go home without me." How could I, so far on foot? "Go and sing your lovesick songs to your lean English misses! They will thank you with a cup of abominable tea, and you will be in Paradise! This is *my* Paradise, and I shall stay until the angel comes to open it."

He was very cross and unreasonable, and those were just the times when one loved him most, so I waited and enveloped my throat in my pocket-handkerchief and sang a passage or two just to prevent my voice from becoming stiff in that damp air.

"Be still! Silence yourself!" he cried. "I cannot hear if anyone is coming."

Someone came at last, a rough-looking sort of keeper, or *guardiano* as they are called there, who looked at us as though he thought we were mad. One of us certainly was, but it was not I. Marcello spoke pretty good Italian, with a French accent, it is true, but the man understood him, especially as he held his purse in his hand. I heard him say a great many impetuously persuasive things all in one breath, then he slipped a gold piece into the *guardiano*'s horny hand, and the two turned towards the house, the man shrugging his shoulders in a resigned sort of way, and Marcello called out to me over his shoulder—

"Go home in the cab, or you will be late for your horrible English party! I am going to stay here tonight." *Ma foi!* I took his permission and left him; for a tenor voice is as tyrannical as a jealous woman. Besides, I was furious, and yet I laughed. His was the artist temperament, and appeared to us by turns absurd, sublime, and intensely irritating; but this last never for long, and we all felt that were we more like him our pictures would be worth more. I had not got as far as the city gate when my temper had cooled, and I began to reproach myself for leaving him in that lonely place with his purse full of money, for he was not poor at all, and tempting the dark *guardiano* to murder him. Nothing could be easier than to kill him in his sleep and bury him away somewhere under the olive trees or in some old vault of a ruined catacomb, so common on the borders of the Campagna. There were sure to be a hundred convenient places. I stopped the coachman and told him to turn back, but he shook his head and said something about having to be in the Piazza of St. Peter at eight o'clock. His horse began to go lame, as though he had understood his master and was his accomplice. What could I do? I said to myself that it was fate, and let him take me back to the Villa Medici, where I had to pay him a pretty sum for our crazy expedition, and then he rattled off, the horse not lame at all, leaving me bewildered at this strange afternoon.

I did not sleep well that night, though my tenor song had been applauded, and the English misses had caressed me much. I tried not to think of Marcello, and he did not trouble me much until I went to bed; but then I could not sleep, as I have told you.

I fancied him already murdered, and being buried in the darkness by the *guardiano*. I saw the man dragging his body, with the beautiful head thumping against the stones, down dark passages, and at last leaving it all bloody and covered with earth under a black arch in a recess, and coming back to count the gold pieces. But then again I fell asleep, and dreamed that Marcello was standing at the gate and stamping his foot; and then I slept no more, but got up as soon as the dawn came, and dressed myself and went to my studio at the end of the laurel walk. I took down my painting jacket, and remembered how he had pulled it off my shoulders. I took up the brushes he had washed for me; they were only half cleaned after all, and stiff with paint and soap. I felt glad to be angry with him, and *sacré*'d a little, for it made me sure that he was yet alive if I could scold at him. Then I pulled out my study of his head for my picture of Mucius Scaevola holding his hand in the flame, and then I forgave him; for who could look upon that face and not love it?

I worked with the fire of friendship in my brush, and did my best to endow the features with the expression of

scorn and obstinacy I had seen at the gate. It could not
have been more suitable to my subject! Had I seen it for
the last time? You will ask me why I did not leave my
work and go to see if anything had happened to him, but
against this there were several reasons. Our yearly exhibi-
tion was not far off and my picture was barely painted in,
and my comrades had sworn that it would not be ready. I
was expecting a model for the King of the Etruscans; a
man who cooked chestnuts in the Piazza Montanara,
and who had consented to stoop to sit to me as a great
favour; and then, to tell the truth, the morning was beginning to dispel my fancies. I had a good northern light
to work by, with nothing sentimental about it, and I was
not fanciful by nature; so when I sat down to my easel I
told myself that I had been a fool, and that Marcello was
perfectly safe: the smell of the paints helping me to feel
practical again. Indeed, I thought every moment that he
would come in, tired of his caprice already, and even was
preparing and practising a little lecture for him. Some
one knocked at my door, and I cried *"Entrez!"* thinking it
was he at last, but no, it was Pierre Magnin.

"There is a curious man, a man of the country, who
wants you," he said. "He has your address on a dirty piece
of paper in Marcello's handwriting, and a letter for you,
but he won't give it up. He says he must see 'Il Signor
Martino.' He'd make a superb model for a murderer!
Come and speak to him, and keep him while I get a
sketch of his head."

I followed Magnin through the garden, and outside,

for the porter had not allowed him to enter. I found the
guardiano of yesterday. He showed his white teeth, and
said, "Good day, signore," like a Christian; and here in
Rome he did not look half so murderous, only a stupid,
brown, country fellow. He had a rough peasant-cart waiting, and he had tied up his shaggy horse to a ring in the
wall. I held out my hand for the letter and pretended to
find it difficult to read, for I saw Magnin standing with his
sketch-book in the shadow of the entrance hall. The note
said this: I have it still and I will copy it. It was written in
pencil on a leaf torn from his pocketbook.

Mon vieux! *I have passed a good night here, and the
man will keep me as long as I like. Nothing will happen to me, except that I shall be divinely quiet, and I
already have a famous motif in my head. Go to my
lodgings and pack up some clothes and all my manu-
scripts, with plenty of music paper and a few bottles of
Bordeaux, and give them to my messenger. Be quick
about it!*

    *Fame is preparing to descend upon me! If you care
to see me, do not come before eight days. The gate will
not be opened if you come sooner. The guardiano is my
slave, and he has instructions to kill any intruder who
in the guise of a friend tries to get in uninvited. He will
do it, for he has confessed to me that he has murdered
three men already.*

(Of course this was a joke. I knew Marcello's way.)

When you come, go to the poste restante *and fetch my*
letters. Here is my card to legitimate you. Don't forget
pens and a bottle of ink! Your Marcello.

There was nothing for it but to jump into the cart, tell
Magnin, who had finished his sketch, to lock up my studio, and go bumping off to obey these commands. We
drove to his lodgings in the Via del Governo Vecchio,
and there I made a bundle of all that I could think of; the
landlady hindering me by a thousand questions about
when the Signore would return. He had paid for the
rooms in advance, so she had no need to be anxious
about her rent. When I told her where he was, she shook
her head, and talked a great deal about the bad air out
there, and said "Poor Signorino!" in a melancholy way, as
though he were already buried, and looked mournfully
after us from the window when we drove away. She irri-
tated me, and made me feel superstitious. At the corner
of the Via del Tritone I jumped down and gave the man
a franc out of pure sentimentality, and cried after him,
"Greet the Signore!" but he did not hear me, and jogged
away stupidly whilst I was longing to be with him.
Marcello was a cross to us sometimes, but we loved him
always.

The eight days went by sooner than I had thought they
would, and Thursday came, bright and sunny, for my ex-

pedition. At one o'clock I descended into the Piazza di Spagna, and made a bargain with a man who had a well-fed horse, remembering how dearly Marcello's want of good sense had cost me a week ago, and we drove off at a good pace to the Vigna Marziali, as I was almost forgetting to say that it was called. My heart was beating, though I did not know why I should feel so much emotion. When we reached the iron gate the *guardiano* answered my ring directly, and I had no sooner set foot in the long flower-walk than I saw Marcello hastening to meet me.

"I knew you would come," he said, drawing my arm within his, and so we walked towards the little grey house, which had a sort of portico and several balconies, and a sun-dial on its front. There were grated windows down to the ground floor, and the place, to my relief, looked safe and habitable. He told me that the man did not sleep there, but in a little hut down towards the Campagna, and that he, Marcello, locked himself in safely every night, which I was also relieved to know.

"What do you get to eat?" said I.

"Oh, I have goat's flesh, and dried beans and polenta, with pecorino cheese, and there is plenty of black bread and sour wine," he answered smilingly. "You see I am not starved."

"Do not overwork yourself, *mon vieux*," I said. "You are worth more than your opera will ever be."

"Do I look overworked?" he said, turning his face to

me in the broad, outdoor light. He seemed a little of-
fended at my saying that about his opera, and I was foolish to do it.

I examined his face critically, and he looked at me
half defiantly. "No, not yet," I answered rather unwillingly, for I could not say that he did; but there was a restless, inward look in his eyes, and an almost imperceptible
shadow lay around them. It seemed to me as though the
full temples had grown slightly hollow, and a sort of faint
mist lay over his beauty, making it seem strange and far
off. We were standing before the door, and he pushed
it open, the *guardiano* following us with slow, loud-
resounding steps.

"Here is my Paradise," said Marcello, and we entered
the house, which was like all the others of its kind.
A hall, with stucco bas-reliefs, and a stairway adorned
with antique fragments, gave access to the upper rooms.
Marcello ran up the steps lightly, and I heard him lock a
door somewhere above and draw out the key, then he
came and met me on the landing.

"This," he said, "is my workroom," and he threw open
a low door. The key was in the lock, so this room could
not be the one I heard him close. "Tell me I shall not
write like an angel here!" he cried. I was so dazzled by
the flood of bright sunshine after the dusk of the passage,
that I blinked like an owl at first, and then I saw a large
room, quite bare except for a rough table and chair, the
chair covered with manuscript music.

"You are looking for the furniture," he said, laughing. "It is outside. Look here!" And he drew me to a rickety door of worm-eaten wood and coarse greenish glass, and flung it open on to a rusty iron balcony. He was right; the furniture was outside, that is to say, a divine view met my eyes. The Sabine Mountains, the Alban Hills, and broad Campagna, with its mediaeval towers and ruined aqueducts, and the open plain to the sea. All this glowing and yet calm in the sunlight. No wonder he could write there! The balcony ran round the corner of the house, and to the right I looked down upon an alley of ilexes, ending in a grove of tall laurel trees—very old, apparently. There were bits of sculpture and some ancient sarcophagi standing gleaming against them, and even from so high I could hear a little stream of water pouring from an antique mask into a long, rough trough. I saw the brown *guardiano* digging at his cabbages and onions, and I laughed to think that I could fancy him a murderer! He had a little bag of relics, which dangled to and fro over his sun-burned breast, and he looked very innocent when he sat down upon an old column to eat a piece of black bread with an onion which he had just pulled out of the ground, slicing it with a knife not at all like a dagger. But I kept my thoughts to myself, for Marcello would have laughed at them. We were standing together, looking down at the man as he drank from his hands at the running fountain, and Marcello now leaned down over the balcony, and called out a long "Ohé!" The lazy *guardiano* looked up, nodded, and then got up slowly from the stone where he had been half-kneeling to reach the jet of water.

"We are going to dine," Marcello explained. "I have been waiting for you." Presently we heard the man's heavy tread upon the stairs, and he entered bearing a strange meal in a basket.

There came to light pecorino cheese made from ewe's milk, black bread of the consistency of a stone, a great bowl of salad apparently composed of weeds, and a sausage which filled the room with a strong smell of garlic. Then he disappeared and came back with a dish full of ragged-looking goat's flesh cooked together with a mass of smoking polenta, and I am not sure that there was not oil in it.

"I told you I lived well, and now you see!" said Marcello. It was a terrible meal, but I had to eat it, and was glad to have some rough, sour wine to help me, which tasted of earth and roots. When we had finished I said, "And your opera! How are you getting on?"

"Not a word about that!" he cried. "You see how I have written!" And he turned over a heap of manuscript. "But do not talk to me about it. I will not lose my ideas in words." This was not like Marcello, who loved to discuss his work, and I looked at him astonished.

"Come," he said, "we will go down into the garden, and you shall tell me about the comrades. What are they doing? Has Magnin found a model for his Clytemnestra?"

I humoured him, as I always did, and we sat upon a

stone bench behind the house, looking towards the laurel grove, talking of the pictures and the students. I wanted to walk down the ilex alley, but he stopped me.

"If you are afraid of the damp, don't go down there," he said. "The place is like a vault. Let us stay here and be thankful for this heavenly view."

"Well, let us stay here," I answered, resigned as ever. He lit a cigar and offered me one in silence. If he did not care to talk, I could be still too. From time to time he made some indifferent observation, and I answered it in the same tone. It almost seemed to me as though we, the old heart-comrades, had become strangers who had not known each other a week, or as though we had been so long apart that we had grown away from each other. There was something about him which escaped me. Yes, the days of solitude had indeed put years and a sort of shyness, or rather ceremony, between us! It did not seem natural to me now to clap him on the back, and make the old, harmless jokes at him. He must have felt the constraint too, for we were like children who had looked forward to a game, and did not know now what to play at.

At six o'clock I left him. It was not like parting with Marcello. I felt rather as though I should find my old friend in Rome that evening, and here only left a shadowy likeness of him. He accompanied me to the gate, and pressed my hand, and for a moment the true Marcello looked out of his eyes; but we called out no last word to each other as I drove away. I had only said, "Let me know when you want me," and he said, *"Merci!"* and all the way back to Rome I felt a chill upon me, his hand had been so cold, and I thought and thought what could be the matter with him.

That evening I spoke out my anxiety to Pierre Magnin, who shook his head and declared that malaria fever must be taking hold of him, and that people often begin to show it by being a little odd.

"He must not stay there! We must get him away as soon as possible," I cried.

"We both know Marcello, and that nothing can make him stir against his will," said Pierre. "Let him alone, and he will get tired of his whim. It will not kill him to have a touch of malaria, and some evening he will turn up amongst us as merry as ever."

But he did not. I worked hard at my picture and finished it, but for a few touches, and he had not yet appeared. Perhaps it was the extreme application, perhaps the sitting out in that damp place, for I insist upon tracing it to something more material than emotion. Well, whatever it was, I fell ill; more ill than I had ever been in my life. It was almost twilight when it overtook me, and I remember it distinctly, though I forget what happened afterwards, or, rather, I never knew, for I was found by Magnin quite unconscious, and he has told me that I remained so for some time, and then became delirious, and talked of nothing but Marcello. I have told you that it was very nearly twilight; but just at the moment when the sun is gone the colours show in their true value. Artists know this, and I was putting last touches here and there to my picture and especially to my head of Mucius Scaevola, or rather, Marcello.

The rest of the picture came out well enough; but that head, which should have been the principal one, seemed faded and sunk in. The face appeared to grow paler and paler, and to recede from me; a strange veil spread over it, and the eyes seemed to close. I am not easily frightened, and I know what tricks some peculiar methods of colour will play by certain lights, for the moment I spoke of had gone, and the twilight greyness had set in; so I stepped back to look at it. Just then the lips, which had become almost white, opened a little, and sighed! An illusion, of course. I must have been very ill and quite delirious already, for to my imagination it was a real sigh, or, rather, a sort of exhausted gasp. Then it was that I fainted, I suppose, and when I came to myself I was in my bed, with Magnin and Monsieur Sutton standing by me, and a Sœur de Charité moving softly about among medicine bottles, and speaking in whispers. I stretched out my hands, and they were thin and yellow, with long, pale nails; and I heard Magnin's voice, which sounded very far away, say, *"Dieu Merci!"* And now Monsieur Sutton will tell you what I did not know until long afterwards.

II

ROBERT SUTTON'S ACCOUNT OF WHAT
HAPPENED AT THE VIGNA MARZIALI

I am attached to Detaille, and was very glad to be of use to him, but I never fully shared his admiration for Marcello Souvestre, though I appreciated his good points. He was certainly very promising—I must say that. But he was an odd, flighty sort of fellow, not of the kind which we English care to take the trouble to understand. It is my business to write stories, but not having need of such characters I have never particularly studied them. As I say, I was glad to be of use to Detaille, who is a thorough good fellow, and I willingly gave up my work to go and sit by his bedside. Magnin knew that I was a friend of his, and very properly came to me when he found that Detaille's illness was a serious one and likely to last for a long time. I found him perfectly delirious, and raving about Marcello.

"Tell me what the *motif* is! I know it is a *Marche Funèbre!*" And here he would sing a peculiar melody, which, as I have a knack at music, I noted down, it being like nothing I had heard before. The Sister of Charity looked at me with severe eyes; but how could she know that all is grist for our mill, and that observation becomes with us a mechanical habit? Poor Detaille kept repeating this curious melody over and over, and then would stop and seem to be looking at his picture, crying that it was fading away.

"Marcello! Marcello! You are fading too! Let me come to you!" He was as weak as a baby, and could not have moved from his bed unless in the strength of delirium.

"I cannot come!" he went on. "They have tied me down." And here he made as though he were trying to gnaw through a rope at his wrists, and then burst into tears. "Will no one go for me and bring me a word from you? Ah! if I could know that you are alive!"

Magnin looked at me. I knew what he was thinking. He would not leave his comrade, but I must go. I don't mind acknowledging that I did not undertake this unwillingly. To sit by Detaille's bedside and listen to his ravings enervated me, and what Magnin wanted struck me as troublesome but not uninteresting to one of my craft, so I agreed to go. I had heard all about Marcello's strange seclusion from Magnin and Detaille himself, who lamented over it openly in his simple way at supper at the Academy, where I was a frequent guest.

I knew that it would be useless to ring at the gate of the Vigna Marziali. Not only should I not be admitted, but I should arouse Marcello's anger and suspicion, for I did not for a moment believe that he was not alive, though I thought it very possible that he was becoming a little crazy, as his countrymen are so easily put off their balance. Now, odd people are oddest late in the day and at evening time. Their nerves lose the power of resistance then, and the real man gets the better of them. So I determined to try to discover something at night, reflecting also that I should be safer from detection then. I knew his liking for wandering about when he ought to be in his bed, and I did not doubt that I should get a glimpse of him, and that was really all I needed.

My first step was to take a long walk out of the Porta San Giovanni, and this I did in the early morning, tramping along steadily until I came to an iron gate on the right of the road, with "Vigna Marziali" over it; and then I walked straight on, never stopping until I had reached a little bushy lane running down towards the Campagna to the right. It was pebbly, and quite shut in by luxuriant ivy and elder bushes, and it bore deep traces of the last heavy rains. These had evidently been effaced by no footprints, so I concluded that it was little used. Down this path I made my way cautiously, looking behind and before me, from a habit contracted in my lonely wanderings in the Abruzzi. I had a capital revolver with me—an old friend—and I feared no man; but I began to feel a dramatic interest in my undertaking, and determined that it should not be crossed by any disagreeable surprises. The lane led me further down the plain than I had reckoned upon, for the bushy edge shut out the view; and when I had got to the bottom and faced round, the Vigna Marziali was lying quite far to my left. I saw at a glance that behind the grey casino an alley of ilexes ended in a laurel grove; then there were plantations of kitchen stuff, with a sort of thatched cabin in their midst, probably that of a gardener. I looked about for a kennel, but saw none, so there was no watchdog. At the end of this primitive kitchen garden was a broad patch of grass, bounded by a fence, which I could take at a spring. Now, I knew my way, but I could not resist tracing it out a little further. It was well that I did so; for I found just within the fence a sunken stream; rather full at the time, in consequence of the rains, too deep to wade and too broad to jump. It struck me that it would be easy enough to take a board from the fence and lay it over for a bridge. I measured the breadth with my eye, and decided the board would span it; then I went back as I had come, and returned to find Detaille still raving.

As he could understand nothing it seemed to me rather a fool's errand to go off in search of comfort for him; but a conscious moment might come, and moreover, I began to be interested in my undertaking; and so I agreed with Magnin that I should go and take some food and rest and return to the Vigna that night. I told my landlady that I was going into the country and should return the next day, and I went to Nazarri's and laid in a stock of sandwiches and filled my flask with something they called sherry, for, though I was no great wine-drinker, I feared the night chill.

It was about seven o'clock when I started, and I retraced my morning's steps exactly. As I reached the lane, it occurred to me that it was still too light for me to pass unobserved over the stream, and I made a place for myself under the hedge and lay down, quite screened by the thick curtain of tangled overhanging ivy.

I must have been out of training, and tired by the morning's walk, for I fell asleep. When I awoke it was night; the stars were shining, a dank mist made its way down my throat, and I felt stiff and cold. I took a pull at my flask, finding it nasty stuff, but it warmed me. Then I rang my repeater, which struck a quarter to eleven, got up and shook myself free of the leaves and brambles, and went on down the lane. When I got to the fence I sat down and thought the thing over. What did I expect to discover? What *was* there to discover? Nothing! Nothing but that Marcello was alive; and that was no discovery at all for I felt sure of it. I was a fool, and had let myself be allured by the mere stage nonsense and mystery of the business, and a mouse would creep out of this mountain of precautions! Well, at least I could turn it to account by describing my own absurd behaviour in some story yet to be written, and, as it was not enough for a chapter, I would add to it by further experience. "Come along!" I said to myself. "You're an ass, but it may prove instructive." I raised the top board from the fence noiselessly. There was a little stile there, and the boards were easily moved. I laid down my bridge with some difficulty, and stepped carefully across, and made my way to the laurel grove as quickly and noiselessly as possible.

There all was thick darkness, and my eyes only grew slowly accustomed to it. After all there was not much to see; some stone seats in a semicircle, and some fragments of columns set upright with antique busts upon them. Then a little to the right a sort of arch, with apparently some steps descending into the ground, probably the entrance to some discovered branch of a catacomb. In the midst of the enclosure, not a very large one, stood a stone table, deeply fixed in the earth. No one was there; of that I felt certain, and I sat down, having now got used to the gloom, and fell to eat my sandwiches, for I was desperately hungry.

Now that I had come so far, was nothing to take place to repay me for my trouble? It suddenly struck me that it was absurd to expect Marcello to come out to meet me and perform any mad antics he might be meditating there before my eyes for my especial satisfaction. Why had I supposed that something would take place in the grove I do not know, except that this seemed a fit place for it. I would go and watch the house, and if I saw a light anywhere I might be sure he was within. Any fool might have thought of that, but a novelist lays the scene of his drama and expects his characters to slide about in the grooves like puppets. It is only when mine surprise me that I feel they are alive. When I reached the end of the ilex alley I saw the house before me. There were more cabbages and onions after I had left the trees, and I saw that in this open space I could easily be perceived by any one standing on the balcony above. As I drew back again under the ilexes, a window above, not the one on the bal-

cony, was suddenly lighted up; but the light did not remain long, and presently a gleam shone through the
glass oval over the door below.

I had just time to spring behind the thickest trunk
near me when the door opened. I took advantage of its
creaking to creep up the slanting tree like a cat, and lie
out upon a projecting branch.

As I expected, Marcello came out. He was very pale,
and moved mechanically like a sleepwalker. I was
shocked to see how hollow his face had become as he
held the candle still lighted in his hand, and it cast deep
shadows on his sunken cheeks and fixed eyes, which
burned wildly and seemed to see nothing. His lips were
quite white, and so drawn that I could see his gleaming
teeth. Then the candle fell from his hand, and he came
slowly and with a curiously regular step on into the darkness of the ilexes, I watching him from above. But I
scarcely think he would have noticed me had I been
standing in his path. When he had passed I let myself
down and followed him. I had taken off my shoes, and
my tread was absolutely noiseless; moreover, I felt sure
he would not turn around.

On he went with the same mechanical step until he
reached the grove. There I knelt behind an old sarcophagus at the entrance, and waited. What would he do? He
stood perfectly still, not looking about him, but as though
the clockwork within him had suddenly stopped. I felt
that he was becoming psychologically interesting, after
all. Suddenly he threw up his arms as men do when they

are mortally wounded on the battle-field, and I expected to see him fall at full length. Instead of this he made a step forward.

I looked in the same direction, and saw a woman, who must have concealed herself there while I was waiting before the house, come from out of the gloom, and as she slowly approached and laid her head upon his shoulder, the outstretched arms clasped themselves closely around her, so that her face was hidden upon his neck.

So this was the whole matter, and I had been sent off on a wild-goose chase to spy out a common love affair! His opera and his seclusion for the sake of work, his tyrannical refusal to see Detaille unless he sent for him—all this was but a mask to a vulgar intrigue which, for reasons best known to himself, could not be indulged in in the city. I was thoroughly angry! If Marcello passed his time mooning about in that damp hole all night, no wonder that he looked so wretchedly ill, and seemed half mad! I knew very well that Marcello was no saint. Why should he be? But I had not taken him for a fool! He had had plenty of romantic episodes, and as he was discreet without being uselessly mysterious, no one had ever unduly pried into them, nor should we have done so now. I said to myself that that mixture of French and Italian blood was at the bottom of it; French flimsiness and light-headedness and Italian love of cunning! I looked back upon all the details of my mysterious expedition. I suppose at the root of my anger lay a certain dramatic disappointment at not finding him lying murdered, and I despised myself for all the trouble I had taken to this ridiculous end: just to see him holding a woman in his arms. I could not see her face, and her figure was enveloped from head to foot in something long and dark; but I could make out that she was tall and slender, and that a pair of white hands gleamed from her drapery. As I was looking intently, for all my indignation, the couple moved on, and still clinging to one another descended the steps. So even the solitude of the lonely laurel grove could not satisfy Marcello's insane love of secrecy! I kept still awhile; then I stole to where they had disappeared, and listened; but all was silent, and I cautiously struck a match and peered down. I could see the steps for a short distance below me, and then the darkness seemed to rise and swallow them. It must be a catacomb as I had imagined, or an old Roman bath, perhaps, which Marcello had made comfortable enough, no doubt, and as likely as not they were having a nice little cold supper there. My empty stomach told me that I could have forgiven him even then could I have shared it; I was in truth frightfully hungry as well as angry, and sat down on one of the stone benches to finish my sandwiches.

The thought of waiting to see this love-sick pair return to upper earth never for a moment occurred to me. I had found out the whole thing, and a great humbug it was! Now I wanted to get back to Rome before my temper had cooled, and to tell Magnin on what a fool's errand he had sent me. If he liked to quarrel with me, all the better!

All the way home I composed cutting French

speeches, but they suddenly cooled and petrified like a
gust of lava from a volcano when I discovered that the
gate was closed. I had never thought of getting a pass, and
Magnin ought to have warned me. Another grievance
against the fellow! I enjoyed my resentment, and it kept
me warm as I patrolled up and down. There are houses,
and even small eating-shops outside the gate, but no light
was visible, and I did not care to attract attention by
pounding at the doors in the middle of the night; so I
crept behind a bit of wall. I was getting used to hiding by
this time, and made myself as comfortable as I could
with my ulster, took another pull at my flask, and waited.
At last the gate was opened and I slipped through, trying
not to look as though I had been out all night like a ban-
dit. The guard looked at me narrowly, evidently wondering at my lack of luggage. Had I had a knapsack I might
have been taken for some innocently mad English
tourist indulging in the mistaken pleasure of trudging in
from Frascati or Albano; but a man in an ulster, with his
hands in his pockets, sauntering in at the gate of the city
at break of day as though returning from a stroll, naturally puzzled the officials, who looked at me and
shrugged their shoulders.

Luckily I found an early cab in the Piazza of the
Lateran, for I was dead-beat, and was soon at my lodgings
in the Via della Croce, where my landlady let me in very
speedily. Then at last I had the comfort of throwing off
my clothes, all damp with the night dew, and turning in.
My wrath had cooled to a certain point, and I did not fear

to lower its temperature too greatly by yielding to an over-whelming desire for sleep. An hour or two could make no great difference to Magnin—let him fancy me still hanging about the Vigna Marziali! Sleep I must have, no matter what he thought.

I slept long, and was awakened at last by my landlady, Sora Nanna, standing over me, and saying, "There is a Signore who wants you."

"It is I, Magnin!" said a voice behind her. "I could not wait for you to come!" He looked haggard with anxiety and watching.

"Detaille is raving still," he went on, "only worse than before. Speak, for Heaven's sake! Why don't you tell me something?" And he shook me by the arm as though he thought I was still asleep.

"Have you nothing to say? You must have seen some-thing! Did you see Marcello?"

"Oh! Yes, I saw him."

"Well?"

"Well, he was very comfortable—quite alive. He had a woman's arms around him."

I heard my door violently slammed to, a ferocious *"Sacré gamin!"* and then steps springing down the stairs. I felt perfectly happy at having made such an impression, and turned and resumed my broken sleep with almost a kindly feeling towards Magnin, who was at that moment probably tearing up the Spanish Scalinata two steps at a time, and making himself horribly hot. It could not help Detaille, poor fellow! He could not understand my news.

When I had slept long enough I got up, refreshed myself with a bath and something to eat, and went off to see Detaille. It was not his fault that I had been made a fool of, so I felt sorry for him.

I found him raving just as I had left him the day before, only worse, as Magnin said. He persisted in continually crying, "Marcello, take care! No one can save you!" in hoarse, weak tones, but with the regularity of a knell, keeping up a peculiar movement with his feet, as though he were weary with a long road, but must press forward to his goal. Then he would stop and break into childish sobs.

"My feet are so sore," he murmured piteously, "and I am so tired! But I will come! They are following me, but I am strong!" Then a violent struggle with his invisible pursuers, in which he would break off into that singing of his, alternating with the warning cry. The singing voice was quite another from the speaking one. He went on and on repeating the singular air which he had himself called "A Funeral March," and which had become intensely disagreeable to me. If it was one indeed, it surely was intended for no Christian burial. As he sang, the tears kept trickling down his cheeks, and Magnin sat wiping them away as tenderly as a woman. Between his song he would clasp his hands, feebly enough, for he was very weak when the delirium did not make him violent, and cry in heart-rending tones, "Marcello, I shall never see you again! Why did you leave us?" At last, when he stopped for a moment, Magnin left his side, beckoning the Sister to take it, and drew me into the other room, closing the door behind him.

"Now tell me exactly how you saw Marcello," said he; so I related my whole absurd experience—forgetting, however, my personal irritation, for he looked too wretched and worn for anybody to be angry with him. He made me repeat several times my description of Marcello's face and manner as he had come out of the house. That seemed to make more impression upon him than the love-business.

"Sick people have strange intuitions," he said gravely, "and I persist in thinking that Marcello is very ill and in danger. *Tenez!*" And here he broke off, went to the door, and called, "*Ma sœur!*" under his breath. She understood, and after having drawn the bedclothes straight, and once more dried the trickling tears, she came noiselessly to where we stood, the wet handkerchief still in her hand. She was a singularly tall and strong-looking woman, with piercing black eyes and a self-controlled manner. Strange to say, she bore the adopted name of Claudius, instead of a more feminine one.

"*Ma sœur*," said Magnin, "at what o'clock was it that he sprang out of bed and we had to hold him for so long?"

"Half-past eleven and a few minutes," she answered promptly. Then he turned to me.

"At what time did Marcello come out into the garden?"

"Well, it might have been half-past eleven," I answered unwillingly. "I should say that three-quarters of an hour might possibly have passed since I rang my repeater. Mind you, I won't swear it!" I hate to have people try to prove mysterious coincidences, and this was just what they were attempting.

"Are you sure of the hour, *ma sœur?*" I asked, a little tartly.

She looked at me calmly with her great, black eyes, and said:

"I heard the Trinità de' Monti strike the half-hour just before it happened."

"Be so good as to tell Monsieur Sutton exactly what took place," said Magnin.

"One moment, monsieur," and she went swiftly and softly to Detaille, raised him on her strong arm, and held a glass to his lips, from which he drank mechanically. Then she came and stood where she could watch him through the open door.

"He hears nothing," she said, as she hung the handkerchief to dry over a chair, and then she went on: "It was half-past eleven, and my patient had been very uneasy— that is to say, more so even than before. It might have been four or five minutes after the clock had finished striking that he became suddenly quite still, and then began to tremble all over, so that the bed shook with him." She spoke admirable English, as many of the Sisters do, so I need not translate, but will give her own words.

"He went on trembling until I thought he was going to have a fit, and told Monsieur Magnin to be ready to go for the doctor, when just then the trembling stopped, he became perfectly stiff, his hair stood up upon his head, and his eyes seemed coming out of their sockets, though he could see nothing, for I passed the candle before them. All at once he sprang out of his bed and rushed to the door. I did not know he was so strong. Before he got there I had him in my arms, for he has become very light, and I carried him back to bed again, though he was struggling, like a child. Monsieur Magnin came in from the next room just as he was trying to get up again, and we held him down until it was past, but he screamed Monsieur Souvestre's name for a long time after that. Afterwards he was very cold and exhausted, of course, and I gave him some beef-tea, though it was not the hour for it."

"I think you had better tell the Sister all about it," said Magnin turning to me. "It is best that the nurse should know everything."

"Very well," said I, "though I do not think it's much in her line." She answered me herself: "Everything which concerns our patients is our business. Nothing shocks me." Thereupon she sat down and thrust her hands into her long sleeves, prepared to listen. I repeated the whole affair as I had done to Magnin. She never took her brilliant eyes from off my face, and listened as coolly as though she had been a doctor hearing an account of a difficult case, though to me it seemed almost sacrilege to be describing the behaviour of a love-stricken youth to a Sister of Charity.

"What do you say to that, *ma sœur*?" asked Magnin, when I had done. "I say nothing, monsieur. It is sufficient that I know it," and she withdrew her hands from her sleeves, took up the handkerchief, which was dry by this time, and returned quietly to her place at the bedside.

"I wonder if I have shocked her, after all?" I said to Magnin.

"Oh, no," he answered. "They see many things, and a *sœur* is as abstract as a confessor; they do not allow themselves any personal feelings. I have seen Sœur Claudius listen perfectly unmoved to the most abominable ravings, only crossing herself beneath her cape at the most hideous blasphemies. It was late summer when poor Justin Revol died. You were not here." Magnin put his hand to his forehead.

"You are looking ill yourself," I said. "Go and try to sleep, and I will stay."

"Very well," he answered, "but I cannot rest unless you promise to remember everything he says, that I may hear it when I wake," and he threw himself down on the hard sofa like a sack, and was asleep in a moment; and I, who had felt so angry with him but a few hours ago, put a cushion under his head and made him comfortable.

I sat down in the next room and listened to Detaille's monotonous ravings, while Sœur Claudius read in her book of prayers. It was getting dusk, and several of the academicians stole in and stood over the sick man and shook their heads. They looked around for Magnin, but I pointed to the other room with my finger on my lips, and they nodded and went away on tiptoe.

It required no effort of memory to repeat Detaille's words to Magnin when he woke, for they were always the same. We had another Sister that night, and as Sœur Claudius was not to return till the next day at midday, I offered to share the watch with Magnin, who was getting very nervous and exhausted, and who seemed to think that some such attack might be expected as had occurred the night before. The new Sister was a gentle, delicate-looking little woman, with tears in her soft brown eyes as she bent over the sick man, and crossed herself from time to time, grasping the crucifix which hung from the beads at her waist. Nevertheless she was calm and useful, and as punctual as Sœur Claudius herself in giving the medicines.

The doctor had come in the evening, and prescribed a change in these. He would not say what he thought of his patient, but only declared that it was necessary to wait for a crisis. Magnin sent for some supper, and we sat over it together in the silence, neither of us hungry. He kept looking at his watch.

"If the same thing happens tonight, he will die!" said he, and laid his head on his arms.

"He will die in a most foolish cause, then," I said angrily, for I thought he was going to cry, as those Frenchmen have a way of doing, and I wanted to irritate him by way of a tonic; so I went on —

"It would be dying for a *vaurien* who is making an ass of himself in a ridiculous business which will be over in a week! Souvestre may get as much fever as he likes! Only don't ask me to come and nurse him."

"It is not the fever," said he slowly. "It is a horrible nameless dread that I have; I suppose it is listening to Detaille that makes me nervous. Hark!" he added. "It strikes eleven. We must watch!"

"If you really expect another attack you had better warn the Sister," I said; so he told her in a few words what might happen.

"Very well, monsieur," she answered, and sat down quietly near the bed, Magnin at the pillow and I near him. No sound was to be heard but Detaille's ceaseless lament.

And now, before I tell you more, I must stop to entreat you to believe me. It will be almost impossible for you to do so, I know, for I have laughed myself at such tales, and no assurances would have made me credit them. But I, Robert Sutton, swear that this thing happened. More I cannot do. It is the truth.

We had been watching Detaille intently. He was lying with closed eyes, and had been very restless. Suddenly he became quite still, and then began to tremble, exactly as Sœur Claudius had described. It was a curious, uniform trembling, apparently in every fibre, and his iron bedstead shook as though strong hands were at its head and foot. Then came the absolute rigidity she had also described, and I do not exaggerate when I say that not only did his short-cropped hair seem to stand erect, but that it literally did so. A lamp cast the shadow of his profile against the wall to the left of his bed, and as I looked at the immovable outline which seemed painted on the wall, I saw the hair slowly rise until the line where it joined the forehead was quite a different one—abrupt instead of a smooth sweep. His eyes opened wide and were frightfully fixed, then as frightfully strained, but they certainly did not see us.

We waited breathlessly for what might follow. The little Sister was standing close to him, her lips pressed together and a little pale, but very calm. "Do not be frightened, *ma sœur*," whispered Magnin, and she answered in a business-like tone, "No, monsieur," and drew still nearer to her patient, and took his hands, which were stiff as those of a corpse, between her own to warm them. I laid mine upon his heart; it was beating so imperceptibly that I almost thought it had stopped, and as I leaned my face to his lips I could feel no breath issue from them. It seemed as though the rigour would last forever.

Suddenly, without any transition, he hurled himself with enormous force, and literally at one bound, almost into the middle of the room, scattering us aside like leaves in the wind. I was upon him in a moment, grappling with him with all my strength, to prevent him from reaching the door. Magnin had been thrown backwards against the table, and I heard the medicine bottles crash with his fall. He had flung back his hand to save himself, and rushed to help me with blood dripping from a cut in his wrist. The little Sister sprang to us. Detaille had thrown her violently back upon her knees, and now, with a nurse's instinct, she tried to throw a shawl over his bare breast. We four must have made a strange group!

Four? *We were five!* Marcello Souvestre stood before us, just within the door! We all saw him, for he was there. His bloodless face was turned towards us unmoved; his hands hung by his side as white as his face; only his eyes had life in them; they were fixed on Detaille.

"Thank God you have come at last!" I cried. "Don't stand there like a fool! Help us, can't you?" But he never moved. I was furiously angry, and, leaving my hold, sprang upon him to drag him forwards. My outstretched hands struck hard against the door, and I felt a thing like a spider's web envelop me. It seemed to draw itself over my mouth and eyes, and to blind and choke me, and then to flutter and tear and float from me.

Marcello was gone!

Detaille had slipped from Magnin's hold, and lay in a heap upon the floor, as though his limbs were broken. The Sister was trembling violently as she knelt over him and tried to raise his head. We gazed at one another, stooped and lifted him in our arms, and carried him back to his bed, while Sœur Marie quietly collected the broken phials.

"You saw it, *ma sœur?*" I heard Magnin whisper hoarsely.

"Yes, monsieur!" she only answered, in a trembling voice, holding on to her crucifix. Then she said in a professional tone—

"Will monsieur let me bind up his wrist?" And though her fingers trembled and his hand was shaking, the bandage was an irreproachable one.

Magnin went into the next room, and I heard him throw himself heavily into a chair. Detaille seemed to be sleeping. His breath came regularly; his eyes were closed with a look of peace about the lids, his hands lying in a natural way upon the quilt. He had not moved since we laid him there. I went softly to where Magnin was sitting in the dark. He did not move, but only said: "Marcello is dead!"

"He is either dead or dying," I answered, "and we must go to him."

"Yes," Magnin whispered, "we must go to him, but we shall not reach him."

"We will go as soon as it is light," I said, and then we were still again.

When the morning came at last he went and found a comrade to take his place, and only said to Sœur Marie, "It is not necessary to speak of this night," and at her quiet "You are right, monsieur," we felt we could trust her. Detaille was still sleeping. Was this the crisis the doctor had expected? Perhaps; but surely not in such fearful form. I insisted upon my companion having some breakfast before we started, and I breakfasted myself, but I cannot say I tasted what passed between my lips.

We engaged a closed carriage, for we did not know what we might bring home with us, though neither of us spoke out his thoughts. It was early morning still when we reached the Vigna Marziali, and we had not exchanged a word all the way. I rang at the bell, while the coachman looked on curiously. It was answered promptly by the *guardiano*, of whom Detaille has already told you.

"Where is the Signore?" I asked through the gate.

"*Chi lo sa?*" he answered. "He is here, of course; he has not left the Vigna. Shall I call him?"

"*Call him?*" I knew that no mortal voice could reach Marcello now, but I tried to fancy he was still alive.

"No," I said. "Let us in. We want to surprise him; he will be pleased."

The man hesitated, but he finally opened the gate, and we entered, leaving the carriage to wait outside. We went straight to the house; the door at the back was wide open. There had been a gale in the night, and it had torn some leaves and bits of twigs from the trees and blown them into the entrance hall. They lay scattered across the threshold, and were evidence that the door had remained open ever since they had fallen. The *guardiano* left us, probably to escape Marcello's anger at having let us in, and we went up the stairs unhindered, Magnin foremost, for he knew the house better than I, from Detaille's description. He had told him about the corner room with the balcony, and we pretended that Marcello might be there, absorbed betimes in his work, but we did not call him.

He was not there. His papers were strewn over the table as though he had been writing, but the inkstand was dry and full of dust; he could not have used it for days. We went silently into the other chambers. Perhaps he was still asleep? But, no! We found his bed untouched, so he could not have lain in it that night. The rooms were all unlocked but one, and this closed door made our hearts beat. Marcello could scarcely be there, however, for there was no key in the lock; I saw the daylight shining through the key-hole. We called his name, but there came no answer. We knocked loudly; still no sign from within; so I put my shoulder to the door, which was old and cracked in several places, and succeeded in bursting it open.

Nothing was there but a sculptor's modelling-stand, with something upon it covered with a white cloth, and the modelling-tools on the floor. At the sight of the cloth, still damp, we drew a deep breath. It could have hung there for many hours, certainly not for twenty-four. We did not raise it. "He would be vexed," said Magnin, and I nodded, for it is accounted almost a crime in the artist's world to unveil a sculptor's work behind his back. We expressed no surprise at the fact of his modelling: a ban seemed to lie upon our tongues. The cloth hung tightly to the object beneath it, and showed us the outline of a woman's head and rounded bust, and so veiled we left her. There was a little winding stair leading out of the passage, and we climbed it, to find ourselves in a sort of belvedere, commanding a superb view. It was a small, open terrace, on the roof of the house, and we saw at a glance that no one was there.

We had now been all over the casino, which was small and simply built, being evidently intended only for short summer use. As we stood leaning over the balustrade we could look down into the garden. No one was there but the *guardiano*, lying amongst his cabbages with his arms behind his head, half asleep. The laurel grove had been in my mind from the beginning, only it had seemed more natural to go to the house first. Now we descended the stairs silently and directed our steps thither.

As we approached it, the *guardiano* came towards us lazily.

"Have you seen the Signore?" he asked, and his stupidly placid face showed me that he, at least, had no hand in his disappearance.

"No, not yet," I answered, "but we shall come across him somewhere, no doubt. Perhaps he has gone to take a walk, and we will wait for him. What is this?" I went on, trying to seem careless. We were standing now by the little arch of which you know.

"This?" said he. "I have never been down there, but they say it is something old. Do the Signori want to see it? I will fetch a lantern."

I nodded, and he went off to his cabin. I had a couple of candles in my pocket, for I had intended to explore the place, should we not find Marcello. It was there that he had disappeared that night, and my thoughts had been busy with it; but I kept my candles concealed, reflecting that they would give our search an air of premeditation which would excite curiosity.

"When did you see the Signore last?" I asked, when he had returned with the lantern.

"I brought him his supper yesterday evening."

"At what o'clock?"

"It was the Ave Maria, Signore," he replied. "He always sups then."

It would be useless to put any further questions. He was evidently utterly unobserving, and would lie to please us.

"Let me go first," said Magnin, taking the lantern. We set our feet upon the steps; a cold air seemed to fill our lungs and yet to choke us, and a thick darkness lay beneath. The steps, as I could see by the light of my candle, were modern, as well as the vaulting above them. A tablet was let into the wall, and in spite of my excitement I paused to read it, perhaps because I was glad to delay whatever awaited us below. It ran thus:

"Questo antico sepolcro Romano scoprì il Conte Marziali nell' anno 1853, e piamente conservò." In plain English:

"Count Marziali discovered this ancient Roman sepulchre in the year 1853, and piously preserved it."

I read it more quickly than it has taken time to write here, and hurried after Magnin, whose footsteps sounded faintly below me. As I hastened, a draught of cold air extinguished my candle, and I was trying to make my way down by feeling along the wall, which was horribly dark and clammy, when my heart stood still at a cry from far beneath me—a cry of horror!

"Where are you?" I shouted; but Magnin was calling my name, and could not hear me. "I am here. I am in the dark!"

I was making haste as fast as I could, but there were several turnings.

"I have found him!" came up from below.

"Alive?" I shouted. No answer.

One last short flight brought me face to face with the gleam of the lantern. It came from a low doorway, and within stood Magnin peering into the darkness. I knew by his face, as he held the light high above him, that our fears were realized.

Yes; Marcello was there. He was lying stretched upon the floor, staring at the ceiling, dead, and already stiff, as I could see at a glance. We stood over him, saying not a word, then I knelt down and felt him, for mere form's sake, and said, as though I had not known it before, "He has been dead for some hours."

"Since yesterday evening," said Magnin in a horror-stricken voice, yet with a certain satisfaction in it, as though to say, "You see, I was right."

Marcello was lying with his head slightly thrown back, no contortions in his handsome features; rather the look of a person who has quietly died of exhaustion—who has slipped unconsciously from life to death. His collar was thrown open and a part of his breast, of a ghastly white, was visible. Just over the heart was a small spot.

"Give me the lantern," I whispered, as I stooped over it. It was a very little spot, of a faint purplish-brown, and must have changed colour within the night.

I examined it intently, and should say that the blood had been sucked to the surface, and then a small prick or incision made. The slight subcutaneous effusion led me to this conclusion. One tiny drop of coagulated blood closed the almost imperceptible wound. I probed it with the end of one of Magnin's matches. It was scarcely more than skin deep, so it could not be the stab of a stiletto, however slender, or the track of a bullet. Still, it was strange, and with one impulse we turned to see if no one were concealed there, or if there were no second exit. It would be madness to suppose that the murderer, if there was one, would remain by his victim. Had Marcello been making love to a pretty *contadina*, and was this some jealous lover's vengeance? But it was not a stab. Had one drop of poison in the little wound done this deadly work?

We peered about the place, and I saw that Magnin's eyes were blinded by tears and his face as pale as that upturned one on the floor, whose lids I had vainly tried to close. The chamber was low, and beautifully ornamented with stucco bas-reliefs, in the manner of the well-known one not far from there upon the same road. Winged genii, griffins, and arabesques, modelled with marvellous lightness, covered the walls and ceiling. There was no other door than the one we had entered by. In the centre stood a marble sarcophagus, with the usual subjects sculptured upon it, on the one side Hercules conducting a veiled figure, on the other a dance of nymphs and fauns. A space in the middle contained the following inscription, deeply cut in the stone, and still partially filled with red pigment:

D. M.

VESPERTILIAE•THC•

ΑΙΜΑΤΟΠΩΤΙΔΟC • Q • FLAVIVS •

VIX•IPSE•SOSPES•MON•

POSVIT

"What is this?" whispered Magnin. It was only a pickaxe and a long crowbar, such as the country people use in hewing out their blocks of "tufa," and his foot had struck against them. Who could have brought them here? They must belong to the *guardiano* above, but he said that he had never come here, and I believed him, knowing the Italian horror of darkness and lonely places; but what had Marcello wanted with them? It did not occur to us that archaeological curiosity could have led him to attempt to open the sarcophagus, the lid of which had evidently never been raised, thus justifying the expression "piously preserved."

As I rose from examining the tools my eyes fell upon the line of mortar where the cover joined to the stone below, and I noticed that some of it had been removed, perhaps with the pickaxe which lay at my feet. I tried it with my nails and found that it was very crumbly. Without a word I took the tool in my hand, Magnin instinctively following my movements with the lantern. What impelled us I do not know. I had myself no thought, only an irresistible desire to see what was within. I saw that much of the mortar had been broken away, and lay in small fragments upon the ground, which I had not noticed before. It did not take long to complete the work. I snatched the lantern from Magnin's hand and set it upon the ground, where it shone full upon Marcello's dead face, and by its light I found a little break between the two masses of stone and managed to insert the end of my crowbar, driving it in with a blow of the pickaxe. The stone chipped and then cracked a little. Magnin was shivering.

"What are you going to do?" he said, looking around at where Marcello lay.

"Help me!" I cried, and we two bore with all our might upon the crowbar. I am a strong man, and I felt a sort of blind fury as the stone refused to yield. What if the bar should snap? With another blow I drove it in still further, then using it as a lever, we weighed upon it with our outstretched arms until every muscle was at its highest tension. The stone moved a little, and almost fainting we stopped to rest.

From the ceiling hung the rusty remnant of an iron chain which must once have held a lamp. To this, by scrambling upon the sarcophagus, I contrived to make fast the lantern.

"Now!" said I, and we heaved again at the lid. It rose, and we alternately heaved and pushed until it lost its balance and fell with a thundering crash upon the other side; such a crash that the walls seemed to shake, and I was for a moment utterly deafened, while little pieces of stucco rained upon us from the ceiling. When we had paused to recover from the shock we leaned over the sarcophagus and looked in.

The light shone full upon it, and we saw—how is it possible to tell? We saw lying there, amidst folds of mouldering rags, the body of a woman, perfect as in life, with faintly rosy face, soft crimson lips, and a breast of living pearl, which seemed to heave as though stirred by some delicious dream. The rotten stuff swathed about her was in ghastly contrast to this lovely form, fresh as the morning! Her hands lay stretched at her side, the pink palms were turned a little outwards, her eyes were closed as peacefully as those of a sleeping child, and her long hair, which shone red-gold in the dim light from above, was wound around her head in numberless finely plaited tresses, beneath which little locks escaped in rings upon her brow. I could have sworn that the blue veins on that divinely perfect bosom held living blood!

We were absolutely paralyzed, and Magnin leaned gasping over the edge as pale as death, paler by far than this living, almost smiling face to which his eyes were glued. I do not doubt that I was as pale as he at this inexplicable vision. As I looked the red lips seemed to grow redder. They *were* redder! The little pearly teeth showed between them. I had not seen them before, and now a clear ruby drop trickled down to her rounded chin and from there slipped sideways and fell upon her neck. Horror-struck I gazed upon the living corpse, till my eyes could not bear the sight any longer. As I looked away my glance fell once more upon the inscription, but now I could see—*and read*—it all. "To Vespertilia"—that was in Latin, and even the Latin name of the woman suggested a thing of evil flitting in the dusk. But the full horror of the nature of that thing had been veiled to Roman eyes under the Greek τῆζ αἱματοπωίδοζ, "the blooddrinker, the vampire woman." And Flavius—her lover—*vix ipse sospes*, "himself hardly saved" from that deadly embrace, had buried her here, and set a seal upon her sepulchre, trusting to the weight of stone and the strength of clinging mortar to imprison for ever the beautiful monster he had loved.

"Infamous murderess!" I cried. "You have killed Marcello!" And a sudden, vengeful calm came over me.

"Give me the pickaxe," I said to Magnin; I can hear myself saying it still. He picked it up and handed it to me as in a dream; he seemed little better than an idiot, and the beads of sweat were shining on his forehead. I took my knife, and from the long wooden handle of the pickaxe I cut a fine, sharp stake. Then I clambered, scarcely feeling any repugnance, over the side of the sarcophagus, my feet amongst the folds of Vespertilia's decaying winding-sheet, which crushed like ashes beneath my boot.

I looked for one moment at that white breast, but only to choose the loveliest spot, where the network of azure veins shimmered like veiled turquoises, and then with one blow I drove the pointed stake deep down through the breathing snow and stamped it in with my heel.

An awful shriek, so ringing and horrible that I thought my ears must have burst; but even then I felt neither fear nor horror. There are times when these cannot touch us. I stopped and gazed once again at the face, now undergoing a fearful change—fearful and final!

"Foul vampire!" I said quietly in my concentrated rage. "You will do no more harm now!" And then, without looking back upon her cursed face, I clambered out of the horrible tomb.

We raised Marcello, and slowly carried him up the steep stairs—a difficult task, for the way was narrow and he was so stiff. I noticed that the steps were ancient up to the end of the second flight; above, the modern passage was somewhat broader. When we reached the top, the *guardiano* was lying upon one of the stone benches; he did not mean us to cheat him out of his fee. I gave him a couple of francs.

"You see that we have found the Signore," I tried to say in a natural voice. "He is very weak, and we will carry him to the carriage." I had thrown my handkerchief over Marcello's face, but the man knew as well as I did that he was dead. Those stiff feet told their own story, but Italians are timid of being involved in such affairs. They have a childish dread of the police, and he only answered, "Poor Signorino! He is very ill; it is better to take him to Rome," and kept cautiously clear of us as we went up to the ilex alley with our icy burden, and he did not go to the gate with us, not liking to be observed by the coachman who was dozing on his box. With difficulty we got Marcello's corpse into the carriage, the driver turning to look at us suspiciously. I explained we had found our friend very ill, and at the same time slipped a gold piece into his hand, telling him to drive to the Via del Governo Vecchio. He pocketed the money, and whipped his horses into a trot, while we sat supporting the stiff body, which swayed like a broken doll at every pebble in the road. When we reached the Via del Governo Vecchio at last, no one saw us carry him into the house. There was no step before the door, and we drew up so close to it that it was possible to screen our burden from sight. When we had brought him into his room and laid him upon his bed, we noticed that his eyes were closed; from the movement of the carriage, perhaps, though that was scarcely possible. The landlady behaved very much as I had expected her to do, for, as I told you, I know the Italians. She pretended, too, that the Signore was very ill, and made a pretence of offering to fetch a doctor, and when I thought it best to tell her that he was dead, declared that it must have happened that very moment, for she had seen him look at us and close his eyes again. She had always told him that he ate too little and that he would be ill. Yes, it was weakness and that bad air out there which had killed him; and then he worked too hard. When she had successfully established this fiction, which we were glad enough to agree to, for neither did we wish for the publicity of an inquest, she ran out and fetched a gossip to come and keep her company.

So died Marcello Souvestre, and so died Vespertilia the blood-drinker at last.

There is not much more to tell. Marcello lay calm and beautiful upon his bed, and the students came and stood silently looking at him, then knelt down for a moment to say a prayer, crossed themselves, and left him for ever.

We hastened to the Villa Medici, where Detaille was sleeping, and Sister Claudius watching him with a satisfied look on her strong face. She rose noiselessly at our entrance, and came to us at the threshold.

"He will recover," said she, softly. She was right. When he awoke and opened his eyes he knew us directly, and Magnin breathed a devout "Thank God!"

"Have I been ill, Magnin?" he asked, very feebly.

"You have had a little fever," answered Magnin, promptly, "but it is over now. Here is Monsieur Sutton come to see you."

"Has Marcello been here?" was the next question. Magnin looked at him very steadily.

"No," he only said, letting his face tell the rest.

"Is he dead, then?" Magnin only bowed his head.

"Poor friend!" Detaille murmured to himself, then closed his heavy eyes and slept again.

A few days after Marcello's funeral we went to the fatal Vigna Marziali to bring back the objects which had belonged to him. As I laid the manuscript score of the opera carefully together, my eye fell upon a passage which struck me as the identical one which Detaille had so constantly sung in his delirium, and which I noted down. Strange to say, when I reminded him of it later, it was perfectly new to him, and he declared that Marcello had not let him examine his manuscript. As for the veiled bust in the other room, we left it undisturbed, and to crumble away unseen.

THE VAMPIRE

◆◆◆

VASILE ALECSANDRI

Near the cliff's sharp edge, on high
Standing out against the sky,
Dost thou see a ruined cross
Weatherstained, o'ergrown by moss,
Gloomy, desolate, forsaken,
By unnumbered tempests shaken?

Not a blade of grass grows nigh it,
Not a peasant lingers by it.
E'en the sombre bird of night
Shuns it in her darksome flight,
Startled by the piteous groan
That arises from the stone.

All around, on starless nights,
Myriad hosts of livid lights
Flicker fretfully, revealing
At its foot a phantom, kneeling
Whilst it jabbers dismal plaints,
Cursing God and all the saints.

Tardy traveller, beware
Of that spectre gibbering there;
Close your eyes, and urge your steed
To the utmost of his speed;—
For beneath that cross, I ween,
Lies a Vampyre's corpse obscene!

Though the night is black and cold
Love's fond story, often told,
Floats in whispers through the air.
Stalwart youth and maiden fair
Seal sweet vows of ardent passion
With their lips, in lovers' fashion.

Restless, pale, a shape I see
Hov'ring nigh; what may it be?
'Tis a charger, white as snow,
Pacing slowly to and fro
Like a sentry. As he turns
Haughtily the sward he spurns.

"Leave me not, beloved, tonight!
Stay with me till morning's light!"
Weeping, thus besought the maid;
"Love, my soul is sore afraid!
Brave not the dread Vampyre's power,
Mightiest at this mystic hour!"

Not a word he spake, but prest
The sobbing maiden to his breast;
Kissed her lips and cheeks and eyes
Heedless of her tears and sighs;
Waved his hand, with gesture gay,
Mounted—smiled—and rode away.

Who rides across the dusky plain
Tearing along with might and main
Like some wild storm-fiend, in his flight
Nursed on the ebony breast of Night?
'Tis he, who left her in her need—
Her lover, on his milk-white steed!

The blast in all its savage force
Strives to o'erthrow the gallant horse
That snorts defiance to his foe
And struggles onward. See! below
The causeway, 'long the river-side
A thousand flutt'ring flamelets glide!

Now they approach and now recede,
Still followed by the panting steed;
He nears the ruined cross! A crash,
A piteous cry, a heavy splash,
And in the rocky river-bed
Rider and horse lie crushed and dead.

Then from those dismal depths arise
Blaspheming yells and strident cries
Re-echoing through the murky air.
And, like a serpent from its lair,
Brandishing high a blood-stained glaive
The Vampyre rises from his grave!

— TRANSLATED INTO ENGLISH BY
WILLIAM BEATTY-KINGSTON

DUTY

✦✦✦

ED GORMAN

Earlier this morning, just as the sun had begun to burn
the dew off the farm fields, Keller got out his old
Schwinn and set off. In less than a minute, he'd left behind the tar-paper shack where he lived with a goat,
three chickens he'd never had the heart to eat, four cats,
and a hamster. The hamster had been Timmy's.

Today he traveled the old two-lane highway. The sun
hot on his back, he thought of how it used to be on this
stretch of asphalt, the bright red convertibles with the
bright pink blondes in them and the sound of rock and
roll waving like a banner in the wind. Or the green John
Deere tractors moving snail-slow, trailing infuriated city
drivers behind.

The old days. Before the change. He used to sit in a
chair in front of his shack and talk to his wife, Martha,
and his son, Timmy, till Timmy went to sleep in
Martha's lap. Then Keller would take the boy inside and
lay him gently in bed and kiss the boy-moist brow good
night. The Kellers had always been referred to locally,
and not unkindly, as "that hippie family." Keller had

worn the tag as a badge of honor. In a world obsessed with money and power, he'd wanted to spend his days discovering again and again the simple pleasures of starry nights, of clear quick country streams, of mountain music strummed on an old six-string and accompanied by owls and kitties and crocuses. Somehow back in time he'd managed to get himself an advanced degree in business and finance. But after meeting Martha, the happiest and most contented person he'd ever known, he'd followed her out here and he never once yearned for the treacherous world he'd deserted.

He thought of these things as he angled the Schwinn down the center of the highway, his golden collie, Andy, running alongside, appreciative of the exercise. Across Keller's shoulder was strapped his ancient backpack, the one he'd carried twenty years ago in college. You could see faintly where the word *Adidas* had been.

He rode on. The Schwinn's chain was loose and banged noisily sometimes, and so on a particularly hard bump the front fender sometimes rubbed the tire. He fixed the bike methodically, patiently, at least once a week, but the Schwinn was like a wild boy and would never quite be tamed. Timmy had been that way.

The trip took two hours. By that time, Andy was tired of running, his pink tongue lolling out of his mouth, exhausted, and Keller was tired of pedaling.

The farmhouse was up a high sloping hill, east of the highway.

From his backpack Keller took his binoculars. He

spent ten minutes scanning the place. He had no idea what he was looking for. He just wanted to reassure himself that the couple who'd sent the message with Conroy—a pig farmer ten miles to the west of Keller's—were who and what they claimed to be.

He saw a stout woman in a faded housedress hanging laundry on a backyard clothesline. He saw a sun-reddened man in blue overalls moving among a waving carpet of white hungry chickens, throwing them golden kernels of corn. He saw a windmill turning with rusty dignity in the southern wind.

After returning his binoculars to his backpack, he mounted the Schwinn again, patted Andy on the head, and set off up the steep gravel hill.

The woman saw Keller first. He had come around the edge of the big two-story frame house when she was just finishing with her laundry.

She looked almost angry when she saw who he was.

She didn't speak to him; instead, she called out in a weary voice for her husband. Somehow, the man managed to hear her above the squawking chickens. He set down the tin pan that held the kernels of corn, then walked over and stood by his wife.

"You're a little early," the farmer said. His name was Dodds, Alcie Dodds, and his wife was Myrna. Keller used to see them at the potluck dinners the community held back before the change.

"I wasn't sure how long it would take. Guess I left a little before I needed to."

"You enjoy what you do, Mr. Keller? Does it give you pleasure?" Myrna Dodds said.

"Now, Myrna, don't be—"

"I just want him to answer the question. I just want him to answer honestly."

By now, Keller was used to being treated this way. It was, he knew, a natural reaction.

Alcie Dodds said, "She hasn't had much sleep the last couple of nights, Keller. You know what I'm saying."

Keller nodded.

"You want a cup of coffee?" Alcie Dodds said.

"I'd appreciate it."

Suddenly the woman started crying. She put her hands to her face and simply began wailing, her fleshy body shaking beneath the loose-fitting housedress.

Keller saw such grief everywhere he went. He wished there was something he could do about it.

Dodds went over and slid his arm around his wife. "Why don't you go in and see Beth, honey?"

Mention of the name only caused the woman to begin sobbing even more uncontrollably.

She took her hands from her face and glared at Keller. "I hope you rot in hell, Mr. Keller. I hope you rot in hell."

Shadows cooled the kitchen. The air smelled of the stew bubbling on the stove, of beef and tomatoes and onions and paprika.

The two men sat at a small kitchen table beneath a funeral home calendar that had a picture of Jesus as a young and very handsome bearded man. By now, they were on their second cup of coffee.

"Sorry about the missus."

"I understand. I'd feel the same way."

"We always assume it won't happen to us."

"Ordinarily, they don't get out this far. It isn't worth it for them. They stick to cities, or at least areas where the population is heavy."

"But they do get out here," Dodds said. "More often than people like to admit."

Keller sighed. He stared down into his coffee cup. "I guess that's true."

"I hear it happened to you."

"Yes."

"Your boy."

"Right."

"The fucking bastards. The fucking bastards." Dodds made a large fist and brought it down thunderously on the table that smelled of the red-and-white checkered oil-cloth. In the window above the sink the sky was very blue and the blooming trees very green.

After a time, Dodds said, "You ever seen one? In person, I mean?"

"No."

"We did once. We were in Chicago. We were supposed to get back to our hotel room before dusk, before they came out into the streets but we got lost. Anybody ever tell you about their smell?"

"Yes."

"It's like rotting meat. You can't believe it. Especially when a lot of them are in one place at the same time. And they've got these sores all over them. Like leprosy. We made it back to the hotel all right, but before we did we saw these two young children—they'd turned already—they found this old lady and they started chasing her, having a good time with her, really prolonging it, and then she tripped in the street and one of them knelt beside her and went to work. You heard about how they puke afterward?"

"Yes. The shock to their digestive systems. All the blood."

"Never saw anybody puke like this. And the noise they made when they were puking. Sickening. Then the old lady got up and let out this cry. I've never heard anything even close to it. Just this loud animal noise. She was already starting to turn."

Keller finished his coffee.

"You want more?"

"No, thanks, Mr. Dodds."

"You want a Pepsi? Got a six-pack we save for special occasions." He shrugged. "I'm not much of a liquor drinker."

"No, thanks, Mr. Dodds."

Dodds drained his own coffee. "Can I ask you something?"

"Sure."

It was time to get it over with. Dodds was stalling. Keller didn't blame him.

"You ever find that you're wrong?"

"How so, Mr. Dodds?"

"You know, that you think they've turned but they really haven't?"

Keller knew what Dodds was trying to say, of course. He was trying to say—to whatever God existed—please let it be a mistake. Please let it not be what it seems to be.

"Not so far, I haven't, Mr. Dodds. I'm sorry."

"You know how it's going to be on her, don't you, on my wife?"

"Yes, I'm afraid I do, Mr. Dodds."

"She won't ever be the same."

"No, I don't suppose she will."

Dodds stared down at his hands and turned them into fists again. Under his breath, he said, "Fucking bastards."

"Maybe we'd better go have a look, Mr. Dodds."

"You sure you don't want another cup of coffee?"

"No, thanks, Mr. Dodds. I appreciate the offer, though."

Dodds led him through the cool, shadowy house. The place was old. You could tell that by all the mahogany trim and the height of the ceilings and the curve of the time-swollen floor. But even given its age it was a pleasant and comfortable place, a nook of sweet shade on a hot day.

Down the hall Keller could hear Mrs. Dodds singing, humming really, soft noises rather than words.

"Forgive her if she acts up again, Mr. Keller."

Keller nodded.

And it was then the rock came sailing through the window in the front room. The smashing glass had an almost musical quality to it on the hot silent afternoon.

"What the hell was that?" Dodds wondered.

He turned around and ran back down the pink wallpapered hall and right out the front door, almost slamming the screen door in Keller's face.

There were ten of them on the lawn, in the shade of the elm, six men, four women. Two of the men held carbines.

"There he is," one of the men said.

"That sonofabitch Keller," another man said.

"You people get out of here, and now," Dodds said, coming down off the porch steps. "This is my land."

"You really gonna let him do it, Alcie?" a man said.

"That's my business," Dodds said, pawing at the front of his coveralls.

A pretty woman leaned forward. "I'm sorry we came, Alcie. The men just wouldn't have it any other way. Us women just came along to make sure there wasn't no violence."

"Speak for yourself, honey," a plump woman in a man's checkered shirt and jeans said. "Personally, I'd like to cut Keller's balls off and feed 'em to my pigs."

Two of the men laughed at her. She'd said it to impress them and she'd achieved her end.

"Go on, now, before somethin' is said or done that can't be unsaid or undone," Dodds said.

"Your wife want this done?" the man with the second carbine said. He answered his own question: "Bet she don't. Bet she fought you on it all the way."

A soft breeze came. It was an afternoon for drinking lemonade and watching monarch butterflies and seeing the foals in the pasture running up and down the summer green hills. It was not an afternoon for angry men with carbines.

"You heard me now," Dodds said.

"How 'bout you, chickenshit? You got anything to say for yourself, Keller?"

"Goddamnit, Davey—" Dodds started to say.

"Won't use my gun, Alcie. Don't need it."

And with that the man named Davey tossed his carbine to one of the other men and then stepped up near the steps where Dodds and Keller stood.

Keller recognized Davey. He ran the feed and grain in town and was a legendary tavern bully. God forbid you should ever beat him at snooker. He had freckles like a pox and fists like anvils.

"You hear what I asked you, chickenshit?"

"Davey—" Dodds started to say again.

Keller stepped down off the steps. He was close enough to smell the afternoon beer on Davey's breath.

"This wasn't easy for Mr. Dodds, Davey," Keller said. He spoke so softly Davey's friends had to lean forward to hear. "But it's his decision to make. His and his wife's."

"You enjoy it, don't you, chickenshit?" Davey said. "You're some kind of pervert who gets his kicks that way, aren't you?"

Behind him, his friends started cursing Keller, and that only emboldened Davey all the more.

He threw a big roundhouse right and got Keller right in the mouth.

Keller started to drop to the ground, black spots alternating with yellow spots before his eyes, and then Davey raised his right foot and kicked Keller square in the chest.

"Kill that fucker, Davey! Kill that fucker!" one of the men with the carbines shouted.

And then, on the sinking afternoon, the shotgun was fired.

The bird shot got so close to Davey that it tore tiny holes in his right sleeve, like something that had been gnawed on by a puppy.

"You heard my husband," Mrs. Dodds said, standing on the porch with a sawed-off double barrel that looked to be one mean and serious weapon. "You get off our land."

Davey said, "We was only tryin' to help you, missus. We knew you didn't want—"

But she silenced him. "I was wrong about Keller here. If he didn't care about them, he couldn't do it. He had to do it to his own wife and son, or are you forgetting that?"

Davey said, "But—"

And Mrs. Dodds leveled the shotgun right at his chest. "You think I won't kill you, Davey, you're wrong."

Davey's wife took him by the sleeve. "C'mon, honey; you can't see she's serious."

But Davey had one last thing to say. "It ain't right what he does. Don't you know that, Mrs. Dodds? It ain't right!"

But Mrs. Dodds could only sadly shake her head. "You know what'd become of 'em if he didn't do it, don't you? Go into the city sometime and watch 'em. Then tell me you'd want one of your own to be that way."

Davey's wife tugged on his sleeve again. Then she looked up at Mrs. Dodds and said, "I'm sorry for this, Mrs. Dodds. I really am. The boys here just had too much to drink and—" She shook her head. "I'm sorry."

And in ones and twos they started drifting back to the pickup trucks they'd parked on the downslope side of the gravel drive.

"It's a nice room," Keller said twenty minutes later. And it was. The wallpaper was blue. Teddy bears and unicorns cavorted across it. There was a tiny table and chairs and a globe and a set of junior encyclopedias, things she would grow up to use someday. Or would have, anyway.

In the corner was the baby's bed. Mrs. Keller stood in front of it, protecting it. "I'm sorry how I treated you when you first came."

"I know."

"And I'm sorry Davey hit you."

"Not your fault."

By now he realized that she was not only stalling. She was also doing something else—pleading. "You look at little Beth and you be sure."

"I will."

"I've heard tales of how sometimes you think they've turned but it's just some other illness with the same symptoms."

"I'll be very careful."

Mr. Dodds said, "You want us to leave the room?"

"It'd be better for your wife."

And then she spun around and looked down into the baby's bed where her seven-month-old daughter lay discolored and breathing as if she could not catch her breath, both primary symptoms of the turning.

She picked the infant up and clutched it to her chest. And began sobbing so loudly, all Keller could do was put his head down.

It fell to Mr. Dodds to pry the baby from his wife's grip and to lead Mrs. Dodds from the baby's room.

On his way out, starting to cry a man's hard embarrassed tears, Mr. Dodds looked straight at Keller and said, "Just be sure, Mr. Keller. Just be sure."

Keller nodded that he'd be sure.

The room smelled of sunlight and shade and baby powder.

The bed had the sort of slatted sides you could pull up or down. He put it down and leaned over to the baby. She was very pretty, chunky, blond, with a cute little mouth. She wore diapers. They looked very white compared to the blue, asphyxiated color of her skin.

His examination was simple. The Dodds could easily have done it themselves, but of course they didn't want to. It would only have confirmed their worst fears.

He opened her mouth. She started to cry. He first examined her gums and then her teeth. The tissue on the former had started to harden and scab; the latter had started to elongate.

The seven-month-old child was in the process of turning.

Sometimes they roamed out here from the cities and took what they could find. One of them had broken into the Dodds' two weeks ago and had stumbled on the baby's room.

He worked quickly, as he always did, as he'd done with his wife and son when they'd been ambushed in the woods one day and had then started to turn.

All that was left of civilization was in the outlands such as these. Even though you loved them, you could not let them turn because the life ahead for them was so unimaginably terrible. The endless hunt for new bodies, the feeding frenzies, the constant illness that was a part of the condition and the condition was forever—

No, if you loved them, you had only one choice.

In this farming community, no one but Keller could bring himself to do what was necessary. They always deluded themselves that their loved ones hadn't really been infected, hadn't really begun turning—

And so it fell to Keller.

He rummaged quickly through his Adidas backpack now, finding hammer and wooden stake.

He returned to the bed and leaned over and kissed the little girl on the forehead. "You'll be with God, honey," he said. "You'll be with God."

He stood up straight, took the stake in his left hand and set it against her heart, and then with great sad weariness raised the hammer.

He killed her as he killed them all, clean and quick, hot infected blood splattering his face and shirt, her final cry one more wound in his soul.

On the porch, Mrs. Dodds inside in her bedroom, Mr. Dodds put his hand on Keller's shoulder and said, "I'll pray for you, Mr. Keller."

"I'll be needing your prayers, Mr. Dodds," Keller said, and then nodded good-bye and left.

In half an hour, he was well down the highway again, Andy getting another good run for the day, pink tongue lolling.

In his backpack he could feel the sticky hammer and stake, the same tools he used over and over again as the sickness of the cities spread constantly outward.

In a while it began to rain. He was still thinking of the little Dodds girl, of her innocent eyes there at the very last.

He did not seem to notice the rain, or the soft quick darkness.

He rode on, the bicycle chain clattering, the front wheel wobbling from the twisted fender, and Andy stopping every quarter mile or so to shake the rain off.

The fucking sonsofbitches, he thought.

The fucking sonsofbitches.

THE MEN & WOMEN OF RIVENDALE

•••

STEVE RASNIC TEM

The thing he would remember most about his days, his weeks at the Rivendale resort—had it really been weeks?—was not the enormous lobby and dining room, nor the elaborately carved mahogany woodwork framing the library, nor even the men and women of Rivendale themselves, with their bright eyes and pale, almost hairless, heads and hands. The thing he would remember most was the room he and Cathy stayed in, the way she looked when she curled up in bed, her bald head rising weakly over her shoulders, the way the dark brocade curtains hung so heavily, trapping dust and light in their intricate folds.

Frank thought he had spent days staring into those folds. He had only two places to look in that room: at the cancer-ridden sack his wife had become, her giant eyes, her grotesque, baby-like face, so stripped of age since she had begun her decline. Or at the curtains, adrift constantly with shadows. They were of a dark, burgundy-colored material, and he never knew if they had darkened with dust and age or if they were meant to be just that shade. If he examined the curtains at close range he could make out the tiny leaf and shell patterns embroidered over the entire surface. From a distance, when he sat in the chair or lay on the bed, they looked like hundreds of tiny, hungry mouths.

Cathy had told him little about the place before they came—that it was a resort in Pennsylvania, in the countryside south of Erie, and that it used to have a hot springs. He hadn't asked, but he wondered what happened to the spring water when it left such a place. As if somebody somewhere had turned a tap. It didn't make any sense to him; natural things shouldn't work that way.

Her ancestors, the family Rivendale, had run the place when it was still a resort. Now many, perhaps all, of her relatives lived in the Rivendale Resort Hotel, or in cottages spotted around the sprawling grounds. Probably several dozen cottages in all. It had been quite a jolt when Frank walked into the place, stumbling over the entrance rug with their luggage wedged under his arms, and saw all these Rivendales sitting around the fireplace in the lobby. It wasn't as if they were clones, or anything like that. But there was this uneasy sort of family resemblance. Something about the fleshtones, the shape of the hands, the perpetually arched eyebrows, the sharp angle at which they held their heads, the irregular pink splotches on their cheeks. It gave him a little chill. After a few days at Rivendale he recognized part of the reason for that chill: the cancer had molded Cathy into a fuzzy copy of a Rivendale.

Frank remembered her as another woman entirely: her hair had been long and honey-brown, and there had been real color in her cheeks. She had been lively, her movements strong and fluid, an incredibly sleek, beautiful woman who could have been a model, though such a public display would have appalled her and, he knew without asking, would have disgraced the Rivendale name.

Cathy had told him that filling up with cancer was like roasting under a hot sun sometimes. The dusty rooms and dark chambers of Rivendale cooled her. They would stay at Rivendale as long as possible, she had said. She could hide from nurses and doctors there.

She wouldn't have surgery. She was a Rivendale; it didn't fit. She washed herself in radiation and, after Frank met these other Rivendales with their scrubbed and antiseptic flesh, the thought came to him: she'd over-bathed.

She never looked or smelled bad, as he'd expected. The distortions the growing cancer made within the skin that covered it were more subtle than that. Sometimes she complained of her legs suddenly weakening. Sometimes she would scream in the middle of the night. He'd look at her pale form and try to see through her translucent flesh, find the cancer feeding and thriving there.

One result of her treatments was that Cathy's belly blew up. She looked at least six months pregnant, maybe more. It had never occurred to either of them to have children. They'd always had too much to do; a child didn't have a place in the schedule. Sometimes now Frank dreamed he was wheeling her into the delivery room, running, trying to get her to the doctors before her terrible labor ceased. A tall doctor in a brilliant white mask always met him at the wide, swinging doors. The doctor took Cathy away from him but blocked Frank from seeing what kind of child they delivered from her heaving, discolored belly.

Nine months after the cancer was diagnosed, the invitation from the Rivendales was delivered. Cathy, who'd barely mentioned her family in all the years they'd been married, welcomed it with a grim excitement he'd never seen in her before. Frank discovered the invitation in the trash later that afternoon. "Come to Rivendale" was all it said.

One of the uncles greeted her at the desk, although "greeted" was probably the wrong word. He checked her in, as if this were still a resort. Even gave her a room key with the resort tag still attached, although now the leather was cracked and the silver lettering hard to read. Only a few of the relatives had bothered to look up from their reading, their mouths twitching as if they were attempting speech after years of muteness. But no one spoke; no one welcomed them. As far as Frank could tell, no one in the crowded, quiet lobby was speaking to anyone else.

They'd gone up to their room immediately; the trip had exhausted Cathy. Then Frank spent his first of many evenings sitting up in the old chair, staring at Cathy curled up on the bed, and staring at the curtains breathing the breeze from the window, the indecipherable embroidered patterns shifting restlessly.

The next morning they were awakened by a bell ringing downstairs. The sound was so soft Frank at first thought it was a dream, wind-chimes tinkling outside. But Cathy was up immediately, and dressing. Frank did the same, suddenly not wanting to initiate any action by himself. When another bell rang Cathy opened the door and started downstairs, and Frank followed her.

Two places were set for them at one of the long, linen-draped tables. "Cathy" and "Frank," the place cards read. He wondered briefly if there might be someone else staying here by those names, so surprised he was to see his name written on the card in floral script. But Cathy took her chair immediately, and he sat down beside her.

There was a silent toast. When the uncle who had met them at the desk tapped his glass of apple wine lightly with a fork the rest raised their glasses silently to the air, then a beat later tipped them back to drink. Cathy drank in time with the others, and that simple bit of coordination and exaggerated manners made Frank uneasy. He remained one step behind all the others, watching them over the lip of his glass. They didn't seem aware of each other, but they were almost, though not quite, synchronized.

He glanced at Cathy; her cheek had grown pale and taut as she drank. She wasn't eating real food anymore, only a special formula she took like medicine to sustain her. Although her skin was almost baby-smooth now, the lack of fat had left wrinkles that deepened as she moved. Death lines.

After breakfast they lingered by the enormous dining room window. Cathy watched as the Rivendales drifted across the front lawn in twos and threes. Their movements were slow and languid like ancient fish in shallow, sun-drenched waters.

"Shouldn't we introduce ourselves around?" Frank said softly. "I mean, we were invited by someone. How do these people even know who we are?"

"Oh, they know, Frank. Hush now; the Rivendales have always had their own way of doing things. Someone will come to us in time. Meanwhile, we enjoy ourselves."

"Sure."

They took a long walk around the grounds. The pool was closed and covered with canvas. The shuffleboard courts were cracked, the cracks pulled further apart by grass and tree roots. And the tennis courts . . . the tennis courts were his first inkling that perhaps he should be trying to convince her of the need to return home.

The tennis courts at Rivendale were built atop a slight, tree-shaded rise behind the main building. He heard the yowling and screeching as they climbed the rise, so loud that he couldn't make out any individual voices. It frightened him so that he grabbed Cathy by the arm and started back down. But she seemed unperturbed by the noise and shrugged away from him, continuing to walk toward the trees, her pace unchanging.

"Cathy . . . I don't think . . ." But she was oblivious to him.

So Frank followed her, reluctantly. As they neared the fenced enclosure the howling increased, and Frank knew that it wasn't people in there making all the noise, but animals, though he had never heard animal sounds quite like those.

As they passed the last tree Frank stopped, unable to proceed; Cathy walked right up to the fence. She pressed close to the wire, but not so close the outstretched paws could touch her.

The tennis courts had become a gigantic cage holding hundreds of cats. An old man stood on a ladder above the wire fence, dumping buckets of feed onto the snarling mass inside. Mesh with glass insulators attached— *electrified*, Frank thought—stretched across the top of the fence.

The old man turned to Frank and stared. He had the arched eyebrows, the pale skin and blotched cheeks. He smiled at Frank, and the shape of the lips seemed to match the shape of the eyebrows. A smile shaped like moth wings, or a bite-pattern in pale cheese, the teeth gleaming snow-white inside.

Cathy spent most of each day in the expansive Rivendale library, checking titles most of the time, but occasionally sitting down to read from a rare and privately-bound old volume. Every few hours one of the uncles, or cousins, would come in and speak to her in a low voice, nod, and leave. The longer he was here the more difficult it became to tell the Rivendales apart, other than male from female. The younger ones mirrored the older ones, and they were all very close in height, weight, and build.

When Cathy wasn't in the library she sat quietly in the parlor or dining room, or up in their own room catnapping or staring up at the ornate ceiling. She would say every day, almost ritualistically, that he was more than welcome to be with her, but he could see nothing here that he might participate in. Sitting in the parlor or dining room was made almost unbearable by the presence of the family, arranged mummy-like around the rooms. Sometimes he would pick up a volume in the library, but invariably discovered it was some sort of laborious tome on trellis and ornate gardening, French architecture, museum catalogs. Or sometimes an old leather-bound novel that read no better. It was impossible to peruse the books without thinking that whatever Cathy was studying must be far more interesting, but on the days he went he never could find the books she had been looking at, as if they had been kept somewhere special, out of his reach.

And for some reason he hesitated to ask after them, or to look over his wife's shoulder as she read. As if he was afraid to.

This growing climate of awkwardness and fear angered Frank so that his neck muscles were always stiff, his head always aching. It was worse because it wasn't entirely unexpected. His relationship with Cathy had been going in this direction for some time. Until he'd met Cathy, he'd almost always been bored. As a child, always needing to be entertained. As an adult, constantly changing lovers and houses and jobs. Now it was happening again, and it frightened him.

The increasing boredom that was beginning to permeate his stay at Rivendale, in fact, had begun to impress on him how completely, utterly bored he had been in his married life. He'd almost forgotten, so preoccupied he'd become with her disease. When Cathy's cancer had first begun, and started to spread, that boredom had dissipated. Perversely, the cancer had brought something new and near-dramatic into their life together. He'd felt bad at first: Cathy, in her baldness, in her body that seemed, impossibly, both emaciated and swollen, had suddenly become sensuous to him again. He wanted to make love to her almost all the time. After the first few times, he had stopped the attempts, afraid to ask her. But as she approached death, his desire increased.

Sometimes Frank sat out on the broad resort lawn, his lounge chair positioned under a low-hanging tree only twenty or so feet away from the library window. He'd watch her as she sat at one of the enormous oak tables, poring over the books, consulting with various elderly Rivendales who drifted in and out of that room in a seemingly endless stream. He'd heard one phrase outside the library, when the Rivendales didn't know he was near, or perhaps he had dreamed his eavesdropping while lying abed late one morning, or falling asleep midafternoon in his hiding place under the tree. "Family histories."

The pale face with the near-hairless pate that floated as if suspended in that library window bore no resemblance to the Cathy he had known, with her dark eyes and nervous gestures and narrow mouth quick to twist ugly and vituperative. They'd discovered it was so much easier to become excited by anger, rage, and all the small cruelties possible in married life, than by love. They'd had a bad fight on their very first date. He found himself asking her out again in the very heat of the argument. She'd stared at him wide-eyed and breathless for some time, then grudgingly accepted.

Throughout the following weeks their fights grew worse. Once he'd slapped her, something he would never have imagined himself doing, and she'd fallen sobbing into his arms. They made love for hours. It became a delirious pattern. The screams, the cries, the ineffectual hitting, then the sweet tickle and swallow of a lust that dragged them red-eyed through the night.

Marriage was a great institution. It gave you the opportunity to experience both sadism and masochism within the privacy and safety of your own home.

"What do you want from me, you bastard!" Cathy's teeth flashed, pinkly . . . Her lipstick was running, he thought. Frank held her head down against the mattress, watching her tongue flicking back and forth over her teeth. He was trapped.

Her leg came up and knocked him off the bed. He tried to roll away but before he could move she had straddled him, pinning him to the floor. "Off! Get off!" He couldn't catch his breath. He suddenly realized her forearm was wedged between his neck and the floor, cutting off the air. His vision blurred quickly and the pressure began to build in his face.

"Frank . . ."

He could barely hear her. He thought he might actually die this time. It was another bad joke; he almost laughed. She was the one who was always talking about dying; she could be damned melodramatic about it. She was the one with the death wish.

He opened his eyes and stared up at her. She was fumbling with his shirt, pulling it loose, ripping the buttons off. Maybe she was trying to save him.

Then he got a better look at her: the feverish eyes, the slackening jawline, tongue flicking, eyes glazed. Now she was tugging frantically at his belt. It all seemed very familiar and ritualized. He searched her eyes and did not think she even saw him.

"Frank . . ."

He woke with a start and stared across the lawn at the library window. Cathy's pale face stared back at him, surrounded by her even paler brethren, their mouths moving soundlessly, fish-like. He thought he could hear the soft clinking of breaking glass, or hundreds of tiny mouths trying their teeth.

The thing he would remember most was this room, and the Rivendales watching. They had a peculiar way of watching; they were very polite about it, for if nothing else they were gentlemen and ladies, these Rivendales. Theirs was an ancient etiquette, developed through practice and interaction with human beings of all eras and climes. Long before he met Cathy they had known him, followed him, for they had intimate knowledge of his type. Or so he imagined it.

Each afternoon there was one who especially drew Frank's attention: an old one, his eyebrows fraying away with the heat like tattered moth wings. He walked the same path each day, wearing it down into a seamless pavement, and only by a slight pause at a particular point on the path did Frank know the old man Rivendale was watching him. Listening to him. And that old one's habitual, everyday patterns were what made Frank wonder if the world might be full of Rivendales, assigned to watch, and recruit.

He was beginning—with excitement—to recognize

them, to guess at what they were. They would always feed, and feed viciously, but their hunger was so great they would never be filled, no matter how many lives they emptied, no matter how many dying relationships they so intimately observed. Like an internal cancer, their bland surfaces concealed an inner, parasitic excitement. They could not generate their own. They couldn't even generate their own kind; they had to infect others in order to multiply.

Frank had always imagined their type to be feral, with impossibly long teeth, and foul, blood-tainted breath. But they had manners, promising a better life, and a cold excitement one need not work for.

He was, after all, one of them. A Rivendale by habit, if not by blood. The thought terrified.

The thing he would remember most was the room, and the way she looked curled up in bed, her bald head rising weakly over her shoulders.

"I have to leave, Cathy. This is crazy."

He'd been packing for fifteen minutes, hoping she'd say something. But the only sounds in the room were those of the shirts and pants being pulled out from drawers and collapsed haphazardly into his suitcase. And the sound the breeze from the window made pushing out the heavy brocade curtains, making the tiny leaf and shell pattern breathe, sigh, the tiny mouths chatter.

And the sound of her last gasp, her last breath trying to escape the confines of the room, escape the family home before their mouths caught her and fed.

"Cathy . . ." Shadows moved behind the bed. It bothered him he couldn't see her eyes. "There was no love anyway . . . you understand what I'm saying?" Tiny red eyes flickered in the darkness. Dozens of pairs. "The fighting is the only thing that kept us together; it kept the boredom away. And I haven't felt like fighting you for some time." The quiet plucked at his nerves. "Cathy?"

He stopped putting his things into the suitcase. He let several pairs of socks fall to the floor. There were tiny red eyes fading into the shadows. And mouths. There was no other excitement out there for him; he couldn't do it on his own. No other defense against the awesome, all-encompassing boredom. The Rivendales had judged him well.

Cathy shifted in the bed. He could see the shadow of her terrible swollen belly as it pushed against the dusty sheets and raised the heavy covers. He could see the paleness of her skin. He could see her teeth. But he could not hear her breathe. He lifted his knee and began the long climb across the bedspread, his hands shaking, yet anxious to give themselves up for her.

He would remember the bite marks in the cool night air, the mouths in the dark brocade. He would remember his last moment of panic just before he gave himself up to this new excitement. The thing he would remember most was the room.

DOCTOR PORTHOS

✦✦✦

BASIL COPPER

I

Nervous debility, the doctor says. And yet Angelina has never been ill in her life. Nervous debility! Something far more powerful is involved here; I am left wondering if I should not call in specialist advice. Yet we are so remote and Dr. Porthos is well spoken of by the local people. Why on earth did we ever come to this house? Angelina was perfectly well until then. It is extraordinary to think that two months can have wrought such a change in my wife.

In the town she was lively and vivacious; yet now I can hardly bear to look at her without profound emotion. Her cheeks are sunken and pale, her eyes dark and tired, her bloom quite gone at twenty-five. Could it be something in the air of the house? It seems barely possible. But in that case Dr. Porthos' ministrations should have proved effective. But so far all his skills have been powerless to produce any change for the better. If it had not been for the terms of my uncle's will we would never have come at all.

Friends may call it cupidity, the world may think what it chooses, but the plain truth is that I needed the money. My own health is far from robust and long hours in the family business—ours is an honoured and well-established counting house—had made it perfectly clear to me that I must seek some other mode of life. And yet I could not afford to retire; the terms of my uncle's will, as retailed to me by the family solicitor, afforded the perfect solution.

An annuity—a handsome annuity to put it bluntly—but with the proviso that my wife and I should reside in the old man's house for a period of not less than five years from the date the terms of the will became effective. I hestitated long; both my wife and I were fond of town life and my uncle's estate was in a remote area, where living for the country people was primitive and amenities few. As I had understood it from the solicitor, the house itself had not even the benefit of gas-lighting; in summer it was not so bad but the long months of winter would be melancholy indeed with only the glimmer of candles and the pale sheen of oil lamps to relieve the gloom of the lonely old place.

I debated with Angelina and then set off one weekend alone for a tour of the estate. I had cabled ahead and after a long and cold railway journey which itself occupied most of the day, I was met at my destination by a horse and chaise. The next part of my pilgrimage occupied nearly four hours and I was dismayed on seeing into what a wild and remote region my uncle had chosen to penetrate in order to select a dwelling.

The night was dark but the moon occasionally burst its veiling of cloud to reveal in feeble detail the contours of rock and hill and tree; the chaise jolted and lurched over an unmade road, which was deeply rutted by the wheels of the few vehicles which had torn up the surface in their passing over many months. My solicitor had wired an old friend, Dr. Porthos, to whose good offices I owed my mode of transport, and he had promised to greet me on arrival at the village nearest the estate.

Sure enough, he came out from under the great porch of the timbered hostelry as our carriage grated into the inn-yard. He was a tall, spare man, with square pince-nez which sat firmly on his thin nose; he wore a many-pleated cape like an ostler and the green top hat, worn rakishly over one eye gave him a somewhat dissipated look. He greeted me effusively but there was something about the man which did not endear him to me.

There was nothing that one could isolate. It was just his general manner; perhaps the coldness of his hand which struck my palm with the clamminess of a fish. Then too, his eyes had a most disconcerting way of looking over the tops of his glasses; they were a filmy grey and their piercing glance seemed to root one to the spot. To my dismay I learned that I was not yet at my destination. The estate was still some way off, said the doctor, and we would have to stay the night at the inn. My ill-temper at his remarks was soon dispelled by the roaring fire and the good food with which he plied me; there were few travellers at this time of year and we were the only ones taking dinner in the vast oak-panelled dining room.

The doctor had been my uncle's medical attendant and though it was many years since I had seen my relative I was curious to know what sort of person he had been.

"The Baron was a great man in these parts," said Porthos. His genial manner emboldened me to ask a question to which I had long been awaiting an answer.

"Of what did my uncle die?" I asked.

Firelight flickered through the gleaming redness of Dr. Porthos' wineglass and tinged his face with amber as he replied simply, "Of a lacking of richness in the blood. A fatal quality in his immediate line, I might say."

I pondered for a moment. "Why do you think he chose me as his heir?" I added.

Dr. Porthos' answer was straight and clear and given without hesitation.

"You were a different branch of the family," he said. "New blood, my dear sir. The Baron was most particular on that account. He wanted to carry on the great tradition."

He cut off any further questions by rising abruptly. "Those were the Baron's own words as he lay dying. And now we must retire as we still have a fair journey before us in the morning."

II

Dr. Porthos' words come back to me in my present trouble. "Blood, new blood . . ." What if this be concerned with those dark legends the local people tell about the house? One hardly knows what to think in this atmosphere. My inspection of the house with Dr. Porthos confirmed my worst fears; sagging lintels, mouldering cornices, worm-eaten panelling. The only servitors a middle-aged couple, husband and wife, who have been caretakers here since the Baron's death; the local people sullen and uncooperative, so Porthos says. Certainly, the small hamlet a mile or so from the mansion had every door and window shut as we clattered past and not a soul was stirring. The house has a Gothic beauty, I suppose, viewed from a distance; it is of no great age, being largely re-built on the remains of an older pile destroyed by fire. The restorer—whether he be my uncle or some older resident I have not bothered to discover—had the fancy of adding turrets, a draw-bridge with castellated towers, and a moated surround. Our footsteps echoed mournfully over this as we turned to inspect the grounds.

I was surprised to see marble statuary and worn obelisks, all tumbled and awry, as though the uneasy dead were bursting from the soil, protruding over an ancient moss-grown wall adjoining the courtyard of the house.

Dr. Porthos smiled sardonically.

"The old family burial ground," he explained. "Your uncle is interred here. He said he likes to be near the house."

III

Well, it is done; we came not two months since and then began the profound and melancholy change of which I have already spoken. Not just the atmosphere— though the very stones of the house seem steeped in evil whispers—but the surroundings, the dark, unmoving trees, even the furniture, seem to exude something inimical to life as we knew it; as it is still known to those fortunate enough to dwell in towns.

A poisonous mist rises from the moat at dusk; it seems to doubly emphasize our isolation. The presence of Angelina's own maid and a handyman who was in my father's employ before me, does little to dispel the ambiance of this place. Even their sturdy matter-of-factness seems affected by a miasma that wells from the pores of the building. It has become so manifest of late that I even welcome the daily visits of Dr. Porthos, despite the fact that I suspect him to be the author of our troubles.

They began a week after our arrival when Angelina failed to awake by my side as usual; I shook her to arouse her and my screams must have awakened the maid. I think I fainted then and came to myself in the great morning room; the bed had been awash with blood, which stained the sheets and pillows around my dear wife's head; Porthos' curious grey eyes had a steely look in them which I had never seen before. He administered a powerful medicine and had then turned to attend to me.

Whatever had attacked Angelina had teeth like the

sharpest canine, Porthos said; he had found two distinct
punctures in Angelina's throat, sufficient to account for
the quantities of blood. Indeed, there had been so much
of it that my own hands and linen were stained with it
where I had touched her; I think it was this which had
made me cry so violently. Porthos had announced that
he would sit up by the patient that night.

Angelina was still asleep, as I discovered when I tiptoed in later. Porthos had administered a sleeping
draught and had advised me to take the same, to settle
my nerves, but I declined. I said I would wait up with
him. The doctor had some theory about rats or other
nocturnal creatures and sat long in the library looking
through some of the Baron's old books on natural history.
The man's attitude puzzles me; what sort of creature
would attack Angelina in her own bedroom? Looking at
Porthos' strange eyes, my old fears are beginning to return, bringing with them new ones.

IV

There have been three more attacks, extending over a
fortnight. My darling grows visibly weaker, though
Porthos had been to the nearest town for more powerful
drugs and other remedies. I am in purgatory; I have not
known such dark hours in my life until now. Yet
Angelina herself insists that we should stay to see this
grotesque nightmare through. The first evening of our
vigil both Porthos and I slept; and in the morning the re-

sult was as the night before. Considerable emissions of
blood and the bandage covering the wound had been removed to allow the creature access to the punctures. I
hardly dare conjecture what manner of beast could have
done this.

I was quite worn out and on the evening of the next
day I agreed to Porthos' suggestion that I should take a
sleeping draught. Nothing happened for several nights
and Angelina began to recover; then the terror struck
again. And so it will go on, my reeling senses tell me. I
daren't trust Porthos and on the other hand I cannot ac-
cuse him before the members of my household. We are
isolated here and any mistake I make might be fatal.

On the last occasion I almost had him. I woke at dawn
and found Porthos stretched on the bed, his long, dark
form quivering, his hands at Angelina's throat. I struck at
him, for I did not know who it was, being half asleep, and
he turned, his grey eyes glowing in the dim room. He had
a hypodermic syringe half full of blood in his hand. I am
afraid I dashed it to the floor and shattered it beneath my
heel.

In my own heart I am convinced I have caught this
creature which has been plaguing us, but how to prove
it? Dr. Porthos is staying in the house now; I dare not
sleep and continually refuse the potions he urgently
presses upon me. How long before he destroys me as well
as Angelina? Was man ever in such an appalling situation since the world began?

I sit and watch Porthos, who stares at me sideways

with those curious eyes, his inexpressive face seeming to hint that he can afford to watch and wait and that his time is coming; my pale wife, in her few intervals of consciousness, sits and fearfully watches both of us. Yet I cannot even confide in her for she would think me mad. I try to calm my racing brain. Sometimes I think I shall go insane altogether, the nights are so long. God help me.

V

It is over. The crisis has come and gone. I have laid the mad demon which has us in thrall. I caught him at it. Porthos writhed as I got my hands at his throat. I would have killed him at his foul work, the syringe glinted in his hand. Now he has slipped aside, eluded me for the moment. My cries brought in the servants who have my express instructions to hunt him down. He shall not escape me this time. I pace the corridors of this worm-eaten mansion and when I have cornered him I shall destroy him. Angelina shall live! And my hands will perform the healing work of his destruction . . . But now I must rest. Already it is dawn again. I will sit in this chair by the pillar, where I can watch the hall. I sleep.

VI

Later. I awake to pain and cold. I am lying on earth. Something slippery trickles over my hand. I open my eyes. I draw my hand across my mouth. It comes away scarlet. I can see more clearly now. Angelina is here too. She looks terrified but somehow sad and composed. She is holding the arm of Dr. Porthos.

He is poised above me, his face looking satanic in the dim light of the crypt beneath the house. He whirls a mallet while shriek after shriek disturbs the silence of this place. Dear Christ, the stake is against MY BREAST!

THE SINGULAR DEATH OF MORTON

◆◆◆

ALGERNON BLACKWOOD

Dusk was melting into darkness as the two men slowly made their way through the dense forest of spruce and fir that clothed the flanks of the mountain. They were weary with the long climb, for neither was in his first youth, and the July day had been a hot one. Their little inn lay further in the valley among the orchards that separated the forest from the vineyards.

Neither of them talked much. The big man led the way, carrying the knapsack, and his companion, older, shorter, evidently the more fatigued of the two, followed with small footsteps. From time to time he stumbled among the loose rocks. An exceptionally observant mind would possibly have divined that his stumbling was not entirely due to fatigue, but to an absorption of spirit that made him careless how he walked.

"All right behind?" the big man would call from time to time, half glancing back.

"Eh? What?" the other would reply, startled out of a reverie.

"Pace too fast?"

"Not a bit. I'm coming." And once he added: "You might hurry on and see to supper, if you feel like it. I shan't be long behind you."

But his big friend did not adopt the suggestion. He kept the same distance between them. He called out the same question at intervals. Once or twice *he* stopped and looked back too.

In this way they came at length to the skirts of the wood. A deep hush covered all the valley; the limestone ridges they had climbed gleamed down white and ghostly upon them from the fading sky. Midway in its journeys, the evening wind dropped suddenly to watch the beauty of the moonlight—to hold the branches still so that the light might slip between and weave its silver pattern on the moss below.

And, as they stood a moment to take it in, a step sounded behind them on the soft pine-needles, and the older man, still a little in the rear, turned with a start as though he had been suddenly called by name.

"There's that girl—again!" he said, and his voice expressed a curious mingling of pleasure, surprise, and—apprehension.

Into a patch of moonlight passed the figure of a young girl, looked at them as though about to stop yet thinking better of it, smiled softly, and moved on out of sight into the surrounding darkness. The moon just caught her eyes and teeth, so that they shone; the rest of her body stood in shadow; the effect was striking—almost as though head and shoulders hung alone in mid air, watching them with this shining smile, then fading away.

"Come on, for heaven's sake," the big man cried. There was impatience in his manner, not unkindness. The other lingered a moment, peering closely into the gloom where the girl had vanished. His friend repeated his injunction, and a moment later the two had emerged upon the high road with the village lights in sight beyond, and the forest left behind them like a vast mantle that held the night within its folds.

For some minutes neither of them spoke; then the big man waited for his friend to draw up alongside.

"About all this valley of the Jura," he said presently, "there seems to me something—rather weird." He shifted the knapsack vigorously on his back. It was a gesture of unconscious protest. "Something uncanny," he added, as he set a good pace.

"But extraordinarily beautiful—"

"It attracts you more than it does me, I think," was the short reply.

"The picturesque superstitions still survive here," observed the older man. "They touch the imagination in spite of oneself."

A pause followed during which the other tried to increase the pace. The subject evidently made him impatient for some reason.

"Perhaps," he said presently. "Though I think myself

it's due to the curious loneliness of the place. I mean, we're in the middle of tourist-Europe here, yet so utterly remote. It's such a neglected little corner of the world. The contradiction bewilders. Then, being so near the frontier, too, with the clock changing an hour a mile from the village, makes one think of time as unreal and imaginary." He laughed. He produced several other reasons as well. His friend admitted their value, and agreed half-heartedly. He still turned occasionally to look back. The mountain ridge where they had climbed was clearly visible in the moonlight.

"Odd," he said, "but I don't see that farmhouse where we got the milk anywhere. It ought to be easily visible from here."

"Hardly—in this light. It was a queer place rather, I thought," he added. He did not deny the curiously suggestive atmosphere of the region, he merely wanted to find satisfactory explanations. "A case in point, I mean. I didn't like it quite—that farmhouse—yet I'm hanged if I know why. It made me feel uncomfortable. That girl appeared so suddenly, although the place seemed deserted. And her silence was so odd. Why in the world couldn't she answer a single question? I'm glad I didn't take the milk. I spat it out. I'd like to know where she got it from, for there was no sign of a cow or a goat to be seen anywhere!"

"I swallowed mine—in spite of the taste," said the other, half smiling at his companion's sudden volubility.

Very abruptly, then, the big man turned and faced his friend. Was it merely an effect of the moonlight, or had his skin really turned pale beneath the sunburn?

"I say, old man," he said, his face grave and serious. "What do you think she was? What made her seem like that, and why the devil do you think she followed us?"

"I think," was the slow reply, "it was *me* she was following."

The words, and particularly the tone of conviction in which they were spoken, clearly were displeasing to the big man, who already regretted having spoken so frankly what was in his mind. With a companion so imaginative, so impressionable, so nervous, it had been foolish and unwise. He led the way home at a pace that made the other arrive five minutes in his rear, panting, limping, and perspiring as if he had been running.

"I'm rather for going on into Switzerland tomorrow, or the next day," he ventured that night in the darkness of their two-bedded room. "I think we've had enough of this place. Eh? What do you think?"

But there was no answer from the bed across the room, for its occupant was sound asleep and snoring.

"Dead tired, I suppose!" he muttered to himself, and then turned over to follow his friend's example. But for a long time sleep refused him. Queer, unwelcome thoughts and feelings kept him awake—of a kind he rarely knew, and thoroughly disliked. It was rubbish, yet it made him uncomfortable, so that his nerves tingled.

He tossed about in the bed. "I'm overtired," he persuaded himself, "that's all."

The strange feelings that kept him thus awake were not easy to analyse, perhaps, but their origin was beyond all question: they grouped themselves about the picture of that deserted, tumble-down châlet on the mountain ridge where they had stopped for refreshment a few hours before. It was a farmhouse, dilapidated and dirty, and the name stood in big black letters against a blue background on the wall above the door: "La Chenille." Yet not a living soul was to be seen anywhere about it; the doors were fastened, windows shuttered; chimneys smokeless; dirt, neglect, and decay everywhere in evidence.

Then, suddenly, as they had turned to go, after much vain shouting and knocking at the door, a face appeared for an instant at a window, the shutter of which was half open. His friend saw it first, and called aloud. The face nodded in reply, and presently a young girl came round the corner of the house, apparently by a back door, and stood staring at them both from a little distance.

And from that very instant, so far as he could remember, these queer feelings had entered his heart—fear, distrust, misgiving. The thought of it now, as he lay in bed in the darkness, made his hair rise. There was something about that girl that struck cold into the soul. Yet she was a mere slip of a thing, very pretty, seductive even, with a certain serpent-like fascination about her eyes and movements; and although she only replied to their questions as to refreshment with a smile, uttering no single word, she managed to convey the impression that she was a managing little person who might make herself very disagreeable if she chose. In spite of her undeniable charm there was about her an atmosphere of something sinister. He himself did most of the questioning, but it was his older friend who had the benefit of her smile. Her eyes hardly ever left his face, and once she had slipped quite close to him and touched his arm.

The strange part of it now seemed to him that he could not remember in the least how she was dressed, or what was the colouring of her eyes and hair. It was almost as though he had *felt*, rather than seen, her presence.

The milk—she produced a jug and two wooden bowls after a brief disappearance round the corner of the house—was—well, it tasted so odd that he had been unable to swallow it, and had spat it out. His friend, on the other hand, savage with thirst, had drunk his bowl to the last drop too quickly to taste it even, and, while he drank, had kept his eyes fixed on those of the girl, who stood close in front of him.

And from that moment his friend had somehow changed. On the way down he said things that were unusual, talking chiefly about the "Chenille," and the girl, and the delicious, delicate flavour of the milk, yet all phrased in such a way that it sounded singular, unfamiliar, unpleasant even. Now that he tried to recall the sentences the actual words evaded him; but the memory of the uneasiness and apprehension they caused him to feel remained. And night ever italicizes such memories!

Then, to cap it all, the girl had followed them. It was wholly foolish and absurd to feel the things he did feel, yet there the feelings were, and what was the good of arguing? That girl frightened him; the change in his friend was in some way or other a danger signal. More than this he could not tell. An explanation might come later, but for the present his chief desire was to get away from the place and to get his friend away, too.

And on this thought sleep overtook him—heavily.

The windows were wide open; outside was a garden with a rather high enclosing wall, and at the far end a gate that was kept locked because it led into private fields and so, by a back way, to the cemetery and the little church. When it was open the guests of the inn made use of it and got lost in the network of fields and vines, for there was no proper route that way to the road or the mountains. They usually ended up prematurely in the cemetery, and got back to the village by passing through the church, which was always open; or by knocking at the kitchen doors of the other houses and explaining their position. Hence the gate was locked now to save trouble.

After several hours of hot, unrefreshing sleep the big man turned in his bed and woke. He tried to stretch, but couldn't; then sat up panting with a sense of suffocation. And by the faint starlight of the summer night, he saw next that his friend was up and moving about the room.

Remembering that sometimes he walked in his sleep, he called to him gently:

"Morton, old chap," he said in a low voice, with a touch of authority in it, "go back to bed! You've walked enough for one day!"

And the figure, obeying as sleep-walkers often will, passed across the room and disappeared among the shadows over his bed. The other plunged and burrowed himself into a comfortable position again for sleep, but the heat of the room, the shortness of the bed, and this tiresome interruption of his slumbers made it difficult to lose consciousness. He forced his eyes to keep shut, and his body to cease from fidgeting, but there was something nibbling at his mind like a spirit mouse that never permitted him to cross the frontier into actual oblivion. He slept with one eye open, as the saying is. Odours of hay and flowers and baked ground stole in through the open window; with them, too, came from time to time sounds—little sounds that disturbed him without being ever loud enough to claim definite attention.

Perhaps, after all, he did lose consciousness for a moment—when, suddenly, a thought came with a sharp rush into his mind and galvanized him once more into utter wakefulness. It amazed him that he had not grasped it before. It was this: the figure he had seen was *not the figure of his friend.*

Alarm gripped him at once before he could think or argue, and a cold perspiration broke out all over his body. He fumbled for matches, couldn't find them; then, remembering there was electric light, he scraped the wall with his fingers—and turned on the little white switch. In the sudden glare that filled the room he saw instantly that his friend's bed was no longer occupied. And his mind, then acting instinctively, without process of conscious reasoning, flew like a flash to their walk of the day—to the tumble-down "Chenille," the glass of milk, the odd behaviour of his friend, and—to the girl.

At the same second he noticed that the odour in the room which hitherto he had taken to be the composite odour of fields, flowers, and night was really something else: it was the odour of freshly turned earth. Immediately on the top of this discovery came another. Those slight sounds he had heard outside the window were not ordinary night-sounds, the murmur of wind and insects: they were footsteps moving softly, stealthily down the little paths of crushed granite.

He was dressed in wonderful short order, noticing as he did so that his friend's night-garments lay upon the bed, and that he, too, had therefore dressed; further— that the door had been unlocked and stood half an inch ajar. There was now no question that he *had* slept again: between the present and the moment when he had seen the figure there had been a considerable interval. A couple of minutes later he had made his way cautiously downstairs and was standing on the garden path in the moonlight. And as he stood there, his mind filled with the stories the proprietor had told a few days before of the superstitions that still lived in the popular imagination and haunted this little, remote pine-clad valley. The thought of that girl sickened him. The odour of newly-turned earth remained in his nostrils and made his gorge rise. Utterly and vigorously he rejected the monstrous fictions he had heard, yet for all that, could not prevent their touching his imagination as he stood there in the early hours of the morning, alone with night and silence. The spell was undeniable; only a mind without sensibility could have ignored it.

He searched the little garden from end to end. Empty! Opposite the high gate he stopped, peering through the iron bars, wet with dew to his hands. Far across the intervening fields he fancied something moved. A second later he was sure of it. Something down there to the right beyond the trees was astir. It was in the cemetery.

And this definite discovery sent a shudder of terror and disgust through him from head to foot. He framed the name of his friend with his lips, yet the sound did not come forth. Some deeper instinct warned him to hold it back. Instead, after incredible efforts, he climbed that iron gate and dropped down into the soaking grass upon the other side. Then, taking advantage of all the cover he could find, he ran, swiftly and stealthily, towards the cemetery. On the way, without quite knowing why he did so, he picked up a heavy stick; and a moment later he stood beside the low wall that separated the fields from the churchyard—stood and stared.

There, beside the tombstones, with their hideous metal wreaths and crowns of faded flowers, he made out the figure of his friend; he was stooping, crouched down upon the ground; behind him rose a couple of bushy yew trees, against the dark of which his form was easily visible. He was not alone; in front of him, bending close over him it seemed, was another figure—a slight, shadowy, slim figure.

This time the big man found his voice and called aloud:

"Morton, Morton!" he cried. "What, in the name of heaven, are you doing? What's the matter—?"

And the instant his deep voice broke the stillness of the night with its clamour, the little figure, half hiding his friend, turned about and faced him. He saw a white face with shining eyes and teeth as the form rose; the moonlight painted it with its own strange pallor; it was weird, unreal, horrible; and across the mouth, downwards from the lips to the chin, ran a deep stain of crimson.

The next moment the figure slid with a queer, gliding motion towards the trees, and disappeared among the yews and tombstones in the direction of the church. The heavy stick, hurled whirling after it, fell harmlessly half way, knocking a metal cross from its perch upon an upright grave; and the man who had thrown it raced full speed towards the huddled-up figure of his friend, hardly noticing the thin, wailing cry that rose trembling through the night air from the vanished form. Nor did he notice more particularly that several of the graves, newly made, showed signs of recent disturbance, and that the odour of turned earth he had noticed in the room grew stronger. All his attention was concentrated upon the figure at his feet.

"Morton, man, get up! Wake for God's sake! You've been walking in—"

Then the words died upon his lips. The unnatural attitude of his friend's shoulders, and the way the head dropped back to show the neck, struck him like a blow in the face. There was no sign of movement. He lifted the body up and carried it, all limp and unresisting, by ways he never remembered afterwards, back to the inn.

It was all a dreadful nightmare—a nightmare that carried over its ghastly horror into waking life. He knew that the proprietor and his wife moved busily to and fro about the bed, and that in due course the village doctor was upon the scene, and that he was giving a muddled and feverish description of all he knew, telling how his friend was a confirmed sleep-walker and all the rest. But he did not realize the truth until he saw the face of the doctor as he straightened up from the long examination.

"Will you wake him?" he heard himself asking, "or let him sleep it out till morning?" And the doctor's expression, even before the reply came to confirm it, told him the truth. "Ah, monsieur, your friend will not ever wake again, I fear! It is the heart, you see; *hélas*, it is sudden failure of the heart!"

The final scenes in the little tragedy which thus brought his holiday to so abrupt and terrible a close need no description, being in no way essential to this strange story. There were one or two curious details, however, that came to light afterwards. One was, that for some weeks before there had been signs of disturbance among newly-made graves in the cemetery, which the authorities had been trying to trace to the nightly wanderings of the village madman — in vain; and another, that the morning after the death a trail of blood had been found across the church floor, as though someone had passed through from the back entrance to the front. A special service was held that very week to cleanse the holy building from the evil of that stain; for the villagers, deep in their superstitions, declared that nothing human had left that trail; nothing could have made those marks but a vampire disturbed at midnight in its awful occupation among the dead.

Apart from such idle rumours, however, the bereaved carried with him to this day certain other remarkable details which cannot be so easily dismissed. For he had a brief conversation with the doctor, it appears, that impressed him profoundly. And the doctor, an intelligent man, prosaic as granite into the bargain, had questioned him rather closely as to the recent life and habits of his dead friend. The account of their climb to the "Chenille" he heard with an amazement he could not conceal.

"But no such châlet exists," he said. "There is no 'Chenille.' A long time ago, fifty years or more, there was such a place, but it was destroyed by the authorities on account of the evil reputation of the people who lived there. They burnt it. Nothing remains today but a few bits of broken wall and foundation."

"Evil reputation—?"

The doctor shrugged his shoulders. "Travellers, even peasants, disappeared," he said. "An old woman lived there with her daughter, and poisoned milk was supposed to be used. But the neighbourhood accused them of worse than ordinary murder—"

"In what way?"

"Said the girl was a vampire," answered the doctor shortly.

And, after a moment's hesitation, he added, turning his face away as he spoke:

"It was a curious thing, though, that tiny hole in your friend's throat, small as a pin-prick, yet so deep. And the heart—did I tell you?—was almost completely drained of blood."

LIGEIA

•••

EDGAR ALLAN POE

*And the will therein lieth, which dieth not. Who knoweth
the mysteries of the will, with its vigór? For God is but a
great will pervading all things by nature of its intentness.
Man doth not yield himself to the angels, nor unto death
utterly, save only through the weakness of his feeble will.*
— JOSEPH GLANVILL

I cannot, for my soul, remember how, when, or even precisely where, I first became acquainted with the lady
Ligeia. Long years have since elapsed, and my memory is
feeble through much suffering. Or, perhaps, I cannot
now bring these points to mind, because, in truth, the
character of my beloved, her rare learning, her singular
yet placid cast of beauty, and the thrilling and enthralling
eloquence of her low musical language, made their way
into my heart by paces so steadily and stealthily progres-
sive, that they have been unnoticed and unknown. Yet I
believe that I met her first and most frequently in some
large, old, decaying city near the Rhine. Of her family —
I have surely heard her speak. That it is of a remotely ancient date cannot be doubted. Ligeia! Ligeia! Buried in

studies of a nature more than all else adapted to deaden impressions of the outward world, it is by that sweet word alone—by Ligeia—that I bring before mine eyes in fancy the image of her who is no more.

And now, while I write, a recollection flashes upon me that I have *never known* the paternal name of her who was my friend and my betrothed, and who became the partner of my studies, and finally the wife of my bosom. Was it a playful charge on the part of my Ligeia? Or was it a test of my strength of affection, that I should institute no inquiries upon this point? Or was it rather a caprice of my own—a wildly romantic offering on the shrine of the most passionate devotion? I but indistinctly recall the fact itself—what wonder that I have utterly forgotten the circumstances which originated or attended it? And, indeed, if ever that spirit which is entitled *Romance*—if ever she, the wan and the misty-winged *Ashtophet* of idolatrous Egypt, presided, as they tell, over marriages ill-omened, then most surely she presided over mine.

There is one dear topic, however, on which my memory fails me not. It is the *person* of Ligeia. In stature she was tall, somewhat slender, and, in her latter days, even emaciated. I would in vain attempt to portray the majesty, the quiet ease of her demeanor, or the incomprehensible lightness and elasticity of her footfall. She came and departed as a shadow. I was never made aware of her entrance into my closed study, save by the dear music of her low sweet voice, as she placed her marble hand upon my shoulder. In beauty of face no maiden

ever equalled her. It was the radiance of an opium
dream—an airy and spirit-lifting vision more wildly divine than the phantasies which hovered about the slum-
bering souls of the daughters of Delos. Yet her features
were not of that regular mould which we have been
falsely taught to worship in the classical labors of the hea-
then. "There is no exquisite beauty," says Bacon, Lord
Verulam, speaking truly of all the forms and *genera* of
beauty, "without some *strangeness* in the proportion."
Yet, although I saw that the features of Ligeia were not of
a classic regularity—although I perceived that her loveliness was indeed "exquisite" and felt that there was much
of "strangeness" pervading it, yet I have tried in vain to
detect the irregularity and to trace home my own perception of "the strange." I examined the contour of the lofty
and pale forehead—it was faultless—how cold indeed
that word when applied to a majesty so divine!—the skin
rivalling the purest ivory, the commanding extent and re-
pose, the gentle prominence of the regions above the
temples; and then the raven-black, the glossy, the luxuriant, and naturally-curling tresses, setting forth the full
force of the Homeric epithet, "hyacinthine!" I looked
at the delicate outlines of the nose—and nowhere but
in the graceful medallions of the Hebrews had I beheld
a similar perfection. There were the same luxurious
smoothness of surface, the same scarcely perceptible ten-
dency to the aquiline, the same harmoniously curved
nostrils speaking the free spirit. I regarded the sweet
mouth. Here was indeed the triumph of all things

heavenly—the magnificent turn of the short upper lip—
the soft, voluptuous slumber of the under—the dimples
which sported, and the color which spoke—the teeth
glancing back, with a brilliancy almost startling, every ray
of the holy light which fell upon them in her serene and
placid yet most exultingly radiant of all smiles. I scrutinized the formation of the chin—and, here too, I found
the gentleness of breadth, the softness and the majesty,
the fulness and the spirituality of the Greek—the contour which the god Apollo revealed but in a dream, to
Cleomenes, the son of the Athenian. And then I peered
into the large eyes of Ligeia.

For eyes we have no models in the remotely antique.
It might have been, too, that in these eyes of my beloved
lay the secret to which Lord Verulam alludes. They were,
I must believe, far larger than the ordinary eyes of
our own race. They were even fuller than the fullest of
the gazelle eyes of the tribe of the valley of Nourjahad.
Yet it was only at intervals—in moments of intense
excitement—that this peculiarity became more than
slightly noticeable in Ligeia. And at such moments was
her beauty—in my heated fancy thus it appeared perhaps—the beauty of beings either above or apart from the
earth—the beauty of the fabulous Houri of the Turk. The
hue of the orbs was the most brilliant of black, and, far
over them, hung jetty lashes of great length. The brows,
slightly irregular in outline, had the same tint. The
"strangeness," however, which I found in the eyes was of
a nature distinct from the formation, or the color, or the

brilliancy of the features, and must, after all, be referred
to the *expression*. Ah, word of no meaning! Behind whose
vast latitude of mere sound we intrench our ignorance of
so much of the spiritual. The expression of the eyes of
Ligeia! How for long hours have I pondered upon it!
How have I, through the whole of a midsummer night,
struggled to fathom it! What was it—that something
more profound than the well of Democritus—which lay
far within the pupils of my beloved? What *was* it? I was
possessed with a passion to discover. Those eyes! Those
large, those shining, those divine orbs! They became to
me twin stars of Leda, and I to them devoutest of as-
trologers.

There is no point, among the many incomprehensible anomalies of the science of mind, more thrillingly ex-
citing than the fact—never, I believe, noticed in the
schools—that in our endeavors to recall to memory
something long forgotten, we often find ourselves *upon
the very verge* of remembrance, without being able, in the
end, to remember. And thus how frequently, in my intense scrutiny of Ligeia's eyes, have I felt approaching the
full knowledge of their expression—felt it approaching—
yet not quite be mine—and so at length entirely depart!
And (strange, oh, strangest mystery of all!) I found, in the
commonest objects of the universe, a circle of analogies
to that expression. I mean to say that, subsequently to the
period when Ligeia's beauty passed into my spirit, there
dwelling as in a shrine, I derived, from many existences
in the material world, a sentiment such as I felt always

around, within me, by her large and luminous orbs. Yet not the more could I define that sentiment, or analyze, or even steadily view it. I recognized it, let me repeat, sometimes in the survey of a rapidly growing vine—in the contemplation of a moth, a butterfly, a chrysalis, a stream of running water. I have felt it in the ocean—in the falling of a meteor. I have felt it in the glances of unusually aged people. And there are one or two stars in heaven (one especially, a star of the sixth magnitude, double and changeable, to be found near the large star in Lyra) in a telescopic scrutiny of which I have been made aware of the feeling. I have been filled with it by certain sounds from stringed instruments, and not unfrequently by passages from books. Among innumerable other instances, I well remember something in a volume of Joseph Glanvill, which (perhaps merely from its quaintness— who shall say?) never failed to inspire me with the sentiment: "And the will therein lieth, which dieth not. Who knoweth the mysteries of the will, with its vigor? For God is but a great will pervading all things by nature of its intentness. Man doth not yield himself to the angels, nor unto death utterly, save only through the weakness of his feeble will."

Length of years and subsequent reflection have enabled me to trace, indeed, some remote connection between this passage in the English moralist and a portion of the character of Ligeia. An *intensity* in thought, action, or speech was possibly, in her, a result, or at least an index, of that gigantic volition which, during our long intercourse, failed to give other and more immediate evidence of its existence. Of all the women whom I have ever known, she, the outwardly calm, the ever-placid Ligeia, was the most violently a prey to the tumultuous vultures of stern passion. And of such passion I could form no estimate save by the miraculous expansion of those eyes which at once so delighted and appalled me,—by the almost magical melody, modulation, distinctness, and placidity of her very low voice,—and by the fierce energy (rendered doubly effective by contrast with her manner of utterance) of the wild words which she habitually uttered.

I have spoken of the learning of Ligeia: it was immense—such as I have never known in woman. In the classical tongues was she deeply proficient, and as far as my own acquaintance extended in regard to the modern dialects of Europe, I have never known her at fault. Indeed upon any theme of the most admired because simply the most abstruse of the boasted erudition of the Academy, have I *ever* found Ligeia at fault? How singularly—how thrillingly, this one point in the nature of my wife has forced itself, at this late period only, upon my attention! I said her knowledge was such as I have never known in woman—but where breathes the man who has traversed, and successfully, *all* the wide areas of moral, physical, and mathematical science? I saw not then what I now clearly perceive, that the acquisitions of Ligeia were gigantic, were astounding; yet I was sufficiently aware of her infinite supremacy to resign myself,

with a child-like confidence, to her guidance through
the chaotic world of metaphysical investigation at which
I was most busily occupied during the earlier years of our
marriage. With how vast a triumph—with how vivid a
delight—with how much of all that is ethereal in hope
did I *feel*, as she bent over me in studies but little sought—
but less known—that delicious vista by slow degrees ex-
panding before me, down whose long, gorgeous, and all
untrodden path, I might at length pass onward to the goal
of a wisdom too divinely precious not to be forbidden!

How poignant, then, must have been the grief with
which, after some years, I beheld my well-grounded
expectations take wings to themselves and fly away!
Without Ligeia I was but as a child groping benighted.
Her presence, her readings alone, rendered vividly luminous the many mysteries of the transcendentalism in
which we were immersed. Wanting the radiant lustre of
her eyes, letters, lambent and golden, grew duller than
Saturnian lead. And now those eyes shone less and less
frequently upon the pages over which I pored. Ligeia
grew ill. The wild eyes blazed with a too—too glorious
effulgence; the pale fingers became of the transparent
waxen hue of the grave; and the blue veins upon the lofty
forehead swelled and sank impetuously with the tides of
the most gentle emotion. I saw that she must die—and I
struggled desperately in spirit with the grim Azrael. And
the struggles of the passionate wife were, to my astonishment, even more energetic than my own. There had
been much in her stern nature to impress me with the

belief that, to her, death would have come without its terrors; but not so. Words are impotent to convey any just
idea of the fierceness of resistance with which she wres-
tled with the Shadow. I groaned in anguish at the pitiable
spectacle. I would have soothed—I would have rea-
soned; but in the intensity of her wild desire for life—for
life—*but* for life—solace and reason were alike the uttermost of folly. Yet not until the last instance, amid the
most convulsive writhings of her fierce spirit, was shaken
the external placidity of her demeanor. Her voice grew
more gentle—grew more low—yet I would not wish to
dwell upon the wild meaning of the quietly uttered
words. My brain reeled as I hearkened, entranced to a
melody more than mortal—to assumptions and aspira-
tions which mortality had never before known.

That she loved me I should not have doubted; and I
might have been easily aware that, in a bosom such as
hers, love would have reigned no ordinary passion. But in
death only was I fully impressed with the strength of her
affection. For long hours, detaining my hand, would she
pour out before me the overflowing of a heart whose
more than passionate devotion amounted to idolatry.
How had I deserved to be so blessed by such confes-
sions?—how had I deserved to be so cursed with the removal of my beloved in the hour of her making them?
But upon this subject I cannot bear to dilate. Let me say
only, that in Ligeia's more than womanly abandonment
to a love, alas! all unmerited, all unworthily bestowed, I
at length recognized the principle of her longing, with so

wildly earnest a desire, for the life which was now fleeing so rapidly away. It is this wild longing—it is this eager vehemence of desire for life—*but* for life—that I have no power to portray—no utterance capable of expressing.

At high noon of the night in which she departed, beckoning me, peremptorily, to her side, she bade me repeat certain verses composed by herself not many days before. I obeyed her. They were these:—

> Lo! 'tis a gala night
> > Within the lonesome latter years!
> An angel throng, bewinged, bedight
> > In veils, and drowned in tears,
> Sit in a theatre, to see
> > A play of hopes and fears,
> While the orchestra breathes fitfully
> > The music of the spheres.
>
> Mimes, in the form of God on high,
> > Mutter and mumble low,
> And hither and thither fly;
> > Mere puppets they, who come and go
> At bidding of vast formless things
> > That shift the scenery to and fro,
> Flapping from out their condor wings
> > Invisible Woe!
>
> That motley drama!—oh, be sure
> > It shall not be forgot!

> With its Phantom chased for evermore,
>> By a crowd that seize it not,
> Through a circle that ever returneth in
>> To the self-same spot;
> And much of Madness, and more of Sin,
>> And Horror, the soul of the plot!
>
> But see, amid the mimic rout
>> A crawling shape intrude!
> A blood-red thing that writhes from out
>> The scenic solitude!
> It writhes!—it writhes!—with mortal pangs
>> The mimes become its food,
> And the seraphs sob at vermin fangs
>> In human gore imbued.
>
> Out—out are the lights—out all!
>> And over each quivering form,
> The curtain, a funeral pall,
>> Comes down with the rush of a storm—
> And the angels, all pallid and wan,
>> Uprising, unveiling, affirm
> That the play is the tragedy, "Man,"
>> And its hero, the conqueror Worm.

"O God!" half shrieked Ligeia, leaping to her feet and extending her arms aloft with a spasmodic movement, as I made an end of these lines—"O God! O Divine Father!—shall these things be undeviatingly so?—shall this conqueror be not once conquered? Are we not part and parcel in Thee? Who—who knoweth the mysteries of the will with its vigor? Man doth not yield him to the angels, *nor unto death utterly*, save only through the weakness of his feeble will."

And now, as if exhausted with emotion, she suffered her white arms to fall, and returned solemnly to her bed of death. And as she breathed her last sighs, there came mingled with them a low murmur from her lips. I bent to them my ear, and distinguished, again, the concluding words of the passage in Glanvill: "*Man doth not yield himself to the angels, nor unto death utterly, save only through the weakness of his feeble will.*"

She died: and I, crushed into the very dust with sorrow, could no longer endure the lonely desolation of my dwelling in the dim and decaying city by the Rhine. I had no lack of what the world calls wealth. Ligeia had brought me far more, very far more, than ordinarily falls to the lot of mortals. After a few months, therefore, of weary and aimless wandering, I purchased and put in some repair, an abbey, which I shall not name, in one of the wildest and least frequented portions of fair England. The gloomy and dreary grandeur of the building, the almost savage aspect of the domain, the many melancholy and time-honored memories connected with both, had much in unison with the feelings of utter abandonment which had driven me into that remote and unsocial region of the country. Yet although the external abbey, with its verdant decay hanging about it, suffered but little al-

teration, I gave way, with a child-like perversity, and per-
chance with a faint hope of alleviating my sorrows, to a
display of more than regal magnificence within. For such
follies, even in childhood, I had imbibed a taste, and
now they came back to me as if in the dotage of grief.
Alas, I feel how much even of incipient madness might
have been discovered in the gorgeous and fantastic
draperies, in the solemn carvings of Egypt, in the wild
cornices and furniture, in the Bedlam patterns of the carpets of tufted gold! I had become a bounden slave in the
trammels of opium, and my labors and my orders had
taken a coloring from my dreams. But these absurdities I
must not pause to detail. Let me speak only of that one
chamber, ever accursed, whither, in a moment of mental
alienation, I led from the altar as my bride—as the successor of the unforgotten Ligeia—the fair-haired and
blue-eyed Lady Rowena Trevanion, of Tremaine.

There is no individual portion of the architecture and
decoration of that bridal chamber which is not now visibly before me. Where were the souls of the haughty family of the bride, when, through thirst of gold, they
permitted to pass the threshold of an apartment so be-
decked, a maiden and a daughter so beloved? I have said,
that I minutely remember the details of the chamber—
yet I am sadly forgetful on topics of deep moment; and
here there was no system, no keeping, in the fantastic display, to take hold upon the memory. The room lay in a
high turret of the castellated abbey, was pentagonal in
shape, and of capacious size. Occupying the whole

southern face of the pentagon was the sole window—an
immense sheet of unbroken glass from Venice—a single
pane, and tinted of a leaden hue, so that the rays of either
the sun or moon passing through it, fell with a ghastly
lustre on the objects within. Over the upper portion of
this huge window, extended the trellis-work of an aged
vine, which clambered up the massy walls of the turret.
The ceiling, of gloomy-looking oak, was excessively lofty,
vaulted, and elaborately fretted with the wildest and most
grotesque specimens of a semi-Gothic, semi-Druidical
device. From out the most central recess of this melancholy vaulting, depended, by a single chain of gold with
long links, a huge censer of the same metal, Saracenic in
pattern, and with many perforations so contrived that
there writhed in and out of them, as if endued with a serpent vitality, a continual succession of parti-colored fires.

Some few ottomans and golden candelabra, of Eastern figure, were in various stations about; and there was
the couch, too—the bridal couch—of an Indian model,
and low, and sculptured of solid ebony, with a pall-like
canopy above. In each of the angles of the chamber stood
on end a gigantic sarcophagus of black granite, from the
tombs of the kings over against Luxor, with their aged
lids full of immemorial sculpture. But in the draping of
the apartment lay, alas! the chief phantasy of all. The
lofty walls, gigantic in height—even unproportionably
so—were hung from summit to foot, in vast folds, with a
heavy and massive-looking tapestry—tapestry of a material which was found alike as a carpet on the floor, as a

covering for the ottomans and the ebony bed, as a canopy
for the bed and as the gorgeous volutes of the curtains
which partially shaded the window. The material was the
richest cloth of gold. It was spotted all over, at irregular
intervals, with arabesque figures, about a foot in diame-
ter, and wrought upon the cloth in patterns of the most
jetty black. But these figures partook of the true character
of the arabesque only when regarded from a single point
of view. By a contrivance now common, and indeed
traceable to a very remote period of antiquity, they were
made changeable in aspect. To one entering the room,
they bore the appearance of simple monstrosities; but
upon a further advance, this appearance gradually departed; and, step by step, as the visitor moved his station
in the chamber, he saw himself surrounded by an endless succession of the ghastly forms which belong to the
superstition of the Norman, or arise in the guilty slumbers of the monk. The phantasmagoric effect was vastly
heightened by the artificial introduction of a strong continual current of wind behind the draperies—giving a
hideous and uneasy animation to the whole.

In halls such as these—in a bridal chamber such as
this—I passed, with the Lady of Tremaine, the unhal-
lowed hours of the first month of our marriage—passed
them with but little disquietude. That my wife dreaded
the fierce moodiness of my temper—that she shunned
me, and loved me but little—I could not help perceiving; but it gave me rather pleasure than otherwise. I
loathed her with a hatred belonging more to demon than

to man. My memory flew back (oh, with what intensity of regret!) to Ligeia, the beloved, the august, the beautiful, the entombed. I revelled in recollections of her purity, of her wisdom, of her lofty—her ethereal nature, of her passionate, her idolatrous love. Now, then, did my spirit fully and freely burn with more than all the fires of her own. In the excitement of my opium dreams (for I was habitually fettered in the shackles of the drug), I would call aloud upon her name, during the silence of the night, or among the sheltered recesses of the glens by day, as if, through the wild eagerness, the solemn passion, the consuming ardor of my longing for the departed, I could restore her to the pathways she had abandoned—ah, *could* it be for ever?—upon the earth.

About the commencement of the second month of the marriage, the Lady Rowena was attacked with sudden illness, from which her recovery was slow. The fever which consumed her rendered her nights uneasy; and in her perturbed state of half-slumber, she spoke of sounds, and of motions, in and about the chamber of the turret, which I concluded had no origin save in the distemper of her fancy, or perhaps in the phantasmagoric influences of the chamber itself. She became at length convalescent—finally, well. Yet but a brief period elapsed, ere a second more violent disorder again threw her upon a bed of suffering; and from this attack her frame, at all times feeble, never altogether recovered. Her illnesses were, after this epoch, of alarming character, and of more alarming recurrence, defying alike the knowledge and the great exertions of her physicians. With the increase of the chronic disease, which had thus, apparently, taken too sure hold upon her constitution to be eradicated by human means, I could not fail to observe a similar increase in the nervous irritation of her temperament, and in her excitability by trivial causes of fear. She spoke again, and now more frequently and pertinaciously, of the sounds—of the slight sounds—and of the unusual motions among the tapestries, to which she had formerly alluded.

One night, near the closing in of September, she pressed this distressing subject with more than usual emphasis upon my attention. She had just awakened from an unquiet slumber, and I had been watching, with feelings half of anxiety, half of vague terror, the workings of her emaciated countenance. I sat by the side of her ebony bed, upon one of the ottomans of India. She partly arose, and spoke, in an earnest low whisper, of sounds which she *then* heard, but which I could not hear—of motions which she *then* saw, but which I could not perceive. The wind was rushing hurriedly behind the tapestries, and I wished to show her (what, let me confess it, I could not *all* believe) that those almost inarticulate breathings, and those very gentle variations of the figures upon the wall, were but the natural effects of that customary rushing of the wind. But a deadly pallor, overspreading her face, had proved to me that my exertions to reassure her would be fruitless. She appeared to be fainting, and no attendants were within call. I remembered where was deposited a decanter of light wine which had been ordered by her physicians, and hastened across the chamber to procure it. But, as I stepped beneath the light of the censer, two circumstances of a startling nature attracted my attention. I had felt that some palpable although invisible object had passed lightly by my person; and I saw that there lay upon the golden carpet, in the very middle of the rich lustre thrown from the censer, a shadow—a faint, indefinite shadow of angelic aspect— such as might be fancied for the shadow of a shade. But I was wild with the excitement of an immoderate dose of opium, and heeded these things but little, nor spoke of them to Rowena. Having found the wine, I recrossed the chamber, and poured out a gobletful, which I held to the lips of the fainting lady. She had now partially recovered, however, and took the vessel herself, while I sank upon an ottoman near me, with my eyes fastened upon her person. It was then that I became distinctly aware of a gentle footfall upon the carpet, and near the couch; and in a second thereafter, as Rowena was in the act of raising the wine to her lips, I saw, or may have dreamed that I saw, fall within the goblet, as if from some invisible spring in the atmosphere of the room, three or four large drops of a brilliant and ruby-colored fluid. If this I saw—not so Rowena. She swallowed the wine unhesitatingly, and I forbore to speak to her of a circumstance which must, after all, I considered, have been but the suggestion of a vivid imagination, rendered morbidly active by the terror of the lady, by the opium, and by the hour.

Yet I cannot conceal it from my own perception that, immediately subsequent to the fall of the ruby-drops, a rapid change for the worse took place in the disorder of my wife; so that, on the third subsequent night, the hands of her menials prepared her for the tomb, and on the fourth, I sat alone, with her shrouded body, in that fantastic chamber which had received her as my bride. Wild visions, opium-engendered, flitted, shadow-like, before me. I gazed with unquiet eye upon the sarcophagi in the angles of the room, upon the varying figures of the drapery, and upon the writhing of the parti-colored fires in the censer overhead. My eyes then fell, as I called to mind the circumstances of a former night, to the spot beneath the glare of the censer where I had seen the faint traces of the shadow. It was there, however, no longer; and breathing with greater freedom, I turned my glances to the pallid and rigid figure upon the bed. Then rushed upon me a thousand memories of Ligeia—and then came back upon my heart, with the turbulent violence of a flood, the whole of that unutterable woe with which I had regarded *her* thus enshrouded. The night waned; and still, with a bosom full of bitter thoughts of the one only and supremely beloved, I remained gazing upon the body of Rowena.

It might have been midnight, or perhaps earlier, or later, for I had taken no note of time, when a sob, low, gentle, but very distinct, startled me from my reverie. I *felt* that it came from the bed of ebony—the bed of death. I listened in an agony of superstitious terror—but there was no repetition of the sound. I strained my vision to detect any motion in the corpse—but there was not the slightest perceptible. Yet I could not have been deceived. I *had* heard the noise, however faint, and my soul was awakened within me. I resolutely and perseveringly kept my attention riveted upon the body. Many minutes elapsed before any circumstance occurred tending to throw light upon the mystery. At length it became evident that a slight, a very feeble, and barely noticeable tinge of color had flushed up within the cheeks, and along the sunken small veins of the eyelids. Through a species of unutterable horror and awe, for which the language of mortality has no sufficiently energetic expression, I felt my heart cease to beat, my limbs grow rigid where I sat. Yet a sense of duty finally operated to restore my self-possession. I could no longer doubt that we had been precipitate in our preparations—that Rowena still lived. It was necessary that some immediate exertion be made; yet the turret was altogether apart from the portion of the abbey tenanted by the servants—there were none within call—I had no means of summoning them to my aid without leaving the room for many minutes—and this I could not venture to do. I therefore struggled alone in my endeavors to call back the spirit still hovering. In a short period it was certain, however, that a relapse had taken place; the color disappeared from both eyelid and cheek, leaving a wanness even more than that of marble;

the lips became doubly shrivelled and pinched up in the ghastly expression of death; a repulsive clamminess and coldness overspread rapidly the surface of the body; and all the usual rigorous stiffness immediately supervened. I fell back with a shudder upon the couch from which I had been so startlingly aroused, and again gave myself up to passionate waking visions of Ligeia. An hour thus elapsed, when (could it be possible?) I was a second time aware of some vague sound issuing from the region of the bed.

I listened—in extremity of horror. The sound came again—it was a sigh. Rushing to the corpse, I saw—distinctly saw—a tremor upon the lips. In a minute afterward they relaxed, disclosing a bright line of the pearly teeth. Amazement now struggled in my bosom with the profound awe which had hitherto reigned there alone. I felt that my vision grew dim, that my reason wandered; and it was only by a violent effort that I at length succeeded in nerving myself to the task which duty thus once more had pointed out. There was now a partial glow upon the forehead and upon the cheek and throat; a perceptible warmth pervaded the whole frame; there was even a slight pulsation at the heart. The lady *lived*; and with redoubled ardor I betook myself to the task of restoration. I chafed and bathed the temples and the hands, and used every exertion which experience, and no little medical reading, could suggest. But in vain. Suddenly, the color fled, the pulsation ceased, the lips resumed the expression of the dead, and, in an instant af-

terward, the whole body took upon itself the icy chilli-
ness, the livid hue, the intense rigidity, the sunken outline, and all the loathsome peculiarities of that which has
been, for many days, a tenant of the tomb.

And again I sank into visions of Ligeia—and again
(what marvel that I shudder while I write?), *again* there
reached my ears a low sob from the region of the ebony
bed. But why shall I minutely detail the unspeakable hor-
rors of that night? Why shall I pause to relate how, time
after time, until near the period of the gray dawn, this
hideous drama of revivification was repeated; how each
terrific relapse was only into a sterner and apparently
more irredeemable death; how each agony wore the aspect of a struggle with some invisible foe; and how each
struggle was succeeded by I know not what of wild
change in the personal appearance of the corpse? Let me
hurry to a conclusion.

The greater part of the fearful night had worn away,
and she who had been dead once again stirred—and now
more vigorously than hitherto, although arousing from a
dissolution more appalling in its utter hopelessness than
any. I had long ceased to struggle or to move, and remained sitting rigidly upon the ottoman, a helpless prey
to a whirl of violent emotions, of which extreme awe was
perhaps the least terrible, the least consuming. The
corpse, I repeat, stirred, and now more vigorously than
before. The hues of life flushed up with unwonted energy into the countenance—the limbs relaxed—and,
save that the eyelids were yet pressed heavily together,

and that the bandages and draperies of the grave still im-
parted their charnel character to the figure, I might have
dreamed that Rowena had indeed shaken off, utterly, the
fetters of Death. But if this idea was not, even then, altogether adopted, I could at least doubt no longer, when,
arising from the bed, tottering, with feeble steps, with
closed eyes, and with the manner of one bewildered in a
dream, the thing that was enshrouded advanced boldly
and palpably into the middle of the apartment.

I trembled not—I stirred not—for a crowd of unutterable fancies connected with the air, the stature, the demeanor, of the figure, rushing hurriedly through my
brain, had paralyzed—had chilled me into stone. I
stirred not—but gazed upon the apparition. There was a
mad disorder in my thoughts—a tumult unappeasable.
Could it, indeed, be the *living* Rowena who confronted
me? Could it, indeed, be Rowena *at all*—the fair-haired,
the blue-eyed Lady Rowena Trevanion of Tremaine?
Why, *why* should I doubt it? The bandage lay heavily
about the mouth—but then might it not be the mouth of
the breathing Lady of Tremaine? And the cheeks—there
were the roses as in her noon of life—yes, these might indeed be the fair cheeks of the living Lady of Tremaine.
And the chin, with its dimples, as in health, might it not
be hers?—but *had she then grown taller since her malady*? What inexpressible madness seized me with that
thought? One bound, and I had reached her feet!
Shrinking from my touch, she let fall from her head, un-
loosened, the ghastly cerements which had confined it,

and there streamed forth into the rushing atmosphere of the chamber huge masses of long and dishevelled hair; *it was blacker than the raven wings of midnight!* And now slowly opened *the eyes* of the figure which stood before me. "Here then, at least," I shrieked aloud, "can I never—can I never be mistaken—these are the full, and the black, and the wild eyes—of my lost love—of the lady—of the Lady Ligeia."

WHEN IT WAS MOONLIGHT

•••

MANLY WADE WELLMAN

Let my heart be still a moment, and this mystery explore.
— THE RAVEN

His hand, as slim as a white claw, dipped a quillful of ink
and wrote in one corner of the page the date — 3 March
1842. Then:

THE PREMATURE BURIAL
by Edgar A. Poe.

He hated his middle name, the name of his miserly and
spiteful stepfather. For a moment he considered crossing
out even the initial; then he told himself that he was
only wool-gathering, putting off the drudgery of writing.
And write he must, or starve — the Philadelphia *Dollar
Newspaper* was clamouring for the story he had promised. Well, today he had heard a tag of gossip — his
mother-in-law had it from a neighbour — that revived in
his mind a subject always fascinating.

He began rapidly to write, in a fine copperplate hand:

> There are certain themes of which the interest is all-
> absorbing, but which are entirely too horrible for the
> purposes of legitimate fiction . . .

This would really be an essay, not a tale, and he could
do it justice. Often he thought of the whole world as a
vast fat cemetery, close set with tombs in which not all
the occupants were at rest—too many struggled unavail-
ingly against their smothering shrouds, their locked and
weighted coffin lids. What were his own literary labours,
he mused, but a struggle against being shut down and
throttled by a society as heavy and grim and senseless as
clóds heaped by a sexton's spade?

He paused, and went to the slate mantelshelf for a
candle. His kerosene lamp had long ago been pawned,
and it was dark for midafternoon, even in March. Elsewhere in the house his mother-in-law swept busily, and
in the room next to his sounded the quiet breathing of his
invalid wife. Poor Virginia slept, and for the moment
knew no pain. Returning with his light, he dipped more
ink and continued down the sheet:

> To be buried while alive is, beyond question, the most
> terrific of these extremes which has ever fallen to the
> lot of mere mortality. That it has frequently, very fre-
> quently, fallen will scarcely be denied . . .

Again his dark imagination savoured the tale he had
heard that day. It had happened here in Philadelphia, in

this very quarter, less than a month ago. A widower had gone, after weeks of mourning, to his wife's tomb, with flowers. Stooping to place them on the marble slab, he had heard noise beneath. At once joyful and aghast, he fetched men and crowbars, and recovered the body, all untouched by decay. At home that night, the woman returned to consciousness.

So said the gossip, perhaps exaggerated, perhaps not. And the house was only six blocks away from Spring Garden Street, where he sat.

Poe fetched out his notebooks and began to marshal bits of narrative for his composition—a gloomy tale of resurrection in Baltimore, another from France, a genuinely creepy citation from the *Chirurgical Journal* of Leipzig; a sworn case of revival, by electrical impulses, of a dead man in London. Then he added an experience of his own, romantically embellished, a dream adventure of his boyhood in Virginia. Just as he thought to make an end, he had a new inspiration.

Why not learn more about that reputed Philadelphia burial and the one who rose from seeming death? It would point up his piece, give it a timely local climax, ensure acceptance—he could hardly risk a rejection. Too, it would satisfy his own curiosity. Laying down the pen, Poe got up. From a peg he took his wide black hat, his old military cloak that he had worn since his ill-fated cadet days at West Point. Huddling it round his slim little body, he opened the front door and went out.

March had come in like a lion and, lion-like, roared

and rampaged over Philadelphia. Dry, cold dust blew up into Poe's full grey eyes, and he hardened his mouth under the gay dark moustache. His shins felt goosefleshy; his striped trousers were unseasonably thin and his shoes badly needed mending. Which way lay his journey?

He remembered the name of the street, and something about a ruined garden. Eventually he came to the place, or what must be the place—the garden was certainly ruined, full of dry, hardy weeds that still stood in great ragged clumps after the hard winter. Poe forced open the creaky gate, went up the rough-flagged path to the stoop. He saw a bronzed nameplate—"Gauber," it said. Yes, that was the name he had heard. He swung the knocker loudly, and thought he caught a whisper of movement inside. But the door did not open.

"Nobody lives there, Mr. Poe," said someone from the street. It was a grocery boy, with a heavy basket on his arm. Poe left the doorstep. He knew the lad; indeed he owed the grocer eleven dollars.

"Are you sure?" Poe prompted.

"Well"—and the boy shifted the weight of his burden—"if anybody lived there, they'd buy from our shop, wouldn't they? And I'd deliver, wouldn't I? But I've had this job for six months, and never set foot inside that door."

Poe thanked him and walked down the street, but did not take the turn that would lead home. Instead he sought the shop of one Pemberton, a printer and friend, to pass the time of day and ask for a loan.

Pemberton could not lend even one dollar—times were hard—but offered a drink of Monongahela whiskey, which Poe forced himself to refuse; then a supper of crackers, cheese, and garlic sausage, which Poe thankfully shared. At home, unless his mother-in-law had begged or borrowed from the neighbours, would be only bread and molasses. It was past sundown when the writer shook hands with Pemberton, thanked him with warm courtesy for his hospitality, and ventured into the evening.

Thank Heaven, it did not rain. Poe was saddened by storms. The wind abated and the March sky was clear save for a tiny fluff of scudding cloud and a banked dark line at the horizon, while up rose a full moon the colour of frozen cream. Poe squinted from under his hat brim at the shadow-pattern on the disc. Might he not write another story of a lunar voyage—like the one about Hans Pfaall, but dead serious this time? Musing thus, he walked along the dusk-filling street until he came again opposite the ruined garden, the creaky gate, and the house with the doorplate marked: "Gauber."

Hello, the grocery boy had been wrong. There was light inside the front window, water-blue light—or was there? Anyway, motion—yes, a figure stooped there, as if to peer out at him.

Poe turned in at the gate, and knocked at the door once again.

Four or five moments of silence; then he heard the old lock grating. The door moved inwards, slowly and noisily. Poe fancied that he had been wrong about the blue light; for he saw only darkness inside. A voice spoke:

"Well, sir."

The two words came huskily but softly, as though the door-opener scarcely breathed. Poe swept off his broad black hat and made one of his graceful bows.

"If you will pardon me . . ." He paused, not knowing whether he addressed man or woman. "This is the Gauber residence?"

"It is," was the reply, soft, hoarse, and sexless. "Your business, sir?"

Poe spoke with official crispness; he had been a sergeant-major of artillery before he was twenty-one, and knew how to inject the proper note. "I am here on public duty," he announced. "I am a journalist, tracing a strange report."

"Journalist?" repeated his interrogator. "Strange report? Come in, sir."

Poe complied, and the door closed abruptly behind him, with a rusty snick of the lock. He remembered being in jail once, and how the door of his cell had slammed just so. It was not a pleasant memory. But he saw more clearly, now he was inside—his eyes got used to the tiny trickle of moonlight.

He stood in a dark hallway, all panelled in wood, with no furniture, drapes, or pictures. With him was a woman, in full skirt and down-drawn lace cap, a woman as tall as he and with intent eyes that glowed as from within. She neither moved nor spoke, but waited for him to tell her more of his errand.

Poe did so, giving his name and, stretching a point, claiming to be a sub-editor of the *Dollar Newspaper*, definitely assigned to the interview. "And now, madam, concerning this story that is rife concerning a premature burial . . ."

She had moved very close, but as his face turned towards her she drew back. Poe fancied that his breath had blown her away like a feather; then, remembering Pemberton's garlic sausage, he was chagrined. To confirm his new thought, the woman was offering him wine—to sweeten his breath.

"Would you take a glass of canary, Mr. Poe," she invited, and opened a side door. He followed her into a room papered in pale blue. Moonglow, drenching it, reflected from that paper and seemed an artificial light. That was what he had seen from outside. From an undraped table his hostess lifted a bottle, poured wine into a metal goblet, and offered it.

Poe wanted that wine, but he had recently promised his sick wife, solemnly and honestly, to abstain from even a sip of the drink that so easily upset him. Through thirsty lips he said: "I thank you kindly, but I am a temperance man."

"Oh," and she smiled. Poe saw white teeth. Then: "I am Elva Gauber—Mrs. John Gauber. The matter of which you ask I cannot explain clearly, but it is true. My husband was buried, in the Eastern Lutheran Church-yard . . ."

"I had heard, Mrs. Gauber, that the burial concerned a woman."

"No, my husband. He had been ill. He felt cold and quiet. A physician, a Dr. Mechem, pronounced him dead, and he was interred beneath a marble slab in his family vault." She sounded weary, but her voice was calm. "This happened shortly after the New Year. On Valentine's Day, I brought flowers. Beneath his slab he stirred and struggled. I had him brought forth. And he lives—after a fashion—today."

"Lives today?" repeated Poe. "In this house?"

"Would you care to see him? Interview him?"

Poe's heart raced, his spine chilled. It was his peculiar-ity that such sensations gave him pleasure. "I would like nothing better," he assured her, and she went to another door, an inner one.

Opening it, she paused on the threshold, as though summoning her resolution for a plunge into cold, swift water. Then she started down a flight of steps.

Poe followed, unconsciously drawing the door shut behind him.

The gloom of midnight, of prison—yes, of the tomb—fell at once upon those stairs. He heard Elva Gauber gasp:

"No—the moonlight—let it in . . ." And then she fell, heavily and limply, rolling downstairs.

Aghast, Poe quickly groped his way after her. She lay

against a door at the foot of the flight, wedged against the panel. He touched her—she was cold and rigid, without motion or elasticity of life. His thin hand groped for and found the knob of the lower door, flung it open. More dim reflected moonlight, and he made shift to drag the woman into it.

Almost at once she sighed heavily, lifted her head, and rose. "How stupid of me," she apologized hoarsely.

"The fault was mine," protested Poe. "Your nerves, your health, have naturally suffered. The sudden dark— the closeness—overcame you." He fumbled in his pocket for a tinderbox. "Suffer me to strike a light."

But she held out a hand to stop him. "No, no. The moon is sufficient." She walked to a small oblong pane set in the wall. Her hands, thin as Poe's own, with long grubby nails, hooked on the sill. Her face, bathed in the full light of the moon, strengthened and grew calm. She breathed deeply, almost voluptuously. "I am quite recovered," she said. "Do not fear for me. You need not stand so near, sir."

He had forgotten that garlic odour, and drew back contritely. She must be as sensitive to the smell as . . . as . . . what was it that was sickened and driven by garlic? Poe could not remember, and he took time to note that they were in a basement, stone-walled and with a floor of dirt. In one corner water seemed to drip, forming a dank pool of mud. Close to this, set into the wall, showed a latched trapdoor of planks, thick and wide, cleated cross-wise, as though to cover a window. But no window would be set so low. Everything smelt earthy and close, as though fresh air had been shut out for decades.

"Your husband is here?" he inquired.

"Yes." She walked to the shutter-like trap, unlatched it, and drew it open.

The recess beyond was black as ink, and from it came a feeble mutter. Poe followed Elva Gauber, and strained his eyes. In a little stone-flagged nook a bed had been made up. Upon it lay a man, stripped almost naked. His skin was as white as dead bone, and only his eyes, now opening, had life. He gazed at Elva Gauber and past her at Poe.

"Go away," he mumbled.

"Sir," ventured Poe formally, "I have come to hear of how you came to life in the grave . . ."

"It's a lie," broke in the man on the pallet. He writhed halfway to a sitting posture, labouring upwards as against a crushing weight. The wash of moonlight showed how wasted and fragile he was. His face stared and snarled bare-toothed, like a skull. "A lie, I say!" he cried, with a sudden strength that might well have been his last. "Told by this monster who is not—my wife . . ."

The shutter-trap slammed upon his cries. Elva Gauber faced Poe, withdrawing a pace to avoid his garlic breath.

"You have seen my husband," she said. "Was it a pretty sight, sir?"

He did not answer, and she moved across the dirt to

the stair doorway. "Will you go up first?" she asked. "At the top, hold the door open, that I may have"—she said "life," or, perhaps, "light." Poe could not be sure which.

Plainly she, who had almost welcomed his intrusion at first, now sought to lead him away. Her eyes, compelling as shouted commands, were fixed upon him. He felt their power, and bowed to it.

Obediently he mounted the stairs, and stood with the upper door wide open. Elva Gauber came up after him. At the top her eyes seized his. Suddenly Poe knew more than ever before about the mesmeric impulses he loved to write about. "I hope," she said measuredly, "that you have not found your mission fruitless. I live here alone— seeing nobody, caring for the poor thing that was once my husband, John Gauber. My mind is not clear. Perhaps my manners are not good. Forgive me, and goodnight."

Poe found himself ushered from the house and outside the wind was howling again. The front door closed behind him, and the lock grated.

The fresh air, the whip of gale in his face, and the absence of Elva Gauber's impelling gaze suddenly brought him back, as though from sleep, to a realization of what had happened—or what had not happened.

He had come out, on this uncomfortable March evening, to investigate the report of a premature burial. He had seen a ghastly thing, that had called the gossip a lie. Somehow, then, he had been drawn abruptly away—

stopped from full study of what might be one of the strangest adventures it was ever a writer's good fortune to know. Why was he letting things drop at this stage?

He decided not to let them drop. That would be worse than staying away altogether.

He made up his mind, formed quickly a plan. Leaving the doorstep, he turned from the gate, slipped quickly around the house. He knelt by the foundation at the side, just where a small oblong pane was set flush with the ground.

Bending his head, he found that he could see plainly inside, by reason of the flood of moonlight—a phenomenon, he realized, for generally an apartment was disclosed only by light within. The open doorway to the stairs, the swamp mess of mud in the corner, the outflung trapdoor, were discernible. And something stood or huddled at the exposed niche—something that bent itself upon and above the frail white body of John Gauber.

Full skirt, white cap—it was Elva Gauber. She bent herself down, her face was touching the face or shoulder of her husband.

Poe's heart, never the healthiest of organs, began to drum and race. He pressed closer to the pane, for a better glimpse of what went on in the cellar. His shadow cut away some of the light. Elva Gauber turned to look.

Her face was as pale as the moon itself. Like the moon, it was shadowed in irregular patches. She came quickly, almost running, towards the pane where Poe crouched. He saw her, plainly and at close hand.

Dark, wet, sticky stains lay upon her mouth and cheeks. Her tongue roved out, licking at the stains—

Blood!

Poe sprang up and ran to the front of the house. He forced his thin, trembling fingers to seize the knocker, to swing it heavily again and again. When there was no answer, he pushed heavily against the door itself—it did not give. He moved to a window, rapped on it, pried at the sill, lifted his fist to smash the glass.

A silhouette moved beyond the pane, and threw it up. Something shot out at him like a pale snake striking— before he could move back, fingers had twisted in the front of his coat. Elva Gauber's eyes glared into his.

Her cap was off, her dark hair fallen in disorder. Blood still smeared and dewed her mouth and jowls.

"You have pried too far," she said, in a voice as measured and cold as the drip from icicles. "I was going to spare you, because of the odour about you that repelled me—the garlic. I showed you a little, enough to warn any wise person, and let you go. Now . . ."

Poe struggled to free himself. Her grip was immovable, like the clutch of a steel trap. She grimaced in triumph, yet she could not quite face him—the garlic still clung to his breath.

"Look in my eyes," she bade him. "Look—you cannot refuse, you cannot escape. You will die, with John—and the two of you, dying, shall rise again like me. I'll have two fountains of life while you remain—two companions after you die."

"Woman," said Poe, fighting against her stabbing gaze, "you are mad."

She snickered gustily. "I am sane, and so are you. We both know that I speak the truth. We both know the futility of your struggle." Her voice rose a little. "Through a chink in the tomb, as I lay dead, a ray of moonlight streamed and struck my eyes. I woke. I struggled. I was set free. Now at night, when the moon shines—Ugh! Don't breathe that herb in my face!"

She turned her head away. At that instant it seemed to Poe that a curtain of utter darkness fell and with it sank down the form of Elva Gauber.

He peered into the sudden gloom. She was collapsed across the window sill, like a discarded puppet in its booth. Her hand still twisted in the bosom of his coat, and he pried himself loose from it, finger by steely, cold finger. Then he turned to flee from this place of shadowed peril to body and soul.

As he turned, he saw whence had come the dark. A cloud had come up from its place on the horizon—the fat, sooty bank he had noted there at sundown—and now it obscured the moon. Poe paused, in mid-retreat, gazing.

His thoughtful eye gauged the speed and size of the cloud. It curtained the moon, would continue to curtain it for—well, ten minutes. And for that ten minutes Elva Gauber would lie motionless, lifeless. She had told the truth about the moon giving her life. Hadn't she fallen like one slain on the stairs when they were darkened? Poe began grimly to string the evidence together.

It was Elva Gauber, not her husband, who had died and gone to the family vault. She had come back to life, or a mockery of life, by touch of the moon's rays. Such light was an unpredictable force—it made dogs howl, it flogged madmen to violence, it brought fear, or black sorrow, or ecstasy. Old legends said that it was the birth of fairies, the transformation of werewolves, the motive power of broom-riding witches. It was surely the source of the strength and evil animating what had been the corpse of Elva Gauber—and he, Poe, must not stand there dreaming.

He summoned all the courage that was his, and scrambled in at the window through which clumped the woman's form. He groped across the room to the cellar door, opened it, and went down the stairs, through the door at the bottom, and into the stone-walled basement.

It was dark, moonless still. Poe paused only to bring forth his tinderbox, strike a light, and kindle the end of a tightly twisted linen rag. It gave a feeble steady light, and he found his way to the shutter, opened it, and touched the naked, wasted shoulder of John Gauber.

"Get up," he said. "I've come to save you."

The skull-face feebly shifted its position to meet his gaze. The man managed to speak, moaningly:

"Useless. I can't move—unless she lets me. Her eyes keep me here—half-alive. I'd have died long ago, but somehow . . ."

Poe thought of a wretched spider, paralysed by the sting of a mud-wasp, lying helpless in its captive's close den until the hour of feeding comes. He bent down, holding his blazing tinder close. He could see Gauber's neck, and it was a mass of tiny puncture wounds, some of them still beaded with blood drops fresh or dried. He winced but bode firm in his purpose.

"Let me guess the truth," he said quickly. "Your wife was brought home from the grave, came back to a seeming of life. She put a spell on you, or played a trick— made you a helpless prisoner. That isn't contrary to nature, that last. I've studied mesmerism."

"It's true," John Gauber mumbled.

"And nightly she comes to drink your blood?"

Gauber weakly nodded. "Yes. She was beginning just now, but ran upstairs. She will be coming back."

"Good," said Poe bleakly. "Perhaps she will come back to more than she expects. Have you ever heard of vampires? Probably not, but I have studied them, too. I began to guess, I think, when first she was so repelled by the odour of garlic. Vampires lie motionless by day and walk and feed at night. They are creatures of the moon— their food is blood. Come."

Poe broke off, put out his light, and lifted the man in his arms. Gauber was as light as a child. The writer carried him to the slanting shelter of the closed-in staircase, and there set him against the wall stones. The poor fellow would be well hidden.

Next Poe flung off his coat, waistcoat, and shirt. Heaping his clothing in a deeper shadow of the stairway, he stood up, stripped to the waist. His skin was almost as bloodlessly pale as Gauber's, his chest and arms almost as gaunt. He dared believe that he might pass momentarily for the unfortunate man.

The cellar sprang full of light again. The cloud must be passing from the moon. Poe listened. There was a dragging sound above, then footsteps.

Elva Gauber, the blood drinker by night, had revived.

Now for it. Poe hurried to the niche, thrust himself in, and pulled the trapdoor shut after him.

He grinned, sharing a horrid paradox with the blackness around him. He had heard all the fabled ways of destroying vampires — transfixing stakes, holy water, prayer, fire. But he, Edgar Allan Poe, had evolved a new way. Myriads of tales whispered frighteningly of fiends lying in wait for normal men, but who had ever heard of a normal man lying in wait for a fiend? Well, he had never considered himself normal, in spirit, or brain, or taste.

He stretched out, feet together, hands crossed on his bare midriff. Thus it would be in the tomb, he found himself thinking. To his mind came a snatch of poetry by a man named Bryant, published long ago in a New England review — "Breathless darkness, and the narrow house." It was breathless and dark enough in this hole, Heaven knew, and narrow as well. He rejected, almost hysterically, the implication of being buried. To break the ugly spell that daunted him where thought of Elva Gauber failed, he turned sideways to face the wall, his naked arm lying across his cheek and temple.

As his ear touched the musty bedding, it brought to

him once again the echo of footsteps, footsteps descending the stairs. They were rhythmic, confident. They were eager.

Elva Gauber was coming to seek again her interrupted repast.

Now she was crossing the floor. She did not pause or turn aside—she had not noticed her husband, lying under the cadet cloak in the shadow of the stairs. The noise came straight to the trapdoor, and he heard her fumbling for the latch.

Light, blue as skimmed milk, poured into his nook. A shadow fell in the midst of it, full upon him. His imagination, ever out-stripping reality, whispered that the shadow had weight, like lead—oppressive, baleful.

"John," said the voice of Elva Gauber in his ear, "I've come back. You know why—you know what for." Her voice sounded greedy, as though it came through loose, trembling lips. "You're my only source of strength now. I thought tonight, that a stranger—but he got away. He had a cursed odour about him, anyway."

Her hand touched the skin of his neck. She was prodding him, like a butcher fingering a doomed beast.

"Don't hold yourself away from me, John," she was commanding, in a voice of harsh mockery. "You know it won't do any good. This is the night of the full moon, and I have power for anything, anything!" She was trying to drag his arm away from his face. "You won't gain by—" She broke off, aghast. Then, in a wild dry-throated scream:

"You're not John!"

Poe whipped over on his back, and his bird-claw hands shot out and seized her—one hand clinching upon her snaky disorder of dark hair, the other digging its fingertips into the chill flesh of her arm.

The scream quivered away into a horrible breathless rattle. Poe dragged his captive violently inwards, throwing all his collected strength into the effort. Her feet were jerked from the floor and she flew into the recess, hurtling above and beyond Poe's recumbent body. She struck the inner stones with a crashing force that might break bones, and would have collapsed upon Poe; but, at the same moment, he had released her and slid swiftly out upon the floor of the cellar.

With frantic haste he seized the edge of the back-flung trapdoor. Elva Gauber struggled upon hands and knees, among the tumbled bedclothes in the niche; then Poe had slammed the panel shut.

She threw herself against it from within, yammering and wailing like an animal in a trap. She was almost as strong as he, and for a moment he thought that she would burst out of the niche. But, sweating and wheezing, he bore against the planks with his shoulder, bracing his feet against the earth. His fingers found the latch, lifted it, forced it into place.

"Dark," moaned Elva Gauber from inside. "Dark—no moon—" Her voice trailed off.

Poe went to the muddy pool in the corner, thrust in his hands. The mud was slimy but workable. He pushed a double handful of it against the trapdoor, sealing cracks and edges. Another handful, another. Using his palms like trowels, he coated the boards with thick mud.

"Gauber," he said breathlessly, "how are you?"

"All right—I think." The voice was strangely strong and clear. Looking over his shoulder, Poe saw that Gauber had come upright of himself, still pale but apparently steady. "What are you doing?" Gauber asked.

"Walling her up," jerked out Poe, scooping still more mud. "Walling her up forever, with her evil."

He had a momentary flash of inspiration, a symbolic germ of a story; in it a man sealed a woman into such a nook of the wall, and with her an embodiment of active evil—perhaps in the form of a black cat.

Pausing at last to breathe deeply, he smiled to himself. Even in the direst of danger, the most heart-breaking moment of toil and fear, he must ever be coining up new plots for stories.

"I cannot thank you enough," Gauber was saying to him. "I feel that all will be well—if only she stays there."

Poe put his ear to the wall. "Not a whisper of motion, sir. She's shut off from moonlight—from life and power. Can you help me with my clothes? I feel terribly chilled."

His mother-in-law met him on the threshold when he returned to the house in Spring Garden Street. Under the white widow's cap, her strong-boned face was drawn with worry.

"Eddie, are you ill?" She was really asking if he had been drinking. A look reassured her. "No," she answered herself, "but you've been away from home so long. And you're dirty, Eddie—filthy. You must wash."

He let her lead him in, pour hot water into a basin. As he scrubbed himself, he formed excuses, a banal lie about a long walk for inspiration, a moment of dizzy weariness, a stumble into a mud puddle.

"I'll make you some nice hot coffee, Eddie," his mother-in-law offered.

"Please," he responded and went back to his own room with the slate mantelpiece. Again he lighted the candle, sat down, and took up his pen.

His mind was embellishing the story inspiration that had come to him at such a black moment, in the cellar of the Gauber house. He'd work on that tomorrow. The *United States Saturday Post* would take it, he hoped. Title? He would call it simply "The Black Cat."

But to finish the present task! He dipped his pen in ink. How to begin? How to end? How, after writing and publishing such an account, to defend himself against the growing whisper of his insanity?

He decided to forget it, if he could—at least to seek healthy company, comfort, quiet—perhaps even to write some light verse, some humorous articles and stories. For the first time in his life, he had had enough of the macabre.

Quickly he wrote a final paragraph:

There are moments when, even to the sober eye of
Reason, the world of our sad Humanity may assume
the semblance of a Hell—but the imagination of man
is no Carathis, to explore with impunity its every cav-
ern. Alas! The grim legion of sepulchral terrors cannot be regarded as altogether fanciful—but, like the
Demons in whose company Afrasiab made his voyage
down the Oxus, they must sleep, or they will devour
us—they must be suffered to slumber, or we will
perish.

That would do for the public, decided Edgar Allan Poe.
In any case, it would do for the Philadelphia *Dollar
Newspaper.* His mother-in-law brought in the coffee.

FOUR WOODEN STAKES

✦✦✦

VICTOR ROMAN

There it lay on the desk in front of me, that missive so simple in wording, yet so perplexing, so urgent in tone.

> *Jack, Come at once for old time's sake. Am all alone.*
> *Will explain upon arrival. Remson.*

Having spent the past three weeks in bringing to a successful termination a case that had puzzled the police and two of the best detective agencies in the city, I decided that I was entitled to a rest, so I ordered two suitcases packed and went in search of a timetable. It was several years since I had seen Remson Holroyd; in fact I had not seen him since we had matriculated from college together. I was curious to know how he was getting along, to say nothing of the little diversion he promised me in the way of a mystery.

The following afternoon found me standing on the platform of the little town of Charing, a village of about fifteen hundred souls. Remson's place was about ten miles from there so I stepped forward to the driver of a shay and asked if he would kindly take me to the Holroyd estate. He clasped his hands in what seemed a silent prayer, shuddered slightly, then looked at me with an air of wonder, mingled with suspicion.

"I don't know what ye wants to go out there for, stranger, but if ye'll take the advice o' a God-fearing man, ye'll turn back whence ye come from. There be some mighty fearful tales concernin' that place floatin' around, and more'n one tramp's been found near there so weak from loss of blood and fear he could hardly crawl. They's somethin' there. Be it man or beast I don't know, but as for me, I wouldn't drive ye out there for a hundred dollars cash."

This was not at all encouraging, but I was not to be influenced by the talk of a superstitious old gossip, so I cast about for a less impressionable rustic who would undertake the trip to earn the ample reward I promised at the end of my ride. To my chagrin, they all acted like the first; some crossed themselves fervently, while others gave me one wild look and ran, as if I were in alliance with the devil.

By now my curiosity was thoroughly aroused, and I was determined to see the thing through to a finish if it cost me my life. So, casting a last, contemptuous look upon those poor souls, I stepped out briskly in the direction pointed out to me. However, I had gone but a scant two miles when the weight of the suitcases began to tell, and I slackened pace considerably.

The sun was just disappearing beneath the treetops

when I caught my first glimpse of the old homestead,
now deserted but for its one occupant. Time and the elements had laid heavy hands upon it, for there was hardly
a window that could boast its full quota of panes, while
the shutters banged and creaked with a noise dismal
enough to daunt even the strong of heart.

About one hundred yards back I discerned a small
building of grey stone, pieces of which seemed to be lying all around it, partly covered by the dense growth of
vegetation that overran the entire countryside. On closer
observation I realized that the building was a crypt, while
what I had taken to be pieces of the material scattered
around were really tombstones. Evidently this was the
family burying ground. But why had certain members
been interred in a mausoleum while the remainder of
the family had been buried in the ground in the usual
manner?

Having observed thus much, I turned my steps
towards the house, for I had no intention of spending the
night with naught but the dead for company. Indeed, I
began to realize just why those simple country folk had
refused to aid me, and a hesitant doubt began to assert itself as to the expedience of my being here, when I might
have been at the shore or at the country club enjoying
life to the full.

By now the sun had completely slid from view, and in
the semi-darkness the place presented an even drearier
aspect than before. With a great display of bravado I
stepped upon the veranda, slammed my suitcases upon a

seat very much the worse for wear, and pulled lustily at the knob.

Peal after peal reverberated through the house, echoing and reechoing from room to room, till the whole structure rang. Then all was still once more, save for the sighing of the wind and the creaking of the shutters.

A few minutes passed, and the sound of footsteps approaching the door reached my ears. Another interval, and the door was cautiously opened a few inches, while a head, shrouded by the darkness, scrutinized me closely. Then the door was flung wide, and Remson (I hardly knew him, so changed was he) rushed forward and throwing his arms around me thanked me again and again for heeding his plea, till I thought he would go into hysterics.

I begged him to brace up, and the sound of my voice seemed to help him, for he apologized rather shamefacedly for his discourtesy and led the way along the wide hall. There was a fire blazing merrily away in the sitting room, and after partaking generously of a repast, for I was famished after my long walk, I was seated in front of it, facing Remson and waiting to hear his story.

"Jack," he began, "I'll start at the beginning and try and give you the facts in their proper sequence. Five years ago my family circle consisted of five persons: my grandfather, my father, two brothers, and myself, the baby of the family. My mother died, you know, when I was a few weeks old. Now . . ."

His voice broke and for a moment he was unable to continue.

"There's only myself left," he went on, "and so help me God, I'm going too, unless you can solve this damnable mystery that hovers over this house, and put an end to that something which took my kin and is gradually taking me.

"Grandad was the first to go. He spent the last few years of his life in South America. Just before leaving there he was attacked while asleep by one of those huge bats. Next morning he was so weak that he couldn't walk. That awful thing had sucked his life blood away. He arrived here, but was sickly until his death a few weeks later. The doctors couldn't agree as to the cause of death, so they laid it to old age and let it go at that. But I knew better. It was his experience in the south that had done for him. In his will he asked that a crypt be built immediately and his body interred therein. His wish was carried out, and his remains lie in that little grey vault that you may have noticed if you cut around behind the house. Then my dad began failing and just pined away until he died. What puzzled the doctors was the fact that right up until the end he consumed enough food to sustain three men, yet he was so weak he lacked the strength to drag his legs over the floor. He was buried, or rather interred, with Grandad. The same symptoms were in evidence in the cases of George and Fred. They are both lying in the vault. And now, Jack, I'm going, too, for of late my appetite has increased to alarming proportions, yet I am as weak as a kitten."

"Nonsense!" I chided. "We'll just leave this place for a while and take a trip somewhere, and when you return you'll laugh at your fears. It's all a case of overwrought nerves, and there is certainly nothing strange about the deaths you speak of. Probably due to some hereditary disease. More than one family has passed out in a hurry just on that account."

"Jack, I only wish I could think so, but somehow I know better. And as for leaving here, I just can't. Understand, I hate the place; I loathe it, but I can't get away. There is a morbid fascination about the place which holds me. If you want to be a real friend, just stay with me for a couple of days and if you don't find anything, I'm sure the sight of you and the sound of your voice will do wonders for me."

I agreed to do my best, although I was hard put to it to keep from smiling at his fears, so apparently groundless were they. We talked on other subjects for several hours, then I proposed bed, saying that I was very tired after my journey and subsequent walk. Remson showed me to my room, and after seeing that everything was as comfortable as possible, he bade me good night.

As he turned to leave the room the flickering light from the lamp fell on his neck and I noticed two small punctures in the skin. I questioned him regarding them, but he replied that he must have beheaded a pimple and that he hadn't noticed them before. He again said good night and left the room.

I undressed and tumbled into bed. During the night I was conscious of an overpowering feeling of suffocation—as if some great burden was lying on my chest which I could not dislodge; and in the morning when I awoke, I experienced a curious sensation of weakness. I arose, not without an effort, and began divesting myself of my sleeping suit.

As I folded the jacket, I noticed a thin line of blood on the collar. I felt my neck, a terrible fear overwhelming me. It pained slightly at the touch. I rushed to examine it in the mirror. Two tiny dots rimmed with blood—my blood—and on my neck! No longer did I chuckle at Remson's fears, for *it*, the thing, had attacked me as I slept!

I dressed as quickly as my condition would permit and went downstairs, thinking to find my friend there. He was not about, so I looked outside, but he was not in evidence. There was but one answer to the question. He had not yet risen. It was nine o'clock, so I resolved to awaken him.

Not knowing which room he occupied, I entered one after another in a fruitless search. They were all in various stages of disorder, and the thick coating of dust on the furniture showed that they had been untenanted for some time. At last, in a bedroom on the north side of the third floor, I found him.

He was lying spread-eagle fashion across the bed, still in his pajamas, and as I leaned forward to shake him, my eyes fell on two drops of blood, splattered on the coverlet. I crushed back a wild desire to scream and shook Remson rather roughly. His head rolled to one side, and the hellish perforations on his throat showed up vividly. They looked fresh and raw, and had increased to much greater dimensions. I shook him with increased vigor, and at last he opened his eyes stupidly and looked around. Then, seeing me, he said in a voice loaded with anguish, resignation, and despair:

"It's been here again, Jack. I can't hold out much longer. May God take my soul when I go."

So saying, he fell back again from sheer weakness. I left him and went about preparing myself some breakfast. I thought it best not to destroy his faith in me by telling him that I, too, had suffered at the hands of his persecutor.

A walk brought me some peace of mind if not a solution, and when I returned about noon to the big house, Remson was up and about. Together we prepared a really excellent meal. I was hungry and did justice to my share; but after I had finished, my friend continued eating until I thought he must either disgorge or burst. Then after putting things to rights, we strolled about the long hall, looking at the oil paintings, many of which were very valuable.

At one end of the hall I discovered a portrait of an old gentleman, evidently a dandy of his day. He wore his hair in the long, flowing fashion adopted by the old school and sported a carefully trimmed moustache and Vandyke beard. Remson noticed my interest in the painting and came forward.

"I don't wonder that picture holds your interest, Jack. It has a great fascination for me, also. At times I sit for hours, studying the expression on that face. I sometimes think that he has something to tell me, but of course that's all tommy rot. But I beg your pardon, I haven't introduced the old gent yet, have I? This is my grandad. He was a great old boy in his day, and he might be living yet but for that cursed bloodsucker. Perhaps it is such a creature that is doing for me; what do you think?"

"I wouldn't like to venture an opinion, Remson, but unless I'm badly mistaken we must dig deeper for an explanation. We'll know tonight, however. You retire as usual and I'll keep a close watch and we'll solve the riddle or die in the attempt."

Remson said not a word but silently extended his hand. I clasped it in a firm embrace and in each other's eyes we read complete understanding. To change the trend of thought I questioned him on the servant problem.

"I've tried time and again to get servants that would stay," he replied, "but about the third day they would begin acting queer, and the first thing I'd know, they'd have skipped, bag and baggage."

That night I accompanied my friend to his room and remained until he had disrobed and was ready to retire. Several of the window panes were cracked and one was entirely missing. I suggested boarding up the aperture, but he declined, saying that he rather enjoyed the night air, so I dropped the matter.

As it was still early, I sat by the fire in the sitting room and read for an hour or two. I confess that there were many times when my mind wandered from the printed page before me and chills raced up and down my spine as some new sound was borne to my ears. The wind had risen, and was whistling through the trees with a peculiar whining sound. The creaking of the shutters tended to further the eerie effect, and in the distance could be heard the hooting of numerous owls, mingled with the cries of miscellaneous night fowl and other nocturnal creatures.

As I ascended the two flights of steps, the candle in my hand casting grotesque shadows on the walls and ceiling, I had little liking for my job. Many times in the course of duty I had been called upon to display courage, but it took more than mere courage to keep me going now.

I extinguished the candle and crept forward to Remson's room, the door of which was closed. Being careful to make no noise I knelt and looked in at the keyhole. It afforded me a clear view of the bed and two of the windows in the opposite wall. Gradually my eye became accustomed to the darkness and I noticed a faint reddish glow outside one of the windows. It apparently emanated from nowhere. Hundreds of little specks danced and whirled in the spot of light, and as I watched them, fascinated, they seemed to take on the form of a human face.

The features were masculine, as was also the arrangement of the hair. Then the mysterious glow disappeared.

So great had the strain been on me that I was wet from perspiration, although the night was quite cool. For a moment I was undecided whether to enter the room or to stay where I was and use the keyhole as a means of observation. I concluded that to remain where I was would be the better plan, so I once more placed my eye to the hole.

Immediately my attention was drawn to something moving where the light had been. At first, owing to the poor light, I was unable to distinguish the general outline and form of the thing; then I saw. It was a man's head.

I will swear it was the exact reproduction of that picture I had seen in the hall that very morning. But, oh, the difference in expression! The lips were drawn back in a snarl, disclosing two sets of pearly white teeth, the canines overdeveloped and remarkably sharp. The eyes, an emerald green in color, stared in a look of consuming hate. The hair was sadly disarranged while on the beard was a large clot of what seemed to be congealed blood.

I noticed thus much, then the head melted from my sight and I transferred my attention to a great bat that circled round and round, his huge wings beating a tattoo on the glass. Finally he circled round the broken pane and flew straight through the hole made by the missing glass. For a few moments he was shut off from my view, then he reappeared and began circling round my friend, who lay sound asleep, blissfully ignorant of all that was occurring.

Nearer and nearer it drew, then swooped down and fastened itself on Remson's throat, just over the jugular vein.

At this I rushed into the room and made a wild dash for the thing that had come night after night to gorge itself on my friend, but to no avail. It flew out of the window and away, and I turned my attention to the sleeper.

"Remson, old man, get up."

He sat up like a shot. "What's the matter, Jack? Has it been here?"

"Never mind just now," I replied. "Just dress as hurriedly as possible. We have a little work before us this evening."

He glanced questioningly towards me, but followed my command without argument. I turned and cast my eye about the room for a suitable weapon. There was a stout stick lying in the corner and I made toward it.

"Jack!"

I wheeled about.

"What is it? Damn it, haven't you any sense, almost scaring a man to death?"

He pointed a shaking finger towards the window.

"There! I swear I saw him. It was my grandad, but oh, how disfigured!"

He threw himself upon the bed and began sobbing. The shock had completely unnerved him.

"Forgive me, old man," I pleaded, "I was too quick. Pull yourself together and we may get to the bottom of things tonight, yet."

I handed him my flask. He took a generous swallow and squared up. When he had finished dressing we left the house. There was no moon out, and it was pitch dark.

I led the way, and soon we came to within ten yards of the little grey crypt. I stationed Remson behind a tree with instructions to just use his eyes, and I took up my stand on the other side of the vault, after making sure that the door into it was closed and locked. For the greater part of an hour we waited without results, and I was about ready to call it off when I perceived a white figure flitting between the trees about fifty yards off.

Slowly it advanced, straight towards us, and as it drew closer I looked not *at* it, but *through* it. The wind was blowing strongly, yet not a fold in the long shroud quivered. Just outside the vault it paused and looked around. Even knowing as I did about what to expect, it came as a decided shock when I looked into the eyes of the old Holroyd, deceased these past five years. I heard a gasp and knew that Remson had seen, too, and had recognized. Then the spirit, ghost, or whatever it was, passed into the crypt through the crack between the door and the jamb, a space not one-sixteenth of an inch wide.

As it disappeared, Remson came running forward, his face wholly drawn of color.

"What was it, Jack? What was it? I know it resembled Grandad, but it couldn't have been he. He's been dead five years."

"Let's go back to the house," I answered, "and I'll do my best to explain things to the best of my ability. I may be wrong, of course, but it won't hurt to try my remedy. Remson, what we are up against is a vampire. Not the female species usually spoken of today, but the real thing. I noticed you had an old edition of the Encyclopedia on your shelf. If you'll bring me volume XXIV I'll be able to explain more fully the meaning of the word."

He left the room and returned, carrying the desired book. Turning to page 52, I read—

Vampire. A term apparently of Serbian origin originally applied in Eastern Europe to blood-sucking ghosts, but in modern usage transferred to one or more species of blood-sucking bats inhabiting South America . . . In the first-mentioned meaning a vampire is usually supposed to be the soul of a dead man which quits the buried body by night to suck the blood of living persons. Hence, when the vampire's grave is opened his corpse is found to be fresh and rosy from the blood thus absorbed . . . They are accredited with the power of assuming any form they may so desire, and often fly about as specks of dust, pieces of down or straw, etc. . . . To put an end to his ravages, a stake is driven through him, or his head cut off, or his heart torn out, or boiling water and vinegar poured over the grave . . . The persons who turn vampires are wizards, witches, suicides, and those who have come to a violent end. Also, the death of anyone resulting from these vampires will cause that person to join their hellish throng . . . See Calumet's "Dissertation on the Vampires of Hungary."

I looked at Remson. He was staring straight into the

fire. I knew that he realized the task before us and was steeling himself to it. Then he turned to me.

"Jack, we'll wait till morning."

That was all. I understood and he knew. There we sat, each struggling with his own thoughts, until the first faint glimmers of light came struggling through the trees and warned us of approaching dawn.

Remson left to fetch a sledge-hammer and a large knife with its edge honed to a razorlike keenness. I busied myself making four wooden stakes, shaped like wedges. He returned, bearing the horrible tools, and we struck out towards the crypt. We walked rapidly, for had either of us hesitated an instant I verily believe both would have fled. However, our duty lay clearly before us. Remson unlocked the door and swung it outwards. With a prayer on our lips we entered.

As if by mutual understanding, we both turned to the coffin on our left. It belonged to the grandfather. We unplaced the lid, and there lay the old Holroyd. He appeared to be sleeping. His face was full of color, and he had none of the stiffness of death. The hair was matted, the moustache untrimmed, and on the beard were matted stains of a dull brownish hue.

But it was his eyes that attracted me. They were greenish, and they glowed with an expression of fiendish malevolence such as I had never seen before. The look of baffled rage on the face might well have adorned the features of the devil in his hell.

Remson swayed and would have fallen, but I forced

some whisky down his throat and he took a grip on himself. He placed one of the stakes directly over its heart, then shut his eyes and prayed that the good God above take this soul that was to be delivered to Him.

I took a step backward, aimed carefully, and swung the sledge-hammer with all my strength. It hit the wedge squarely, and a terrible scream filled the place, while the blood gushed out of the open wound, up and over us, staining the walls and our clothes. Without hesitating, I swung again, and again, and again, while it struggled vainly to rid itself of that awful instrument of death. Another swing and the stake was driven through.

The thing squirmed about in the narrow confines of the coffin, much after the manner of a dismembered worm, and Remson proceeded to sever the head from the body, making a rather crude but effectual job of it. As the final stroke of the knife cut the connection a scream issued from the mouth; and the whole corpse fell away into dust, leaving nothing but a wooden stake lying in a bed of bones.

This finished, we despatched the remaining three. Simultaneously as if struck by the same thought, we felt our throats. The slight pain was gone from mine, and the wounds had entirely disappeared from my friend's, leaving not even a scar.

I wished to place before the world the whole facts contingent upon the mystery and the solution, but Remson prevailed upon me to hold my peace.

Some years later Remson died a Christian death and

with him went the only confirmation of my tale. However, ten miles from the little town of Charing there sits an old house, forgotten these many years, and near it is a little grey crypt. Within are four coffins; and in each lies a wooden stake, stained a brownish hue, and bearing the fingerprints of the deceased Remson Holroyd.

BLOOD-LUST

◆◆◆

DION FORTUNE

I

I have never been able to make up my mind whether Dr. Taverner should be the hero or the villain of these histories. That he was a man of the most selfless ideals could not be questioned, but in his methods of putting these ideals into practice he was absolutely unscrupulous. He did not evade the law, he merely ignored it, and though the exquisite tenderness with which he handled his cases was an education in itself, yet he would use that wonderful psychological method of his to break a soul to pieces, going to work as quietly and methodically and benevolently as if bent upon the cure of his patient.

The manner of my meeting with this strange man was quite simple. After being gazetted out of the R.A.M.C. I went to a medical agency and inquired what posts were available.

I said: "I have come out of the Army with my nerves

shattered. I want some quiet place till I can pull myself together."

"So does everybody else," said the clerk.

He looked at me thoughtfully. "I wonder whether you would care to try a place we have had on our books for some time. We have sent several men down to it but none of them would stop."

He sent me round to one of the tributaries of Harley Street, and there I made the acquaintance of the man who, whether he was good or bad, I have always regarded as the greatest mind I ever met.

Tall and thin, with a parchment-like countenance, he might have been any age from thirty-five to sixty-five. I have seen him look both ages within the hour. He lost no time in coming to the point.

"I want a medical superintendent for my nursing home," he told me. "I understand that you have specialized, as far as the Army permitted you to, in mental cases. I am afraid you will find my methods very different from the orthodox ones. However, as I sometimes succeed where others fail, I consider I am justified in continuing to experiment, which I think, Dr. Rhodes, is all any of my colleagues can claim to do."

The man's cynical manner annoyed me, though I could not deny that mental treatment is not an exact science at the present moment. As if in answer to my thought he continued:

"My chief interest lies in those regions of psychology

which orthodox science has not as yet ventured to explore. If you work with me you will see some queer things, but all I ask of you is, that you should keep an open mind and a shut mouth."

This I undertook to do, for, although I shrank instinctively from the man, yet there was about him such a curious attraction, such a sense of power and adventurous research, that I determined at least to give him the benefit of the doubt and see what it might lead to. His extraordinarily stimulating personality, which seemed to key my brain to concert pitch, made me feel that he might be a good tonic for a man who had lost his grip on life for the time being.

"Unless you have elaborate packing to do," he said, "I can motor you down to my place. If you will walk over with me to the garage I will drive you round to your lodgings, pick up your things, and we shall get in before dark."

We drove at a pretty high speed down the Portsmouth road till we came to Thursley, and, then, to my surprise, my companion turned off to the right and took the big car by a cart track over the heather.

"This is Thor's Ley, or field," he said, as the blighted country unrolled before us. "The old worship is still kept up about here."

"The Catholic faith?" I inquired.

"The Catholic faith, my dear sir, is an innovation. I was referring to the pagan worship. The peasants about here still retain bits of the old ritual; they think that it brings them luck, or some such superstition. They have no knowledge of its inner meaning." He paused a moment, and then turned to me and said with extraordinary emphasis: "Have you ever thought what it would mean if a man who had the Knowledge could piece that ritual together?"

I admitted I had not. I was frankly out of my depth, but he had certainly brought me to the most unchristian spot I had ever been in in my life.

His nursing home, however, was in delightful contrast to the wild and barren country that surrounded it. The garden was a mass of colour, and the house, old and rambling and covered with creepers, as charming within as without; it reminded me of the East, it reminded me of the Renaissance, and yet it had no style save that of warm rich colouring and comfort.

I soon settled down to my job, which I found exceedingly interesting. As I have already said, Taverner's work began where ordinary medicine ended, and I had under my care cases such as the ordinary doctor would have referred to the safe keeping of an asylum, as being nothing else but mad. Yet Taverner, by his peculiar methods of work, laid bare causes operating both within the soul and in the shadowy realm where the soul has its dwelling, that threw an entirely new light upon the problem, and often enabled him to rescue a man from the dark influences that were closing in upon him. The affair of the sheep-killing was an interesting example of his methods.

II

One showery afternoon at the nursing home we had a call from a neighbour—not a very common occurrence, for Taverner and his ways were regarded somewhat askance. Our visitor shed her dripping mackintosh, but declined to loosen the scarf which, warm as the day was, she had twisted tightly round her neck.

"I believe you specialize in mental cases," she said to my colleague. "I should very much like to talk over with you a matter that is troubling me."

Taverner nodded, his keen eyes watching her for symptoms.

"It concerns a friend of mine—in fact, I think I may call him my *fiancé*, for, although he has asked me to release him from his engagement, I have refused to do so; not because I should wish to hold a man who no longer loved me, but because I am convinced that he still cares for me, and there is something which has come between us that he will not tell me of.

"I have begged him to be frank with me and let us share the trouble together, for the thing that seems an insuperable obstacle to him may not appear in that light to me; but you know what men are when they consider their honour is in question." She looked from one to the other of us smiling. No woman ever believes that her men folk are grown up; perhaps she is right. Then she leant forward and clasped her hands eagerly. "I believe I have found the key to the mystery. I want you to tell me whether it is possible or not."

"Will you give me particulars?" said Taverner.

Clearly and concisely she gave us what was required.

"We got engaged while Donald was stationed here for his training (that would be nearly five years ago now), and there was always the most perfect harmony between us until he came out of the Army, when we all began to notice a change in him. He came to the house as often as ever, but he always seemed to want to avoid being alone with me. We used to take long walks over the moors together, but he has absolutely refused to do this recently. Then, without any warning, he wrote and told me he could not marry me and did not wish to see me again, and he put a curious thing in his letter. He said: 'Even if I should come to you and ask you to see me, I beg you not to do it.'

"My people thought he had got entangled with some other girl, and were furious with him for jilting me, but I believe there is something more in it than that. I wrote to him, but could get no answer, and I had come to the conclusion that I must try and put the whole thing out of my life, when he suddenly turned up again. Now, this is where the queer part comes in.

"We heard the fowls shrieking one night, and thought a fox was after them. My brothers turned out armed with golf clubs, and I went too. When we got to the hen-house we found several fowls with their throats torn as if a rat had been at them; but the boys discovered that the hen-house door had been forced open, a thing no rat could do. They said a gipsy must have been trying to steal the birds, and told me to go back to the house. I was return-ing by way of the shrubberies when someone suddenly stepped out in front of me. It was quite light, for the moon was nearly full, and I recognized Donald. He held out his arms and I went to him, but, instead of kissing me, he suddenly bent his head and—look!"

She drew her scarf from her neck and showed us a semicircle of little blue marks on the skin just under the ear, the unmistakable print of human teeth.

"He was after the jugular," said Taverner. "Lucky for you he did not break the skin."

"I said to him: 'Donald, what are you doing?' My voice seemed to bring him to himself, for he let me go and tore off through the bushes. The boys chased him but did not catch him, and we have never seen him since."

"You have informed the police, I suppose?" said Taverner.

"Father told them someone had tried to rob the hen-roost, but they do not know who it was. You see, I did not tell them I had seen Donald."

"And you walk about the moors by yourself, knowing that he may be lurking in the neighbourhood?"

She nodded.

"I should advise you not to, Miss Wynter; the man is

probably exceedingly dangerous, especially to you. We will send you back in the car."

"You think he has gone mad? That is exactly what I think. I believe he knew he was going mad, and that was why he broke off our engagement. Dr. Taverner, is there nothing that can be done for him? It seems to me that Donald is not mad in the ordinary way. We had a house-maid once who went off her head, and the whole of her seemed to be insane, if you can understand; but with Donald it seems as if only a little bit of him were crazy, as if his insanity were outside himself. Can you grasp what I mean?"

"It seems to me you have given a very clear description of a case of psychic interference—what was known in scriptural days as 'being possessed by a devil,'" said Taverner.

"Can you do anything for him?" the girl inquired eagerly.

"I may be able to do a good deal if you can get him to come to me."

On our next day at the Harley Street consulting-room we found that the butler had booked an appointment for a Captain Donald Craigie. We discovered him to be a personality of singular charm—one of those highly-strung, imaginative men who have the makings of an artist in them. In his normal state he must have been a delightful companion, but as he faced us across the consulting-room desk he was a man under a cloud.

"I may as well make a clean breast of this matter," he said. "I suppose Beryl told you about their chickens?"

"She told us that you tried to bite her."

"Did she tell you I bit the chickens?"

"No."

"Well, I did."

Silence fell for a moment. Then Taverner broke it.

"When did this trouble first start?"

"After I got shell-shock. I was blown right out of a trench, and it shook me up pretty badly. I thought I had got off lightly, for I was only in hospital about ten days, but I suppose this is the aftermath."

"Are you one of those people who have a horror of blood?"

"Not especially so. I didn't like it, but I could put up with it. We had to get used to it in the trenches; someone was always getting wounded, even in the quietest times."

"And killed," put in Taverner.

"Yes, and killed," said our patient.

"So you developed a blood hunger?"

"That's about it."

"Underdone meat and all the rest of it, I suppose?"

"No, that is no use to me. It seems a horrible thing to say, but it is fresh blood that attracts me, blood as it comes from the veins of my victim."

"Ah!" said Taverner. "That puts a different complexion on the case."

"I shouldn't have thought it could have been much blacker."

"On the contrary, what you have just told me renders the outlook much more hopeful. You have not so much a blood lust, which might well be an effect of the subconscious mind, as a vitality hunger which is quite a different matter."

Craigie looked up quickly. "That's exactly it. I have never been able to put it into words before, but you have hit the nail on the head."

I saw that my colleague's perspicuity had given him great confidence.

"I should like you to come down to my nursing home for a time and be under my personal observation," said Taverner.

"I should like to very much, but I think there is something further you ought to know before I do so. This thing has begun to affect my character. At first it seemed something outside myself, but now I am responding to it, almost helping, and trying to find out ways of gratifying it without getting myself into trouble. That is why I went for the hens when I came down to the Wynters' house. I was afraid I should lose my self-control and go for Beryl. I did in the end, as it happened, so it was not much use. In fact I think it did more harm than good, for I seemed to get into much closer touch with 'It' after I had yielded to the impulse. I know that the best thing I could do would be to do away with myself, but I daren't. I feel that after I am dead I should have to meet—whatever it is—face to face."

"You need not be afraid to come down to the nursing home," said Taverner. "We will look after you."

After he had gone Taverner said to me: "Have you ever heard of vampires, Rhodes?"

"Yes, rather," I said. "I used to read myself to sleep with *Dracula* once when I had a spell of insomnia."

"That," nodding his head in the direction of the departing man, "is a singularly good specimen."

"Do you mean to say you are going to take a revolting case like that down to Hindhead?"

"Not revolting, Rhodes, a soul in a dungeon. The soul may not be very savoury, but it is a fellow creature. Let it out and it will soon clean itself."

I often used to marvel at the wonderful tolerance and compassion Taverner had for erring humanity.

"The more you see of human nature," he said to me once, "the less you feel inclined to condemn it, for you realize how hard it has struggled. No one does wrong because he likes it, but because it is the lesser of the two evils."

III

A couple of days later I was called out of the nursing home office to receive a new patient. It was Craigie. He had got as far as the door-mat, and there he had stuck. He seemed so thoroughly ashamed of himself that I had not the heart to administer the judicious bullying which is usual under such circumstances.

"I feel as if I were driving a baulking horse," he said. "I want to come in, but I can't."

I called Taverner and the sight of him seemed to relieve our patient.

"Ah," he said, "you give me confidence. I feel that I can defy 'It,' " and he squared his shoulders and crossed the threshold. Once inside, a weight seemed lifted from his mind, and he settled down quite happily to the routine of the place. Beryl Wynter used to walk over almost every afternoon, unknown to her family, and cheer him up; in fact he seemed on the high road to recovery.

One morning I was strolling round the grounds with the head gardener, planning certain small improvements, when he made a remark to me which I had reason to remember later.

"You would think all the German prisoners should have been returned by now, wouldn't you, sir? But they haven't. I passed one the other night in the lane outside the back door. I never thought that I should see their filthy field-grey again."

I sympathized with his antipathy; he had been a prisoner in their hands, and the memory was not one to fade.

I thought no more of his remark, but a few days later I was reminded of it when one of our patients came to me and said:

"Dr. Rhodes, I think you are exceedingly unpatriotic

to employ German prisoners in the garden when so many discharged soldiers cannot get work."

I assured her that we did not do so, no German being likely to survive a day's work under the superintendence of our ex-prisoner head gardener.

"But I distinctly saw the man going round the greenhouses at shutting-up time last night," she declared. "I recognized him by his flat cap and grey uniform."

I mentioned this to Taverner.

"Tell Craigie he is on no account to go out after sundown," he said, "and tell Miss Wynter she had better keep away for the present."

A night or two later, as I was strolling round the grounds smoking an after-dinner cigarette, I met Craigie hurrying through the shrubbery.

"You will have Dr. Taverner on your trail," I called after him.

"I missed the post-bag," he replied, "and I am going down to the pillar-box."

Next evening I again found Craigie in the grounds after dark. I bore down on him.

"Look here, Craigie," I said, "if you come to this place you must keep the rules, and Dr. Taverner wants you to stay indoors after sundown."

Craigie bared his teeth and snarled at me like a dog. I took him by the arm and marched him into the house, and reported the incident to Taverner.

"The creature has re-established its influence over

him," he said. "We cannot evidently starve it out of existence by keeping it away from him; we shall have to use other methods. Where is Craigie at the present moment?"

"Playing the piano in the drawing-room," I replied.

"Then we will go up to his room and unseal it."

As I followed Taverner upstairs he said to me: "Did it ever occur to you to wonder why Craigie jibbed on the doorstep?"

"I paid no attention," I said. "Such a thing is common enough with mental cases."

"There is a sphere of influence, a kind of psychic bell-jar, over this house to keep out evil entities, what might in popular language be called a 'spell.' Craigie's familiar could not come inside, and did not like being left behind. I thought we might be able to tire it out by keeping Craigie away from its influences, but it has got too strong a hold over him, and he deliberately co-operates with it. Evil communications corrupt good manners, and you can't keep company with a thing like that and not be tainted, especially if you are a sensitive Celt like Craigie."

When we reached the room Taverner went over to the window and passed his hand across the sill, as if sweeping something aside.

"There," he said. "It can come in now and fetch him out, and we will see what it does."

At the doorway he paused again and made a sign on the lintel.

"I don't think it will pass that," he said.

When I returned to the office I found the village policeman waiting to see me.

"I should be glad if you would keep an eye on your dog, sir," he said. "We have been having complaints of sheep-killing lately, and whatever animal is doing it is working in a three-mile radius with this as the centre."

"Our dog is an Airedale," I said. "I should not think he is likely to be guilty. It is usually collies that take to sheep-killing."

At eleven o'clock we turned out the lights and herded our patients off to bed. At Taverner's request I changed into an old suit and rubber-soled tennis shoes and joined him in the smoking-room, which was under Craigie's bedroom. We sat in the darkness awaiting events.

"I don't want you to do anything," said Taverner, "but just to follow and see what happens."

We had not long to wait. In about a quarter-of-an-hour we heard a rustling in the creepers, and down came Craigie hand over fist, swinging himself along by the great ropes of wisteria that clothed the wall. As he disappeared into the shrubbery I slipped after him, keeping in the shadow of the house.

He moved at a stealthy dog-trot over the heather paths towards Frensham.

At first I ran and ducked, taking advantage of every patch of shadow, but presently I saw that this caution was unnecessary. Craigie was absorbed in his own affairs, and thereupon I drew up closer to him, following at a distance of some sixty yards.

He moved at a swinging pace, a kind of loping trot that put me in mind of a blood-hound. The wide, empty levels of that forsaken country stretched out on either side of us, belts of mist filled the hollows, and the heights of Hindhead stood out against the stars. I felt no nervousness; man for man, I reckoned I was a match for Craigie, and, in addition, I was armed with what is technically known as a "soother"—two feet of lead gas-piping inserted in a length of rubber hose-pipe. It is not included in the official equipment of the best asylums, but can frequently be found in a keeper's trouser-leg.

If I had known what I had to deal with I should not have put so much reliance on my "soother." Ignorance is sometimes an excellent substitute for courage.

Suddenly out of the heather ahead of us a sheep got up, then the chase began. Away went Craigie in pursuit, and away went the terrified wether. A sheep can move remarkably fast for a short distance, but the poor wool-encumbered beast could not keep the pace, and Craigie ran it down, working in gradually lessening circles. It stumbled, went to its knees, and he was on it. He pulled its head back, and whether he used a knife or not I could not see, for a cloud passed over the moon, but dimly luminous in the shadow, I saw something that was semi-transparent pass between me and the dark, struggling mass among the heather. As the moon cleared the clouds I made out the flat-topped cap and field-grey uniform of the German Army.

I cannot possibly convey the sickening horror of that

sight—the creature that was not a man assisting the man who, for the moment, was not human.

Gradually the sheep's struggles weakened and ceased. Craigie straightened his back and stood up; then he set off at his steady lope towards the east, his grey familiar at his heels.

How I made the homeward journey I do not know. I dared not look behind lest I should find a Presence at my elbow; every breath of wind that blew across the heather seemed to be cold fingers on my throat; fir trees reached out-long arms to clutch me as I passed under them, and heather bushes rose up and assumed human shapes. I moved like a runner in a nightmare, making prodigious efforts after a receding goal.

At last I tore across the moonlit lawns of the house, regardless who might be looking from the windows, burst into the smoking-room and flung myself face downwards on the sofa.

IV

"Tut, tut!" said Taverner. "Has it been as bad as all that?"

I could not tell him what I had seen, but he seemed to know.

"Which way did Craigie go after he left you?" he asked.

"Towards the moonrise," I told him.

"And you were on the way to Frensham? He is head-

ing for the Wynters' house. This is very serious, Rhodes.
We must go after him; it may be too late as it is. Do you
feel equal to coming with me?"

He gave me a stiff glass of brandy, and we went to get
the car out of the garage. In Taverner's company I felt secure. I could understand the confidence he inspired in
his patients. Whatever that grey shadow might be, I felt
he could deal with it and that I should be safe in his
hands.

We were not long in approaching our destination.

"I think we will leave the car here," said Taverner,
turning into a grass-grown lane. "We do not want to rouse
them if we can help it."

We moved cautiously over the dew-soaked grass into
the paddock that bounded one side of the Wynters' garden. It was separated from the lawn by a sunk fence, and
we could command the whole front of the house and easily gain the terrace if we so desired. In the shadow of a
rose pergola we paused. The great trusses of bloom,
colourless in the moonlight, seemed a ghastly mockery
of our business.

For some time we waited, and then a movement
caught my eye.

Out in the meadow behind us something was moving
at a slow lope; it followed a wide arc, of which the house
formed the focus, and disappeared into a little coppice
on the left. It might have been imagination, but I
thought I saw a wisp of mist at its heels.

We remained where we were, and presently he came round once more, this time moving in a smaller circle — evidently closing in upon the house. The third time he reappeared more quickly, and this time he was between us and the terrace.

"Quick! Head him off," whispered Taverner. "He will be up the creepers next round."

We scrambled up the sunk fence and dashed across the lawn. As we did so a girl's figure appeared at one of the windows; it was Beryl Wynter. Taverner, plainly visible in the moonlight, laid his finger on his lips and beckoned her to come down.

"I am going to do a very risky thing," he whispered, "but she is a girl of courage, and if her nerve does not fail we shall be able to pull it off."

In a few seconds she slipped out of a side door and joined us, a cloak over her nightdress.

"Are you prepared to undertake an exceedingly unpleasant task?" Taverner asked her. "I can guarantee you will be perfectly safe so long as you keep your head, but if you lose your nerve you will be in grave danger."

"Is it to do with Donald?" she inquired.

"It is," said Taverner. "I hope to be able to rid him of the thing that is overshadowing him and trying to obsess him."

"I have seen it," she said. "It is like a wisp of grey vapour that floats just behind him. It has the most awful face you ever saw. It came up to the window last night, just the face only, while Donald was going round and round the house."

"What did you do?" asked Taverner.

"I didn't do anything. I was afraid that if someone found him he might be put in an asylum, and then we should have no chance of getting him well."

Taverner nodded.

" 'Perfect love casteth out fear,' " he said. "You can do the thing that is required of you."

He placed Miss Wynter on the terrace in full moonlight.

"As soon as Craigie sees you," he said, "retreat round the corner of the house into the yard. Rhodes and I will wait for you there."

A narrow doorway led from the terrace to the back premises, and just inside its arch Taverner bade me take my stand.

"Pinion him as he comes past you and hang on for your life," he said. "Only mind he doesn't get his teeth into you; these things are infectious."

We had hardly taken up our positions when we heard the loping trot come round once more, this time on the terrace itself. Evidently he caught sight of Miss Wynter, for the stealthy padding changed to a wild scurry over the gravel, and the girl slipped quickly through the archway and sought refuge behind Taverner. Right on her heels came Craigie. Another yard and he would have had her, but I caught him by the elbows and pinioned him securely. For a moment we swayed and struggled across the dew-drenched flagstones, but I locked him in an old wrestling grip and held him.

"Now," said Taverner, "if you will keep hold of Craigie I will deal with the other. But first of all we must get it away from him, otherwise it will retreat on to him, and he may die of shock. Now, Miss Wynter, are you prepared to play your part?"

"I am prepared to do whatever is necessary," she replied. Taverner took a scalpel out of a pocket case and made a small incision in the skin of her neck, just under the ear. A drop of blood slowly gathered, showing black in the moonlight.

"That is the bait," he said. "Now go close up to Craigie and entice the creature away; get it to follow you and draw it out into the open."

As she approached us Craigie plunged and struggled in my arms like a wild beast, and then something grey and shadowy drew out of the gloom of the wall and hovered for a moment at my elbow. Miss Wynter came nearer, walking almost into it.

"Don't go too close," cried Taverner, and she paused.

Then the grey shape seemed to make up its mind; it drew clear of Craigie and advanced towards her. She retreated towards Taverner, and the Thing came out into the moonlight. We could see it quite clearly from its flat-topped cap to its knee-boots; its high cheek-bones and slit eyes pointed its origin to that south-eastern corner of

Europe where strange tribes still defy civilization and keep up their still stranger beliefs.

The shadowy form drifted onwards, following the girl across the yard, and when it was some twenty feet from Craigie, Taverner stepped out quickly behind it, cutting off its retreat. Round it came in a moment, instantly conscious of his presence, and then began a game of "puss-in-the-corner." Taverner was trying to drive it into a kind of psychic killing-pen he had made for its reception. Invisible to me, the lines of psychic force which bounded it were evidently plainly perceptible to the creature we were hunting. This way and that way it slid in its efforts to escape, but Taverner all the time herded it towards the apex of the invisible triangle, where he could give it its *coup de grâce*.

Then the end came. Taverner leapt forward. There was a Sign then a Sound. The grey form commenced to spin like a top. Faster and faster it went, its outlines merging into a whirling spiral of mist; then it broke. Out into space went the particles that had composed its form, and with the almost soundless shriek of supreme speed the soul went to its appointed place.

Then something seemed to lift. From a cold hell of limitless horror the flagged space became a normal back yard, the trees ceased to be tentacled menaces, the gloom of the wall was no longer an ambuscade, and I knew that never again would a grey shadow drift out of the darkness upon its horrible hunting.

I released Craigie, who collapsed in a heap at my feet. Miss Wynter went to rouse her father, while Taverner and I got the insensible man into the house.

What masterly lies Taverner told to the family I have never known, but a couple of months later we received, instead of the conventional fragment of wedding cake, a really substantial chunk, with a note from the bride to say it was to go in the office cupboard, where she knew we kept provisions for those nocturnal meals that Taverner's peculiar habits imposed upon us.

It was during one of these midnight repasts that I questioned Taverner about the strange matter of Craigie and his familiar. For a long time I had not been able to refer to it; the memory of that horrible sheep-killing was a thing that would not bear recalling.

"You have heard of vampires," said Taverner. "That was a typical case. For close on a hundred years they have been practically unknown in Europe—Western Europe that is—but the War has caused a renewed outbreak, and quite a number of cases have been reported.

"When they were first observed—that is to say, when some wretched lad was caught attacking the wounded, they took him behind the lines and shot him, which is not a satisfactory way of dealing with a vampire, unless you also go to the trouble of burning his body, according to the good old-fashioned way of dealing with practitioners of black magic. Then our enlightened generation came to the conclusion that they were not dealing with a crime, but with a disease, and put the unfortunate individual afflicted with this horrible obsession into an asylum, where he did not usually live very long, the supply of his peculiar nourishment being cut off. But it never struck anybody that they might be dealing with more than one factor—that what they were really contending with was a gruesome partnership between the dead and the living."

"What in the world do you mean?" I asked.

"We have two physical bodies, you know," said Taverner, "the dense material one, with which we are all familiar, and the subtle etheric one, which inhabits it, and acts as the medium of the life forces, whose functioning would explain a very great deal if science would only condescend to investigate it. When a man dies, the etheric body, with his soul in it, draws out of the physical form and drifts about in its neighbourhood for about three days, or until decomposition sets in, and then the soul draws out of the etheric body also, which in turn dies, and the man enters upon the first phase of his post mortem existence, the purgatorial one.

"Now, it is possible to keep the etheric body together almost indefinitely if a supply of vitality is available, but, having no stomach which can digest food and turn it into energy, the thing has to batten on someone who has, and develops into a spirit parasite which we call a vampire.

"There is a pretty good working knowledge of black magic in Eastern Europe. Now, supposing some man who has this knowledge gets shot, he knows that in three days' time, at the death of the etheric body, he will have to face his reckoning, and with his record he naturally does not want to do it, so he establishes a connection with the subconscious mind of some other soul that still has a body, provided he can find one suitable for his purposes. A very positive type of character is useless; he has to find one of a negative type, such as the lower class of medium affords. Hence one of the many dangers of mediumship to the untrained. Such a negative condition may be temporarily induced by, say, shell-shock, and it is possible then for such a soul as we are considering to obtain an influence over a being of much higher type— Craigie, for instance—and use him as a means of obtaining its gratification."

"But why did not the creature confine its attentions to Craigie, instead of causing him to attack others?"

"Because Craigie would have been dead in a week if it had done so, and then it would have found itself minus its human feeding bottle. Instead of that it worked *through* Craigie, getting him to draw extra vitality from others and pass it on to itself; hence it was that Craigie had a vitality hunger rather than a blood hunger, though the fresh blood of a victim was the means of absorbing the vitality."

"Then that German we all saw—?"

"Was merely a corpse who was insufficiently dead."

A CASE OF ALLEGED VAMPIRISM

◆◆◆

LUIGI CAPUANA

"It's no laughing matter!" said Lelio Giorgi.

"Why shouldn't I laugh?" replied Mongeri. "*I* don't believe in ghosts."

"Neither did I, once . . . and I'd still rather not," went on Giorgi. "That's why I've come to see you. You might be able to explain whatever it is that's making my life a misery and wrecking my marriage."

"*Whatever it is?* You mean whatever you *imagine* it is. You're not well. It's true that a hallucination is itself a fact, but what it represents has no reality outside yourself. Or, to put it better, it's the externalization of a sensation, a sort of projection of yourself, so that the eye sees what it in fact does not see, and the ear hears sounds that were never made. Previous impressions, often stored up unconsciously, project themselves rather like events in dreams. We still don't know how or why. We dream, and that's the right word, with our eyes wide open. But one has to distinguish between split-second hallucinations which don't necessarily indicate any organic or psychic disturbance, and those of a more persistent nature. . . . But of course that's not the case with you."

"But it *is*, with me *and* my wife."

"You don't understand. What we scientists call persistent hallucinations are those experienced by the insane. I don't have to give you an example. . . . The fact that you both suffer the same hallucinations is just a case of simple induction. You probably must have influenced your wife's nervous system."

"No. She was the first."

"Then you mean that your nervous system, having a greater receptivity, was the one to be influenced. And don't turn up your poetical nose at what you please to call my scientific jargon. It has its uses."

"If you would just let me get a word in edgeways . . ."

"Some things are best let well alone. Do you want a scientific explanation? Well, the answer is that for the moment you wouldn't get anything of the sort. We are in the realm of hypotheses. One today, a different one tomorrow, and a different one the day after. You are a curious lot, you artists! When you feel like it you make fun of Science, you undervalue the whole business of experiment, research, and hypothesis that makes it progress; then when a case comes along that interests you personally you want a clear, precise, and categorical answer. And there are scientists who play the game, out of conviction or vanity. But I'm not one of them. You want the plain truth? Science is the greatest proof of our own ignorance. To calm you down I can talk of hallucinations, of induction, receptivity. Words! Words! The more I study the more I despair of ever knowing anything for certain. It seems to happen on purpose; no sooner do scientists get a kick out of some new law they've discovered than along comes some new fact, some discovery, that upsets the lot. You need to take it easy, just let life flow by; what's happened to you and your wife has happened to so many others. It will pass. Why must you try and find out how and why it happened? Are you scared of dreams?"

"If you'd just let me tell you . . ."

"Go on then, tell me, if you want to get it off your chest. But I warn you, it can only make matters worse. The only way to get over it, is to busy yourself with other things, get away from it. Find a new devil to drive out the old—it's a good saying."

"We did all that. It wasn't any good. The first signs . . . the first manifestations, happened in the country, in our villa at Foscolara. We ran away from it, but the very night that we came back to town . . ."

"It's natural. What distraction could you find in your own house? You ought to travel, stay in hotels, one day here, another day there; spend the whole day sightseeing, looking at churches, museums, go to the theatre, come back late at night, tired out. . . ."

"We did all that too, but . . ."

"Just the two of you, on your own. You should have been with a friend, a party. . . ."

"But we were; it wasn't any good."

"It all depends on the party!"

"But they were a lively crowd. . . ."

"Selfish, you mean, and there you were, isolated, I know. . . ."

"But we were lively too, when we were with them. But you can hardly expect them to have come and slept with us. . . ."

"Then you *were* asleep? Really I don't know what you mean any more, dreams or hallucinations. . . ."

"To hell with your dreams and hallucinations. We were wide awake and completely sound in mind and body, just as I am now, if you would only let me get a word in edgeways. . . ."

"As you wish."

"Well, you could at least let me give you the facts."

"I know. I can imagine it all. The books are full of them. There could be small differences in detail . . . but they don't count. The essentials are the same."

"Can't I even have the satisfaction of . . ."

"You can. Hundreds of them. You are one of those who seem to want to lay up troubles for themselves, even make them worse. . . . I'm sorry, that's stupid! But if it would please you . . ."

"Quite frankly, you seem to me to be scared."

"Scared of what? A nice idea!"

"Scared of having to change your mind. You've just said, 'I do not believe in ghosts.' And what if I force you to believe in them?"

"All right then. It would be a blow. What do you expect? We scientists are like that, we're men after all.

When our way of seeing things, of judging them, takes a knock, the intellect refuses to follow the senses. Even intelligence is a matter of habit. But now you have me with my back to the wall. All right then. Let's hear your precious facts."

"Well," said Lelio Giorgi with a sigh, "you know already the unhappy background to my years in America. Luisa's parents were against our marrying—and they may well have been right, they were thinking above all of the economic situation of their future son-in-law—they had no faith in my abilities, and were doubtful about my future as a poet. That slim volume of early verse was my worst enemy. I haven't even written, let alone published, any more from that day to this, yet even now you called me 'poetical.' The label stuck. Oh well."

"Just like you writers to go right back to the remote beginning."

"Don't get impatient. Listen. I had no news of Luisa for the three years I was in Buenos Aires. Then came that rich uncle's will, after he had nothing to do with me while he was alive. I came back to Europe, hurried to London, and flew here with £200,000 in my pocket, only to find that Luisa had been married for six months! And I was as much in love with her as ever. The poor girl must have given in to family pressure. At that time I might have done anything. . . . All these details are important. . . . I was stupid enough, however, to write her a letter full of violent reproaches. I never thought that it could have fallen into the hands of her husband. The next day he turned up at my house, having realized the folly of my behaviour, and determined to persuade me to calm down. He was calm himself.

" 'I have come to give you your letter back,' he said. 'I opened it by mistake, not out of inquisitiveness; and it's just as well I did. I am assured that you are a gentleman. I have every respect for your distress, but I do trust you have no intention of needlessly disturbing the peace of a family. If you can bring yourself to think things over you will realize that nobody wished to harm you intentionally. It was pure misfortune. You must see now where your duty lies, and I can tell you quite plainly that I am determined to defend my domestic happiness at all costs.'

"He was pale as he spoke, and his voice trembled.

" 'I must apologize for my indiscretion,' I replied, 'and to reassure you I can add that tomorrow I shall be leaving for Paris.' I must have been even paler than him, the words would hardly come. I held out my hand, he shook it. And I kept my word. Six months later I received a telegram from Luisa: 'I am a widow. I still love you. And you?' Her husband had been dead for two months."

"Such is life; it's an ill wind. . . ."

"And that's what I somewhat selfishly thought; but it isn't always true. I had never been so happy in my life as I was on my wedding night and during the following months. We both of us avoided any mention of *him.*

Luisa had destroyed every trace. Not out of ingratitude, for he had done everything to make her happy, but because she was afraid that even the slightest memory would have upset me. And she was right. Sometimes the thought that someone else, however legitimately, had once possessed her, made me tremble from head to foot. I could scarcely hide it from her. Often she must have sensed this, and her lovely eyes were clouded with tears. But how radiant she looked on the day she felt sure enough to tell me of the expected arrival of a child. I remember it clearly, we were drinking coffee, I was standing and she was sitting down, with a look of touching weariness. And that was the first time she had ever made any reference to the past: 'How glad I am that this didn't happen *then*!' she exclaimed.

"A loud crash was heard at the door, as if someone had struck it a blow with their fist. We leapt up. I rushed out to see what had happened, imagining it was one of the servants, but the adjoining room was empty."

"It could have been one of the beams in the house shrinking in the heat."

"That was how I explained it to Luisa, seeing how upset she was, but I was not convinced myself. I felt somehow disturbed. We waited some minutes, nothing happened. But from then onwards I noticed that Luisa avoided being left on her own; she was still upset, though she would not admit it and I dared not question her."

"And now I see how you were both influencing each other, without realizing it."

"Not at all. A few days later I was laughing at the whole episode, and thought that Luisa's agitated state of mind was due to her condition. Then even she seemed to calm down. Eventually the child was born. After a few months, however, I noticed that the old feeling of fear and terror had returned. At night, all of a sudden, she would cling to me, cold and trembling. 'What is it? Are you ill?' I would ask anxiously. 'I'm frightened, didn't you hear?' 'No.' 'Don't you hear?' she insisted the following night. 'No.' Though this time I had heard the sound of footsteps in the room, pacing up and down, by the bed: I said 'no' so as not to frighten her any more. I raised my head and looked around, 'It must be a mouse in the room. . . .' 'I'm afraid! . . . I'm afraid! . . .' And for several nights, at the same time, the same shuffling, the same uncanny coming and going, up and down, by the bed. We lay and waited for it!"

"And your jangling nerves did the rest."

"You know me; I'm not the sort to get worked up easily. I put up a brave show, because of Luisa; I tried to explain things: echoes of distant sounds, accidental resonances in the structure of the villa. . . . We went back to town. But that very night the phenomena turned up again worse than before. Twice the bedstead was shaken violently. I peered out. 'It's he! It's he!' stammered Luisa, huddled under the bedclothes."

"If you don't mind my saying so," interrupted Mongeri, "*I* wouldn't marry a widow for all the gold in the world! Something of the dead husband always remains with her, in spite of everything. Your wife wasn't seeing his ghost. 'It's *he*' is the 'he' of the sensations he left behind him, purely physiological."

"Well, maybe so," replied Lelio Giorgi. "But in that case where do *I* come in?"

"Suggestion. Now it seems perfectly plain."

"Suggestion only at specified times in the middle of the night?"

"Just waiting for it to happen would be enough."

"Well then, how can the phenomena vary every time when my imagination isn't working at all?"

"That's what you think; the Unconscious at work."

"Do let me go on. Keep your explanations until I've finished. Just note that the following morning we were able to discuss the matter with relative calm. Luisa described her impressions and I told her of mine, in such a way that I was convinced that it could not have been an unpleasant trick played on us by our over-excited imaginations; the same blow on the bedstead, the same tugging at the sheets in the same circumstances, when I was trying to comfort her with a kiss and prevent her from crying, as if this itself had provoked the malice of the invisible person. Then one night Luisa flung her arms round my neck and whispered in my ear in a voice that made me shudder: 'He spoke!' 'What did he say?' 'I couldn't hear. Now! He said: You're mine!' And as I held her closer I felt her being dragged violently away from me by two powerful hands, and I had to give way in spite of her resistance."

"What resistance could she offer to what must have been her own behaviour?"

"All right. . . . But I felt it too, a something trying to stop her coming into contact with me. . . . I saw her flung back with a jolt . . . then she tried to get to her feet, to go to the child, who was sleeping in the cot at the foot of the bed. Then we heard the cot wheels squeaking and saw it tossed across the room, blankets flying in all directions; that wasn't a hallucination. We picked things up, made up the cot, and soon they were flying through the air again and the child was whimpering with fear. Three nights later it was even worse. Luisa seemed drawn completely under *his* evil spell. She seemed unaware of me when I spoke to her, as if I were no longer there. She seemed to be talking to *him* and I could tell from her replies what he was saying to her. 'But can it be his fault that you are dead?' 'No, no, no, how could you think so? *I*, poison you? That's monstrous!' 'And what can the child have done to harm you?' 'But why are you unhappy? I have prayed for you . . .' 'Why don't you want my prayers? You want *me*, but how can you, you're dead!' I tried without success to shake her from the trance. Then she came to. 'Did you hear that?' she said. 'He says I poisoned him. *You* wouldn't believe that of me. . . . O God! What about the child? He'll kill him. Did you hear?' I heard nothing, but I was well aware that Luisa was not raving. She wept, clutching the child to her. 'What shall we do? What shall we do?' "

"But the child was all right. That must have reassured her."

"What can you expect? This sort of thing would upset even the most strong-minded. I myself am not superstitious; but I'm not a free-thinker either. I just don't have much time for religion. But in a case like this, and with my wife saying, 'I'll pray for you,' I naturally thought of calling in a priest."

"You had him exorcize it?"

"No, but I had a blessing said in the house, with a fine sprinkling of holy water . . . as much to influence poor Luisa, if it really were a case of nerves, as anything. Luisa is a religious person. You can laugh; I'd like to have seen what you would have done in my place."

"What about the holy water?"

"Useless. No effect at all."

"Not a bad idea, though. Some nervous diseases can be cured that way. We had a case of a man who thought his nose was being stretched. The doctor went through all the motions of an operation, without actually doing anything, and the man was cured."

"But the holy water in fact made things worse. The next night . . . My God! I can't bear to think of it. This time *he* seemed to be taking everything out on the child. . . . It was awful. When Luisa saw . . ."

"Or thought she saw . . ."

"Saw, man, saw . . . And *I* saw too, almost. She couldn't get near the cot, something was holding her back. There she was, stretching out her hands to the child, while that *thing*—she described it to me—bent over the baby and did something horrible, its lips pressed to his mouth, sucking his blood. . . . For three nights this ghastly process has been repeated, and the poor little thing . . . you wouldn't recognize him. . . . He used to be so plump and rosy, and now . . . in only three nights . . . he's wasted away. This can't be imagination. Come and see for yourself."

"So it could really be? . . ."

Mongeri thought for a few minutes, frowning. The sarcastic and somewhat pitying smile with which he had listened to Lelio Giorgi had vanished all of a sudden. Then he looked up and said:

"So it could really be? . . . Listen. I can't explain anything because I'm convinced there is no explanation. One can't be more skeptical than that. But I could give you some advice, which might make you laugh, coming from me. . . . Anyway, that's up to you."

"I'll do as you suggest, at once."

"You would need several days for what you have to do. I'll help you to cut it as short as possible. I don't doubt the facts you've put before me. And I ought to add that since Science has come to examine this kind of problem, it, too, has been less skeptical. It has now become a question of trying to see this sort of thing as a natural phenomenon; but a physical problem, not a spiritual one. That's not our province; we leave that to priests or spiritualists. We are concerned with the flesh, blood, and bone that go to make an individual and disintegrate into their original elements when he dies. But then the question arises, does this disintegration, this cessation of organic function end instantaneously with death, annulling all individuality, or does this persist, in some cases, for any amount of time after death? One is beginning to suspect that this could be the case. And Science is on the verge of coming round to popular beliefs. I have been studying for three years now the empirical remedies of 'old wives' and witches and I am coming to the conclusion that they are in fact the remnants of the ancient secret sciences and also, even more likely, of the instincts we can still observe in animals. When man was closer to animals he knew instinctively the medicinal value of certain herbs, but as he evolved away from them he lost this primitive use of certain faculties, and the tradition died out. Only the honest peasant women, in whom it was more deeply rooted, preserved some of these natural medicines; and I think that Science should study them, for every superstition contains something more than mere popular error. I'm sorry about this digression. . . . What scientists now admit, that the existence of an individual does not cease at death, but only when actual decomposition of the body has taken place, popular superstition has already acknowledged through the belief in vampires, and has even offered a remedy. Vampires are individuals, rare but not unheard of, who persist after death. You may look surprised, but this is a case, and not the only one, where science and popular superstition, or rather, primitive intuition, find themselves at one. And what is the only defense against this evil thing, this disembodied individual sucking the blood and life-force from healthy individuals? The complete destruction of its former body. Where vampires have been known to occur the victims have run to the grave, dug up the body, and burned it; then the vampire really does die, and the visitations cease. Now you were saying that your child . . ."

"Come and see him, you wouldn't recognize him. Luisa is going crazy. And I'm not far off myself. I keep saying to myself that it can't be true, it couldn't possibly happen; I even think: 'Well, if she did poison him, it was for my sake, it shows how much she loves me. . . .' But it won't work, the thought repels me, *she* repels me even . . . all *his* doing! And the reproaches go on, I can tell by her replies. 'What? Poison you? . . . How can you believe such a thing?' Life has become impossible, for months now we have gone on like this. You are the first person I have dared to confide in. I'm desperate, I need help. . . . And we would have put up with everything if it weren't for the child."

"As a friend and as a scientist, I give you this advice: Have the body cremated. Your wife will easily get permission, and I will help you to speed up the formalities. And Science herself would not be ashamed to have recourse to somewhat empirical methods, trying out a remedy which might well be a superstition in appearance only, seeking out the truth by unconventional methods.

Cremate the body. Seriously," he added, seeing from the look in his friend's eye that he feared he was being treated like one of the ignorant populace.

"But what about the child?" cried Lelio Giorgi, wringing his hands. "One night I lost my temper and threw myself at him yelling, 'Get out! For God's sake get out!' But I was stopped dead in my tracks, unable to move, mumbling, with the words drying up in my throat. You can't imagine. . . ."

"Would you allow me to accompany you tonight?"

"I hardly dared to ask you such a favour. . . . But perhaps it would upset him even more; would you leave it until tomorrow?"

But the next day he returned in such shattered state that Mongeri really wondered if he had gone out of his mind.

"He knows!" stammered Lelio Giorgi. "God, what a night! He swore he would do the most terrible things if we dared to . . ."

"All the more reason for daring," replied Mongeri.

"If you had seen the cot tossed about! I don't know how the poor child survived! Luisa had to get down on her knees to him, weeping, 'I will be yours, all yours, only please don't hurt the child!' And I felt at that moment that every link with her was broken, that she belonged to him again and not to me."

"Calm down! We shall get rid of him. Let me come round tonight."

Mongeri went, thinking, convinced that his presence would keep the vampire away. "It's always the case, a neutral, indifferent force will counteract the unknown thing. We don't yet know how or why, but continued observation and study will show."

And in the early hours of the night this seemed to be the case. Luisa looked anxiously around but nothing happened. The child slept untroubled in his cot, pale and wan. Lelio Giorgi did his best to conceal his worry, but kept glancing fearfully from his wife to the complacent Mongeri. They kept up a conversation on various topics. Mongeri was describing some highly amusing incident on one of his holidays; he was a good talker, without any of his professional pomposity, and he hoped to distract the attention of both of them, so that if the phenomenon did occur he could observe it uninterrupted, when suddenly, as he glanced at the cot, he noticed a slight movement, which could not have been caused by either of the parents, since they were sitting at the other side of the room. He stopped, and they leapt to their feet. By the time they had followed his gaze to the cot it was rocking with some violence. Luisa cried, "O heavens, my poor child!" and rushed towards the cot, but was stopped short and sank back onto the couch. Pale as death, she rolled her eyes in terror and muttered something unintelligible, on the point of suffocating.

"It's nothing!" said Mongeri, rising himself, and grasping the hand of Lelio, who was shaken with terror. Then Luisa, with a violent shudder, returned to her normal self though with her attention fixed on some invisible person, listening to words they could not hear but at which they could guess from the sense of her replies.

"Why do you say that I keep on wanting to hurt you? . . . But I've prayed for you. . . . No, I can't do anything about it, you're dead. . . . But how can you say I've poisoned you if you are not dead? . . . That I was plotting it with him? . . . That he sent me the poison? . . . But how can you? I kept my promise! . . . I did! It's absurd! . . . All right, I won't say you are dead any more . . . no, no more. . . ."

"This is a case of spontaneous trance!" said Mongeri. "Leave it to me."

He took Luisa by the wrists and said in a loud voice: "Come now!" At the sound of the robust, angry, and masculine voice with which she replied Mongeri was taken aback. She had drawn herself up with such a hard, truculent expression that she seemed another person. Her gentle, timid beauty had completely vanished.

"What do you want? Why must you interfere?"

Mongeri pulled himself together. The habitual reserve of the scientist might have made him fear that he too had come under the influence of an overheated imagination, but for the sight of the cot rocking to and fro and this sudden uncanny phenomenon of the personification of the fantasma. He drew himself up, angry for having been startled by the harsh masculine voice, and said sharply: "Stop that! Stop it at once!"

There was such a note of command in his voice, enough to dominate, as he thought, the young woman's mind, that he was surprised at the sardonic laugh with which she replied.

"Stop that! At once!" he replied in stronger tones.

"Aha! Another poisoner! You were in on this too?"

"That's a damned lie!"

Mongeri could not prevent himself from replying as if to a living person. His mind, already troubled, in spite of his efforts to remain calm and impartial, received another shock when he felt himself struck twice on the shoulder by an invisible fist, and turning towards the lamp, saw silhouetted against the light a greyish, wasted hand that seemed almost like smoke from the candle.

"You see? You see?" cried Giorgi with a sob in his voice.

Suddenly everything stopped. Luisa came out of her trance and looked around her as if waking from a natural sleep, questioning her husband and Mongeri with a pathetic movement of the head. They too were amazed and gazed around, speechless, overcome by the sense of peace and serenity. No one dared to break the silence. Only a slight sound of moaning from the cot made them turn in that direction. The baby whimpered and struggled under the pressure that was forcing something against his mouth. . . . Then without warning that, too, stopped, and nothing more happened.

The next morning, on his way home, Mongeri was thinking not only about the folly of scientists who fail to examine cases which coincide with popular superstition, but also of what he had said to his friend two days previously: *I wouldn't marry a widow for all the gold in the world.*

As a scientist he had acquitted himself well, carrying out the experiment to its logical conclusion, without considering the humiliating consequences of failure if the experiment (the cremation of the body of Luisa's first husband) had failed. But notwithstanding the fact that the experiment had confirmed a popular superstition, and that from the day of the cremation the visitations had stopped completely, to the great relief of the good Lelio Giorgi and his Luisa, in his report, not yet published, he did not write with complete sincerity. He could not say, "The facts are such, and such is the result of the remedy: popular superstition has triumphed over the narrow-mindedness of science; the vampire died as soon as the body was cremated." No, he restricted his narrative with so many "if's" and "but's" and confused it with so many "hallucinations," "suggestions," and "inductions," simply to confirm what he had already admitted: that even intelligence is a matter of habit, and that having to change his mind had shaken him.

And what is even more curious, his own life became somewhat incoherent, for he who had once sworn that he would not marry a widow for all the gold in the world, married one for far less, a pension of a mere £7,000! And when his friend Lelio Giorgi ingenuously remarked, "What? You!" he replied, "But her husband has been dead for the past seven years, not a scrap of him remains," without realizing that in so saying, he was contradicting the author of that learned paper, "A Case of Alleged Vampirism," namely, himself.

MIDNIGHT MASS

◆◆◆

F. PAUL WILSON

I

It had been almost a full minute since he'd slammed the brass knocker against the heavy oak door. That should have been proof enough. After all, wasn't the knocker in the shape of a cross? But no, they had to squint through their peephole and peer through the sidelights that framed the door.

Rabbi Zev Wolpin sighed and resigned himself to the scrutiny. He couldn't blame people for being cautious, but this seemed a bit overly so. The sun was in the west and shining full on his back; he was all but silhouetted in it. What more did they want?

I should maybe take off my clothes and dance naked?

He gave a mental shrug and savored the damp sea air. At least it was cool here. He'd bicycled from Lakewood, which was only ten miles inland from this same ocean but at least twenty degrees warmer. The bulk of the huge Tudor retreat house stood between him and the Atlantic, but the ocean's briny scent and rhythmic rumble were everywhere.

Spring Lake. An Irish Catholic seaside resort since before the turn of the century. He looked around at its carefully restored Victorian houses, the huge mansions arrayed here along the beach front, the smaller homes set in neat rows running straight back from the ocean. Many of them were still occupied. Not like Lakewood. Lakewood was an empty shell.

Not such a bad place for a retreat, he thought. He wondered how many houses like this the Catholic Church owned.

A series of clicks and clacks drew his attention back to the door as numerous bolts were pulled in rapid succession. The door swung inward, revealing a nervous-looking young man in a long black cassock. As he looked at Zev his mouth twisted and he rubbed the back of his wrist across it to hide a smile.

"And what should be so funny?" Zev asked.

"I'm sorry. It's just—"

"I know," Zev said, waving off any explanation as he glanced down at the wooden cross slung on a cord around his neck. "I know."

A bearded Jew in a baggy black serge suit wearing a yarmulke and a cross. Hilarious, no?

So, *nu*? This was what the times demanded, this was what it had come to if he wanted to survive. And Zev did want to survive. Someone had to live to carry on the tra-

ditions of the Talmud and the Torah, even if there were
hardly any Jews left alive in the world.

Zev stood on the sunny porch, waiting. The priest
watched him in silence.

Finally Zev said, "Well, may a wandering Jew come
in?"

"I won't stop you," the priest said, "but surely you
don't expect me to invite you."

Ah, yes. Another precaution. The vampire couldn't
cross the threshold of a home unless he was invited in, so
don't invite. A good habit to cultivate, he supposed.

He stepped inside and the priest immediately closed
the door behind him, relatching all the locks one by one.
When he turned around Zev held out his hand.

"Rabbi Zev Wolpin, Father. I thank you for allowing
me in."

"Brother Christopher, sir," he said, smiling and shaking Zev's hand. His suspicions seemed to have been completely allayed. "I'm not a priest yet. We can't offer you
much here, but—"

"Oh, I won't be staying long. I just came to talk to
Father Joseph Cahill."

Brother Christopher frowned. "Father Cahill isn't
here at the moment."

"When will he be back?"

"I—I'm not sure. You see—"

"Father Cahill is on another bender," said a stentorian
voice behind Zev.

He turned to see an elderly priest facing him from the far end of the foyer. White-haired, heavyset, wearing a black cassock. "I'm Rabbi Wolpin."

"Father Adams," the priest said, stepping forward and extending his hand.

As they shook Zev said, "Did you say he was on 'another' bender? I never knew Father Cahill to be much of a drinker."

"Apparently there was a lot we never knew about Father Cahill," the priest said stiffly.

"If you're referring to that nastiness last year," Zev said, feeling the old anger rise in him, "I for one never believed it for a minute. I'm surprised anyone gave it the slightest credence."

"The veracity of the accusation was irrelevant in the final analysis. The damage to Father Cahill's reputation was a *fait accompli.* Father Palmeri was forced to request his removal for the good of St. Anthony's parish."

Zev was sure that sort of attitude had something to do with Father Joe being on "another bender."

"Where can I find Father Cahill?"

"He's in town somewhere, I suppose, making a spectacle of himself. If there's any way you can talk some sense into him, please do. Not only is he killing himself with drink but he's become quite an embarrassment to the priesthood and to the Church."

Which bothers you more? Zev wanted to ask but held his tongue. "I'll try."

He waited for Brother Christopher to undo all the locks, then stepped toward the sunlight.

"Try Morton's down on Seventy-one," the younger man whispered as Zev passed.

Zev rode his bicycle south on 71. It was almost strange to see people on the streets. Not many, but more than he'd ever see in Lakewood again. Yet he knew that as the vampires consolidated their grip on the world and infiltrated the Catholic communities, there'd be fewer and fewer day people here as well.

He thought he remembered passing a place named Morton's on his way to Spring Lake. And then up ahead he saw it, by the railroad track crossing, a white stucco one-story box of a building with "Morton's Liquors" painted in big black letters along the side.

Father Adams' words echoed back to him: . . . *on another bender* . . .

Zev pushed his bicycle to the front door and tried the knob. Locked up tight. A look inside showed a litter of trash and empty shelves. The windows were barred; the back door was steel and locked as securely as the front. So where was Father Joe?

Then he spotted the basement window at ground level by the overflowing trash dumpster. It wasn't latched. Zev went down on his knees and pushed it open.

Cool, damp, musty air wafted against his face as he

peered into the Stygian blackness. It occurred to him that he might be asking for trouble by sticking his head inside, but he had to give it a try. If Father Cahill wasn't here, Zev would begin the return trek to Lakewood and write this whole trip off as wasted effort.

"Father Joe?" he called. "Father Cahill?"

"That you again, Chris?" said a slightly slurred voice. "Go home, will you? I'll be all right. I'll be back later."

"It's me, Joe. Zev. From Lakewood."

He heard shoes scraping on the floor and then a familiar face appeared in the shaft of light from the window.

"Well I'll be damned. It *is* you! Thought you were Brother Chris come to drag me back to the retreat house. Gets scared I'm gonna get stuck out after dark. So how ya doin', Reb? Glad to see you're still alive. Come on in!"

Zev saw that Father Cahill's eyes were glassy and he swayed ever so slightly, like a skyscraper in the wind. He wore faded jeans and a black Bruce Springsteen *Tunnel of Love* Tour sweatshirt.

Zev's heart twisted at the sight of his friend in such condition. Such a mensch like Father Joe shouldn't be acting like a *shikker*. Maybe it was a mistake coming here. Zev didn't like seeing him like this.

"I don't have that much time, Joe. I came to tell you—"

"Get your bearded ass down here and have a drink or I'll come up and drag you down."

"All right," Zev said. "I'll come in but I won't have a drink."

He hid his bike behind the dumpster, then squeezed through the window. Father Joe helped him to the floor. They embraced, slapping each other on the back. Father Joe was a taller man, a giant from Zev's perspective. At six-four he was ten inches taller; at thirty-five he was a quarter-century younger; he had a muscular frame, thick brown hair, and—on better days—clear blue eyes.

"You're grayer, Zev, and you've lost weight."

"Kosher food is not so easily come by these days."

"All kinds of food is getting scarce." He touched the cross slung from Zev's neck and smiled. "Nice touch. Goes well with your zizith."

Zev fingered the fringe protruding from under his shirt. Old habits didn't die easily.

"Actually, I've grown rather fond of it."

"So what can I pour you?" the priest said, waving an arm at the crates of liquor stacked around him. "My own private reserve. Name your poison."

"I don't want a drink."

"Come on, Reb. I've got some nice hundred-proof Stoli here. You've got to have at least *one* drink—"

"Why? Because you think maybe you shouldn't drink alone?"

Father Joe smiled. "Touché."

"All right," Zev said. "*Bissel.* I'll have *one* drink on the condition that you *don't* have one. Because I wish to talk to you."

The priest considered that a moment, then reached for the vodka bottle.

"Deal."

He poured a generous amount into a paper cup and handed it over. Zev took a sip. He was not a drinker and when he did imbibe he preferred his vodka ice cold from a freezer. But this was tasty. Father Cahill sat back on a crate of Jack Daniel's and folded his arms.

"*Nu?*" the priest said with a Jackie Mason shrug.

Zev had to laugh. "Joe, I still say that somewhere in your family tree is Jewish blood."

For a moment he felt light, almost happy. When was the last time he had laughed? Probably more than a year now, probably at their table near the back of Horovitz's deli, shortly before the St. Anthony's nastiness began, well before the vampires came.

Zev thought of the day they'd met. He'd been standing at the counter at Horovitz's waiting for Yussel to wrap up the stuffed derma he had ordered when this young giant walked in. He towered over the other rabbis in the place, looked as Irish as Paddy's pig, and wore a Roman collar. He said he'd heard this was the only place on the whole Jersey Shore where you could get a decent corned beef sandwich. He ordered one and cheerfully warned that it better be good. Yussel asked him what could he know about good corned beef and the priest replied that he grew up in Bensonhurst. Well, about half the people in Horovitz's on that day—and on any other day for that matter—grew up in Bensonhurst and before you knew it they were all asking him if he knew such-and-such a store and so-and-so's deli.

Zev then informed the priest—with all due respect to Yussel Horovitz behind the counter—that the best corned beef sandwich in the world was to be had at Shmuel Rosenberg's Jerusalem Deli in Bensonhurst. Father Cahill said he'd been there and agreed one hundred per cent.

Yussel served him his sandwich then. As he took a huge bite out of the corned beef on rye, the normal *tummel* of a deli at lunchtime died away until Horovitz's was as quiet as a *shoul* on Sunday morning. Everyone watched him chew, watched him swallow. Then they waited. Suddenly his face broke into this big Irish grin.

"I'm afraid I'm going to have to change my vote," he said. "Horovitz's of Lakewood makes the best corned beef sandwich in the world."

Amid cheers and warm laughter, Zev led Father Cahill to the rear table that would become theirs and sat with this canny and charming gentile who had so easily won over a roomful of strangers and provided such a *mechaieh* for Yussel. He learned that the young priest was the new assistant to Father Palmeri, the pastor at St. Anthony's Catholic church at the northern end of Lakewood. Father Palmeri had been there for years but Zev had never so much as seen his face. He asked Father Cahill—who wanted to be called Joe—about life in Brooklyn these days and they talked for an hour.

During the following months they would run into each other so often at Horovitz's that they decided to meet regularly for lunch, on Mondays and Thursdays.

They did so for years, discussing religion—Oy, the religious discussions!—politics, economics, philosophy, life in general. During those lunchtimes they solved most of the world's problems. Zev was sure they'd have solved them all if the scandal at St. Anthony's hadn't resulted in Father Joe's removal from the parish.

But that was in another time, another world. The world before the vampires took over.

Zev shook his head as he considered the current state of Father Joe in the dusty basement of Morton's Liquors.

"It's about the vampires, Joe," he said, taking another sip of the Stoli. "They've taken over St. Anthony's."

Father Joe snorted and shrugged.

"They're in the majority now, Zev, remember? They've taken over everything. Why should St. Anthony's be different from any other parish in the world?"

"I didn't mean the parish. I meant the church."

The priest's eyes widened slightly. "The church? They've taken over the building itself?"

"Every night," Zev said. "Every night they are there."

"That's a holy place. How do they manage that?"

"They've desecrated the altar, destroyed all the crosses. St. Anthony's is no longer a holy place."

"Too bad," Father Joe said, looking down and shaking his head sadly. "It was a fine old church." He looked up again, at Zev. "How do you know about what's going on at St. Anthony's? It's not exactly in your neighborhood."

"A neighborhood I don't exactly have anymore."

Father Joe reached over and gripped his shoulder with a huge hand.

"I'm sorry, Zev. I heard how your people got hit pretty hard over there. Sitting ducks, huh? I'm really sorry."

Sitting ducks. An appropriate description. Oh, they'd been smart, those bloodsuckers. They knew their easiest targets. Whenever they swooped into an area they singled out Jews as their first victims, and among Jews they picked the Orthodox first of the first. Smart. Where else would they be less likely to run up against a cross? It worked for them in Brooklyn, and so when they came south into New Jersey, spreading like a plague, they headed straight for the town with one of the largest collections of yeshivas in North America.

But after the Bensonhurst holocaust the people in the Lakewood communities did not take quite so long to figure out what was happening. The Reformed and Conservative synagogues started handing out crosses at Shabbes—too late for many but it saved a few. Did the Orthodox congregations follow suit? No. They hid in their homes and shules and yeshivas and read and prayed.

And were liquidated.

A cross, a crucifix—they held power over the vampires, drove them away. His fellow rabbis did not want to accept that simple fact because they could not face its devastating ramifications. To hold up a cross was to negate two thousand years of Jewish history, it was to say that the Messiah had come and they had missed him.

Did it say that? Zev didn't know. Argue about it later. Right now, people were dying. But the rabbis had to argue it now. And as they argued, their people were slaughtered like cattle.

How Zev railed at them, how he pleaded with them! Blind, stubborn fools! If a fire was consuming your house, would you refuse to throw water on it just because you'd always been taught not to believe in water? Zev had arrived at the rabbinical council wearing a cross and had been thrown out—literally sent hurtling through the front door. But at least he had managed to save a few of his own people. Too few.

He remembered his fellow Orthodox rabbis, though. All the ones who had refused to face the reality of the vampires' fear of crosses, who had forbidden their students and their congregations to wear crosses, who had watched those same students and congregations die en masse only to rise again and come for them. And soon those very same rabbis were roaming their own community, hunting the survivors, preying on other yeshivas, other congregations, until the entire community was liquidated and incorporated into the brotherhood of the vampire. The great fear had come to pass: they'd been assimilated.

The rabbis could have saved themselves, could have saved their people, but they would not bend to the reality of what was happening around them. Which, when Zev thought about it, was not at all out of character. Hadn't they spent generations learning to turn away from the rest of the world?

Those early days of anarchic slaughter were over. Now that the vampires held the ruling hand, the blood-letting had become more organized. But the damage to Zev's people had been done—and it was irreparable. Hitler would have been proud. His Nazi "final solution" was an afternoon picnic compared to the work of the vampires. They did in months what Hitler's Reich could not do in all the years of the Second World War.

There's only a few of us now. So few and so scattered. A final Diaspora.

For a moment Zev was almost overwhelmed by grief, but he pushed it down, locked it back into that place where he kept his sorrows, and thought of how fortunate it was for his wife Chana that she died of natural causes before the horror began. Her soul had been too gentle to weather what had happened to their community.

"Not as sorry as I, Joe," Zev said, dragging himself back to the present. "But since my neighborhood is gone, and since I have hardly any friends left, I use the daylight hours to wander. So call me the Wandering Jew. And in my wanderings I meet some of your old parishioners."

The priest's face hardened. His voice became acid.

"Do you, now? And how fares the remnant of my devoted flock?"

"They've lost all hope, Joe. They wish you were back."

He laughed. "Sure they do! Just like they rallied behind me when my name and honor were being dragged through the muck last year. Yeah, they want me back. I'll bet!"

"Such anger, Joe. It doesn't become you."

"Bullshit. That was the old Joe Cahill, the naive turkey who believed all his faithful parishioners would back him up. But now Palmeri tells the bishop the heat is getting too much for him, the bishop removes me, and the people I dedicated my life to all stand by in silence as I'm railroaded out of my parish."

"It's hard for the commonfolk to buck a bishop."

"Maybe. But I can't forget how they stood quietly by while I was stripped of my position, my dignity, my integrity, of everything I wanted to be . . ."

Zev thought Joe's voice was going to break. He was about to reach out to him when the priest coughed and squared his shoulders. "Meanwhile, I'm a pariah over here in the retreat house. A goddam leper. Some of them actually believe—" He broke off in a growl. "Ah, what's the use? It's over and done. Most of the parish is dead anyway, I suppose. And if I'd stayed there I'd probably be dead too. So maybe it worked out for the best. And who gives a shit anyway."

He reached for the bottle of Glenlivet next to him.

"No-no!" Zev said. "You promised!"

Father Joe drew his hand back and crossed his arms across his chest.

"Talk on, O bearded one. I'm listening."

Father Joe had certainly changed for the worse. Morose, bitter, apathetic, self-pitying. Zev was beginning to wonder how he could have called this man a friend.

"They've taken over your church, desecrated it. Each night they further defile it with butchery and blasphemy. Doesn't that mean anything to you?"

"It's Palmeri's parish. I've been benched. Let him take care of it."

"Father Palmeri is their leader."

"He should be. He's their pastor."

"No. He leads the vampires in the obscenities they perform in the church."

Father Joe stiffened and the glassiness cleared from his eyes.

"Palmeri? He's one of them?"

Zev nodded. "More than that. He's the local leader. He orchestrates their rituals."

Zev saw rage flare in the priest's eyes, saw his hands ball into fists, and for a moment he thought the old Father Joe was going to burst through.

Come on, Joe. Show me that old fire.

But then he slumped back onto the crate.

"Is that all you came to tell me?"

Zev hid his disappointment and nodded. "Yes."

"Good." He grabbed the Scotch bottle. "Because I need a drink."

Zev wanted to leave, yet he had to stay, had to probe a little bit deeper and see how much of his old friend was left, and how much had been replaced by this new, bitter, alien Joe Cahill. Maybe there was still hope. So they talked on.

Suddenly he noticed it was dark.

"*Gevalt!*" Zev said. "I didn't notice the time!"

Father Joe seemed surprised too. He ran to the window and peered out.

"Damn! Sun's gone down!" He turned to Zev. "Lakewood's out of the question for you, Reb. Even the retreat house is too far to risk now. Looks like we're stuck here for the night."

"We'll be safe?"

He shrugged. "Why not? As far as I can tell I'm the only one who's been in here for months, and only in the daytime. Be pretty odd if one of those human leeches should decide to wander in here tonight."

"I hope so."

"Don't worry. We're okay if we don't attract attention. I've got a flashlight if we need it, but we're better off sitting here in the dark and shooting the breeze till sunrise." Father Joe smiled and picked up a huge silver cross, at least a foot in length, from atop one of the crates. "Besides, we're armed. And frankly, I can think of worse places to spend the night."

He stepped over to the case of Glenlivet and opened a fresh bottle. His capacity for alcohol was enormous.

Zev could think of worse places too. In fact he had spent a number of nights in much worse places since the holocaust. He decided to put the time to good use.

"So, Joe. Maybe I should tell you some more about what's happening in Lakewood."

After a few hours their talk died of fatigue. Father Joe gave Zev the flashlight to hold and stretched out across a couple of crates to sleep. Zev tried to get comfortable enough to doze but found sleep impossible. So he listened to his friend snore in the darkness of the cellar.

Poor Joe. Such anger in the man. But more than that—hurt. He felt betrayed, wronged. And with good reason. But with everything falling apart as it was, the wrong done to him would never be righted. He should forget about it already and go on with his life, but apparently he couldn't. Such a shame. He needed something to pull him out of his funk. Zev had thought news of what had happened to his old parish might rouse him, but it seemed only to make him want to drink more. Father Joe Cahill, he feared, was a hopeless case.

Zev closed his eyes and tried to rest. It was hard to get comfortable with the cross dangling in front of him, so he took it off but laid it within easy reach. He was drifting toward a doze when he heard a noise outside. By the dumpster. Metal on metal.

My bicycle!

He slipped to the floor and tiptoed over to where Father Joe slept. He shook his shoulder and whispered.

"Someone's found my bicycle!"

The priest snorted but remained sleeping. A louder clatter outside made Zev turn, and as he moved his elbow struck a bottle. He grabbed for it in the darkness but missed. The sound of smashing glass echoed through the basement like a cannon shot. As the odor of Scotch whiskey replaced the musty ambiance, Zev listened for further sounds from outside. None came.

Maybe it had been an animal. He remembered how raccoons used to raid his garbage at home . . . when he'd had a home . . . when he'd had garbage . . .

Zev stepped to the window and looked out. Probably an animal. He pulled the window open a few inches and felt cool night air wash across his face. He pulled the flashlight from his coat pocket and aimed it through the opening.

Zev almost dropped the light as the beam illuminated a pale, snarling demonic face, baring its fangs and hissing. He fell back as the thing's head and shoulders lunged through the window, its back-curved fingers clawing at him, missing. Then it launched itself the rest of the way through, hurtling toward Zev.

He tried to dodge but he was too slow. The impact knocked the flashlight from his grasp and it went rolling across the floor. Zev cried out as he went down under the snarling thing. Its ferocity was overpowering, irresistible. It straddled him and lashed at him, batting his fending arms aside, its clawed fingers tearing at his collar to free his throat, stretching his neck to expose the vulnerable flesh, its foul breath gagging him as it bent its fangs toward him. Zev screamed out his helplessness.

II

Father Joe awoke to the cries of a terrified voice.

He shook his head to clear it and instantly regretted the move. His head weighed at least two hundred pounds, and his mouth was stuffed with foul-tasting cotton. Why did he keep doing this to himself? Not only did it leave him feeling lousy, it gave him bad dreams. Like now.

Another terrified shout, only a few feet away.

He looked toward the sound. In the faint light from the flashlight rolling across the floor he saw Zev on his back, fighting for his life against—

Damn! This was no dream! One of those bloodsuckers had got in here!

He leaped over to where the creature was lowering its fangs toward Zev's throat. He grabbed it by the back of the neck and lifted it clear of the floor. It was surprisingly heavy but that didn't slow him. Joe could feel the anger rising in him, surging into his muscles.

"Rotten piece of filth!"

He swung the vampire by its neck and let it fly against the cinderblock wall. It impacted with what should have been bone-crushing force, but it bounced off, rolled on the floor, and regained its feet in one motion, ready to attack again. Strong as he was, Joe knew he was no match for a vampire's power. He turned, grabbed his big silver crucifix, and charged the creature.

"Hungry? Eat this!"

As the creature bared its fangs and hissed at him, Joe shoved the long lower end of the cross into its open mouth. Blue-white light flickered along the silver length of the crucifix, reflecting in the creature's startled, agonized eyes as its flesh sizzled and crackled. The vampire let out a strangled cry and tried to turn away but Joe wasn't through with it yet. He was literally seeing red as rage poured out of a hidden well and swirled through him. He rammed the cross deeper down the thing's gullet. Light flashed deep in its throat, illuminating the pale tissues from within. It tried to grab the cross and pull it out but the flesh of its fingers burned and smoked wherever they came in contact with the cross.

Finally Joe stepped back and let the thing squirm and scrabble up the wall and out the window into the night. Then he turned to Zev. If anything had happened—

"Hey, Reb!" he said, kneeling beside the older man. "You all right?"

"Yes," Zev said, struggling to his feet. "Thanks to you."

Joe slumped onto a crate, momentarily weak as his rage dissipated. *This is not what I'm about,* he thought. But it had felt so damn good to let it loose on that vampire. Too good. And that worried him.

I'm falling apart . . . like everything else in the world.

"That was too close," he said to Zev, giving the older man's shoulder a fond squeeze.

"Too close for that vampire for sure," Zev said, replacing his yarmulke. "And would you please remind me, Father Joe, that in the future if ever I should maybe get my blood sucked and become a vampire that I should stay far away from you."

Joe laughed for the first time in too long. It felt good.

They climbed out at first light. Joe stretched his cramped muscles in the fresh air while Zev checked on his hidden bicycle.

"Oy," Zev said as he pulled it from behind the dumpster. The front wheel had been bent so far out of shape that half the spokes were broken. "Look what he did. Looks like I'll be walking back to Lakewood."

But Joe was less interested in the bike than in the whereabouts of their visitor from last night. He knew it couldn't have got far. And it hadn't. They found the vampire—or rather what was left of it—on the far side of the dumpster: a rotting, twisted corpse, blackened to a crisp and steaming in the morning sunlight. The silver crucifix still protruded from between its teeth.

Joe approached and gingerly yanked his cross free of the foul remains.

"Looks like you've sucked your last pint of blood," he said and immediately felt foolish.

Who was he putting on the macho act for? Zev certainly wasn't going to buy it. Too out of character. But then, what *was* his character these days? He used to be a parish priest. Now he was a nothing. A less than nothing.

He straightened up and turned to Zev.

"Come on back to the retreat house, Reb. I'll buy you breakfast."

But as Joe turned and began walking away, Zev stayed and stared down at the corpse.

"They say they don't wander far from where they spent their lives," Zev said. "Which means it's unlikely this fellow was Jewish if he lived around here. Probably Catholic. Irish Catholic, I'd imagine."

Joe stopped and turned. He stared at his long shadow. The hazy rising sun at his back cast a huge hulking shape before him, with a dark cross in one shadow hand and a smudge of amber light where it poured through the unopened bottle of Scotch in the other.

"What are you getting at?" he said.

"The Kaddish would probably not be so appropriate so I'm just wondering if maybe someone should give him the last rites or whatever it is you people do when one of you dies."

"He wasn't one of us," Joe said, feeling the bitterness rise in him. "He wasn't even human."

"Ah, but he used to be before he was killed and became one of them. So maybe now he could use a little help."

Joe didn't like the way this was going. He sensed he was being maneuvered.

"He doesn't deserve it," he said and knew in that instant he'd been trapped.

"I thought even the worst sinner deserved it," Zev said.

Joe knew when he was beaten. Zev was right. He shoved the cross and bottle into Zev's hands—a bit roughly, perhaps—then went and knelt by the twisted cadaver. He administered a form of the final sacrament. When he was through he returned to Zev and snatched back his belongings.

"You're a better man than I am, Gunga Din," he said as he passed.

"You act as if they're responsible for what they do after they become vampires," Zev said as he hurried along beside him, panting as he matched Joe's pace.

"Aren't they?"

"No."

"You're sure of that?"

"Well, not exactly. But they certainly aren't human anymore, so maybe we shouldn't hold them accountable on human terms."

Zev's reasoning tone flashed Joe back to the conversations they used to have in Horovitz's deli.

"But Zev, we know there's some of the old personality left. I mean, they stay in their home towns, usually in the basements of their old houses. They go after people they knew when they were alive. They're not just dumb predators, Zev. They've got the old consciousness they had when they were alive. Why can't they rise above it? Why can't they . . . resist?"

"I don't know. To tell the truth, the question has never occurred to me. A fascinating concept: an undead refusing to feed. Leave it to Father Joe to come up with something like that. We should discuss this on the trip back to Lakewood."

Joe had to smile. So *that* was what this was all about.

"I'm not going back to Lakewood."

"Fine. Then we'll discuss it now. Maybe the urge to feed is too strong to overcome."

"Maybe. And maybe they just don't try hard enough."

"This is a hard line you're taking, my friend."

"I'm a hard-line kind of guy."

"Well, you've become one."

Joe gave him a sharp look. "You don't know what I've become."

Zev shrugged. "Maybe true, maybe not. But do you truly think you'd be able to resist?"

"Damn straight."

Joe didn't know whether he was serious or not. Maybe he was just mentally preparing himself for the day when he might actually find himself in that situation.

"Interesting," Zev said as they climbed the front steps of the retreat house. "Well, I'd better be going. I've a long walk ahead of me. A long, *lonely* walk all the way back to Lakewood. A long, lonely, possibly *dangerous* walk back for a poor old man who—"

"All right, Zev! All *right!*" Joe said, biting back a laugh. "I get the point. You want me to go back to Lakewood. Why?"

"I just want the company," Zev said with pure innocence.

"No, really. What's going on in that Talmudic mind of yours? What are you cooking?"

"Nothing, Father Joe. Nothing at all."

Joe stared at him. Damn it all if his interest wasn't piqued. What was Zev up to? And what the hell? Why not go? He had nothing better to do.

"All right, Zev. You win. I'll come back to Lakewood with you. But just for today. Just to keep you company. And I'm not going anywhere near St. Anthony's, okay? Understood?"

"Understood, Joe. Perfectly understood."

"Good. Now wipe that smile off your face and we'll get something to eat."

III

Under the climbing sun they walked south along the deserted beach, barefooting through the wet sand at the edge of the surf. Zev had never done this. He liked the feel of the sand between his toes, the coolness of the water as it sloshed over his ankles.

"Know what day it is?" Father Joe said. He had his sneakers slung over his shoulder. "Believe it or not, it's the Fourth of July."

"Oh, yes. Your Independence Day. We never made much of secular holidays. Too many religious ones to observe. Why should I not believe it's this date?"

Father Joe shook his head in dismay. "This is Manasquan Beach. You know what this place used to look like on the Fourth before the vampires took over? Wall-to-wall bodies."

"Really? I guess maybe sun-bathing is not the fad it used to be."

"Ah, Zev! Still the master of the understatement. I'll say one thing, though: the beach is cleaner than I've ever seen it. No beer cans or hypodermics." He pointed ahead. "But what's that up there?"

As they approached the spot, Zev saw a pair of naked bodies stretched out on the sand, one male, one female, both young and short-haired. Their skin was bronzed and glistened in the sun. The man lifted his head and stared at them. A blue crucifix was tattooed in the center of his forehead. He reached into the knapsack beside him and withdrew a huge, gleaming, nickel-plated revolver.

"Just keep walking," he said.

"Will do," Father Joe said. "Just passing through."

As they passed the couple, Zev noticed a similar tattoo on the girl's forehead. He noticed the rest of her too. He felt an almost-forgotten stirring deep inside him.

"A very popular tattoo," he said.

"Clever idea. That's one cross you can't drop or lose. Probably won't help you in the dark, but if there's a light on it might give you an edge."

They turned west and made their way inland, finding Route 70 and following it into Ocean County via the Brielle Bridge.

"I remember nightmare traffic jams right here every summer," Father Joe said as they trod the bridge's empty span. "Never thought I'd miss traffic jams."

They cut over to Route 88 and followed it all the way into Lakewood. Along the way they found a few people out and about in Bricktown and picking berries in Ocean County Park, but in the heart of Lakewood . . .

"A real ghost town," the priest said as they walked Forest Avenue's deserted length.

"Ghosts," Zev said, nodding sadly. It had been a long walk and he was tired. "Yes. Full of ghosts."

In his mind's eye he saw the shades of his fallen brother rabbis and all the yeshiva students, beards, black suits, black hats, crisscrossing back and forth at a determined pace on weekdays, strolling with their wives on Shabbes, their children trailing behind like ducklings.

Gone. All gone. Victims of the vampires. Vampires themselves now, most of them. It made him sick at heart to think of those good, gentle men, women, and children curled up in their basements now to avoid the light of day, venturing out in the dark to feed on others, spreading the disease . . .

He fingered the cross slung from his neck. *If only they had listened!*

"I know a place near St. Anthony's where we can hide," he told the priest.

"You've traveled enough today, Reb. And I told you, I don't care about St. Anthony's."

"Stay the night, Joe," Zev said, gripping the young priest's arm. He'd coaxed him this far; he couldn't let him get away now. "See what Father Palmeri's done."

"If he's one of them he's not a priest anymore. Don't call him Father."

"*They* still call him Father."

"Who?"

"The vampires."

Zev watched Father Joe's jaw muscles bunch.

Joe said, "Maybe I'll just take a quick trip over to St. Anthony's myself—"

"No. It's different here. The area is thick with them— maybe twenty times as many as in Spring Lake. They'll get you if your timing isn't just right. I'll take you."

"You need rest, pal."

Father Joe's expression showed genuine concern. Zev was detecting increasingly softer emotions in the man since their reunion last night. A good sign perhaps?

"And rest I'll get when we get to where I'm taking you."

IV

Father Joe Cahill watched the moon rise over his old church and wondered at the wisdom of coming back. The casual decision made this morning in the full light of day seemed reckless and foolhardy now at the approach of midnight.

But there was no turning back. He'd followed Zev to the second floor of this two-story office building across the street from St. Anthony's, and here they'd waited for dark. Must have been a law office once. The place had been vandalized, the windows broken, the furniture trashed, but there was an old Temple University Law School degree on the wall, and the couch was still in one piece. So while Zev caught some Z's, Joe sat and sipped a little of his Scotch and did some heavy thinking.

Mostly he thought about his drinking. He'd done too much of that lately, he knew; so much so that he was afraid to stop cold. So he was taking just a touch now, barely enough to take the edge off. He'd finish the rest later, after he came back from that church over there.

He'd stared at St. Anthony's since they'd arrived. It too had been extensively vandalized. Once it had been a beautiful little stone church, a miniature cathedral, really; very Gothic with all its pointed arches, steep roofs, crocketed spires, and multifoil stained glass windows. Now the windows were smashed, the crosses which had topped the steeple and each gable were gone, and anything resembling a cross in its granite exterior had been defaced beyond recognition.

As he'd known it would, the sight of St. Anthony's brought back memories of Gloria Sullivan, the young, pretty church volunteer whose husband worked for

United Chemical International in New York, commuting in every day and trekking off overseas a little too often. Joe and Gloria had seen a lot of each other around the church offices and had become good friends. But Gloria had somehow got the idea that what they had went beyond friendship, so she showed up at the rectory one night when Joe was there alone. He tried to explain that as attractive as she was, she was not for him. He had taken certain vows and meant to stick by them. He did his best to let her down easy but she'd been hurt. And angry.

That might have been that, but then her six-year-old son Kevin had come home from altar boy practice with a story about a priest making him pull down his pants and touching him. Kevin was never clear on who the priest had been, but Gloria Sullivan was. Obviously it had been Father Cahill—any man who could turn down the heartfelt offer of her love and her body had to be either a queer or worse. And a child molester was worse.

She took it to the police and to the papers.

Joe groaned softly at the memory of how swiftly his life had become hell. But he had been determined to weather the storm, sure that the real culprit eventually would be revealed. He had no proof—still didn't—but if one of the priests at St. Anthony's was a pederast, he knew it wasn't him. That left Father Alberto Palmeri, St. Anthony's fifty-five-year-old pastor. Before Joe could get to the truth, however, Father Palmeri requested that Father Cahill be removed from the parish, and the bishop complied. Joe had left under a cloud that had followed him to the retreat house in the next county and hovered over him till this day. The only place he'd found even brief respite from the impotent anger and bitterness that roiled under his skin and soured his gut every minute of every day was in the bottle—and that was sure as hell a dead end.

So why had he agreed to come back here? To torture himself? Or to get a look at Palmeri and see how low he had sunk?

Maybe that was it. Maybe seeing Palmeri wallowing in his true element would give him the impetus to put the whole St. Anthony's incident behind him and rejoin what was left of the human race—which needed him now more than ever.

And maybe it wouldn't.

Getting back on track was a nice thought, but over the past few months Joe had found it increasingly difficult to give much of a damn about anyone or anything.

Except maybe Zev. He'd stuck by Joe through the worst of it, defending him to anyone who would listen. But an endorsement from an Orthodox rabbi had meant diddly in St. Anthony's. And yesterday Zev had biked all the way to Spring Lake to see him. Old Zev was all right.

And he'd been right about the number of vampires here too. Lakewood was *crawling* with the things. Fascinated and repelled, Joe had watched the streets fill with them shortly after sundown.

But what had disturbed him more were the creatures who'd come out *before* sundown.

The humans. Live ones.

The collaborators.

If there was anything lower, anything that deserved true death more than the vampires themselves, it was the still-living humans who worked for them.

Someone touched his shoulder and he jumped. It was Zev. He was holding something out to him. Joe took it and held it up in the moonlight: a tiny crescent moon dangling from a chain on a ring.

"What's this?"

"An earring. The local Vichy wear them."

"Vichy? Like the Vichy French?"

"Yes. Very good. I'm glad to see that you're not as culturally illiterate as the rest of your generation. Vichy humans—that's what I call the collaborators. These earrings identify them to the local nest of vampires. They are spared."

"Where'd you get them?"

Zev's face was hidden in the shadows. "Their previous owners . . . lost them. Put it on."

"My ear's not pierced."

A gnarled hand moved into the moonlight. Joe saw a long needle clasped between the thumb and index finger.

"That I can fix," Zev said.

"Maybe you shouldn't see this," Zev whispered as they crouched in the deep shadows on St. Anthony's western flank.

Joe squinted at him in the darkness, puzzled.

"You lay a guilt trip on me to get me here, now you're having second thoughts?"

"It is horrible like I can't tell you."

Joe thought about that. There was enough horror in the world outside St. Anthony's. What purpose did it serve to see what was going on inside?

Because it used to be my church.

Even though he'd only been an associate pastor, never fully in charge, and even though he'd been unceremoniously yanked from the post, St. Anthony's had been his first parish. He was here. He might as well know what they were doing inside.

"Show me."

Zev led him to a pile of rubble under a smashed stained glass window. He pointed up to where faint light flickered from inside.

"Look in there."

"You're not coming?"

"Once was enough, thank you."

Joe climbed as carefully, as quietly as he could, all the while becoming increasingly aware of a growing stench like putrid, rotting meat. It was coming from inside, wafting through the broken window. Steeling himself, he straightened up and peered over the sill.

For a moment he was disoriented, like someone peering out the window of a city apartment and seeing the rolling hills of a Kansas farm. This could not be the interior of St. Anthony's.

In the flickering light of hundreds of sacramental candles he saw that the walls were bare, stripped of all their ornaments, of the plaques for the Stations of the Cross; the dark wood along the wall was scarred and gouged wherever there had been anything remotely resembling a cross. The floor too was mostly bare, the pews ripped from their neat rows and hacked to pieces, their splintered remains piled high at the rear under the choir balcony.

And the giant crucifix that had dominated the space behind the altar—only a portion of it remained. The cross-pieces on each side had been sawed off and so now an armless, life-size Christ hung upside down against the rear wall of the sanctuary.

Joe took in all that in a flash, then his attention was drawn to the unholy congregation that peopled St. Anthony's this night. The collaborators—the Vichy humans, as Zev called them—made up the periphery of the group. They looked like normal, everyday people but each was wearing a crescent moon earring.

But the others, the group gathered in the sanctuary—Joe felt his hackles rise at the sight of them. They surrounded the altar in a tight knot. Their pale, bestial faces, bereft of the slightest trace of human warmth, compassion, or decency, were turned upward. His gorge rose when he saw the object of their rapt attention.

A naked teenage boy—his hands tied behind his back—was suspended over the altar by his ankles. He was sobbing and choking, his eyes wide and vacant with shock, his mind all but gone. The skin had been flayed from his forehead—apparently the Vichy had found an expedient solution to the cross tattoo—and blood ran in a slow stream down his abdomen and chest from his freshly truncated genitals. And beside him, standing atop the altar, a bloody-mouthed creature dressed in a long cassock. Joe recognized the thin shoulders, the graying hair trailing from the balding crown, but was shocked at the crimson vulpine grin he flashed to the things clustered below him.

"Now," said the creature in a lightly accented voice Joe had heard hundreds of times from St. Anthony's pulpit.

Father Alberto Palmeri.

And from the group a hand reached up with a straight razor and drew it across the boy's throat. As the blood flowed down over his face, those below squeezed and struggled forward like hatchling vultures to catch the falling drops and scarlet trickles in their open mouths.

Joe fell away from the window and vomited. He felt Zev grab his arm and lead him away. He was vaguely aware of crossing the street and heading toward the ruined legal office.

V

"Why in God's name did you want me to see that?"

Zev looked across the office toward the source of the words. He could see a vague outline where Father Joe sat on the floor, his back against the wall, the open bottle of Scotch in his hand. The priest had taken one drink since their return, no more.

"I thought you should know what they were doing to your church."

"So you've said. But what's the reason behind that one?"

Zev shrugged in the darkness. "I'd heard you weren't doing well, that even before everything else began falling apart, you had already fallen apart. So when I felt it safe to get away, I came to see you. Just as I expected, I found a man who was angry at everything and letting it eat up his *guderim*. I thought maybe it would be good to give that man something very specific to be angry at."

"You bastard!" Father Joe whispered. "Who gave you the right?"

"Friendship gave me the right, Joe. I should hear that you are rotting away and do nothing? I have no congregation of my own anymore so I turned my attention on you. Always I was a somewhat meddlesome rabbi."

"Still are. Out to save my soul, ay?"

"We rabbis don't save souls. Guide them maybe, hopefully give them direction. But only you can save your soul, Joe."

Silence hung in the air for a while. Suddenly the crescent moon earring Zev had given Father Joe landed in the puddle of moonlight on the floor between them.

"Why do they do it?" the priest said. "The Vichy—why do they collaborate?"

"The first were quite unwilling, believe me. They cooperated because their wives and children were held hostage by the vampires. But before too long the dregs of humanity began to slither out from under their rocks and offer their services in exchange for the immortality of vampirism."

"Why bother working for them? Why not just bare your throat to the nearest bloodsucker?"

"That's what I thought at first," Zev said. "But as I witnessed the Lakewood holocaust I detected the vampires' pattern. They can choose who joins their ranks, so after they've fully infiltrated a population, they change their tactics. You see, they don't want too many of their kind concentrated in one area. It's like too many carnivores in one forest—when the herds of prey are wiped out, the predators starve. So they start to employ a different style of killing. For only when the vampire draws the life's blood from the throat with its fangs does the victim become one of them. Anyone drained as in the manner of that boy in the church tonight dies a true death. He's as dead now as someone run over by a truck. He will not rise tomorrow night."

"I get it," Father Joe said. "The Vichy trade their daylight services and dirty work to the vampires now for immortality later on."

"Correct."

There was no humor in the soft laugh that echoed across the room from Father Joe.

"Swell. I never cease to be amazed at our fellow human beings. Their capacity for good is exceeded only by their ability to debase themselves."

"Hopelessness does strange things, Joe. The vampires know that. So they rob us of hope. That's how they beat us. They transform our friends and neighbors and leaders into their own, leaving us feeling alone, completely cut off. Some of us can't take the despair and kill ourselves."

"Hopelessness," Joe said. "A potent weapon."

After a long silence, Zev said, "So what are you going to do now, Father Joe?"

Another bitter laugh from across the room.

"I suppose this is the place where I declare that I've found new purpose in life and will now go forth into the world as a fearless vampire killer."

"Such a thing would be nice."

"Well screw that. I'm only going as far as across the street."

"To St. Anthony's?"

Zev saw Father Joe take a swig from the Scotch bottle and then screw the cap on tight.

"Yeah. To see if there's anything I can do over there."

"Father Palmeri and his nest might not like that."

"I told you, don't call him Father. And screw *him*.

Nobody can do what he's done and get away with it. I'm taking my church back."

In the dark, behind his beard, Zev smiled.

VI

Joe stayed up the rest of the night and let Zev sleep. The old guy needed his rest. Sleep would have been impossible for Joe anyway. He was too wired. He sat up and watched St. Anthony's.

They left before first light, dark shapes drifting out the front doors and down the stone steps like parishioners leaving a predawn service. Joe felt his back teeth grind as he scanned the group for Palmeri, but he couldn't make him out in the dimness. By the time the sun began to peek over the rooftops and through the trees to the east, the street outside was deserted.

He woke Zev and together they approached the church. The heavy oak and iron front doors, each forming half of a pointed arch, were closed. He pulled them open and fastened the hooks to keep them open. Then he walked through the vestibule and into the nave.

Even though he was ready for it, the stench backed him up a few steps. When his stomach settled, he forced himself ahead, treading a path between the two piles of shattered and splintered pews. Zev walked beside him, a handkerchief pressed over his mouth.

Last night he had thought the place a shambles. He

saw now that it was worse. The light of day poked into all the corners, revealing everything that had been hidden by the warm glow of the candles. Half a dozen rotting corpses hung from the ceiling—he hadn't noticed them last night—and others were sprawled on the floor against the walls. Some of the bodies were in pieces. Behind the chancel rail a headless female torso was draped over the front of the pulpit. To the left stood the statue of Mary. Someone had fitted her with foam rubber breasts and a huge dildo. And at the rear of the sanctuary was the armless Christ hanging head down on the upright of his cross.

"My church," he whispered as he moved along the path that had once been the center aisle, the aisle brides used to walk down with their fathers. "Look what they've done to my church!"

Joe approached the huge block of the altar. Once it had been backed against the far wall of the sanctuary, but he'd had it moved to the front so that he could celebrate Mass facing his parishioners. Solid Carrara marble, but you'd never know it now. So caked with dried blood, semen, and feces it could have been made of styrofoam.

His revulsion was fading, melting away in the growing heat of his rage, drawing the nausea with it. He had intended to clean up the place but there was so much to be done, too much for two men. It was hopeless.

"Fadda Joe?"

He spun at the sound of the strange voice. A thin fig-

ure stood uncertainly in the open doorway. A man of
about fifty edged forward timidly.

"Fadda Joe, izat you?"

Joe recognized him now. Carl Edwards. A twitchy little man who used to help pass the collection basket at
10:30 Mass on Sundays. A transplantee from Jersey
City—hardly anyone around here was originally from
around here. His face was sunken, his eyes feverish as he
stared at Joe.

"Yes, Carl. It's me."

"Oh, tank God!" He ran forward and dropped to his
knees before Joe. He began to sob. "You come back!
Tank God, you come back!"

Joe pulled him to his feet.

"Come on now, Carl. Get a grip."

"You come back ta save us, ain'tcha? God sent ya here
to punish him, din't He?"

"Punish whom?"

"Fadda Palmeri! He's one a dem! He's da woist a alla
dem! He—"

"I know," Joe said. "I know."

"Oh, it's so good to have ya back, Fadda Joe! We ain't
knowed what to do since da suckers took ova. We been
prayin' fa someone like youse an' now ya here. It's a freak-
in' miracle!"

Joe wanted to ask Carl where he and all these people
who seemed to think they needed him now had been
when he was being railroaded out of the parish. But that
was ancient history.

"Not a miracle, Carl," Joe said, glancing at Zev. "Rabbi Wolpin brought me back." As Carl and Zev shook hands, Joe said, "And I'm just passing through."

"Passing t'rough? No. Dat can't be! Ya gotta stay!"

Joe saw the light of hope fading in the little man's eyes. Something twisted within him, tugging him.

"What can I do here, Carl? I'm just one man."

"I'll help! I'll do whatever ya want! Jes' tell me!"

"Will you help me clean up?"

Carl looked around and seemed to see the cadavers for the first time. He cringed and turned a few shades paler.

"Yeah . . . sure. Anyting."

Joe looked at Zev. "Well? What do you think?"

Zev shrugged. "I should tell you what to do? My parish it's not."

"Not mine either."

Zev jutted his beard at Carl. "I think maybe he'd tell you differently."

Joe did a slow turn. The vaulted nave was utterly silent except for the buzzing of the flies around the cadavers.

A massive clean-up job. But if they worked all day they could make a decent dent in it. And then—

And then what?

Joe didn't know. He was playing this by ear. He'd wait and see what the night brought.

"Can you get us some food, Carl? I'd sell my soul for a cup of coffee."

Carl gave him a strange look.

"Just a figure of speech, Carl. We'll need some food if we're going to keep working."

The man's eyes lit again.

"Dat means ya staying?"

"For a while."

"I'll getcha some food," he said excitedly as he ran for the door. "An' coffee. I know someone who's still got coffee. She'll part wit' some of it for Fadda Joe." He stopped at the door and turned. "Ay, an' Fadda, I neva believed any a dem tings dat was said aboutcha. Neva."

Joe tried but he couldn't hold it back.

"It would have meant a lot to have heard that from you last year, Carl."

The man lowered his eyes. "Yeah. I guess it woulda. But I'll make it up to ya, Fadda. I will. You can take dat to da bank."

Then he was out the door and gone. Joe turned to Zev and saw the old man rolling up his sleeves.

"*Nu?*" Zev said. "The bodies. Before we do anything else, I think maybe we should move the bodies."

VII

By early afternoon, Zev was exhausted. The heat and the heavy work had taken their toll. He had to stop and rest. He sat on the chancel rail and looked around. Nearly eight hours' work and they'd barely scratched the surface. But the place did look and smell better.

Removing the flyblown corpses and scattered body

parts had been the worst of it. A foul, gut-roiling task that had taken most of the morning. They'd carried the corpses out to the small graveyard behind the church and left them there. Those people deserved a decent burial but there was no time for it today.

Once the corpses were gone, Father Joe had torn the defilements from the statue of Mary and then they'd turned their attention to the huge crucifix. It took a while but they finally found Christ's plaster arms in the pile of ruined pews. They were still nailed to the sawn-off crosspiece of the crucifix. While Zev and Father Joe worked at jury-rigging a series of braces to reattach the arms, Carl found a mop and bucket and began the long, slow process of washing the fouled floor of the nave.

Now the crucifix was intact again—the life-size plaster Jesus had his arms reattached and was once again nailed to his refurbished cross. Father Joe and Carl had restored him to his former position of dominance. The poor man was upright again, hanging over the center of the sanctuary in all his tortured splendor.

A grisly sight. Zev could never understand the Catholic attachment to these gruesome statues. But if the vampires loathed them, then Zev was for them all the way.

His stomach rumbled with hunger. At least they'd had a good breakfast. Carl had returned from his food run this morning with bread, cheese, and two thermoses of hot coffee. He wished now they'd saved some. Maybe there was a crust of bread left in the sack. He headed back to the vestibule to check and found an aluminum pot and a paper bag sitting by the door. The pot was full of beef stew and the sack contained three cans of Pepsi.

He poked his head out the doors but no one was in sight on the street outside. It had been that way all day— he'd spy a figure or two peeking in the front doors; they'd hover there for a moment as if to confirm that what they had heard was true, then they'd scurry away. He looked at the meal that had been left. A group of the locals must have donated from their hoard of canned stew and precious soft drinks to fix this. Zev was touched.

He called Father Joe and Carl.

"Tastes like Dinty Moore," Father Joe said around a mouthful of the stew.

"It is," Carl said. "I recognize da little potatoes. Da ladies of the parish must really be excited about youse comin' back to break inta deir canned goods like dis."

They were feasting in the sacristy, the small room off the sanctuary where the priests had kept their vestments—a clerical Green Room, so to speak. Zev found the stew palatable but much too salty. He wasn't about to complain, though.

"I don't believe I've ever had anything like this before."

"I'd be real surprised if you had," said Father Joe. "I

doubt very much that something that calls itself Dinty Moore is kosher."

Zev smiled but inside he was suddenly filled with a great sadness. Kosher . . . how meaningless now seemed all the observances which he had allowed to rule and circumscribe his life. Such a fierce proponent of strict dietary laws he'd been in the days before the Lakewood holocaust. But those days were gone, just as the Lakewood community was gone. And Zev was a changed man. If he hadn't changed, if he were still observing, he couldn't sit here and sup with these two men. He'd have to be elsewhere, eating special classes of specially prepared foods off separate sets of dishes. But really, wasn't division what holding to the dietary laws in modern times was all about? They served a purpose beyond mere observance of tradition. They placed another wall between observant Jews and outsiders, keeping them separate even from other Jews who didn't observe.

Zev forced himself to take a big bite of the stew. Time to break down all the walls between people . . . while there was still enough time and people left alive to make it matter.

"You okay, Zev?" Father Joe asked.

Zev nodded silently, afraid to speak for fear of sobbing. Despite all its anachronisms, he missed his life in the good old days of last year. Gone. It was all gone. The rich traditions, the culture, the friends, the prayers. He felt adrift—in time and in space. Nowhere was home.

"You sure?" The young priest seemed genuinely concerned.

"Yes, I'm okay. As okay as you could expect me to feel after spending the better part of the day repairing a crucifix and eating non-kosher food. And let me tell you, that's not so okay."

He put his bowl aside and straightened from his chair.

"Come on, already. Let's get back to work. There's much yet to do."

VIII

"Sun's almost down," Carl said.

Joe straightened from scrubbing the altar and stared west through one of the smashed windows. The sun was out of sight behind the houses there.

"You can go now, Carl," he said to the little man. "Thanks for your help."

"Where youse gonna go, Fadda?"

"I'll be staying right here."

Carl's prominent Adam's apple bobbed convulsively as he swallowed.

"Yeah? Well den, I'm staying too. I tol' ya I'd make it up to ya, din't I? An' besides, I don't tink the suckas'll like da new, improved St. Ant'ny's too much when dey come back tonight, d'you? I don't even tink dey'll get t'rough da doors."

Joe smiled at the man and looked around. Luckily it

was July when the days were long. They'd had time to make a difference here. The floors were clean, the crucifix was restored and back in its proper position, as were most of the Stations of the Cross plaques. Zev had found them under the pews and had taken the ones not shattered beyond recognition and rehung them on the walls. Lots of new crosses littered those walls. Carl had found a hammer and nails and had made dozens of them from the remains of the pews.

"No, I don't think they'll like the new decor one bit. But there's something you can get us if you can, Carl. Guns. Pistols, rifles, shotguns, anything that shoots."

Carl nodded slowly. "I know a few guys who can help in dat department."

"And some wine. A little red wine if anybody's saved some."

"You got it."

He hurried off.

"You're planning Custer's last stand, maybe?" Zev said from where he was tacking the last of Carl's crude crosses to the east wall.

"More like the Alamo."

"Same result," Zev said with one of his shrugs.

Joe turned back to scrubbing the altar. He'd been at it for over an hour now. He was drenched with sweat and knew he smelled like a bear, but he couldn't stop until it was clean.

An hour later he was forced to give up. No use. It wouldn't come clean. The vampires must have done something to the blood and foulness to make the mixture seep into the surface of the marble like it had.

He sat on the floor with his back against the altar and rested. He didn't like resting because it gave him time to think. And when he started to think he realized that the odds were pretty high against his seeing tomorrow morning.

At least he'd die well fed. Their secret supplier had left them a dinner of fresh fried chicken by the front doors. Even the memory of it made his mouth water. Apparently someone was *really* glad he was back.

To tell the truth, though, as miserable as he'd been, he wasn't ready to die. Not tonight, not any night. He wasn't looking for an Alamo or a Little Big Horn. All he wanted to do was hold off the vampires till dawn. Keep them out of St. Anthony's for one night. That was all. That would be a statement—*his* statement. If he found an opportunity to ram a stake through Palmeri's rotten heart, so much the better, but he wasn't counting on that. One night. Just to let them know they couldn't have their way everywhere with everybody whenever they felt like it. He had surprise on his side tonight, so maybe it would work. One night. Then he'd be on his way.

"What the fuck have you *done*?"

Joe looked up at the shout. A burly, long-haired man in jeans and a flannel shirt stood in the vestibule staring at the partially restored nave. As he approached, Joe noticed his crescent moon earring.

A Vichy.

Joe balled his fists but didn't move.

"Hey, I'm talking to you, mister. Are you responsible for this?"

When all he got from Joe was a cold stare, he turned to Zev.

"Hey, you! Jew! What the hell do you think *you're* doing?" He started toward Zev. "You get those fucking crosses off—"

"Touch him and I'll break you in half," Joe said in a low voice.

The Vichy skidded to a halt and stared at him.

"Hey, asshole! Are you crazy? Do you know what Father Palmeri will do to you when he arrives?"

"*Father* Palmeri? Why do you still call him that?"

"It's what he wants to be called. And he's going to call you *dog meat* when he gets here!"

Joe pulled himself to his feet and looked down at the Vichy. The man took two steps back. Suddenly he didn't seem so sure of himself.

"Tell him I'll be waiting. Tell him Father Cahill is back."

"You're a priest? You don't look like one."

"Shut up and listen. Tell him Father Joe Cahill is back—and he's pissed. Tell him that. Now get out of here while you still can."

The man turned and hurried out into the growing darkness. Joe turned to Zev and found him grinning through his beard. " 'Father Joe Cahill is back—and he's pissed.' I like that."

"We'll make it into a bumper sticker. Meanwhile let's close those doors. The criminal element is starting to wander in. I'll see if we can find some more candles. It's getting dark in here."

IX

He wore the night like a tuxedo.

Dressed in a fresh cassock, Father Alberto Palmeri turned off County Line Road and strolled toward St. Anthony's. The night was lovely, especially when you owned it. And he owned the night in this area of Lakewood now. He loved the night. He felt at one with it, attuned to its harmonies and its discords. The darkness made him feel so alive. Strange to have to lose your life before you could really feel alive. But this was it. He'd found his niche, his métier.

Such a shame it had taken him so long. All those years trying to deny his appetites, trying to be a member of the other side, cursing himself when he allowed his appetites to win, as he had with increasing frequency toward the end of his mortal life. He should have given in to them completely long ago.

It had taken undeath to free him.

And to think he had been afraid of undeath, had cowered in fear each night in the cellar of the church, surrounded by crosses. Fortunately he had not been as safe as he'd thought and one of the beings he now called brother was able to slip in on him in the dark while he dozed. He saw now that he had lost nothing but his blood by that encounter.

And in trade he'd gained a world.

For now it was his world, at least this little corner of it, one in which he was completely free to indulge himself in any way he wished. Except for the blood. He had no choice about the blood. That was a new appetite, stronger than all the rest, one that would not be denied. But he did not mind the new appetite in the least. He'd found interesting ways to sate it.

Up ahead he spotted dear, defiled St. Anthony's. He wondered what his servants had prepared for him tonight. They were quite imaginative. They'd yet to bore him.

But as he drew nearer the church, Palmeri slowed. His skin prickled. The building had changed. Something was very wrong there, wrong inside. Something amiss with the light that beamed from the windows. This wasn't the old familiar candlelight, this was something else, something more. Something that made his insides tremble.

Figures raced up the street toward him. Live ones. His night vision picked out the earrings and familiar faces of some of his servants. As they neared he sensed the warmth of the blood coursing just beneath their skins. The hunger rose in him and he fought the urge to rip into one of their throats. He couldn't allow himself that pleasure. He had to keep the servants dangling, keep them working for him and the nest. They needed the services of the indentured living to remove whatever obstacles the cattle might put in their way.

"Father! Father!" they cried.

He loved it when they called him Father, loved being one of the undead and dressing like one of the enemy.

"Yes, my children. What sort of victim do you have for us tonight?"

"No victim, Father—trouble!"

The edges of Palmeri's vision darkened with rage as he heard of the young priest and the Jew who had dared to try to turn St. Anthony's into a holy place again. When he heard the name of the priest, he nearly exploded.

"Cahill? Joseph Cahill is back in my church?"

"He was cleaning the altar!" one of the servants said.

Palmeri strode toward the church with the servants trailing behind. He knew that neither Cahill nor the Pope himself could clean that altar. Palmeri had desecrated it himself; he had learned how to do that when he became nest leader. But what else had the young pup dared to do?

Whatever it was, it would be undone. *Now!*

Palmeri strode up the steps and pulled the right door open—and screamed in agony.

The light! The *light*! The LIGHT! White agony lanced through Palmeri's eyes and seared his brain like two hot pokers. He retched and threw his arms across his face as he staggered back into the cool, comforting darkness.

It took a few minutes for the pain to drain off, for the nausea to pass, for vision to return.

He'd never understand it. He'd spent his entire life in the presence of crosses and crucifixes, surrounded by them. And yet as soon as he'd become undead, he was unable to bear the sight of one. As a matter of fact, since he'd become undead, he'd never even *seen* one. A cross was no longer an object. It was a light, a light so excruciatingly bright, so blazingly white that it was sheer agony to look at it. As a child in Naples he'd been told by his mother not to look at the sun, but when there'd been talk of an eclipse, he'd stared directly into its eye. The pain of looking at a cross was a hundred, no, a thousand times worse than that. And the bigger the cross or crucifix, the worse the pain.

He'd experienced monumental pain upon looking into St. Anthony's tonight. That could only mean that Joseph, that young bastard, had refurbished the giant crucifix. It was the only possible explanation.

He swung on his servants.

"Get in there! Get that crucifix down!"

"They've got guns!"

"Then get help. But get it *down*!"

"We'll get guns too! We can—"

"*No!* I want him! I want that priest alive! I want him for myself! Anyone who kills him will suffer a very painful, very long and lingering true death! Is that clear?"

It was clear. They scurried away without answering.

Palmeri went to gather the other members of the nest.

X

Dressed in a cassock and a surplice, Joe came out of the sacristy and approached the altar. He noticed Zev keeping watch at one of the windows. He didn't tell him how ridiculous he looked carrying the shotgun Carl had brought back. He held it so gingerly, like it was full of nitroglycerine and would explode if he jiggled it.

Zev turned, and smiled when he saw him.

"*Now* you look like the old Father Joe we all used to know."

Joe gave him a little bow and proceeded toward the altar.

All right: He had everything he needed. He had the Missal they'd found in among the pew debris earlier today. He had the wine; Carl had brought back about four ounces of sour red barberone. He'd found a smudged surplice and a dusty cassock on the floor of one of the closets in the sacristy, and he wore them now. No hosts, though. A crust of bread left over from breakfast would have to do. No chalice, either. If he'd known he was going to be saying Mass he'd have come prepared. As a last resort he'd used the can opener in the rectory to remove the top from one of the Pepsi cans from lunch. Quite a stretch from the gold chalice he'd used since his ordination, but probably more in line with what Jesus had used at that first Mass—the Last Supper.

He was uncomfortable with the idea of weapons in St. Anthony's but he saw no alternative. He and Zev knew nothing about guns, and Carl knew little more; they'd probably do more damage to themselves than to the Vichy if they tried to use them. But maybe the sight of them would make the Vichy hesitate, slow them down. All he needed was a little time here, enough to get to the consecration.

This is going to be the most unusual Mass in history, he thought.

But he was going to get through it if it killed him. And that was a real possibility. This might well be his last Mass. But he wasn't afraid. He was too excited to be afraid. He'd had a slug of the Scotch—just enough to ward off the DTs—but it had done nothing to quell the buzz of the adrenalin humming along every nerve in his body.

He spread everything out on the white tablecloth he'd taken from the rectory and used to cover the filthy altar. He looked at Carl.

"Ready?"

Carl nodded and stuck the .38 caliber pistol he'd been examining in his belt.

"Been a while, Fadda. We did it in Latin when I was a kid but I tink I can swing it."

"Just do your best and don't worry about any mistakes."

Some Mass. A defiled altar, a crust for a host, a Pepsi can for a chalice, a fifty-year-old, pistol-packing altar boy, and a congregation consisting of a lone, shotgun-carrying Orthodox Jew.

Joe looked heavenward. *You do understand, don't you, Lord, that this was arranged on short notice?*

Time to begin.

He read the Gospel but dispensed with the homily. He tried to remember the Mass as it used to be said, to fit in better with Carl's outdated responses. As he was starting the Offertory the front doors flew open and a group of men entered—ten of them, all with crescent moons dangling from their ears. Out of the corner of his eye he saw Zev move away from the window toward the altar, pointing his shotgun at them.

As soon as they entered the nave and got past the broken pews, the Vichy fanned out toward the sides. They began pulling down the Stations of the Cross, ripping Carl's makeshift crosses from the walls and tearing them apart. Carl looked up at Joe from where he knelt, his eyes questioning, his hand reaching for the pistol in his belt.

Joe shook his head and kept up with the Offertory.

When all the little crosses were down, the Vichy swarmed behind the altar. Joe chanced a quick glance over his shoulder and saw them begin their attack on the newly repaired crucifix.

"Zev!" Carl said in a low voice, cocking his head toward the Vichy. "Stop 'em!"

Zev worked the pump on the shotgun. The sound echoed through the church. Joe heard the activity behind him come to a sudden halt. He braced himself for the shot . . .

But it never came.

He looked at Zev. The old man met his gaze and sadly shook his head. He couldn't do it. To the accompaniment of the sound of renewed activity and derisive laughter behind him, Joe gave Zev a tiny nod of reassurance and understanding, then hurried the Mass toward the Consecration.

As he held the crust of bread aloft, he started at the sound of the life-size crucifix crashing to the floor, cringed as he heard the freshly buttressed arms and crosspiece being torn away again.

As he held the wine aloft in the Pepsi can, the swaggering, grinning Vichy surrounded the altar and brazenly tore the cross from around his neck. Zev and Carl put up a struggle to keep theirs but were overpowered.

And then Joe's skin began to crawl as a new group entered the nave. There had to be at least forty of them, all of them vampires.

And Palmeri was leading them.

XI

Palmeri hid his hesitancy as he approached the altar. The crucifix and its intolerable whiteness were gone, yet something was not right. Something repellent here, something that urged him to flee. What?

Perhaps it was just the residual effect of the crucifix and all the crosses they had used to line the walls. That had to be it. The unsettling aftertaste would fade as the night wore on. Oh, yes. His nightbrothers and sisters from the nest would see to that.

He focused his attention on the man behind the altar and laughed when he realized what he held in his hands.

"Pepsi, Joseph? You're trying to consecrate Pepsi?" He turned to his nest siblings. "Do you see this, my brothers and sisters? Is this the man we are to fear? And look who he has with him! An old Jew and a parish hanger-on!"

He heard their hissing laughter as they fanned out around him, sweeping toward the altar in a wide phalanx. The Jew and Carl—he recognized Carl and wondered how he'd avoided capture for so long—retreated to the other side of the altar where they flanked Joseph. And Joseph . . . Joseph's handsome Irish face so pale and drawn, his mouth drawn into such a tight, grim line. He looked scared to death. And well he should be.

Palmeri put down his rage at Joseph's audacity. He was glad he had returned. He'd always hated the young priest for his easy manner with people, for the way the parishioners had flocked to him with their problems despite the fact that he had nowhere near the experience of their older and wiser pastor. But that was over now. That world was gone, replaced by a nightworld—Palmeri's world. And no one would be flocking to Father Joe for anything when Palmeri was through with him. "Father Joe"—how he'd hated it when the parishioners had started calling him that. Well, their Father Joe would provide superior entertainment tonight. This was going to be *fun*.

"Joseph, Joseph, Joseph," he said as he stopped and smiled at the young priest across the altar. "This futile gesture is so typical of your arrogance."

But Joseph only stared back at him, his expression a mixture of defiance and repugnance. And that only fueled Palmeri's rage.

"Do I repel you, Joseph? Does my new form offend your precious shanty-Irish sensibilities? Does my undeath disgust you?"

"You managed to do all that while you were still alive, Alberto."

Palmeri allowed himself to smile. Joseph probably thought he was putting on a brave front, but the tremor in his voice betrayed his fear.

"Always good with the quick retort, weren't you, Joseph. Always thinking you were better than me, always putting yourself above me."

"Not much of a climb where a child molester is concerned."

Palmeri's anger mounted.

"So superior. So self-righteous. What about your appetites, Joseph? The secret ones? What are they? Do you always hold them in check? Are you so far above the rest of us that you never give in to an improper impulse? I'll bet you think that even if we made you one of us you could resist the blood hunger."

He saw by the startled look in Joseph's face that he had struck a nerve. He stepped closer, almost touching the altar.

"You do, don't you? You really think you could resist it! Well, we shall see about that, Joseph. By dawn you'll be drained—we'll each take a turn at you—and when the sun rises you'll have to hide from its light. When the night comes you'll be one of us. And then all the rules will be off. The night will be yours. You'll be able to do anything and everything you've ever wanted. But the blood hunger will be on you too. You won't be sipping your god's blood, as you've done so often, but *human* blood. You'll thirst for hot, human blood, Joseph. And you'll have to sate that thirst. There'll be no choice. And I want to be there when you do, Joseph. I want to be there to laugh in your face as you suck up the crimson nectar, and keep on laughing every night as the red hunger lures you into infinity."

And it *would* happen. Palmeri knew it as sure as he felt his own thirst. He hungered for the moment when he could rub dear Joseph's face in the muck of his own despair.

"I was about to finish saying Mass," Joseph said coolly. "Do you mind if I finish?"

Palmeri couldn't help laughing this time.

"Did you really think this charade would work? Did you really think you could celebrate Mass on *this*?"

He reached out and snatched the tablecloth from the altar, sending the Missal and the piece of bread to the floor and exposing the fouled surface of the marble.

"Did you really think you could effect the Transubstantiation here? Do you really believe any of that garbage? That the bread and wine actually take on the substance of"—he tried to say the name but it wouldn't form—"the Son's body and blood?"

One of the nest brothers, Frederick, stepped forward and leaned over the altar, smiling.

"Transubstantiation?" he said in his most unctuous voice, pulling the Pepsi can from Joseph's hands. "Does that mean that this is the blood of the Son?"

A whisper of warning slithered through Palmeri's mind. Something about the can, something about the way he found it difficult to bring its outline into focus . . .

"Brother Frederick, maybe you should—"

Frederick's grin broadened. "I've always wanted to sup on the blood of a deity."

The nest members hissed their laughter as Frederick raised the can and drank.

Palmeri was jolted by the explosion of intolerable brightness that burst from Frederick's mouth. The inside of his skull glowed beneath his scalp and shafts of pure white light shot from his ears, nose, eyes—every orifice in his head. The glow spread as it flowed down through his throat and chest and into his abdominal cavity, silhouetting his ribs before melting through his skin. Frederick was liquefying where he stood, his flesh steaming, softening, running like glowing molten lava.

No! This couldn't be happening! Not now when he had Joseph in his grasp!

Then the can fell from Frederick's dissolving fingers and landed on the altar top. Its contents splashed across the fouled surface, releasing another detonation of brilliance, this one more devastating than the first. The glare spread rapidly, extending over the upper surface and running down the sides, moving like a living thing, engulfing the entire altar, making it glow like a corpuscle of fire torn from the heart of the sun itself.

And with the light came blast-furnace heat that drove Palmeri back, back, back until he had to turn and follow the rest of his nest in a mad, headlong rush from St. Anthony's into the cool, welcoming safety of the outer darkness.

XII

As the vampires fled into the night, their Vichy toadies behind them, Zev stared in horrid fascination at the puddle of putrescence that was all that remained of the vampire Palmeri had called Frederick. He glanced at Carl and caught the look of dazed wonderment on his face. Zev touched the top of the altar—clean, shiny, every whorl of the marble surface clearly visible.

There was fearsome power here. Incalculable power. But instead of elating him, the realization only depressed him. How long had this been going on? Did it happen at every Mass? Why had he spent his entire life ignorant of this?

He turned to Father Joe.

"What happened?"

"I—I don't know."

"A miracle!" Carl said, running his palm over the altar top.

"A miracle and a meltdown," Father Joe said. He picked up the empty Pepsi can and looked into it. "You know, you go through the seminary, through your ordination, through countless Masses *believing* in the Transubstantiation. But after all these years . . . to actually *know* . . ."

Zev saw him rub his finger along the inside of the can and taste it. He grimaced.

"What's wrong?" Zev asked.

"Still tastes like sour barberone . . . with a hint of Pepsi."

"Doesn't matter what it tastes like. As far as Palmeri and his friends are concerned, it's the real thing."

"No," said the priest with a small smile. "That's Coke."

And then they started laughing. It wasn't that funny, but Zev found himself roaring along with the other two. It was more a release of tension than anything else. His sides hurt. He had to lean against the altar to support himself.

It took the return of the Vichy to cure the laughter. They charged in carrying a heavy fire blanket. This time Father Joe did not stand by passively as they invaded his church. He stepped around the altar and met them head-on.

He was great and terrible as he confronted them. His giant stature and raised fists cowed them for a few heartbeats. But then they must have remembered that they outnumbered him twelve to one and charged him. He swung a massive fist and caught the lead Vichy square on the jaw. The blow lifted him off his feet and he landed against another. Both went down.

Zev dropped to one knee and reached for the shotgun. He would use it this time, he would shoot these vermin, he swore it!

But then someone landed on his back and drove him to the floor. As he tried to get up he saw Father Joe, surrounded, swinging his fists, laying the Vichy out every time he connected. But there were too many. As the priest went down under the press of them, a heavy boot thudded against the side of Zev's head. He sank into darkness.

XIII

. . . a throbbing in his head, stinging pain in his cheek, and a voice, sibilant yet harsh . . .

". . . now, Joseph. Come on. Wake up. I don't want you to miss this!"

Palmeri's sallow features swam into view, hovering over him, grinning like a skull. Joe tried to move but found his wrists and arms tied. His right hand throbbed, felt twice its normal size; he must have broken it on a Vichy jaw. He lifted his head and saw that he was tied spread-eagle on the altar, and that the altar had been covered with the fire blanket.

"Melodramatic, I admit," Palmeri said, "but fitting, don't you think? I mean, you and I used to sacrifice our god symbolically here every weekday and multiple times on Sundays, so why shouldn't this serve as *your* sacrificial altar?"

Joe shut his eyes against a wave of nausea. This couldn't be happening.

"Thought you'd won, didn't you?" When Joe wouldn't answer him, Palmeri went on. "And even if you'd chased me out of here for good, what would you have accomplished? The world is ours now, Joseph. Feeders and cattle—that is the hierarchy. We are the feeders. And tonight you'll join us. But *he* won't. *Voila!*"

He stepped aside and made a flourish toward the balcony. Joe searched the dim, candlelit space of the nave, not sure what he was supposed to see. Then he picked out Zev's form and he groaned. The old man's feet were lashed to the balcony rail; he hung upside down, his reddened face and frightened eyes turned his way. Joe fell back and strained at the ropes but they wouldn't budge.

"Let him go!"

"What? And let all that good rich Jewish blood go to waste? Why, these people are the Chosen of God! They're a delicacy!"

"Bastard!"

If he could just get his hands on Palmeri, just for a minute.

"Tut-tut, Joseph. Not in the house of the Lord. The Jew should have been smart and run away like Carl."

Carl got away? Good. The poor guy would probably hate himself, call himself a coward the rest of his life, but he'd done what he could. Better to live on than get strung up like Zev.

We're even, Carl.

"But don't worry about your rabbi. None of us will lay a fang on him. He hasn't earned the right to join us. We'll use the razor to bleed him. And when he's dead, he'll be dead for keeps. But not you, Joseph. Oh no, not you." His smile broadened. "You're mine."

Joe wanted to spit in Palmeri's face—not so much as an act of defiance as to hide the waves of terror surging through him—but there was no saliva to be had in his parched mouth. The thought of being undead made him weak. To spend eternity like . . . he looked at the rapt faces of Palmeri's fellow vampires as they clustered under Zev's suspended form . . . like *them*?

He *wouldn't* be like them! He wouldn't allow it!

But what if there was no choice? What if becoming undead toppled a lifetime's worth of moral constraints, cut all the tethers on his human hungers, negated all his mortal concepts of how a life should be lived? Honor, justice, integrity, truth, decency, fairness, love—what if they became meaningless words instead of the footings for his life?

A thought struck him:

"A deal, Alberto," he said.

"You're hardly in a bargaining position, Joseph."

"I'm not? Answer me this: Do the undead ever kill

each other? I mean, has one of them ever driven a stake through another's heart?"

"No. Of course not."

"Are you sure? You'd better be sure before you go through with your plans tonight. Because if I'm forced to become one of you, I'll be crossing over with just one thought in mind: to find you. And when I do I won't stake your heart, I'll stake your arms and legs to the pilings of the Point Pleasant boardwalk where you can watch the sun rise and feel it slowly crisp your skin to charcoal."

Palmeri's smile wavered. "Impossible. You'll be different. You'll want to thank me. You'll wonder why you ever resisted."

"You'd better be sure of that, Alberto . . . for your sake. Because I'll have all eternity to track you down. And I'll find you, Alberto. I swear it on my own grave. Think on that."

"Do you think an empty threat is going to cow me?"

"We'll find out how empty it is, won't we? But here's the deal: Let Zev go and I'll let you be."

"You care that much for an old Jew?"

"He's something you never knew in life, and never will know: he's a friend." *And he gave me back my soul.*

Palmeri leaned closer. His foul, nauseous breath wafted against Joe's face.

"A friend? How can you be friends with a dead man?" With that he straightened and turned toward the balcony. "Do him! *Now!*"

As Joe shouted out frantic pleas and protests, one of the vampires climbed up the rubble toward Zev. Zev did not struggle. Joe saw him close his eyes, waiting. As the vampire reached out with the straight razor, Joe bit back a sob of grief and rage and helplessness. He was about to squeeze his own eyes shut when he saw a flame arc through the air from one of the windows. It struck the floor with a crash of glass and a *woomp!* of exploding flame.

Joe had only heard of such things, but he immediately realized that he had just seen his first Molotov cocktail in action. The splattering gasoline caught the clothes of a nearby vampire who began running in circles, screaming as it beat at its flaming clothes. But its cries were drowned by the roar of other voices, a hundred or more. Joe looked around and saw people—men, women, teenagers—climbing in the windows, charging through the front doors. The women held crosses on high while the men wielded long wooden pikes—broom, rake, and shovel handles whittled to sharp points. Joe recognized most of the faces from the Sunday Masses he had held here for years.

St. Anthony's parishioners were back to reclaim their church.

"Yes!" he shouted, not sure of whether to laugh or cry. But when he saw the rage in Palmeri's face, he laughed. "Too bad, Alberto!"

Palmeri made a lunge at his throat but cringed away as a woman with an upheld crucifix and a man with a pike charged the altar—Carl and a woman Joe recognized as Mary O'Hare.

"Told ya I wun't letcha down, din't I, Fadda?" Carl said, grinning and pulling out a red Swiss Army knife. He began sawing at the rope around Joe's right wrist. "Din't I?"

"That you did, Carl. I don't think I've ever been so glad to see anyone in my entire life. But how—?"

"I told 'em. I run t'rough da parish, goin' house ta house. I told 'em dat Fadda Joe was in trouble an' dat we let him down before but we shoun't let him down again. He come back fa us, now we gotta go back fa him. Simple as dat. And den *dey* started runnin' house ta house, an afore ya knowed it, we had ourselfs a little army. We come ta kick ass, Fadda, if you'll excuse da expression."

"Kick all the ass you can, Carl."

Joe glanced at Mary O'Hare's terror-glazed eyes as she swiveled around, looking this way and that; he saw how the crucifix trembled in her hand. She wasn't going to kick too much ass in her state, but she was *here*, dear God, she was here for him and for St. Anthony's despite the terror that so obviously filled her. His heart swelled with love for these people and pride in their courage.

As soon as his arms were free, Joe sat up and took the knife from Carl. As he sawed at his leg ropes, he looked around the church.

The oldest and youngest members of the parishioner army were stationed at the windows and doors where they held crosses aloft, cutting off the vampires' escape, while all across the nave — chaos. Screams, cries, and an occasional shot echoed through St. Anthony's. The vampires were outnumbered three to one and seemed blinded and confused by all the crosses around them. Despite their superhuman strength, it appeared that some were indeed getting their asses kicked. A number were already writhing on the floor, impaled on pikes. As Joe watched, he saw a pair of the women, crucifixes held before them, backing a vampire into a corner. As it cowered there with its arms across its face, one of the men charged in with a sharpened rake handle held like a lance and ran it through.

But a number of parishioners lay in inert, bloody heaps on the floor, proof that the vampires and the Vichy were claiming their share of victims too.

Joe freed his feet and hopped off the altar. He looked around for Palmeri — he *wanted* Palmeri — but the vampire priest had lost himself in the melée. Joe glanced up at the balcony and saw that Zev was still hanging there, struggling to free himself. He started across the nave to help him.

XIV

Zev hated that he should be hung up here like a salami in a deli window. He tried again to pull his upper body up far enough to reach his leg ropes but he couldn't get close. He had never been one for exercise; doing a sit-up flat on the floor would have been difficult, so what made him think he could do the equivalent maneuver hanging upside down by his feet? He dropped back, exhausted, and felt the blood rush to his head again. His vision swam, his ears pounded, he felt like the skin of his face was going to burst open. Much more of this and he'd have a stroke or worse maybe.

He watched the upside-down battle below and was glad to see the vampires getting the worst of it. These people—seeing Carl among them, Zev assumed they were part of St. Anthony's parish—were ferocious, almost savage in their attacks on the vampires. Months' worth of pent-up rage and fear was being released upon their tormentors in a single burst. It was almost frightening.

Suddenly he felt a hand on his foot. Someone was untying his knots. Thank you, Lord. Soon he would be on his feet again. As the cords came loose he decided he should at least attempt to participate in his own rescue.

Once more, Zev thought. *Once more I'll try.*

With a grunt he levered himself up, straining, stretching to grasp something, anything. A hand came out of the darkness and he reached for it. But Zev's relief turned to horror when he felt the cold clamminess of the thing that clutched him, that pulled him up and over the balcony rail with inhuman strength. His bowels threatened to evacuate when Palmeri's grinning face loomed not six inches from his own.

"It's not over yet, Jew," he said softly, his foul breath clogging Zev's nose and throat. "Not by a long shot!"

He felt Palmeri's free hand ram into his belly and grip his belt at the buckle, then the other hand grab a handful of his shirt at the neck. Before he could struggle or cry out, he was lifted free of the floor and hoisted over the balcony rail.

And the demon's voice was in his ear.

"Joseph called you a friend, Jew. Let's see if he really meant it."

XV

Joe was halfway across the floor of the nave when he heard Palmeri's voice echo above the madness.

"Stop them, Joseph! Stop them now or I drop your friend!"

Joe looked up and froze. Palmeri stood at the balcony rail, leaning over it, his eyes averted from the nave and all its newly arrived crosses. At the end of his outstretched arms was Zev, suspended in mid-air over the splintered remains of the pews, over a particularly large and ragged spire of wood that pointed directly at the middle of Zev's back. Zev's frightened eyes were flashing between Joe and the giant spike below.

Around him Joe heard the sounds of the melée drop a notch, then drop another as all eyes were drawn to the tableau on the balcony.

"A human can die impaled on a wooden stake just as well as a vampire!" Palmeri cried. "And just as quickly if it goes through his heart. But it can take hours of agony if it rips through his gut."

St. Anthony's grew silent as the fighting stopped and each faction backed away to a different side of the church, leaving Joe alone in the middle.

"What do you want, Alberto?"

"First I want all those crosses put away so that I can see!"

Joe looked to his right where his parishioners stood.

"Put them away," he told them. When a murmur of dissent arose, he added, "Don't put them down, just out of sight. Please."

Slowly, one by one at first, then in groups, the crosses and crucifixes were placed behind backs or tucked out of sight within coats.

To his left, the vampires hissed their relief and the Vichy cheered. The sound was like hot needles being forced under Joe's fingernails. Above, Palmeri turned his face to Joe and smiled.

"That's better."

"What do you want?" Joe asked, knowing with a sick crawling in his gut exactly what the answer would be.

"A trade," Palmeri said.

"Me for him, I suppose?" Joe said.

Palmeri's smile broadened. "Of course."

"No, Joe!" Zev cried.

Palmeri shook the old man roughly. Joe heard him say, "Quiet, Jew, or I'll snap your spine!" Then he looked

down at Joe again. "The other thing is to tell your rabble
to let my people go." He laughed and shook Zev again.
"Hear that, Jew? A Biblical reference—Old Testament,
no less!"

"All right," Joe said without hesitation.

The parishioners on his right gasped as one and cries
of "No!" and "You can't!" filled St. Anthony's. A particularly loud voice nearby shouted, "He's only a lousy kike!"

Joe wheeled on the man and recognized Gene Harrington, a carpenter. He jerked a thumb back over his
shoulder at the vampires and their servants.

"You sound like you'd be more at home with them,
Gene."

Harrington backed up a step and looked at his feet.

"Sorry, Father," he said in a voice that hovered on the
verge of a sob. "But we just got you back!"

"I'll be all right," Joe said softly.

And he meant it. Deep inside he had a feeling that he
would come through this, that if he could trade himself
for Zev and face Palmeri one-on-one, he could come out
the victor, or at least battle him to a draw. Now that he
was no longer tied up like some sacrificial lamb, now that
he was free, with full use of his arms and legs again, he
could not imagine dying at the hands of the likes of
Palmeri.

Besides, one of the parishioners had given him a tiny
crucifix. He had it closed in the palm of his hand.

But he had to get Zev out of danger first. That above
all else. He looked up at Palmeri.

"All right, Alberto. I'm on my way up."

"Wait!" Palmeri said. "Someone search him."

Joe gritted his teeth as one of the Vichy, a blubbery, unwashed slob, came forward and searched his pockets. Joe thought he might get away with the crucifix but at the last moment he was made to open his hands. The Vichy grinned in Joe's face as he snatched the tiny cross from his palm and shoved it into his pocket.

"He's clean now!" the slob said and gave Joe a shove toward the vestibule.

Joe hesitated. He was walking into the snake pit unarmed now. A glance at his parishioners told him he couldn't very well turn back now.

He continued on his way, clenching and unclenching his tense, sweaty fists as he walked. He still had a chance of coming out of this alive. He was too angry to die. He prayed that when he got within reach of the ex-priest the smoldering rage at how he had framed him when he'd been pastor, at what he'd done to St. Anthony's since then, would explode and give him the strength to tear Palmeri to pieces.

"No!" Zev shouted from above. "Forget about me! You've started something here and you've got to see it through!"

Joe ignored his friend.

"Coming, Alberto."

Father Joe's coming, Alberto. And he's pissed. Royally pissed.

XVI

Zev craned his neck around, watching Father Joe disappear beneath the balcony.

"Joe! Come back!"

Palmeri shook him again.

"Give it up, old Jew. Joseph never listened to anyone and he's not listening to you. He still believes in faith and virtue and honesty, in the power of goodness and truth over what he perceives as evil. He'll come up here ready to sacrifice himself for you, yet sure in his heart that he's going to win in the end. But he's wrong."

"No!" Zev said.

But in his heart he knew that Palmeri was right. How could Joe stand up against a creature with Palmeri's strength, who could hold Zev in the air like this for so long? Didn't his arms ever tire?

"Yes!" Palmeri hissed. "He's going to lose and we're going to win. We'll win for the same reason we'll always win. We don't let anything as silly and transient as sentiment stand in our way. If we'd been winning below and situations were reversed—if Joseph were holding one of my nest brothers over that wooden spike below—do you think I'd pause for a moment? For a second? Never! That's why this whole exercise by Joseph and these people is futile."

Futile . . . Zev thought. Like much of his life, it seemed. Like all of his future. Joe would die tonight and Zev would live on, a cross-wearing Jew, with the traditions of his past sacked and in flames, and nothing in his future but a vast, empty, limitless plain to wander alone.

There was a sound on the balcony stairs and Palmeri turned his head.

"Ah, Joseph," he said.

Zev couldn't see the priest but he shouted anyway.

"Go back, Joe! Don't let him trick you!"

"Speaking of tricks," Palmeri said, leaning further over the balcony rail as an extra warning to Joe, "I hope you're not going to try anything foolish."

"No," said Joe's tired voice from somewhere behind Palmeri. "No tricks. Pull him in and let him go."

Zev could not let this happen. And suddenly he knew what he had to do. He twisted his body and grabbed the front of Palmeri's cassock while bringing his legs up and bracing his feet against one of the uprights of the brass balcony rail. As Palmeri turned his startled face toward him, Zev put all his strength into his legs for one convulsive backward push against the railing, pulling Palmeri with him. The vampire priest was overbalanced. Even his enormous strength could not help him once his feet came free of the floor. Zev saw his undead eyes widen with terror as his lower body slipped over the railing. As they fell free, Zev wrapped his arms around Palmeri and clutched his cold and surprisingly thin body tight against him.

"What goes through this old Jew goes through you!" he shouted into the vampire's ear.

For an instant he saw Joe's horrified face appear over the balcony's receding edge, heard Joe's faraway shout of "*No!*" mingle with Palmeri's nearer scream of the same word, then there was a spine-cracking jar and a tearing, wrenching pain beyond all comprehension in his chest. In an eyeblink he felt the sharp spire of wood rip through him and into Palmeri.

And then he felt no more.

As roaring blackness closed in he wondered if he'd done it, if this last desperate, foolish act had succeeded. He didn't want to die without finding out. He wanted to know—

But then he knew no more.

XVII

Joe shouted incoherently as he hung over the rail and watched Zev's fall, gagged as he saw the bloody point of the pew remnant burst through the back of Palmeri's cassock directly below him. He saw Palmeri squirm and flop around like a speared fish, then go limp atop Zev's already inert form.

As cheers mixed with cries of horror and the sounds of renewed battle rose from the nave, Joe turned away from the balcony rail and dropped to his knees.

"Zev!" he cried aloud. "Good God, Zev!"

Forcing himself to his feet, he stumbled down the back stairs, through the vestibule, and into the nave. The vampires and the Vichy were on the run, as cowed and demoralized by their leader's death as the parishioners were buoyed by it. Slowly, steadily, they were falling before the relentless onslaught. But Joe paid them scant attention. He fought his way to where Zev lay impaled beneath Palmeri's already rotting corpse. He looked for a sign of life in his old friend's glazing eyes, a hint of a pulse in his throat under his beard, but there was nothing.

"Oh, Zev, you shouldn't have. You shouldn't have."

Suddenly he was surrounded by a cheering throng of St. Anthony's parishioners.

"We did it, Fadda Joe!" Carl cried, his face and hands splattered with blood. "We killed 'em all! We got our church back!"

"Thanks to this man here," Joe said, pointing to Zev.

"No!" someone shouted. "Thanks to *you*!"

Amid the cheers, Joe shook his head and said nothing. Let them celebrate. They deserved it. They'd reclaimed a small piece of the planet as their own, a toe-hold and nothing more. A small victory of minimal significance in the war, but a victory nonetheless. They had their church back, at least for tonight. And they intended to keep it.

Good. But there would be one change. If they wanted their Father Joe to stick around they were going to have to agree to rename the church.

St. Zev's.

Joe liked the sound of that.

Permissions Acknowledgments

✦✦✦

Fan Club Book of Vampires (1981). Reprinted by permission of Brandt & Hochman Literary Agents, Inc.

Manly Wade Wellman: "When It Was Moonlight" by Manly Wade Wellman, copyright © 1940 by Street & Smith, copyright renewed 1968 by Conde Nast. Originally published in *Unknown Worlds*, February 1940. Reprinted by permission of David Drake.

F. Paul Wilson: "Midnight Mass" by F. Paul Wilson, copyright © 1990 by F. Paul Wilson. Reprinted by permission of F. Paul Wilson.